S0-BSB-383

Nanuet Public Library
149 Church Street
Nanuet, NY 10954

AGAINST THE SKY

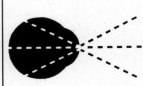

This Large Print Book carries the
Seal of Approval of N.A.V.H.

THE BRODIES OF ALASKA

AGAINST THE SKY

KAT MARTIN

THORNDIKE PRESS
A part of Gale, Cengage Learning

Nanuet Public Library
149 Church Street
Nanuet, NY 10954

GALE
CENGAGE Learning·

Farmington Hills, Mich • San Francisco • New York • Waterville, Maine
Meriden, Conn • Mason, Ohio • Chicago

GALE
CENGAGE Learning®

Copyright © 2015 by Kat Martin.
The Brodies of Alaska.
Thorndike Press, a part of Gale, Cengage Learning.

ALL RIGHTS RESERVED
Thorndike Press® Large Print Core.
The text of this Large Print edition is unabridged.
Other aspects of the book may vary from the original edition.
Set in 16 pt. Plantin.

LIBRARY OF CONGRESS CATALOGING-IN-PUBLICATION DATA

Martin, Kat.
    Against the sky / by Kat Martin. — Large print edition.
        pages cm. — (Thorndike Press large print core) (The Brodies of Alaska)
        ISBN 978-1-4104-7732-3 (hardcover) — ISBN 1-4104-7732-0 (hardcover)
        1. Large type books. I. Title.
    PS3563.A7246A759 2015
    813'.54—dc23   2014048965

Published in 2015 by arrangement with Zebra Books, an imprint of Kensington Publishing Corp.

Printed in Mexico
1 2 3 4 5 6 7 19 18 17 16 15

*To the men and women
in law enforcement
who work so hard to keep us safe.*

CHAPTER ONE

"Earth to earth, ashes to ashes, dust to dust . . ." A rumble of thunder in the sullen gray sky blotted the reverend's next words.

Nick Brodie pulled the collar of his coat up against the wind and impending rain, his gaze traveling to twelve-year-old Jimmy Evans, who stood rigidly in front of his father's grave.

Jimmy and his dad lived in a house not far from the place Nick had purchased a few months back — a log home he had been renting for years for weekend fishing trips. It sat on a secluded piece of property near Fish Lake, a rural Alaska community sixty miles north of Anchorage.

He'd met Jimmy one summer and hired him to work after school and on weekends to look after the place when he wasn't there and to do odd jobs around the property. The boy, big for his age and in many ways older than his years, had lost his mother in a car accident when he was six. Now his dad was gone, heart attack at forty-four years old. Go figure.

Nick felt a rush of pity for the kid who couldn't seem to catch a break.

The reverend's voice held a touch of that same sadness. "The Lord bless and keep this man, Alexander Evans, who has passed into your loving arms, be gracious unto him and give him eternal peace. Amen."

Standing at the front of the small group of mourners, the boy walked up to the grave. The shaggy black hair, cocoa skin, and almond eyes came from his mother's Alaska Native heritage. But his above-average height and solid build came from his dad. The combination resulted in a handsome boy, still a little pudgy, but losing his baby fat as he grew toward manhood.

Reaching down, Jimmy picked up a handful of dirt and tossed it onto the casket, turned to see his aunt walking up beside him. Mary George was his mother's sister, a pretty black-haired woman in her late twenties, who would be staying at the house with Jimmy until the estate was settled and arrangements for her to become his legal guardian could be completed. Resting a hand on his shoulder, Mary led the boy away.

As the mourners dispersed, Nick turned into the wind and started walking back to the big black Ford Explorer he had parked at the edge of the cemetery. He flicked a last sympathetic glance at the kid, who walked forlornly toward the little white Subaru his aunt was driving. He didn't know much about Jimmy's family, but the boy seemed to like his aunt, and there was a chance they would be able to stay in the house at the lake.

Nick hoped so. If Jimmy didn't have to change schools, adjusting to his new life might not be quite as hard on him. Having lost his own mother in his freshman year of high school, his dad a few years later, Nick knew how rough life without your parents could be. If it weren't for his two older brothers, Dylan and Rafe, he would have been one lonely teenage kid.

He looked up at the sky as he slid behind the wheel. Lots of rain in September, even this early in the month. Next month, the snow would begin to fly. Even now, an icy wind slid down the sides of the towering mountains, soon to be white-capped through the long winter months ahead.

Nick started the engine and pulled off the shoulder onto the road. He had a couple of stops to make before he headed home, a

9

crucial one at the cleaners.

His suits and shirts had been hanging in the closet since he'd quit the Anchorage police force five months ago. He needed them cleaned and pressed for the trip he was planning to make. Tomorrow he would be leaving Alaska, heading south for the vacation he had been meaning to take for years.

Until his older brother, Rafe, had shoved an airline ticket into his hand and demanded he use it, he'd only talked about going. Now that he'd made the decision, he couldn't wait to leave.

Thinking about the city he'd never seen but had wanted to visit for years, Nick found himself smiling. Before he'd quit his job, he'd been working as an APD homicide detective. An inheritance he and his brothers had received from the sale of the family ranch in Texas had given him the chance to explore other venues.

Nick had been more than ready. The last case he'd worked involved the murder of three young girls by a serial killer. The haunted looks in the parents' eyes, the unforgettable memories of those small, tortured bodies. The blood and death he'd waded through to solve the crime had been the straw that had broken the camel's back.

He was out of the murder business for good, and nothing was going to lure him back. Nick stepped on the gas, his mind already seeing the bright lights of Las Vegas.

The afternoon was almost gone. Jimmy Evans wandered through his house, thinking of his dad and the funeral, trying to work up his courage.

He needed to talk to Nick. Nick Brodie was the only one he could trust, the only person he could tell the truth about what had happened to his dad. But even if he did, Nick wasn't a cop anymore and Jimmy wasn't sure he would be willing to help.

Closing the door to his bedroom, he flung himself down on the mattress. Through the walls, he could hear his aunt in the living room, saying good-bye to the last of the friends who had been at his dad's funeral and come by the house afterward. Along with the cards and flowers, they'd brought salads and casseroles, enough to feed an army.

Jimmy wasn't hungry. Just the smell of food made him sick. He tried not to think of his dad, the way he had found him four days ago, leaning back in the chair in his office, his eyes open, staring at the ceiling.

A heart attack, the doctors said. But

Jimmy didn't believe them. He knew the truth. Or at least he was pretty sure it was the truth. That was the problem. How could he be certain? And if it was the truth, what would happen to him if someone found out he was the one who had told?

His eyes burned. His dad was dead. He had to do something. Feeling lonely and heartsick, Jimmy stared out the window into the gray skies hanging over the mountains. Maybe he'd talk to Nick tomorrow, ask for his help. That would give him a little more time to think, try to work things out in his head.

Tomorrow, he told himself.

But when he went over to Nick's the next day, the house was locked up tight. Nick Brodie was gone.

CHAPTER TWO

There was no place like Las Vegas, Samantha thought. So many neon lights it hurt your eyes — even in the afternoon. With the September weather finally cooling the temperature down from the hundreds into the nineties, the streets overflowed with tourists.

Giant electronic billboards flashed the names of the most famous entertainers in the world — Garth Brooks, Celine Dion, Shania Twain, and half a dozen others. Even some who were no longer among the living, like Michael Jackson and Elvis Presley, were immortalized in huge stage productions.

But Samantha Hollis wasn't in Vegas to enjoy herself. After a long day working at the Mandalay Convention Center, she pushed through the heavy glass doors of the hotel at five thirty p.m., heading for her room in one of the shiny gold towers.

Even indoors, the lights and sounds overwhelmed the senses, people at blackjack tables laughing as they raked in their winnings, or groaning at a loss, a group clustered around a crap table shouting for the player to roll a seven.

Samantha kept going, making her way toward the huge bank of elevators. Grateful when one of the doors slid open, she walked inside and pressed the button for the thirtieth floor. Though her day at the convention center had been productive, now she was paying the price. Her feet ached, and the constant clanging of the slot machines had given her a headache.

She'd only been in Las Vegas two days and already the place had lost some of its glitter. Probably because she was there to do a job, not have fun. The Super Pet Zoo was in town, the pet industry's biggest and most popular trade show. Samantha was part owner of The Perfect Pup, a chain of four dog-grooming salons in the San Francisco Bay area.

Her best friend, Abigail Dunstan, the woman who had started the company and owned the biggest portion, was back in San Francisco running the business while Samantha was away. Abby was the person who managed the day-to-day operations, made sure the quality of work remained high in all of the shops, made sure the dogs were properly groomed and the clientele happy.

Samantha was the marketing person. Her Internet savvy had grown the salon Abby had started from a single location to four, all of them extremely successful. It was only logical that Samantha should travel to Vegas, see what was happening in the industry, see what she could do to keep the company growing.

She just wished her friend was there with her. It would definitely have been more fun. But Abby had recently met someone — Mr. Tall-blond-and-handsome, Abby called him — and Samantha had a hunch he was the real reason her friend had insisted on staying behind.

The elevator door pinged. "Thirtieth floor," said a computerized female voice. Samantha stepped out and headed down the carpeted hall, pausing only long enough to kick off her high heels and work the kinks out of her sore feet. With a sigh of relief, shoes in hand, she continued down the hall to her suite.

Since the convention center was in the hotel and attendees were getting a very low room rate, Samantha had decided to treat herself and stay in one of the sumptuous Mandalay suites. It had a marble bathroom with a big Jacuzzi tub, and she couldn't wait to get there, fill it, climb in and soak her aching feet, among other tired body parts.

She had almost reached her door when she saw a man walking toward her, big and brawny, weaving a little. His suit was wrinkled, his brown hair mussed and falling over a wide forehead. Obviously he was drunk.

She didn't like the leering grin that appeared on his flushed face as he spotted her and staggered in her direction. Samantha opened her purse and began digging frantically for her key card. She was still searching when the man stopped in front of her.

"Hello there, sweetheart. Aren't you a pretty little thing?"

She ignored him, kept on digging, couldn't find the damned card, prayed she hadn't left it in her room.

"Not talking, huh? I'm Howard." He stuck out a meaty hand she ignored, finally let it drop. "Want me to help you find your key?"

"No, thank you." For once, she wished her purse wasn't so big.

"Say, why don't we go downstairs and have a drink? There's a lot of great restaurants in the hotel. What do you say I buy you dinner?"

His words were thick and faintly slurred,

though Samantha didn't think he was quite as drunk as he had first seemed.

"I have plans." Like a soak in the marble tub and an early evening. "Please leave me alone."

Pain-in-the-ass Howard's bushy eyebrows went up. "No reason to take that attitude." He started crowding her, forcing her back against the door. She wasn't very big and he towered above her.

He moved closer, knocking the shoes out of her hand. "Come on, what do you say?"

"I told you to leave me alone." Samantha set her palms on his barrel chest and tried to push him away. "If you don't leave, I'm going to call security." She pushed, didn't budge him. "Please — I'm just not interested."

"Come on, sweetheart, it's only a drink."

He had her completely boxed in against the door, and though her heart was thrumming away, she was more angry than scared. There were hotel cameras everywhere. In another second, she was going to scream.

She might have done it if Howard hadn't suddenly been jerked away like a jumper on a bungee cord and slammed hard against the wall. In an instant, he was facing the opposite direction, spread-eagled, legs splayed, one of his beefy arms forced up behind his back.

"Time to go home, buddy. The lady has other plans."

"What fucking business is that of yours?"

The second man, tall and broad-shouldered with wavy black hair, cranked the arm up higher, drawing a hiss of pain. "I told you the lady has other plans."

"Don't hurt him," Samantha said. "He's just drunk."

The most amazing blue eyes she had ever seen swung in her direction. "He a friend of yours?"

"Heavens, no. I was just trying to open the door to my room when he walked up and started accosting me."

Her rescuer turned back to good ol' Howard, who seemed to have realized the game was up. "Thanks to the lady, I'm letting you go and not calling the hotel police. If you're smart, you'll walk away, go back to your room and sober up."

Howard stiffened. The arm behind his back got cranked a little higher. Howard hissed and nodded.

"Smart move." Easing up a little, the black-haired man released the drunk and stepped away. With a last angry glance, Howard moved off at a loping stagger down the hall, heading back the way he had come.

"You okay?" her rescuer asked.

Dear God, he was handsome. With his blue eyes, high cheekbones, and straight nose, he was one of the best-looking men she had ever seen. The shadow of a late-afternoon beard along his jaw gave him a slightly dangerous appearance that only made him more attractive.

She managed to drag her gaze away from those arresting blue eyes and found her voice. "Thanks to you, I'm fine. Are you a policeman or something?"

"Used to be. Nick Brodie. Glad I could help."

She smiled. "I'm Samantha Hollis. You came just in time. I really appreciate what you did. Most people would have just kept walking."

"Not where I come from."

"Really? Where's that?"

"Alaska. Up there, people help each other. Sometimes it's a matter of life and death." He looked her up and down. "You aren't very big. That bastard was twice your size."

"As I said, he was mostly just drunk."

"I guess."

Trying to ignore the nerves she was beginning to feel, she opened the purse slung over her shoulder and started searching again for her key. She could feel those amazing blue

19

eyes regarding her with interest.

"I hope I don't sound like the guy who just left, but is there any chance you might like to join me for a drink?"

Surprise had her gaze flashing back to him. "Seriously? You're here by yourself?" Impossible, she thought, for a man who looked as good as he did.

He shrugged a set of impressive shoulders. He was wearing jeans and a crisp white western shirt with snaps on the front, black shoes, though, not cowboy boots.

"I needed a break," he said. "Besides, my brother bought me a plane ticket. I didn't have much choice. How about that drink?"

She should probably say no. She wasn't going to give him what he most likely wanted. On the other hand, a guy who looked the way he did wouldn't have much trouble getting laid.

And she did owe him for coming to her rescue.

Samantha looked up at Nick Brodie and smiled. "You know, after my wrestling match with King Kong, a drink really does sound good."

Nick smiled broadly, all white teeth and sex appeal, and the bottom dropped out of her stomach. Oh, my. Maybe she was making a mistake.

"Sounds good," Nick said. "Let's go."

He wasn't sure why he'd asked her to join him. He wasn't really looking for female companionship. Or maybe he was, but hadn't found anyone worth the effort. He'd come to get away, see the city that had always intrigued him, relax, maybe gamble a little — not too much.

Samantha winced as she shoved her feet back into her high heel shoes, and he remembered seeing them in the hall in front of her door where she had taken them off and dropped them.

He was afraid he'd scare her if he suggested she open the door, go in and get a different pair, but he wanted her to be comfortable.

"I got a hunch those shoes are hurting like hell. Why don't I wait for you by the elevator? Give you time to go in and change?"

The smile she gave him was so full of gratitude, he figured he'd scored another point — besides the one he'd gotten for pulling that big bastard off her.

She opened her purse, found the key she'd been searching for, flashed it in front of the lock and opened the door. "Thanks, Nick. I'll be right there."

He frowned. The lady was way too trusting. He could have pushed her inside and done any damn thing he wanted. He thought she would have learned her lesson with the bruiser who'd been manhandling her.

His frown slowly faded, replaced by another smile. In an odd way, he found her naiveté refreshing. Still, if he got a chance, he'd talk to her, make her understand the need to be careful with strangers. Clearly, his cop instincts hadn't faded, probably never would.

Time ticked past. Standing next to the elevator, he checked his watch. She'd been gone fifteen minutes when he spotted her coming down the hall. She'd changed out of her pale peach linen suit into a short black skirt, pink and black top, and another pair of heels, just as tall but open-toed and apparently more comfortable.

"Thanks for waiting," she said. "I've been working all day. It feels good to get into something that isn't wrinkled."

His eyes ran over her. "You look fantastic." Damned if she didn't. With her heart-shaped face and warm brown eyes, he'd thought she was attractive. Now he could see she was way more than pretty, with a great figure, curves in all the right places, just a hint of cleavage above the neckline of her blouse. She had taken the clips out of her hair, letting the springy, light brown curls that hung down her back tumble softly around her face. He wanted to grab a fistful, see if it felt as silky as it looked.

They got into the elevator, rode it down to the casino. He'd chosen the hotel on the Internet, got a deal on the rates. His suite was a real treat, with a marble bathroom and views out over the city. They headed over to one of the numerous bars, one he'd visited last night that wasn't far from the elevators.

"How about right here?" he suggested. "It's not as noisy as some of the others."

"Perfect." She smiled. "And my feet get a chance to rest."

He smiled back, led her into a quiet corner. Samantha ordered a glass of white wine while he went for a whiskey and Coke. He was mainly a beer drinker, but hey — he was in Vegas.

The waiter brought the drinks and Nick took a sip, enjoyed the burn and the view across the table. The more he looked at Samantha, the more he liked what he saw: pert, slightly upturned nose, big golden-brown eyes, full pink lips, and smooth skin with just a touch of rose.

He watched her sipping her wine, took another drink of whiskey. "You said you were working. So what do you do?"

Samantha smiled and he felt a little kick. "I'm part owner of a chain of dog-grooming parlors in the San Francisco area. Four so far. The Perfect Pup. I'm the marketing person. I'm here for the Super Pet Zoo, hoping to get some new ideas. We're planning to expand."

He imagined her trimming a poodle or washing a big St. Bernard and fought not to smile. "A dog-lover and a businesswoman. Nice combination."

"Actually, it's not what I set out to do in life. When I was a kid I wanted to be a vet, but I ran out of money before I finished college. I took a job with a friend and it morphed into a career. What about you? You said you *were* a policeman — past tense. What are you doing now?"

"At the moment, nothing. I was a homicide detective. I got tired of dealing with criminals and murder. I'm figuring out what I want to do." Which could be anything that didn't involve violence, blood, and death.

She glanced around the bar, at the modern architecture, high ceilings and glass chandeliers, at the red lights illuminating the endless bottles of liquor in the back bar. In the distance, Nick could hear the sounds of the casino, the ringing of slots, the spin of endless wheels.

"Then maybe you came to the right place," she said. "There's plenty to do here to get your mind off the bad stuff you've been dealing with."

"That's exactly what my brother said." He smiled. "And on top of that, now I've met you." He lifted his glass. "Here's to new friends and having a good time in Vegas."

Samantha lifted her wineglass, clinked it against his. "New friends and fun," she said, repeating his toast.

Nick looked at the attractive woman sitting across from him and thought maybe things were finally beginning to swing in his direction.

Nanuet Public Library
149 Church Street
Nanuet, NY 10954

CHAPTER THREE

Samantha was having such a good time with Nick, she didn't realize how late it was getting.

She glanced down at her wristwatch. "Good heavens, it's almost nine o'clock. I've got to work tomorrow. I'd better get going." She started to rise, but Nick caught her arm.

"Neither of us has had dinner," he said reasonably. "There's a great steak house in the hotel — if you like meat, that is. Why don't we eat together?"

Samantha studied the man sitting across from her. So far, Nick Brodie had been a perfect gentleman. They wouldn't be leaving the hotel, so she wouldn't be in any sort of danger, and she *was* having fun.

As if to persuade her, her stomach rumbled right on cue. "All right. Mostly I eat fish and chicken, but I'm sure they'll have something I like."

Nick stood up and held out his hand. Samantha placed hers in his and felt a little rush of awareness. How long had it been since a man had attracted her the way Nick Brodie did? Not since Justin. She'd been swept off her feet by Justin Chapman III, overwhelmed by his blond good looks, Stanford education, and charm. Justin had turned out to be a complete and utter rat.

The memory reminded her to be wary.

They made their way to Charlie Palmer's, which turned out to be kind of old-style, with upholstered red chairs and white linen tablecloths, and extremely expensive.

When she saw the menu prices, her stomach tightened. She told herself she was in Vegas — she deserved to treat herself. But still . . . Something in her face must have revealed her thoughts. Nick reached over and covered the hand she rested on the table.

"This was my idea. My treat, okay?"

She firmly shook her head. "No way. I'm not about to let you pay my share. You don't even have a job."

Nick laughed, a husky, sexy sound, and a little curl of heat slid into her stomach.

"I can afford it," he said. "And besides, I'm an ex-cop, I'm from Alaska, and way too much of a male chauvinist to let a

27

woman pay."

Samantha smiled. She could see by the stubborn set of his jaw and the look in his eyes he was determined. "Fine. But don't say I didn't offer."

His mouth edged up. "You can buy me an after-dinner drink in the bar, how's that?"

It was a trick to keep her from going back upstairs, but Samantha no longer cared. Nick was great company and she loved being with a man who intrigued her in ways no one had in nearly two years.

The conversation never turned dull all the way through dinner. She enjoyed Nick's anecdotes about Alaska and hearing him talk about his two brothers, who also lived in the North. They laughed together at Samantha's pet parlor stories — a definite change from Justin, who seemed to be embarrassed by her employment.

And under it all was that sweep of attraction, the pull she felt whenever she looked into those amazing blue eyes.

As they walked out of the restaurant, Nick asked if she wanted to go listen to some jazz in one of the lounges. Samantha threw caution to the wind and said yes.

It was three in the morning when Nick walked her to the door of her suite; his was on the same floor farther down the hall.

"I know it's late and you have to work tomorrow," he said. "But I've really had a great time and I hate to say good night."

She didn't want the evening to end, either. But she wasn't into hooking up for a one-night stand with a guy she would never see again. "It's been really fun. I'm glad I met you, Nick."

"I'm glad I met you, too, Samantha."

She leaned toward him, went up on her toes and brushed a soft kiss over his lips. Before she could pull away, Nick drew her into his arms and kissed her the way she'd been fantasizing about all night, soft and sexy at first, then hot, wet, and deep. A little whimper escaped when he started kissing the side of her neck.

"You could invite me in," he said softly, tempting her more than she would have expected.

Samantha eased away. "I could, but I'm not going to. You gave me a wonderful evening, one I won't forget. Maybe if we had time to get to know each other, things would be different." She turned, swiped her key card and opened the door. "Good night, Nick." He caught her before she could disappear inside.

"Promise me you won't open your door that way when you're with a stranger. It's really dangerous."

Samantha looked up at him, pleased to think he was worried about her. "You aren't a stranger anymore, and besides you were a cop."

"Just be careful, okay?"

When she nodded, he bent his head and pressed another soft kiss on her lips. "What time are you finished tomorrow?"

Surprise trickled through her. Even knowing she wasn't going to sleep with him, he wanted to see her again. "About five, five thirty."

"This is my first trip to Vegas. Why don't I get tickets to one of the shows? I was thinking the Michael Jackson Cirque du Soleil might be good. Or something else if you'd rather. I'd really like to see you again."

"Are you . . . are you sure?" The real question was, *Are you sure you don't want to take someone who'll sleep with you when the evening's over?*

Nick tipped up her chin, forcing her eyes to his face. "I had a great time tonight. I don't expect anything more. Let me take you to a show."

Samantha grinned. She really wanted to go. "Michael Jackson sounds fabulous."

They exchanged business cards and entered each other's cell numbers on their phones. Nick didn't leave until she was safely inside her room, the door closed and locked behind her.

Samantha leaned against it. She hadn't come to Las Vegas to have a fling. And it looked as though Nick didn't expect her to fall into bed with him. But recalling those hot, sexy kisses and amazing blue eyes, maybe it was time to rethink her plans.

Nick spent the next two nights with Samantha. She was, he thought, the closest to the proverbial *girl next door* he had ever met. Most of the women he knew were the outdoor type. They enjoyed hiking and camping, snowmobiling, skiing, even ice fishing.

Not to say they couldn't be beautiful. Hell, Lisa Graham, the last girl he'd dated, could have entered any beauty pageant in the country. But like most Alaska women, she was athletic and adventurous, had to be to handle the long winters and harsh living conditions.

Samantha was different. At twenty-eight, she was softly feminine, not a callous in sight. She played tennis on occasion, she'd told him, but mostly enjoyed going to movies or plays, shopping, or going out to dinner. Hell, she didn't even know how to snow

31

ski, though she'd said some day she might want to give it a try.

According to her, her favorite treat was a stay in a fancy hotel, or a day at the spa. She loved to cook and garden, enjoyed her family, which included her parents and a brother, all of whom lived in Northern California. Her favorite adventures were found in the pages of a book, she had said.

Samantha was the wholesome type, even had the smattering of freckles across her nose. She was also smart and sexy and fun to be with. Aside from a burning desire to take the lady to bed, Nick enjoyed her company. He was beginning to dread the day he would be leaving to go back home.

But both of them were realists. This was just a whirlwind weekend that wasn't going anywhere. Just an interlude that would soon come to an end.

Their last night in Vegas, Nick took Samantha to see David Copperfield at the MGM Grand, one of the most popular shows in town. Nick found himself enjoying Samantha's excitement as much as he did the show.

"How in the world did he do that?" she whispered when the magician made a tiger disappear on stage.

Nick grinned. "You'd have to ask him. But

if you did, I don't think he'd tell you."

Nick stopped to play the slot machines on the way out of the casino. He handed a twenty to Samantha but she just shook her head.

"I can't take that. If I won, the money would be yours. Besides, I don't much like to gamble. The last time I was here, I lost fifty dollars. Maybe your luck will be better."

Nick played the twenty, which was gone in a heartbeat. Next to him, Samantha pulled a single dollar bill out of her wallet, stuck it into the machine next to his and pulled the handle. The barrel rolled, a 7 came up, then another, and another. An instant later, bells started ringing and Samantha started screaming, her petite frame vibrating with excitement.

"Oh, my God, I won! I won!" She turned those big brown eyes in his direction, laughed and threw her arms around his neck. When she planted a quick kiss on his lips, a shot of lust hit him like a fist. His groin tightened to the point of pain, and it was all he could do not to toss her over his shoulder, carry her upstairs, and haul her into bed.

Instead, he bent his head and captured those soft pink lips in a kiss that was deep and thorough, drawing a grinning audience who clapped their approval when the long kiss ended.

Samantha blushed. Avoiding eye contact, she glanced back at the machine. "How much did I win?"

Nick looked over at the flashing lights. "Looks like five thousand dollars."

"Oh, my God! I've never won anything in my life!"

Nick reached up and plucked the printed receipt out of the machine, handed it to Samantha, who pressed it against her heart.

Grinning like a kid, she waved the slip of paper. "I better collect my winnings before I wake up and find out this was all just a dream."

"Good idea." Nick took her hand. "Otherwise you might be tempted to put some of it back in the machine."

Samantha shook her head, tossing that heavy cascade of nutmeg curls that never failed to stir him. "No way. This goes into my savings account."

Nick just smiled. He was beginning to know her well enough not to be surprised.

They collected her winnings and headed for the cabstand at the front of the casino, both of them smiling, enjoying another great evening. But the hour was getting late and this was their last night in Vegas. Samantha would be leaving at ten in the morning. Nick's flight left at a very early six.

As the cab rolled down Las Vegas Boulevard, carrying them back to the Mandalay Bay, both of them were quiet. Their time together was nearly over. Nick lived in Alaska, Samantha in San Francisco. Both of them were smart enough to know long-distance relationships didn't work.

Neither of them suggested a late-night drink, just continued through the casino, heading for their rooms upstairs. His great time in Vegas had come to an end.

The notion put a dull edge on the evening.

Samantha was quiet as the elevator swept toward her room on the thirtieth floor. All evening she'd been dreading these final moments with the amazingly handsome man who had given her such a wonderful time in Las Vegas.

At the door to her suite, she turned and smiled, but the curve of her lips held a tinge of sadness. For days, they had laughed together, shared personal stories and incredibly passionate kisses, made memories she wouldn't soon forget.

It was time to go home, but if she said good-bye to Nick now, the memories would feel incomplete. She looked up at him and took a breath for courage.

"I've had a great time, Nick. I won't forget this weekend for a very long time."

He reached out and traced a finger down her cheek. "It's been great. I won't forget, either, Samantha."

"We're going home tomorrow. We probably won't see each other again." Her heart was beating, thumping away in her chest, her nerves strung taut. "I want one last memory to take home with me. That is . . . if it's what you want, too."

His broad shoulders tightened. He knew what she was saying, knew she was telling him if he wanted her, she would invite him into her room. Nick didn't hesitate, just moved closer, backing her up against the wall, sinking his hands into her hair to hold her in place for a very thorough kiss. Soft at first, he took it deeper, bolder, hotter, arousing her the way he had every time he'd touched her.

"I want you," he said gruffly, nibbling the side of her neck. "I've wanted you since the moment I saw you in the hall, going toe-to-toe with that big bastard twice your size. But I've got to leave before dawn to catch my plane. Are you sure this is what you want?"

She reached up and cupped his cheek, felt the roughness of his late-evening beard. "The time we've spent together has been perfect — at least for me. I want it to have a perfect ending."

Nick kissed her softly. "I want that, too, Samantha." Taking the key card from her hand, he unlocked the door and shoved it open, waited for her to walk past him into the living room, then followed her into her suite.

Nick put the lock on the door, turned and drew her into his arms. Kissing her deeply, he swept her up against his chest and carried her into the bedroom. As he set her on her feet next to the bed, some of her courage faded.

"I've . . . umm . . . never just hooked up with a guy before. I'm . . . umm . . . kind of nervous. I didn't think I would be, but —"

"We aren't just hooking up," Nick said. "We're making a memory. I promise you, baby, I'll make it a good one." Then he dipped his head and kissed her, and desire slid like honey through her veins.

Nick took his time, nibbling and tasting, then delving deep and plundering till Samantha could barely think. Her body was humming, her lips tingling, her skin sensitive to the slightest touch. She was hot and wet and on fire. The thought occurred that a woman had never been kissed until she'd been kissed by Nick Brodie.

The kiss went on till her knees felt weak, her body pliable and completely at his mercy. It barely registered that he had stripped off the backless white sundress she had been wearing, that she was naked except for her super high heels and a pair of white lace bikini panties she had bought at Victoria's Secret on her way back to the hotel after the convention, an indulgence she had convinced herself had nothing to do with Nick, but actually had everything to do with Nick.

Her gaze locked with his. Completely focused on Nick, when he unbuttoned his shirt, shrugged it off and tossed it away, kicked off his shoes and unzipped his pants, for a moment, she couldn't breathe.

The man was ripped. A long, lean torso corded with muscle, six-pack abs, and shoulders that could fill a door frame. His hair wasn't quite black, she realized, just so dark it looked that way and so did the dusting of hair on his chest that arrowed down into the navy blue slacks hanging low on his hips. As he drew her against him, she could feel the springy texture against her breasts, and goose bumps feathered over her skin.

Lifting her into his arms, he settled her in the middle of the king-size bed, then shed his shoes, pants, and briefs, leaving him naked and fiercely aroused. Samantha's eyes widened at his formidable size and length as he came down over her and started kissing her again, drawing her back into the heat, making her forget everything but him.

"Sweet Jesus, I want you," he whispered against the side of her neck. And dear God, she wanted him, too.

A half dozen hot kisses followed, drugging her completely, stirring a hungry ache that settled deep in her core.

"Nick . . ." she whispered as he touched her there, stroked her, seemed to know exactly how to give her pleasure. "Please . . ."

"Easy, baby, we'll get there." He took his time with her breasts, molding and caressing, making the hunger build. As he settled himself between her legs, she realized he had sheathed himself — she had no idea when. She only knew he felt big and hard as he entered her, slowed at the snug fit, kissed her deeply as he seated himself to the hilt. Then he started to move.

"Nick . . ." Catching the rhythm, Samantha gave herself up to the wild sensations, the two of them moving together as if their lovemaking had been perfectly choreo-graphed. She was hot. So hot. She had never felt this hot before, never felt as if her body was going to come apart.

"Let yourself go, Samantha." The com-manding voice, touched with a hint of tenderness, had her on the edge, then tip-ping into climax.

"Nick," she cried softly, but Nick didn't stop. It wasn't until she had reached a second powerful release that he finally let himself go, his muscles tightening, a growl low in his throat.

Samantha clung to his neck as she began to spiral down, a secret smile locked inside her. Nick had given her a perfect memory, just as she had hoped. Samantha knew she wouldn't forget it — or him — any time soon.

Dressed to leave, the sun not yet up, Nick leaned down and softly kissed Samantha's cheek. He smiled when she didn't stir. He had no doubt he had lived up to his promise. Sex with Samantha Hollis had been fantas-tic. Better than fantastic.

After the first time, he had left her nap-ping and returned to his room for a handful of condoms. His encounter wasn't planned but he had learned to be prepared and —

hey, he was in Vegas. And the truth was, he hadn't had enough of Samantha Hollis. Not nearly enough.

The second time they'd made love, she had been less reserved. The third time, the lady had been a tigress. She was small, but every ounce a woman. Nick could think of a dozen different ways he'd like to have her. If she hadn't had a job waiting for her in San Francisco, he might have suggested they stay another week.

Instead, he headed back to his room and packed the carry-on bag that held all the clothes he'd brought. Wheelng the bag toward the door of his suite, he paused long enough to pick up the phone and call down to the concierge.

"I'd like a bouquet of red roses," he told the man on the other end of the line, then read the address on the card Samantha had given him for The Perfect Pup on Hyde Street in San Francisco.

"What would you like on the note, sir?"

He thought of Samantha and smiled. "Just say, *Thanks for the memories, Nick.*"

Nick hung up the phone.

CHAPTER FOUR

Samantha read the card on the huge bouquet of two dozen red roses one more time. They had come to the shop the day after she got back to San Francisco and she had been admiring them ever since.

She sighed. Her fantasy weekend was over, nothing but memories, as the card reminded her. Once the flowers wilted, thoughts of Nick Brodie would fade along with them. Still, it had been wonderful.

"He must have been something." Her partner, Abigail Dunstan, walked toward her. "You've read that card half a dozen times." Taller by six inches, two years older, red-haired and outspoken, Abby Dunstan was a far different woman from Samantha. And yet they'd been friends ever since she'd started working for Abby at The Perfect Pup four years ago.

Samantha just smiled. "Nick was perfect — or at least he was for three whole days."

She grinned. "Of course, no man is ever completely perfect so it's probably a good thing he's totally out of reach."

"Maybe," Abby said. "But not all men are like that rat-bastard Justin Chapman — *the third,*" she added with a haughty accent and her nose in the air.

Samantha laughed. "I guess not. Doesn't matter. Nick's long gone." Just like his flowers soon would be.

"Well, you'll always have the memories."

"True . . ." She gave a wistful sigh and took a last glance at the roses. "And making them is one thing I'll never regret."

Home once more, Nick spent the first four days prowling the house, watching TV, telling himself he would figure out what he wanted to do with his life, and slowly driving himself crazy.

Off and on, he thought of Samantha, but the long weekend in Vegas seemed a distant fantasy, the woman, a pretty little wet dream that had nothing to do with the reality of his life in Alaska. They had e-mailed back and forth a few times, and Samantha had thanked him for the roses, but that had been days ago. He hadn't heard from her since.

His fifth day back, he heard a knock at the door, looked up from his place on the brown leather sofa in front of his big, flat-screen TV to see his best friend, Cordell Reeves, a detective with the Anchorage PD, standing on his porch. Grateful for the break from doing nothing, Nick walked over and opened the door.

"Hey, man, good to see you. Come on in."

Cord's hazel eyes skimmed over Nick's bare feet, jeans, and the plain white T-shirt he had pulled on that morning. "I see nothing's changed since you got back. You're wearing the same uniform you had on before you left."

"Very funny. You want a cup of coffee or a beer?"

"Coffee sounds good." Cord was a couple of inches shorter, about six feet, same lean build, but his hair was blond instead of dark like Nick's. Before they'd gone to work for the Anchorage PD, they had both been in the military, Nick in the Rangers, Cord a Marine. They had hit it off the first day they'd met and been friends ever since.

Nick led Cord into the kitchen and poured him a cup of coffee from the pot he'd made earlier that morning. Cord took a sip and wrinkled his nose.

"On second thought, I think I'll pass." He dumped the thick black brew in the sink. It smelled like dirty laundry.

"I could make some fresh."

Cord shook his head. "I can't stay long. I just came by to see if you'd come to your senses or if you were still deluding yourself into thinking you want to do something besides work."

"I never said I didn't want to work. I just want to work at something different."

"All right, so while you're looking for something different, how about a temporary job? You know Marvin Baxter? Owns Baxter Security? One of his guys quit without notice, and he's got some rich corporate oil man flying into Anchorage who needs protection. You'd be working eight-hour shifts, rotating with two other guys. You interested?"

Nick glanced over at the TV. He was going to start climbing the walls if he didn't find something to do besides watch Dr. Phil and Ellen Degeneres. Besides, he was tired of thinking of Samantha Hollis and all the things he wanted to do to her luscious little body. Things he would probably be fantasizing about for the rest of his life.

"Yeah, I'm interested. When do I start?"

Cord cocked a dark gold eyebrow. "Aren't you even going to ask me what it pays?"

Nick just grunted. "Another two days, I'd probably do it for free."

Cord chuckled. "I'll tell him you're in. It'll only be for a couple of weeks. Maybe by then, you'll have figured out what you want to do — or get your ass back to working Homicide, where you belong."

"That's not gonna happen." He wanted a change, something that wouldn't give him more nightmares.

"Fine. At least this'll give you something to do."

Nick walked Cord outside, waited beneath the overhanging porch while his friend climbed into his Chevy Silverado pickup and started the engine. The house wasn't much, just a three-bedroom, two-bath wood-frame, but it sat on five forested acres. From the porch you could see Fish Lake, walk down through the trees and be sitting on your dock in a couple of minutes. The cabin had a masculine, outdoor feel, with some great mounted trophy fish on the living room walls, along with old wicker creels and antique rods his dad had given him.

Best of all, the place was his now, bought and paid for with some of the inheritance money he had received from the sale of the ranch.

Cord was just pulling away when Nick spotted Jimmy Evans and his dog, a golden retriever named Duke, walking beneath the pine trees along the road toward the house. Nick hadn't seen the kid since he got back from Vegas. He hoped the boy was doing okay, but the solemn look on Jimmy's face made him wonder.

At least he had another excuse not to watch the f-ing TV.

Or dwell on his lost weekend with Samantha.

Jimmy spotted Nick on the porch and picked up his pace. He'd given his friend a couple of days to get home and settled before he'd come down the hill to see him.

Or at least he'd told himself that was the reason. Mostly, he'd been trying to think what he was going to say.

Nick waved at him from the porch. "Hey, Jimmy!"

Jimmy waved back. "Hey, Nick!" He reached the steps and paused. "Okay if I come in for a minute?"

"Sure, come on up."

Jimmy climbed the stairs, and they walked into the house together. Jimmy sat down on the sofa in front of the river rock fireplace, and Nick sat down in one of the chairs.

"How you doin', buddy?" Nick asked.

Jimmy shrugged his shoulders. "Okay, I guess. Looks like my dad left the house to

47

me and Aunt Mary, so we both get to stay there."

"That's great, Jim. I was hoping it would work out that way."

"I really miss him, you know?"

Nick sat forward in the chair. "I was older when I lost my parents, first my mom and then my dad. But I still miss them. It's hard at first. Eventually, it'll get better."

"Yeah, I guess. The thing is . . . umm . . . I . . . umm . . ."

"What is it, Jim?"

He took a deep breath. He was afraid to tell Nick, afraid of what might happen. But he wasn't a coward and he owed it to his dad. The breath he had been holding rushed out all at once. "I don't think my dad had a heart attack. I think he was murdered."

Nick's black eyebrows went up. Jimmy could tell he didn't believe him. Nick was looking at Jimmy with pity.

"Hey, I know losing your dad was hard," Nick said. "Especially since you've already lost your mom. But dreaming up stories won't make it any easier."

Jimmy's heart was pounding. He could feel it pumping beneath the Aces' hockey team polar bear emblem on his T-shirt. "I'm not making it up, Nick. There was a man . . . he came to see my dad the day before he

48

died. I heard them talking in the study, arguing real loud. I don't know what they were fighting about but I know it was bad. The man said, 'You made a mistake, Alex. Now you're going to pay.' "

"Maybe they were fighting about business," Nick said. "Both of them were angry, so it sounded like the man made a threat."

Jimmy shook his head. "I think it was business, but the man really meant it. When I went into the study, my dad looked like he was going to throw up. His face was pale and kind of blotchy. He pulled out the bottle of whiskey he kept in a drawer in his desk and filled a glass to the brim. His hands were shaking, he was so scared."

"He had a heart attack, Jimmy. There was an autopsy. Maybe the argument triggered it. The stress of his job — who knows? You need to deal with the fact your father's gone and nothing you do is going to bring him back. Maybe you should talk to a counselor or something. I'm sure your school could arrange it."

Jimmy's chest was beginning to hurt. Maybe he was going to have a real heart attack instead of a fake one like his dad. "There are ways to kill people and cover it up, you know. I've seen it on TV. They could have poisoned him or something. You're a cop. You could find out the truth. I don't want some guy murdering my dad and getting away with it."

"Jimmy . . ."

"After the man left, my dad asked me if I'd heard anything. I lied and said I didn't. Dad said even if I had, I couldn't tell anyone. Not ever. He made me promise. I would have kept my word, too. But not now. Not after they killed him. Please say you'll find the man who did it."

Nick came out of his chair and Jimmy stood up, too. "I'm not a cop anymore and even if I were, I wouldn't ask them to reopen the case. There isn't any real evidence. You hearing some guy arguing with your dad isn't enough. I'm sorry, Jimmy. I'll help you any way I can, but not with this."

The beat of Jimmy's heart turned slow and dull. His chest felt heavy. "I was afraid you'd say no."

Nick set a hand on his shoulder. "School's back in session. You're a good student. Take on an extracurricular project. Or if you don't want that, try out for some sport besides just hockey. It'll be easier if you keep yourself busy."

Jimmy said nothing.

"Look, maybe we could go fishing this weekend. What do you say?"

Jimmy swallowed. He wasn't interested in catching fish. He wanted to catch a killer. "Yeah, maybe." Even if Nick wouldn't help, he wasn't going to give up. He was going to find the man who killed his dad. He just wished he knew where to start looking.

CHAPTER FIVE

Three weeks had passed since Samantha's trip to Vegas. Three short weeks and her entire life had changed.

She blinked and tears trickled down her cheeks. "I don't want to be pregnant. I'm not ready to be pregnant. We used protection. It was just for fun. This isn't fair."

It was seven o'clock in the evening. They were sitting in the office she shared with Abby at the back of The Perfect Pup, which was closed for the day, all the dogs freshly groomed and delivered or picked up by their owners. The pleasant scent of doggie shampoo hid the smell of wet dog that usually lingered for a while after the crew had cleaned and scrubbed the place, getting it ready to open in the morning.

Abby handed Samantha a Kleenex. "You said Nick gave you the perfect weekend. Now he's given you the perfect gift."

Samantha let out a wail and started crying again. Her memories were far from perfect now.

Abby patted her on the back. "It's not so bad, honey. You like kids, right? You've always liked kids. Now you're going to have one."

Samantha dabbed the Kleenex beneath her eyes. "I love kids. I'd love to have a baby — someday. After I've fallen in love. After I've gotten married to a man who loves me as much as I love him — when both of us are ready to settle down and have a family."

"You sound like that time's a long ways away."

"It's years away, maybe decades." More tears rolled down her cheeks. She wiped them away and blew her nose.

"Look. You said Nick was perfect. Maybe he's ready to settle down. Maybe Nick Brodie's the man you're looking for."

Samantha's head shot up. "What are you talking about? I'm not looking for a man, and I barely know Nick."

Abby studied her face; then she frowned. "You aren't thinking of not telling him? That would hardly be fair, Samantha."

She sniffed. "If I tell him, he might not even believe it's his. I don't know how he feels about children. I can't expect him to want to raise a child with a woman he's known for three days. Who knows, maybe he's abusive. Maybe he'd be a terrible father. I can't take the risk."

Abby continued to frown. "You aren't . . . you aren't thinking of getting rid of it?"

Horror flashed in her eyes. "Of course not! How could you even say something like that?"

Abby started smiling. "Okay, then. That's what I thought. So you'll call Nick. I doubt very much he's abusive or some kind of pervert. You'll talk to him, tell him about the baby. See what he has to say."

Samantha started shaking her head. "I'm not calling Nick Brodie. No way. Not just out of the blue. I'm the one who's pregnant. I'm the one who has to figure this out."

"Fine, at least e-mail him. Tell him you've been thinking about him. See if he has any interest in continuing the relationship."

She mulled that over. Having a baby was monumental. She needed to make the right decision. To do that she needed to see Nick, maybe find a way to spend some time with him, find out what he was really like. His memory was still fresh in her mind, but as she'd told Abby, she didn't really know him.

Declining supper at the pub down the block with Abby and Mr. Tall-blond-and-handsome, Ron Goldberg, Abby's latest conquest, Samantha left the office and headed for home. It was just around the corner on Green Street, one of those old-style buildings with a garage underneath and apartments on the floors above, each with a big bay window in the living room.

Wearily climbing the stairs, Samantha went in and closed the door, walked across the living room, and flopped down on the burgundy overstuffed sofa.

Fresh tears threatened. She couldn't remember crying this much since high school when she'd failed to be chosen for the cheerleading squad.

She was older now, and wiser — or at least she should be. She thought of the chilled bottle of chardonnay in the fridge she had opened a couple of nights ago. God, she could use a glass of wine — or maybe the rest of the bottle. She scoffed. Who was she kidding? No more alcohol — not for nine long months.

She closed her eyes. She was pregnant. There was nothing to do but accept the fact she was going to have a baby.

Which meant there would be things she needed to buy and lots of bills to pay. Thinking of the money she would have to earn, she released a teary sigh and shoved herself up from the sofa, determined to focus on her job and the Internet marketing plan she had been working on.

Her laptop sat open on a pretty little antique oak desk against the wall, an ornately carved high-backed oak chair in front of it. She loved antiques. Though the kitchen, laundry, and two bathrooms had been remodeled, with its high, molded ceilings and hardwood floors, the apartment still had an old-fashioned flavor. The oak claw-foot coffee table in front of the sofa and her old oak dining table suited the place exactly.

She loved the apartment, which was walking distance to her office at The Perfect Pup, in an area full of neighborhood stores and restaurants. Since the place had two spacious bedrooms, at least she wouldn't have to move after the baby was born.

As she sat down in front of her laptop, depression washed through her. She wished she could get excited about being pregnant, the way a lot of her girlfriends would be. They thought being a single mom was fine. Some of them had even considered paying a sperm donor to give them a baby.

But Samantha was as old-fashioned as her apartment. She believed in marriage first, then kids when the time was right. And even if Nick offered marriage — which she would never accept unless she was actually in love with him — he lived in Alaska. No way was she moving to a frozen tundra like that.

She brushed away a tear. Maybe it was just hormones. Maybe all newly pregnant women were weepy. Maybe tomorrow she would feel better.

Pushing the Start button on her laptop, she waited for the screen to come up, then clicked on her e-mail and watched a line of messages fill the screen.

Her mom had sent a note, just checking in from Sacramento where she and Dad lived. There was a note from her younger brother, Peter, who was a senior at U.C. Davis. He was dating a new girl, he said. Heather was athletic, the way he was, and he really liked her.

What's happening with you, sis? his cheerful note ended.

Samantha answered both messages with a vague reply, telling them she was working hard and things were going great at the shop, saying nothing about the baby.

God in heaven, she wasn't ready for that, at least not yet.

She skimmed the rest of her mail, mostly junk advertising from Internet sites where she had made purchases. On a whim she went to Google and typed in newborn baby clothes. A jillion sites popped up. She clicked on Lollipop Moon just because she liked the name. But seeing the photos of a dozen grinning little kids only made her feel worse.

She turned off the machine, went into the bedroom and flopped down on her four-poster bed. She wasn't really tired, but depression made her lethargic. She napped a while, got up and fixed herself a sandwich, tried to watch TV, finally gave up and went to bed early.

Unfortunately, once it was dark, she couldn't fall asleep. Instead she thought about Nick Brodie and the baby, and what she should do.

By midnight, she had convinced herself. She would wait to tell Nick, maybe even get all the way through the pregnancy before she told him, maybe even wait a few years after that. Nick would be older, more ready to accept the fact he was a father. A DNA test would prove his paternity. He might even be happy about it.

She finally fell asleep sometime after three. The bad news was, when she woke up in the morning, none of the decisions she had made during the night seemed to be the right ones.

At least she wasn't so depressed. She had

always been able to bounce back from adversity. Being optimistic was part of her nature. This situation was no different.

She thought of her sister, Danielle, who had died when Samantha was ten, a subject she rarely allowed herself to think of and almost never mentioned. The pain had been nearly unbearable, even worse for her parents. But unlike other families, the loss of a loved one had pulled them more tightly together. Having a baby would be the same.

Feeling a little more in control, Samantha showered and dressed for work, then went into the kitchen for a quick bowl of Cheerios. Carrying the bowl into the living room, she sat down at her laptop and ate as she pulled up her messages.

The first came from a friend in college she hadn't heard from in over a year. Carrie and Mark were getting married. Carrie was really excited. Samantha slid back into depression.

She clicked up a couple of meaningless e-mails, then her heart jerked and started pounding. nbrodie@gmail.com. *Nick Brodie.* She sat up straighter as she read the note he had sent.

Thinking about you. Can't seem to stop. Told myself not to e-mail you again, tried

59

to convince myself it would be better for both of us if we just went on with our lives. That said, what's the chance you might say yes to a trip up to Anchorage? Say you'll come and I'll have a ticket on Alaska Airlines waiting for you at the S.F. airport counter. What do you think? Nick.

Samantha closed her eyes. She felt as if she'd hit another jackpot like the one she had struck in Las Vegas. Every time she thought of Nick, she felt confused and uncertain. She needed to see him before she could make any sort of reasonable decision about the baby. She needed to find out if her initial opinion of him was correct, find out if he was the kind of man he had seemed. She needed to figure out what he would think about sharing a child with her.

Her stomach rolled and she set her unfinished bowl of cereal aside. Would Nick stand up to his responsibilities? Or would he want nothing to do with the baby? Should she even tell him? She had to go to Alaska to find out.

And Nick was giving her the chance.

For the first time since she had seen that little strip turn pink and the doctor had confirmed her pregnancy, Samantha felt as if things might work out.

She hit the Reply button. I've been thinking about you, too. I'd love to come, but I'd
need some time to get to know you again.
Does that make sense? We kind of did things
in a hurry. Let me know how you feel about
that. Samantha

No way was she hopping back into bed
with him. She was already paying a very
high price for her impulsive behavior the
last time.

Nick must have been sitting at his computer because her mail dinged and a note
from him came right back.

Anchorage is a long way to travel for a
booty call. That wasn't my intention. I'd
like to see you, show you around. I just
finished a temporary assignment. Can you
get off for a couple of weeks?

A couple of weeks. Time enough to decide
what she should do. She thought of Abby.
They'd just started to work on expanding
their marketing plan and tossing around
ideas for adding new services.

But she knew what her best friend would
say. Abby would tell her business could wait,
that deciding what to do about the baby
was more important.

She hit the Reply key. If you're sure I

wouldn't wear out my welcome, I could take that much time. She took a deep breath and hit Send.

A few seconds later, her cell phone rang. Samantha couldn't stop the little thrill that ran through her when she pressed the phone against her ear and heard Nick's deep voice on the other end of the line. A thrill that had nothing to do with the baby and everything to do with Nick Brodie.

Samantha felt a surge of panic at the thought she could be stepping out of the frying pan into a very hot fire.

CHAPTER SIX

It felt good to be working. Or at least temporarily working. The assignment he had taken with Baxter Security had lasted only two weeks, but the bodyguard detail had given him something to do, and he was good at it.

He'd been off since then, but yesterday, the company had called again. The president of Great Northern Petroleum, Bill Foley, had been pleased with the security people Baxter had provided during his visit. He wanted the same guys on his team when he brought his family up in three weeks.

The timing would be perfect. Samantha would be arriving today for a two-week stay. She would be leaving a little before his assignment kicked in. Never a patient man, Nick prowled his living room, trying to speed up time so he could leave for the airport.

He thought of Samantha and the few days

he had spent with her. He had no idea why he had invited her for a visit. With her living so far away, their relationship — or lack of one — was doomed to end in failure.

Still, what he had told her was the truth. He hadn't been able to stop thinking about her. He wanted to see her again, if only to convince himself she wasn't any different from any other woman he'd dated. That it was just a casual fling and nothing more.

Hell, they didn't even have that much in common. He had no idea what there was about her that attracted him so strongly, but something sure as hell had. Maybe the next two weeks would give him the answer.

One thing he knew — it was going to be hell keeping his hands off her. He'd wanted her since the moment he had seen her in the hallway fighting off a guy twice her size, five-foot-two-inches of sweet curves and soft smiles. After nearly a month, he still had erotic dreams about her. But he wasn't going to pressure her into having sex with him. It would happen or it wouldn't. Nick hoped like hell it would.

He checked the heavy wristwatch he'd been wearing since his days as an Army Ranger. Seemed like a lifetime ago. But those years in Iraq and Afghanistan, combined with the time he had spent as a homicide detective, were the reason he had finally left the police force.

Too much blood and death. Too much dealing with the evil side of human nature.

The hands of the watch finally ticked into place. It was time to start the hour-plus drive to the Anchorage airport. Samantha's early morning Alaska Airlines flight out of San Francisco, with a plane change in Portland, Oregon, took about six hours' flying time. She'd be arriving a little after noon. He wasn't sure he should be looking forward so much to seeing her, but he was.

Glad to finally be under way, Nick headed out through the kitchen to the separate garage and climbed into his black Explorer. When he powered open the garage door, started the engine, and began to back out, he spotted Jimmy Evans walking over to the driveway. Nick stopped the car and rolled down the window.

"Hey, buddy, what's up?"

"I gotta talk to you, Nick," the boy said solemnly. "It's important." The kid looked thinner and years older than he had the last time Nick had seen him a couple of weeks ago. Jimmy hadn't shown up that Saturday morning to go fishing. Then Nick had gotten busy with his protection job and hadn't seen the boy since.

A wave of guilt washed over him. He knew the kid was hurting. He wished he could find a way to help. "Listen, buddy, I'm just on my way to the airport to pick up a friend who's coming to visit. I'll be back later this afternoon. How about we talk then?"

Jimmy bit his lip. He glanced anxiously behind him. "You won't forget, will you?"

"I won't forget. If I do — you just come over and remind me, all right?"

The boy looked relieved. "Okay."

"Okay, then." Nick smiled. "See ya there, polar bear." Their inside joke — both being fans of the Aces hockey team — didn't bring the usual smile.

"See ya," Jimmy said darkly.

In his rearview mirror, Nick watched the kid meander up the hill the way he had come, his steps slow and plodding. Jimmy's house was a ways up the road, among a thick stand of pines, a big, expensive home with expansive views of the lake. From Nick's porch, he could just get a glimpse of it through the trees.

Alex Evans had been a successful accountant and it showed in the architectural design of the house and its plush interior. Nick figured it probably felt strangely empty now that Jimmy's dad was gone.

Nick watched the kid disappear out of

sight and vowed to make time for the boy. He hoped Samantha would understand, figured if she was anything like the woman he pictured in his mind, she would.

He would soon find out. Driving the SUV along the winding road around the lake, Nick headed for the Parks Highway. Off to his left the water lapped against a shoreline that was dotted with tall, dark pines. As long as he'd lived in Alaska, he'd never gotten tired of the scenery.

The weather was another story. By the time he reached the highway and turned toward Anchorage, a light mist had started to fall. Nick turned on the windshield wipers and stepped on the gas, eager to get to the city.

It was only a little after noon, Alaska time, when Samantha departed the plane. She should have been tired as she towed her carry-on through the airport toward the baggage claim. She'd had to get up at four in the morning to make the long cab ride to the airport to catch the seven a.m. flight to Anchorage.

She'd tried to sleep on the plane, but her nerves wouldn't ease up and she hadn't been able to do more than nap for a few minutes off and on. Now, as she spotted the tall man with the wavy black hair standing next to the baggage carousel, those nerves kicked up again.

Even from a distance, it was impossible to miss Nick Brodie. Those slashing black brows, high cheekbones and amazing blue eyes, that hard male body that oozed sexual virility. As he started walking toward her with the long, purposeful strides she remembered, it only took an instant to recall why she had tossed caution to the wind and gone to bed with him.

In that same instant, she was also reminded of the consequences.

Her pulse kicked up with nerves. Samantha pasted on a smile and moved toward Nick, came to a halt right in front of him.

"Hi," she said lamely.

Nick smiled, bent his head and very briefly kissed her. "Welcome to Alaska."

"I can't believe I'm really here."

"You're really here, and I'm really glad to see you." He glanced down at the heavy black wristwatch she remembered him wearing in Las Vegas. "It's after twelve," he said. "I thought before we head back to the house, we'd get some lunch. You hungry?"

"Starving. There wasn't much to eat on the plane."

"Now there's an understatement. I know

a place in the city with some good food and amazing views. You'll get your first real look at Alaska."

She thought of the endless forest stretching forever and the miles of empty ocean she had seen from the plane. "I saw some of it on the way."

"Yeah, it's really great," he said, missing her noncommittal tone of voice.

Behind them, the luggage carousel started up, and it didn't take long for her bag to appear. Nick wheeled the larger bag toward the exit while she towed her carry-on.

As they crossed the parking lot, Samantha shivered at the chill in the air and wished she'd worn heavier clothes. Her black leggings, short skirt, low heeled shoes and lightweight sweater weren't warm enough.

But the weather was still nice in the Bay area, would be for at least a little while longer. At least she'd packed jeans, sneakers and socks, and a decent jacket. Abby had talked her into buying a pair of hiking boots, but she'd never had them on.

The air was misting as Nick led the way to a black Ford Explorer, loaded in the bags, then helped her climb up in the passenger seat. The tires were big, pushing the vehicle way off the ground, so she didn't mind his help.

She buckled herself in while Nick rounded the car and slid behind the wheel.

"So where are we going?" she asked, still trying to get a handle on her nerves. There was no hurry, she reminded herself as he started the engine, nothing she needed to do but relax and enjoy her time with Nick, try to get to know him. For the time being, she needed to put everything else on the back burner.

"There's a place downtown . . . Simon and Seafort's. It's been around a while. I think you'll like it."

The restaurant, which called itself a saloon and grill, had an old-fashioned decor that made her feel right at home and helped ease some of her nerves. For the first time, she began to relax.

"We're famous for our seafood," Nick said as she looked at the menu and tried to decide what to order. "Crab cakes here are great. Steamed clams. Sandwiches. Pretty much everything."

Choosing a seafood salad made with fresh grilled salmon, bay shrimp, and Dungeness crab, she discovered he was right, the food was delicious. At least she'd found something good in Alaska.

And she couldn't deny the views from the restaurant, perched on a hill, were spectacular: a silvery ocean stretching for miles, misty clouds hanging over the surface of the water. Alaska might be remote, but the scenery was spectacular. The city itself was hilly, though nothing as steep as the hills in San Francisco. She hadn't expected to find skyscrapers in Anchorage, a welcome sight, even if there weren't that many and the buildings weren't as tall as the ones at home.

They finished the meal, the conversation fairly easy, but as they walked outside, the light mist that had been falling had turned into a full-blown storm.

"It's wet a lot this time of year, but there's still some great stuff to see, and it probably won't snow for a while."

Probably? "It rains quite a bit in San Francisco. I usually don't mind." Besides she hadn't really come to sightsee. "If I remember right, you live in a town called Fish Lake."

"Not much of a town, but yeah, that's right. It's about sixty miles away."

Sixty miles from civilization. "How big is it?"

"Population's about twenty-six hundred. But Wasilla's only twenty miles away from there. It's got nearly eight thousand people. They've got a lot more services there."

"Eight-thousand," she repeated dully,

thinking of the shopping she enjoyed at Neiman Marcus and Saks.

You aren't moving here, she reminded herself. But she couldn't help worrying what Nick would expect when she told him about the child she carried. Would he demand she move up here so that they could share custody?

Samantha suppressed a shiver and focused her attention on the road, determined not to worry about something that was still eight months away.

Nick flicked her a sideways glance and she realized it had been quiet in the car too long.

"So how's the pet-grooming business?" he asked.

Since she liked talking about her job, she was grateful he had chosen the topic. "Really great. We're looking for at least two new locations. I've been studying the competition. Doing a little fieldwork, but working mostly on the Internet. I'm putting together suggestions for services we might add to increase our business."

"Such as?"

"Adding doggie day care, for one thing, along with overnight boarding, and training. We could offer fenced-in grass play areas, heated indoor facilities with doggie beds, even a nighttime snuggle-down with

Milk Bones."

Nick's deep voice boomed out a laugh. "You're kidding, right? San Francisco dogs get a nightly snuggle-down? I think I could go for one of those myself."

She tried to summon a little outrage, but found herself grinning instead. "You're right, it sounds crazy. But I'm just the marketing person. I don't even have a dog. And if that's what people want and they're willing to pay for it, that's what we need to provide."

"So you work a lot on the Internet," he said.

Samantha smiled. "I'm a Google whiz."

Nick cocked a sleek dark eyebrow. "I'll remember that. You never know when it might come in handy."

Samantha relaxed back into her seat. "So tell me about Alaska. You were raised here, right? I know you lost your parents. What about your brothers, what are they like?"

"They're both still up here. My dad moved up from Texas just after Rafe was born. He's the oldest. Rafe lives in Valdez now. He owns a fleet of charter fishing boats. My brother, Dylan, is a float plane pilot. He owns a fishing lodge down on the Panhandle."

"So you're the baby of the family. Maybe

that's the reason you joined the Rangers. You had something to prove to your brothers."

"Could be, I guess. Mostly, I believed in God and country." He smiled. "Still do."

She remembered the way he had saved her that night in Las Vegas. Nick definitely had the hero gene.

"What about Alaska? Why do you like it so much?"

For the next few minutes, Nick talked about the wilderness and what it was like to live here. The freedom, the beauty, the wide-open spaces.

"Best time to see it is in the summer. The contrast between blue water and brilliant white, snow-capped mountains is incredible. Fall's pretty with the leaves changing color. Fall's hunting season. Moose and bear, mostly. It's just about over now."

She thought people should have the right to feed themselves but the idea of actually shooting an animal made her chest feel tight.

"Great fishing almost anywhere up here," Nick continued. "Winters are hard, but you get used to them." He talked about deep snow and sled dogs and ice fishing.

Samantha looked out through the rain-washed windows and felt a rush of despair.

CHAPTER SEVEN

As Nick drove the SUV along the lake road back to his house, he glanced over at Samantha. She seemed different up here, weighed down in a way she hadn't been in Vegas. She was just as pretty as he remembered, with her long, bouncy, nutmeg curls and soft pink lips, just as sexy with her petite figure and perfect curves.

Just catching a glimpse of her sitting next to him reminded him of the hours they had spent in bed and made him want her. Arousal slid through him as he thought of their single brief kiss at the airport, which led right back to thoughts of them in bed.

But he hadn't invited Samantha all the way to Alaska just for sex. Hell, he wasn't sure exactly what had possessed him to e-mail her that morning. They were totally unsuited. Samantha was a city girl, born and bred, through and through, completely out of her element in Alaska. Now that he saw her surrounded by rugged mountains, sweeping forests, and vast expanses of water, he could see how poorly she would fit into a life up here.

A life up here?

Where the hell had that come from? He wasn't planning to marry the woman, just get to know her a little, maybe spend a little more time making love to her.

He shouldn't have invited her. Now he had to find a way to entertain her for two whole weeks.

Nick inwardly sighed as he turned the car into his driveway, pressed the garage door opener, and waited for the door to slide up. As he started to pull inside, he spotted Mary George, Jimmy's aunt, standing on the porch at his front door.

He stopped the car and rolled down the window. "Hang on, Mary, I'll be right there."

Next to him, Samantha sat up a little straighter, her gaze going to the woman on the porch. "Who's that?"

"Her name's Mary George. She lives in a house down the way."

"She's . . . umm . . . very pretty."

"She is, yes." In her late twenties, with her tilted eyes, mocha skin, and above average, statuesque figure, Mary was more than just pretty. She was exotically beautiful. But neither of them had ever felt the spark of mutual attraction. Their only connection was Jimmy.

"Her nephew does odd jobs for me," he explained. "His dad recently died. Mary's his guardian."

"I see."

Her tone, one he hadn't heard from her before, had him turning in her direction. For the first time, he felt a ray of hope that things would improve between them. "Mary and I never clicked. I don't exactly know why." He grinned. "I hope you're jealous."

Samantha's eyebrows shot up. "No, of course not."

"Too bad," he teased, making her laugh for the first time since she'd gotten there. "Come on, I'll introduce you."

Nick parked the Explorer and led Samantha into the house, reminding himself to come back for her luggage after he'd talked to Mary.

He wondered why Mary was there. He'd only met the woman a couple of times, at some of Jimmy's youth hockey games, and of course he had spoken to her at the funeral. Because of Jimmy's size, the kid played with the thirteen-to-fourteen-year-old Bantams, instead of the eleven-to-twelve-year-old Pee Wees.

He thought of the boy whizzing over the ice, a natural at the sport. Mary had always been good with the kid, doing her best to fill in for his deceased mother, Cora, Mary's older sister who had died when Jimmy was six. From the photos Nick had seen, Cora had been even more beautiful than Mary.

He crossed the living room to the front door and pulled it open, invited the woman into his house. "It's good to see you, Mary." He tipped his head toward the petite woman who had walked in behind him. "This is a friend of mine from San Francisco, Samantha Hollis. She flew up for a visit."

Mary just nodded. She was dressed in jeans and a T-shirt while Samantha wore leggings and a sweater. "It's nice to meet you, Samantha."

"You, too, Mary."

Her black eyes returned to Nick. "I'm sorry to bother you, Nick, but I'm looking for Jimmy. He's been gone all day. I know it's Saturday, but he usually checks with me before he takes off on his own. He must have woken up early. He was already gone when I got up to fix breakfast and I haven't seen him since."

"I saw him this morning before I left for the airport. He was fine. He's probably off fishing somewhere with one of his friends."

Mary glanced toward the window. "Probably. Being out of the service area would explain why his phone goes directly to voice mail, but . . ."

"But he's only twelve and you're worried just the same."

"Yes, I am."

"Maybe you should call the police," Samantha suggested.

Nick cast her a glance. "State Troopers this far out, but it's a little too soon for that. Jimmy knows these woods, and even when his father was alive, his dad worked all the time. Jimmy's been on his own a lot. He'll probably be home by dark."

"I'm sure you're right," Mary said. "We're really still getting to know each other, at least as more than just aunt and nephew. I know how upset he's been about his dad. Then a couple of hours ago, Duke came home and Jimmy wasn't with him. They're usually inseparable."

"Duke is his dog?" Samantha asked.

Mary nodded. "A golden retriever. Jimmy loves that dog and Duke loves him."

"Sometimes dogs get bored," Samantha said. "If Jimmy and his friends were fishing, maybe Duke got tired of waiting and decided to come on home."

"Samantha works in the pet-grooming business," Nick explained. "She knows a lot about dogs."

Samantha smiled. "Mostly I'm in marketing. But I work in the shop so I'm around dogs a lot."

"I hope you're right. The thing is, Jimmy hasn't been himself since his father died. I want to help him get through this, but I can't seem to find a way to reach him."

Nick thought about the story Jimmy had told him, how he had convinced himself that his dad had been murdered. He wasn't about to mention that to Mary. He and Jimmy were friends. The kid trusted him. Nick didn't want to lose that trust. He made a mental note to have another talk with the boy, see if he had his head on straight about his father's death.

"Have you considered any sort of therapy?" Samantha asked Mary. Nick caught the concern in her voice. She had shown that same kind of concern for the man who had accosted her when Nick had been in the process of pounding him into the carpet. It was an admirable quality, maybe part of the reason he had asked her to supper that night.

"Maybe a psychologist could help him cope," Samantha finished.

"I've suggested it," Mary said. "His father left money in trust for Jimmy. There's enough to pay whatever a doctor would charge. So far I haven't been able to convince him it's a good idea."

"Maybe you just need to give him a little more time," Samantha said.

"I'll call him tonight," Nick added, "ask him if he wants to go fishing in the morning." He looked over at Samantha, hoping she wouldn't mind. "We could go early, be back before you even woke up."

Her features softened. "I think it's a good idea. With his father gone, having a man to talk to is bound to be good for Jimmy."

An idea struck. "Maybe you'd like to come with us," Nick said. "We'll be taking out the aluminum boat. Once you get the hang of it, fishing's really a lot of fun."

Samantha didn't look all that excited about it. "I think the two of you should go by yourselves. Give you time for some man-talk."

"Maybe you're right." He turned back to Mary. "Tell Jimmy I'm going to call. We'll set something up for tomorrow."

Mary nodded. "Okay. In the meantime, if you hear from him —"

"I'll have him call you, then send him straight home."

"Thanks, Nick."

"No problem. Jimmy's a good kid."

"Yes, he is," Mary said. She headed for the door, stopped and looked back as Nick pulled it open. "Nice to meet you, Samantha. If you get some time, our house isn't that far away. I've usually got a pot of coffee on."

Samantha's smile seemed to come easy. "Thanks, I might just take you up on that."

Mary walked out the door and Nick closed it behind her.

"She seems really nice," Samantha said.

"I think she is. She's single and only in her late twenties, but she stepped right up when Jimmy's father died. It can't be easy turning into an instant mom."

Samantha's gaze went toward the window, her pretty brown eyes following Mary up the hill toward home. "No, it can't," she said softly.

Crammed into the back of some rusty old rattletrap car, Jimmy lay on his side, his knees up under his chin, his wrists and ankles bound with duct tape, a piece of tape stretched over his mouth. His eye was swollen nearly shut, his lip split and throbbing.

The two men who had forced him into the trunk had taken his jacket and the brand-new Reeboks his aunt had bought him at the mall last week.

Jimmy shivered. It was dark in the trunk, and with his arms bound behind him, he could barely move. His jeans were damp and he was freezing. The trunk smelled like dead fish.

Fear slipped through him. After he'd gone to see Nick that morning, the men in the car had picked him up on his way to the bus stop not far from his house. Though he'd put up a pretty good fight, they were bigger and stronger. The next thing he knew he was bound and gagged, tossed into the trunk, and the car was driving away.

Jimmy knew why they had taken him. Using some of the money he'd earned from Nick, he'd been riding the bus into Anchorage after school a couple of days a week and again on Saturday, hanging around the office building on "C" Street where his dad had worked.

He'd been searching for the man his father had been arguing with the day before he died. Jimmy hadn't seen anyone he recognized, but if the argument was about business, the man must have worked with his dad, or been one of his clients.

Two days ago, Jimmy had ridden the elevator up to the tenth floor of his father's office. He had talked to his father's secretary, had asked her about his dad, asked her if his father had been upset about anything lately. Maybe she had told someone he'd been there asking questions. A chill shivered through him. Now these men were going to kill him.

The car speeded up and cold air swept through the rusted-out parts of the trunk, sending a chill over his skin. Jimmy struggled against the tape around his wrists, fought to break the hold on his ankles, but the binding didn't even budge. He'd been in the trunk all day, rolling around inside as the car made a series of stops.

During the day, the vehicle had been parked somewhere for hours before the men returned and started the engine again. He had no idea where they were taking him, or any idea what the men would do to him when they got there.

Dread slithered like a snake down his spine. Someone had murdered his dad. He was sure of that now. These men had come after him because he'd been asking questions, trying to find out who'd killed him. They were probably going to kill him, too.

Jimmy closed his eyes. He wondered if anyone would ever find his body.

He wondered what his dad had discovered

that had made the men so mad.

"You don't need to worry," Nick said to Samantha. "Jimmy's a kid. He's just gone off somewhere and time's slipped away from him."

"If he was my son, I'd call the authorities."

Nick flicked her a glance, saw something in her face. "Something happened to you. What was it?"

Samantha glanced back out the window. If she wanted to get to know Nick, it was only fair that he get to know her.

"I lost my older sister when I was ten. Danielle was twelve. She disappeared when she was walking home from school. They found her body two weeks later. She'd been murdered." Samantha swallowed, tried not to think of the way her parents had walked around like zombies, unable to sleep, unable to talk without crying. How she had felt physically ill and so desperately alone.

"Did they catch the guy?"

Samantha shook her head. "No."

"I'm sorry, Samantha. Being a cop, I've seen what that kind of loss can do to a family."

"It was a terrible time. I still don't like to talk about it. But we stuck together, became even closer as a family."

Nick flashed on the young girl in Anchorage, one of three who had been murdered by a serial killer. He remembered her long, golden-blond hair, matted with dried blood where she lay on the floor. Remembered her parents' terrible grief. The case had played a major role in his leaving the force.

This was different. Jimmy was almost a teenager and he was living in a very safe neighborhood, but worry began to filter through him. He'd be damned glad when the kid got home.

Samantha shook her head. "I know I'm overreacting. I'm sure you're right."

"He isn't handling his dad's death very well. He actually told me he believes his father was murdered. The guy died of a heart attack. I guess Jimmy just didn't want to believe it."

"He'll get past it, just like I did."

Nick nodded. "I'm sure he will. I'd better get your luggage, get you settled in." Turning, he went back out to the car.

He grabbed the bags and walked back into the house. "I'll put these in your room," he said. "Come on. I'll show you where." Leading her down the hall to the room next to his, he carried her bags inside and set them up on the bed.

Inwardly, he sighed. In the back of his mind, he'd been hoping she might suggest staying with him. Looked like there wasn't much chance of that.

By the time Samantha got settled, dusk was moving in, earlier now with summer over, around seven thirty p.m. He wasn't much of a cook, but he could barbeque pretty much anything. Remembering Samantha wasn't a big red meat eater, tonight he was grilling chicken.

As he stood in front of the barbeque on the wooden deck attached to the back of the house, he could see her through the kitchen window, all those bouncy, fine brown curls and a face that made a man think of the girl in high school who had been his first crush. She seemed right at home in his kitchen, standing at the counter, making a salad out of the lettuce and tomatoes he had brought home yesterday.

Since he was five miles from the mini-mart in tiny Fish Lake and twenty miles from a bona fide supermarket, he kept his pantry full, and with company coming, he'd stocked up even more than usual. He headed back into the house to grab a beer, see if Samantha wanted something to drink. "Chicken's looking good," he said. "How's the salad coming?"

She wiped her hands on an apron she had found in one of the kitchen drawers. Green canvas with a picture of an antlered deer on the front. Underneath the deer it said, Get the Buck Out of My Kitchen. Just looking at her wearing it had him fighting a grin.

"Salad's finished. I made blue cheese dressing. I hope that's okay."

"Are you kidding? Blue cheese is my favorite." He inhaled the yeasty aroma of baking. "Something smells good. What is it?"

"I found some canned peaches in the pantry. I used them to bake a cobbler. I figured you don't get much homemade dessert, being a bachelor."

"Oh, man." He walked over and brushed a light kiss over her lips. Even with that brief contact, he felt the rush. Samantha made no comment but her big doe eyes went wide. Apparently, she felt it, too.

"I'd better call Jimmy, make sure he got home. You want a beer or a glass of wine?"

"I'm fine."

Nick pulled his cell phone out of his pocket and punched in Jimmy's number, frowned when the phone still went to voice mail. He dialed the landline at Jimmy's house.

Mary answered, near-panic in her voice.

"Jimmy still isn't home. What . . . what should I do?"

Nick's hand tightened on the phone. Supper would have to wait. "I think it's time you called the police."

CHAPTER EIGHT

The junky old car rounded a corner, throwing Jimmy against the inside of the trunk; then it began to slow. His heart started racing, accelerating till it pounded in his ears.

The crunch of tires on the side of the road made his stomach clench in fear. The engine went off and both car doors opened. He could hear the sound of footfalls heading toward the rear of the car.

"Put your mask on, stupid."

"Fuck you, Virgil."

When the trunk popped up, the men were wearing the same red ski masks they'd had on before. "Okay, kid, the joyride's over." The bigger man, with shaggy brown hair sticking out from beneath the cap and squinty little eyes, grabbed Jimmy's arm and dragged him out of the trunk. Jimmy noticed the gun on the belt at his waist.

The other man had a hooked nose that protruded through the hole in the middle of the mask. He pulled out a pocketknife and flipped it open. The loud click of the blade locking in place echoed in the darkness.

Jimmy froze. Though his legs felt wobbly, when the guy with the knife started toward him, Jimmy crouched, ready to spring and fight to the death.

The big guy cuffed him across the head. "Take it easy, kid. We aren't going to hurt you — not if you do what we say."

Jimmy didn't believe them. He was breathing hard, fighting to hold back his fear, trying to work out a plan, figure out what to do.

The man with the knife came toward him again and Jimmy stiffened. "Relax, boy. I'm just gonna cut the tape." His raspy smoker's voice sent a chill down Jimmy's spine.

To his surprise, the knife sliced cleanly through the duct tape around his wrists, then his ankles. The hook-nosed man pulled tape off his jeans and yanked it off his mouth. Jimmy unwrapped the tape on his wrists.

"Now here's the deal," the big man said, his squinty eyes locked on Jimmy's face. "You been nosing around, digging into things that are none of your business. That's gotta stop. You understand?"

When Jimmy said nothing, the man cuffed

him again, harder this time. "I want to know what your father told you."

Jimmy frowned. "About what?"

The big man eyed him darkly. "If your old man didn't say anything, why are you snooping around?"

Jimmy tried to come up with an answer, something they might believe, but his tongue seemed stuck to the roof of his mouth. "I just . . . I wanted to find out what happened to him."

"That's it?"

He managed to nod, even as he glanced wildly around, looking for a way to escape. He knew where he was. The men had brought him back to Fish Lake. He was maybe a mile from his house.

The hook-nosed man grabbed the front of his T-shirt and hauled him close. "All right, boy. From now on you keep your mouth shut. You don't ask questions. You don't snoop around your dad's office. If you do, what happened to you today won't be piss compared to what'll happen to you the next time."

"And it won't be just you," the big man added. "Your pretty little aunt will get a ride in the trunk — after we've had our fill of her."

"And she won't be coming back," said the

hook-nosed man. "She'll be fish food by the time they find her — and so will you. Got it?"

Jimmy nodded, feeling sick to his stomach. He was in seventh grade. He knew what the men would do to his aunt before they killed her and dumped her in the lake.

The hook-nosed man let go of his T-shirt and backed away. Moonlight gleamed on the gun at his waist.

"When you get home, you tell your aunt you had a fight," the big man said. "Nothing else. Not unless you want her to wind up as dead as your old man."

Jimmy's mouth felt so dry he couldn't speak.

"Now get out of here. Before we decide to make sure you keep your mouth shut forever."

Jimmy bolted toward the cover of the pines just off the road, running full-tilt into the darkness. Any second, he expected to feel the burning pain of a bullet slamming into his back. He didn't stop until he reached a place where the trees were so dense he could barely walk between them, then he crouched in the deep foliage to listen for the sound of the men coming after him.

His heart was pounding so hard he could

feel it inside his chest. No matter how mad his aunt got, he wasn't going to tell her or anyone else what had happened to him. As much as he wanted to find the man who had killed his dad, it wasn't worth losing his aunt Mary, the last family he had left in the world.

Jimmy listened for the sound of the car engine starting. He wasn't leaving his hiding place till he was sure it was safe to go home.

By ten o'clock Mary was in tears. Samantha sat next to her on the sofa in the impressive high-ceilinged living room of the family's log home overlooking the lake.

The State Troopers had come and gone. They had taken a report and promised to increase patrols in the area, begin the preliminaries necessary to assemble a search team. In such a rural location, an accident was more likely than foul play, which was no comfort to Mary.

"I should have called sooner," she said, twisting a Kleenex between her fingers. "I was just so sure he'd come home on his own."

Mary had searched every room in the house, checked the garage, the storage shed, and the forest behind the house. She had phoned all Jimmy's friends several times, but no one had seen the boy all day.

Nick was driving around in the Explorer, checking the mini-mart in the tiny town of Fish Lake, the pizza parlor, walking the shoreline in the areas near the house, checking some of Jimmy's favorite fishing holes.

"Have you looked at his e-mail?" Samantha asked.

"One of the troopers suggested it but I didn't know his password."

"Let's give it a try. We could also take a look at his Facebook account."

Mary came up off the sofa. "All right." She started toward the staircase fashioned out of knotted pine, and Samantha fell in behind her.

Jimmy's second-floor bedroom had a full-size log bed covered by a dark green quilt with a bear pattern on the front. Posters of the *Cars* movie hung on the wall next to one of *G.I. Joe.*

On top of the log dresser, there were photos of Jimmy's dad and mom, a tall man with a lean face and reddish-brown hair, and an exotic-looking woman even more beautiful than Mary. Samantha was surprised to see the bed neatly made and Jimmy's clothes all picked up.

"He's been trying really hard to help me

around the house. I don't think his room was this clean when his dad was still alive."

"My younger brother, Peter, was a real slob when we were kids. He's in college now, but I imagine he isn't much better."

They walked over to the desk against the wall. An Apple laptop sat on top. "His dad bought him his first computer when he was nine years old," Mary said. "Jimmy already knew how to use it. Alex gave him this one for Christmas last year."

The woman glanced up, tears in her eyes. "Alex might have done a lot of things, but he loved his son. If something's happened to Jimmy, I'll never forgive myself."

"Don't say that, Mary. He's a boy. Peter was always doing something he shouldn't. Sometimes I wondered if he'd make it through high school. He's in his twenties now and doing just fine." She didn't mention her sister. Mary was having a hard enough time as it was.

"Let me take a look." Samantha pulled out the chair, sat down at the computer and turned it on. The Password box popped up. "Can you think of something that's important to him? Something he loves?"

"Hockey. He loves to play ice hockey. He's really good at it."

"What's his favorite team?"

96

"The Aces."

Samantha typed in the word. *Incorrect Password* popped up.

"Tell me something about them."

"The polar bear is their mascot. Jimmy has a couple of Aces' T-shirts with bears on the front."

She typed in *polarbear,* then polarbear-aces, got nowhere. She typed in *acespolarbears* and the screen opened up.

"Wow, you did it," Mary said.

"I work with computers a lot. My brother's favorite sport was football. His password is *oaklandraidersrule.*"

They checked Jimmy's e-mail, found mostly junk, a couple of notes from friends he hadn't yet answered. Samantha went on her Facebook page to access Jimmy's, but he hadn't posted anything new. A couple of girls had posted photos of themselves, but if he'd seen them, Jimmy hadn't responded.

"It was worth a try," Samantha said, shutting the machine back down.

"I wish Nick would call. I can't stand this waiting." Mary led the way back downstairs and Jimmy's golden retriever, Duke, fell in beside them, a hopeful look on his doggie face. He accompanied them into the kitchen, toenails tapping on the wide-planked hardwood floors. He lay down on his bed in the corner, clearly waiting for his friend to come home.

Samantha glanced around the kitchen, which was state-of-the-art, with stainless steel appliances and designer lighting. Clearly, Jimmy's father had been a very successful man.

Just as they walked up to the breakfast table, the door from the laundry room swung open and Jimmy walked into the house.

"Jimmy!" Mary's voice came out high and shrill. "Forgodsake, where have you been?"

The boy didn't answer. Duke jumped up and hurried toward him. Jimmy patted him absently on the head and kept walking. He was tall for twelve and muscular, a good-looking kid who was clearly part Alaska Native. Mary spotted his swollen and blackening eye at the same time Samantha did.

As the boy walked past, Mary reached out and caught his arm. "What happened, Jimmy? Who did that to you?"

"I got in a fight, okay? I'm all right. It's no big deal."

"It's a very big deal, Jimmy! Do you have any idea how worried I've been? An hour ago, I called the police!"

His face seemed to turn a shade lighter. "Call them back and tell them I'm okay."

"Are you sure?" Mary asked. "I think you should sit down and let me take a look at you, at least let me put some antiseptic on your lip."

"I didn't hit my head or anything. I'm fine."

"I'll call the troopers," Samantha volunteered, "let them know he's home safe. And I'll see if I can reach Nick."

"Thank you."

As Samantha headed for the phone, Jimmy tipped his head in her direction. "Who's she?"

"Her name is Samantha Hollis. She's a friend of Nick's."

Samantha lifted the phone and dialed 9-1-1. When the dispatch answered, she relayed the information that Jimmy Evans was home, safe and well, answered a couple of other questions, then hung up the phone.

She heard footsteps in the living room, figured it was Nick. "We're in here," she called out to him. "Jimmy's home."

Nick walked in scowling. It was clear he was barely hanging onto his temper. "Where the hell have you been? Your aunt's been frantic."

His scowl deepened as he spotted the boy's black eye and split lip. He reached out and caught Jimmy's chin, tipped his face up. His gaze remained hard, but his deep voice softened. "What happened, Jimmy? Are you in some kind of trouble?"

The boy pulled away. "I'm not in trouble. I got in a fight with one of the kids from school. It's no big deal, okay?"

"Which kid?" Mary asked.

Jimmy didn't answer, just mulishly set his jaw.

"Your aunt asked you a question," Nick said.

"I'm not a rat. We had a fight. That's all I'm saying."

Mary looked at Nick for guidance.

"All right, Jimmy, you don't have to rat out your friend. But I think it's time you talked to someone. I called earlier to ask if you wanted to go fishing in the morning. You can either talk to me tomorrow, or you can go to a counselor. As your guardian, your aunt can make that happen. What's it going to be?"

Seconds ticked past as Jimmy mulled over his choices. Samantha was sure he'd pick talking to Nick. "I'll go to the counselor."

Nick looked surprised, though he tried not to show it. "That's a good idea. In the meantime, you and I are still going fishing. I'll be here to pick you up at six a.m."

Jimmy's eyes widened. "No way. I don't

have to go with you. We made a deal."

"The deal was you don't have to talk to me and you don't. You still have to go fishing with me."

Jimmy opened his mouth to argue, snapped it closed. "Fine."

"And you better be here when I get here. I still have plenty of pull with the department. You give your aunt any more trouble and I'll have you hauled in to detention. Now get some sleep. I'll see you in the morning."

Jimmy's mouth thinned.

"Come on, Samantha, let's go home." With a hand at her waist, Nick guided her out of the house.

Nick helped Samantha into his SUV for the drive down the hill to his house. It had started to rain. This time of year, rainy days were a given.

"What do you think really happened?" Samantha asked. "A fistfight wouldn't explain why he didn't come home all day."

"Maybe he was afraid what his aunt would say when she saw his face, but that's hard to believe. Jimmy's usually the kind of kid who tackles trouble head-on."

"Then what else could it be?"

Nick shook his head. "Worrying his aunt

that way was really out of character." He ran a hand over his jaw. "I don't know, it seemed like he was trying to brazen it out, putting up a tough front, but I got a feeling he was scared."

"Of his aunt?"

Nick shook his head. "No." He sighed. "Hell, he's a kid. Maybe I was reading the whole thing wrong. I'll talk to him in the morning, see if I can get him to open up." He looked over at Samantha as he pulled into the driveway. "I've got a microwave. How about we heat up some of that chicken?"

"That sounds great. I'm really hungry."

"Me, too." But the kind of hunger tightening his groin had nothing to do with food and everything to do with Samantha Hollis. He tried not to remember the softness of her lips, her petite, feminine curves moving beneath him, how snug she felt when he was inside her.

He tried, but by the time he pulled the car into the garage and turned off the engine, helped Samantha down from the vehicle, he was hard as a frigging stone.

Samantha smiled as he led her up on the deck, through the mudroom, into the kitchen. "I imagine after all the excitement, we'll both get a good night's sleep."

He cast her a thunderous look. "You really think so? Because I'll be lying there half the night aching for you, wishing you were in my bed instead of your own."

Her eyes widened. "You said —"

"I know what I said, and I won't break my word. Doesn't mean I don't want you." He leaned over and very softly kissed her, felt his erection stirring beneath his jeans. Samantha returned the kiss, making him even harder, then she pulled away.

"I-I'd better get the chicken out of the fridge and into the microwave." She started walking toward the refrigerator, stopped and turned back. "I'm glad your friend is home safe."

"Yeah, so am I." It took superhuman effort to force his mind off sex and onto the conversation he needed to have with Jimmy in the morning. But the kid was important to him. The thought had him glancing at Samantha. Nick sighed and turned away.

Samantha couldn't sleep. Nick had said he'd be lying in bed, aching for her, wishing she were there with him. She hadn't thought she would be the one aching, unable to sleep.

How could she have forgotten the magnetic pull of the man, the aura of masculinity that had so effortlessly seduced her the first time?

Just looking at that lean-muscled body as he walked around the house made her want him, made her remember those long, purposeful strides that had attracted her before. And those eyes, as blue as a sky in summer. Eyes that should have been cool but instead seemed to burn with an inner heat.

He was the kind of man who touched easily and without conscious thought, the kind who made a woman feel protected and desired. She remembered the taste of him, the feel of his heavy weight pressing her down in the mattress, of his hard length moving inside her. She thought of the heat and the pleasure, and dampness settled in her core.

Clearly being pregnant didn't destroy a woman's sexual desires, or at least not at this early stage.

Samantha shifted beneath the sheet, the cool fabric abrading her nipples, which had peaked just thinking about Nick's mouth closing over them. Her womb clenched. She wanted Nick Brodie just as she had from the moment he had appeared in that Las Vegas hallway.

And yet she needed more from him now than just sexual gratification. She needed to know him, trust him. She had to think of the tiny being growing inside her that would one day become his child.

Samantha sighed into the darkness. She couldn't help thinking of how Nick had handled the situation last night with the boy, Jimmy Evans. Nick had been calm and collected, strong and steady for Mary, but under it all, she had sensed his deep concern.

Nick had been just as relieved as Mary when the boy had walked back into the house unharmed, except for a few cuts and bruises. His concern had surfaced when he had taken a stand with the boy, who clearly needed direction from an older male figure now that his father was gone.

So far Samantha had seen nothing in Nick Brodie's behavior that would lead her to believe he would be anything but a responsible parent.

Then again, few men were happy to have such a huge responsibility thrust upon them by a woman they barely knew.

Samantha heard movement in the bedroom next to hers. Nick was awake, just as he'd said. How long would she be able to resist the urge to go to him, offer him her body as she had before?

But a sexual relationship would change

the dynamic between them, alter her perception in any number of ways. She needed time.

Samantha plumped her pillow, put it over her head, and tried not to wish Nick would storm through the door and demand a place in her bed.

CHAPTER NINE

The aluminum boat rocked as Nick pulled the cord on the motor and the small outboard engine sputtered to life. He grabbed the handle and began to steer the boat toward a different fishing hole, one that he and Jimmy favored. The lake was smooth as glass, just the frothy wake of the propellers behind them, and the occasional silver flash of a fish in the water ahead of them. A cool breeze whispered through the trees along the shore.

Sitting in the bow, rod and reel in hand, the boy had been quiet all morning. Nick hadn't pressed him, just let him ease into the quiet rhythm of two men fishing, relaxing and enjoying the day.

It was one of those crisp fall mornings that were golden in Alaska, the leaves brilliant shades of red, orange, and yellow, the sky a cerulean blue, not a cloud in sight.

If it weren't for the serious expression on

Jimmy's puffy, battered face, Nick might have wished he'd brought Samantha along.

He cut the engine, let the boat drift closer to shore, into a spot where the branches of the trees hung over the water, and rocks on the shoreline provided habitat for grayling or rainbow trout.

Jimmy cast his line into the water like a pro. He'd been fishing since he was a little boy. Nick cast his own line, let it sink into the water.

"How's your face?" he asked casually.

"It's okay."

"How'd the other kid look?"

Jimmy just shrugged.

"What were you guys fighting about?"

Jimmy drilled him with a look. "You said we didn't have to talk."

"We've always talked before. What's different this time?"

Jimmy just shook his head. His expression looked bleak, as if he carried the weight of the world on his thick shoulders.

"You know you can trust me, Jim. If you told me something in confidence, it would stay that way. I give you my word on that."

Jimmy swallowed and glanced away. Nick noticed the hand that held the rod trembled.

"You're scaring me, buddy. We've been friends since I first started coming up here on weekends. If something's going on, you can count on me to help you. You can trust me. You can tell me anything, Jimmy."

The boy looked up. Nick thought he caught the sheen of tears in the kid's dark eyes. "You're a cop. If I told you something bad, you'd have to tell the police."

"I was a cop. I'm not a cop anymore. I'm your friend, Jim. Friends help each other."

Jimmy glanced away. His voice came out little more than a whisper. "I told you once, but you didn't believe me."

Christ. Was this about his father's death? Had the kid told one of his friends, the kid made fun of him and they got into a fight? Maybe seeing a shrink really was the answer.

"If you told one of the kids you thought your dad was murdered, I can see where that could be a problem. Kids can be cruel sometimes. If one of them made fun of you —"

The boy seemed not to hear him, just stared at him with such desolation, Nick felt a clutch in his chest.

"If I tell you what happened, they'll kill her, Nick. They'll kill us both. I can't talk about it. I can't tell you anything, okay? If you're my friend you won't ask any more questions."

Nick's pulse began to slow into a rhythm

109

he recognized only too well. All his cop instincts were suddenly kicking in, his brain analyzing the situation, searching for clues, trying to sort out the facts.

"Okay, I won't ask. I'll start by promising you again that you can trust me to keep this between the two of us — at least until we can find a way to get all of it sorted out. You don't have to tell me anything. I'll just make a few guesses, see if I'm on the right track, okay?"

"Maybe we should go back," Jimmy said nervously, glancing toward the shore.

Nick pulled the cord and started the motor, headed the boat farther out into the lake where no one could possibly hear them. He shut off the engine and casually cast his line into the water, the buzz of the reel a friendly, familiar sound.

"Grayling are good eating," he said. "Be nice to take some home to your aunt for supper."

A shudder rippled through Jimmy. He looked back at the shore, then cast his line into the water on the opposite side of the boat.

"Yesterday morning you came to see me," Nick said easily, keeping his attention on his rod and reel. "You had something you wanted to tell me."

"I just . . . I wanted to talk to you."

"About?"

"I thought . . . I was hoping you would change your mind about helping me."

"Help you look into what happened to your dad?"

Jimmy nodded.

"Why would I do that?"

"I don't know . . . I . . . I've been riding the bus into town, getting off at my dad's office. I thought if I saw the man Dad was arguing with that night in the study, I could get his name. Maybe I could figure out what they were fighting about, see if that was the reason Dad got killed."

"That's what you came over to tell me? That you're still convinced your father was murdered?"

He swallowed. "I figured the man must be a client or someone who worked with my dad at the office. I was watching the parking lot a couple of days a week, but I never saw him."

"Something happened yesterday," Nick said, careful to keep his tone even. "Something that had to do with your father."

Jimmy's head came up and fear flashed in his eyes. "I'm scared, Nick. I don't want to say anything. I don't want anything to happen to Aunt Mary."

Jesus. As much as he wanted to believe the kid was just imagining things, one look at his battered face, the terror he couldn't quite hide, and Nick had a very bad feeling Jimmy had stumbled onto something that put him in serious danger.

"Did they come after you?" he asked gently. "Threaten you? Threaten to hurt your aunt?"

Staring into the bottom of the boat as if it held a world of answers, Jimmy finally glanced up, his black eyes filled with turbulent emotion. "These two guys drove up beside me on the road near the bus stop. They told me to get in the car, but I wouldn't. We had a fight. They tied me up and put tape over my mouth, then drove me around in the trunk of their ratty old car. I thought they were going to kill me."

"Christ, Jimmy."

The boy stared into Nick's face. "They said they'd . . . do things to Mary, you know? Then kill us both and throw us in the lake." He swallowed, tears welling an instant before he blinked them away. "They'll do it, Nick. If you tell anyone, they'll kill us."

Samantha finished checking her e-mail on the laptop she'd brought with her and set up in her bedroom. Her mom had sent a message, asking if she was enjoying her trip to the wilds of Alaska. Samantha wrote back that the scenery was beautiful and it was an interesting place.

She hadn't told anyone in her family the real reason for her trip — that she was pregnant by a man she barely knew and was there to decide the best way to handle it. She just said she had a friend who had invited her up for a couple of weeks and she had decided to accept the invitation.

So far her mom hadn't pressed the issue.

There were a couple of business e-mails. Samantha answered them and also the one from Abby.

How are you doing? What is Nick really like? Is he still perfect?

Samantha replied, Doing fine so far. Nick seems like the guy I met in Vegas. Still figuring things out. Sam

P.S. No man is perfect — as we both know very well. A not-so-veiled reference to some of the men Abby had dated and the rat-bastard Justin Chapman III Samantha had been engaged to marry.

The reply came right back. LOL. But I haven't given up yet. Keep me posted. Ab.

Samantha closed down the machine and went into the kitchen. Nick's house was neat and clean, the leather sofa and chairs and big-screen TV were exactly what she would have expected. The place was a little stark, no throw rugs, no curtains at the kitchen window, typically male, which Nick most certainly was.

She checked the clock up on the wall above the doorway. Nick had said he and Jimmy would be back before lunch. To keep herself occupied, she went into the pantry and pulled out what she needed to make the guys a meal.

She was just cleaning up when Nick walked through the back door, Jimmy right behind him. Both of them looked tired, and though they had fished all morning, neither of them looked the least bit relaxed.

"Catch anything?" Samantha asked, injecting a bright note into her voice.

Jimmy just shook his head.

"Nothing biting," Nick said mildly, but she could read the worry in his face. "We'll have better luck next time."

"I made chicken salad sandwiches from the leftovers last night. There's plenty for all of us. Plus I made some potato soup, and there's leftover peach cobbler I heated up."

"Sounds great," Nick said with a little

114

more enthusiasm. He and Jimmy both shrugged out of their jackets and draped them over the backs of the kitchen chairs.

"Sit down and I'll bring the plates over."

Jimmy sat. Nick crossed the kitchen and walked up behind her, slid his arms around her waist and eased her back against his chest. "I'm starting to feel guilty. I didn't ask you up here to do housework."

"I like cooking. It's liking fishing, I guess. It relaxes me." She smiled. "I'm not high on cleaning, but that's another subject."

Nick flicked a glance at Jimmy, who seemed to understand. "Okay, you cooked, we'll clean."

"Fair enough." She went to work as Nick returned to the table, the two of them sitting side by side, Jimmy tall for twelve but way shorter than Nick's six-foot-two-inch frame. The boy's eye was still swollen and he didn't seem any happier than he had been when he had come home late last night. Samantha wondered if Nick had made any progress with him.

Samantha served the plates and they all ate together. Jimmy started slowly, just picking at his food. But he must have liked what she'd made because he began wolfing it down as if he hadn't eaten in days.

"Take it easy, buddy," Nick said. "It's not

going to escape."

"I didn't have breakfast," Jimmy grumbled with a meaningful glance at Nick, who had roused him out of bed at six. "I wasn't hungry."

Their eyes met and something passed between them. "Go ahead then," Nick said. "A growing boy's gotta eat."

"Besides," Samantha added, "I like it when someone appreciates my cooking."

For the first time, Jimmy smiled. He looked like a little boy instead of a sullen preteen. Remembering that he was grieving for his father, Samantha's heart went out to him.

"Aunt Mary tries real hard," he said, talking around his last bite of chicken salad sandwich, "but she's not a very good cook."

"Maybe I can give her some pointers while I'm here," Samantha said.

Jimmy picked up his fork and shoveled in a bite of cobbler. "That'd be great."

After they finished their lunch and dessert, the guys cleaned up the dirty dishes as promised, and Nick walked Jimmy outside. She couldn't hear what they were saying, but she saw Nick clamp a hand on the boy's shoulder and give it a reassuring squeeze. He waved as the kid started up the hill toward home.

Samantha took it as a good sign — until Nick walked back into the house, the scowl once more on his face.

"If that look is any indication, the fishing trip didn't go too well."

"Jimmy doesn't need a shrink. It might help him get over losing his dad, but that isn't the problem."

"Then what is?"

Nick just shook his head. "It's a confidence I'm afraid I can't share. It's the only way he'd talk to me."

"Too bad. I might have been able to help."

Nick walked up behind her, slid his arms around her waist. "That's not the kind of help I need." He nipped the side of her neck. "What I need is you."

Ignoring the rush of warmth, she turned out of his embrace. "It's too soon, Nick."

He sighed. "I know. Sorry. Listen, I've got something I need to do in my office. Can you entertain yourself for a while?"

"Sure. I've got a good book. What about supper? I was hoping you'd bring home some fish, but since you didn't . . ."

"There's frozen trout in the freezer. Would that work?"

"You bet. Fried or baked?"

Nick grinned. "Fried. Definitely."

Samantha's stomach lifted at the sight of

that grin. Oh, boy, she was in trouble.

"You . . . ahh . . . wouldn't know how to make hush puppies, would you?" Nick asked. "My grandmother used to make them when we visited her in Texas."

"I know how to make them. Consider it done."

Nick cocked a sleek black eyebrow. "I know your plan," he teased. "You're trying to make me fall in love with you by cooking all my favorite meals."

Her smile slid away. "That isn't my plan. I just like to cook."

"Hey, I was kidding." Tugging her back into his arms, he kissed her, softly at first, then deeper. A flood of heat shot all the way to her toes. When Nick deepened the kiss, she leaned into him, gave herself up to the need pouring through her. She felt lost when Nick pulled away.

"I . . . ahh . . . really need to do this," he said.

"Sure." She smiled, worked to bring her speeding heart under control. "I think I'll sit out on the deck for a while."

"Good day for it. I won't be too long." Nick disappeared into his bedroom and Samantha took the novel she'd been reading on the plane out on the deck. It was chilly, but nothing more than she was used to in

San Francisco. And from where she sat, she could see a tiny creek running behind the house. On the opposite side, the mountain rose sharply, forested and beautiful. A hawk soared out over the trees.

She tried to read, but the book didn't hold her interest any more here than it had on the plane. She needed a good mystery novel, or maybe a romantic suspense. She amended that. She had more romance in her life right now than she could handle.

Closing the book, she wandered back inside and down the hall. The door to Nick's bedroom was open. He sat at his computer, engrossed in whatever was on the screen. He didn't even stir as she walked up behind him.

A photo took up the left half of the monitor, an attractive man with reddish-brown hair, well-dressed in a suit and tie, and smiling. She recognized him as the man in the photo she had seen on the dresser in Jimmy's bedroom last night, Jimmy's father. On the other half of the screen was a newspaper article in the *Anchorage Daily News.*

Prominent Accountant Dies of Unexpected Heart Attack. Reading over Nick's shoulder, she skimmed the page, saw the article was about a man named Alexander "Alex" Evans, who had died at the age of forty-four. She figured it had to be Jimmy's dad. Alex had been a partner at Jankowski, Sorenson, Petrova, and Evans, one of the most respected accounting firms in Anchorage.

According to the article, Alex and the other partners were noted philanthropists, making large donations to a number of charities, including the Anchorage Police Department Widows and Orphans Fund.

She started to say something, to let Nick know she had come into the room, when he clicked up another page. It was a photograph in profile of the same man twenty years younger. It appeared to be a police mug shot and in it, the man looked like a hardened criminal, his cheeks sunken in, dark circles around his eyes.

Except that the name beneath the photo wasn't Alexander Evans — it was Alexi Evanko.

Her mind spun. She thought of Jimmy's face, battered and bruised last night, filled with desperation this morning. Nick had said the boy seemed afraid. She thought of what Jimmy had told Nick — that he believed his father had been murdered.

Nick's hands moved over the keyboard, pulling up Evanko's known associates, many of whom also had criminal records, and suddenly she knew.

"Oh, my God, you think Jimmy was right! You think his father was murdered!"

Nick stopped typing and whirled in her direction. "What the hell are you doing in here?"

At the angry look on his face, Samantha had to force herself not to back away. This wasn't the jovial man who had taken her out to dinner in Las Vegas. This was the ex-cop, a dangerous man she had only gotten a glimpse of in the hotel hallway. She couldn't help thinking of the baby she carried. What was Nick Brodie really like?

"Something happened to Jimmy yesterday," she said, ignoring his outburst, determined to brazen it out. "Something that had to do with his father being murdered."

"Dammit, Samantha, you shouldn't have come in here. I told you Jimmy spoke to me in confidence."

"I wasn't spying on you, and besides, you didn't tell me anything — I guessed. I saw Jimmy's face last night and this morning. I saw his father's photo on his dresser and recognized him on the screen. And I can tell by what you've dug up, there's a lot more to Alex Evans than what's in that newspaper article."

"Listen to me, Samantha. If anyone — and I mean anyone — finds out I'm digging

121

into this, Jimmy and his aunt could both wind up dead."

Samantha's breath stalled. *Dead? Murdered like Jimmy's father?* Nick was a detective; he was used to this kind of violence. But she was just a marketing person for a dog-grooming parlor! What was she getting herself into?

A memory arose of Jimmy's battered face and the terrible despair in his eyes. The twelve-year-old boy badly needed help.

Samantha squared her shoulders. "I would never do anything to hurt Jimmy or Mary. They could pull out my fingernails and I wouldn't tell anyone a damned thing about Alexander Evans."

Nick's mouth edged up. "You probably wouldn't. You're a pretty tough lady when push comes to shove."

He was talking about the tussle she'd had with good ol' Howard. Samantha managed to smile.

Nick looked back at the screen. "Alexander Evans, alias Alexi Evanko," he said, resigned that Jimmy's secret was out. And trusting her, she hoped, not to say anything that would put the boy or his aunt in danger.

"The guy's got a criminal record for everything from assault to suspicion of murder. Served eight years in Statesville

Correctional Facility in Illinois, but that was seventeen years ago. Since he got out, he's been a model citizen — or at least he hasn't been in the criminal justice system."

"That's why he changed his name."

"Yeah."

"How did you find out who he really was?"

"Now that I'm off the force, I don't have access to police databases, so I went to Google. I'm not much of a computer whiz, but for this kind of stuff you don't have to be. There're a dozen services online that can dig up information. Instant Checkmate, Public Records Now. It's scary what they can tell you about someone for twenty-nine dollars — anyone whose name you type in. Criminal records, marriages and divorces, address histories, how to make contact. Hell, you can even find out if they've had any speeding tickets."

"So you Googled Alexander Evans. But how did Alexi Evanko's name come up?"

"For the last two hours, I've been checking every Alexander Evans who showed up in my initial search, including any variation of spellings. Alexi Evanko was one of them. Just before you walked in, his old photo showed up. I ran a search and here we are."

"Doesn't mean he was murdered."

"No, but apparently Jimmy spent the day

bound and gagged in the back of some guy's trunk. Two men threatened to kill him and his aunt. That's pretty convincing."

Dear God, poor Jimmy. "Good heavens, yes. So what are you going to do?"

Nick pushed back his chair and came to his feet. "I can't go to the cops — not without putting Jimmy and Mary at risk. We don't have any evidence, and you can see by the article, Evans was highly thought of and pretty deeply connected into the department. He and his partners are big supporters. No way are the police going to take a look at him without cause. I need to dig up as much info as I can and see where it leads."

"How much information did you get from Jimmy?"

"Not much. I wanted to give him a little time before I started battering him with more questions. I don't want him to clam up again."

"Well, you've got a lot more to go on now than you did this morning."

"Yeah," Nick said darkly, glancing back down at the screen. "And none of it's good."

Chapter Ten

"I need to talk to Jimmy," Nick said, raking a hand through his hair. "Maybe he got a description of the car or a license plate number. At least a good look at the men."

They were still standing in his bedroom next to the computer. He tried not to look at Samantha and think of the king-size bed just a few feet away.

"So go talk to him," she said. "You have to figure this out. Jimmy's counting on you."

"I know, but I need more information. I'd like to know how the hell Alexi Evanko turned his life around and became Alexander Evans — respectable CPA and partner in a prestigious accounting firm."

Samantha smiled. "I can help with that. Digging around the Internet all day is what I do for a living. Of course, I'm only collecting market data, not information on a criminal."

"Are you sure you want to get involved?"

She scooted him out of the way, sat down at the desk in front of his machine. "I'm staying in your house, so I'm already involved. Besides, I'm not going to do anything dangerous. I won't get into any files that might alert someone we're snooping around."

Nick started nodding. He could use all the help he could get. "All right, if you're sure. Anything you can come up with is bound to be useful. In the meantime, I'll go talk to Jimmy, see if he has any information I can use."

It was late afternoon by the time Nick left Samantha at work on the computer and walked up the hill to Jimmy's. He'd planned to spend these next two weeks with a woman he enjoyed, one he badly wanted back in his bed, but he couldn't ignore the young boy who needed his help.

Nick sighed as he glanced up at the impressive log home overlooking the lake, climbed the front steps to the wrap-around covered porch, and knocked on the eight-foot door. Wearing jeans and white cotton blouse, her long, shiny black hair pulled back in a ponytail, Mary pulled open the door. She was a stay-at-home mom these days. Apparently Alex Evans had left enough money in trust to provide for his son and his guardian, and that included the expensive house Jimmy and Mary lived in.

Alex had been successful and wealthy. Now that Nick knew the man's background, he wondered how he'd earned his money — and what he had done to get himself killed.

Mary smiled and stepped back to welcome him into the house. "Hi, Nick. Come on in. Jimmy's playing games on the computer up in his room. I'll tell him you're here."

"Why don't I just go on up? Be nice and private up there. Give us a chance to talk."

Mary seemed relieved. "Of course. Go right ahead. His room's down the hall on the right."

"Thanks." Nick climbed the stairs and knocked on Jimmy's door, which was easy to spot with a polar bear on the front and the words *Trespassers Will Be Eaten* underneath. He knocked a second time and Jimmy pulled it open.

"Can I come in?" Nick asked.

Jimmy glanced out into the hall as if he expected to see the entire Anchorage police force. "I guess." He stepped back out of the way and Nick walked in and closed the door.

"How're you doing?"

"Okay." At the foot of the bed, Duke raised his head, thumped his tail a couple of times, then settled back to sleep.

"Your eye looks like hell."

The kid relaxed a little. "I know."

"I came over because I need your help. I need you to tell me about the men you fought with yesterday." He purposely avoided saying *the men who abducted you* because he didn't want to scare the kid any more than he was already.

Jimmy shrugged his shoulders. "They were wearing red ski masks so I couldn't see what they looked like."

"Was there anything about them you remember? Height? Build? The clothes they were wearing? You must have noticed something."

Jimmy stared at him as if he didn't want to remember anything about what had happened.

"Look, we have to figure this out, okay? You and me, working together. You came to me for help in the beginning. Now it's even more important that we find out what happened. You need to do your part and give me as much information as you can."

With a sigh of resignation, Jimmy sat down on the edge of his bed while Nick walked over and pulled out the chair in front of the boy's computer, spun it around and sat down. "So what can you tell me about the men?"

"One was pretty big. Tall, you know, and heavy. He had shaggy brown hair that stuck out from under the bottom of his ski mask and squinty little pig eyes."

"Okay, what about the other one?"

"He was shorter and kind of skinny. He had a long, hooked nose and I think he smoked because he stank like cigarettes and his voice was raspy. One called the other man Virgil, but I couldn't tell which was which."

"That's very good, Jim. You might make a pretty good cop someday."

He grunted. "No thanks."

Nick felt the pull of a smile. "What about their car?"

"It was an old beater, kind of a faded metallic blue. I don't know what kind it was."

"You didn't happen to get the license plate number?"

Jimmy shook his head, moving his short-cropped black hair. "I was too scared to think of it at first. By the time I did, it was dark and I couldn't see it."

"That's okay. You did good. Anything else you can think of?"

"One of them was wearing a gun." His eyes fixed on Nick's face. "They were really bad guys, Nick. I think my dad must have found something out they didn't want him to know and that's why they killed him."

Nick didn't tell him that considering the man's background, there could have been any number of reasons Alex Evans was dead. "We don't know enough yet to draw conclusions, but eventually we'll find out. You just go on with your life the way you have been, like nothing has changed. Go to school, play your after-school sports, go fishing with your friends."

"What if those men come after me again?"

"If they wanted to kill you, Jimmy, they had every chance. As long as you stay away from your father's office and out of trouble, I don't think they'll bother you."

Some of the tension left the boy's thick shoulders. "Okay, then."

"We've got to take this slowly, Jim. We can't afford to stir up anything that would put you and Mary in danger."

"But you're gonna find them, right?"

"Oh, yeah. I'm going to find them. In the meantime, I want you safe."

Jimmy walked Nick downstairs and out the front door. Neither of them spoke along the way. Until Nick figured out what the hell was going on, there wasn't anything left to say.

■ ■ ■ ■

It took a second round of knocking before Samantha realized someone was standing at Nick's front door. Getting up from the computer, she hurried through the living room, paused at the window to see who was out on the porch, saw an attractive blond man, early thirties, close to Nick's age.

"I'm a friend of Nick's," the man called to her through the glass when he spotted her peering out at him.

"He isn't home," she called back.

When he grinned and held up his badge, she felt a sweep of relief.

"Sorry," she said as she unlocked the door she'd locked earlier and pulled it open. "I'm from San Francisco. We don't open our doors to strangers." Especially not when there were murder suspects roaming the area.

"Better to be safe than sorry," the man said, wiping his feet on the mat before he stepped into the living room. "I'm Cord Reeves. Nick and I worked together in Anchorage. He was one helluva detective — before he decided to quit and go on holiday."

She smiled. "I'm not sure Nick thinks of

131

it quite that way. I'm Samantha Hollis. I'm here for a visit."

He glanced around the house. "Where is he?"

"He . . . umm . . . he's running an errand. He shouldn't be too long. Would you like a cup of coffee, or a Coke or something while you wait?"

"How about a beer?"

"Sure." She turned and started for the kitchen.

"I'll get it. I know where the fridge is." Cord disappeared into the other room, then walked back into the living room with a bottle of Bud Light in his hand.

He was even better-looking than she had first thought, with dark blond hair, hazel eyes, and masculine features. He shrugged out of the lightweight jacket he was wearing, leaving him in jeans, hiking boots, and a dark brown T-shirt, filled out very nicely by a set of wide shoulders and a muscular chest. He was shorter than Nick by a couple of inches, but just as well-built.

"So you're the lady Nick met in Las Vegas." Cord tipped up his beer bottle and took a drink.

"That's right."

"He talked about you after he got back, said how much fun the two of you had. I'm not really surprised to see you here."

"I'm just here for a couple of weeks. I . . . always wanted to see Alaska." Not even close to the truth, though now that she was here, she was at least enjoying the scenery.

The front door swung open and Nick walked into the living room. He took one look at Cord, sitting next to her on the sofa casually drinking a beer, and a scowl darkened his face.

"Hey, man," Cord said, coming to his feet. "I didn't know you had company." He tossed Samantha a smile. "And very pretty company at that."

Nick walked over, tugged her up off the sofa, and straight into his arms. Bending his head, he very thoroughly kissed her. When he looked back at Cord, the warning was clear. *Hands off. She belongs to me.*

Samantha would never have believed she'd be attracted to a man with such a ridiculous macho attitude, and yet when she saw the possessive gleam in Nick's eyes, an embarrassing wave of lust rolled through her.

Cord flashed a look at Nick and grinned. *Message received loud and clear.*

"So what brings you all the way out here?" Nick asked as they all sat back down, Cord in the chair this time, Nick on the sofa beside her.

"Boredom, I guess you could say." He turned to Samantha. "I've got a cabin up near Hatcher's Pass. Friday night, I drove up there for the weekend, did some hiking yesterday, just kind of relaxed. Thought I might as well drop by before I head back to the city."

"I should have gotten out more while the weather was nicer," Nick said. "Looks like it's going to be getting colder during the week."

"Be snowing before you know it," Cord said. They talked for a while about the protection job Nick would be taking at the end of Samantha's visit.

"It's something to do," Nick said. "Beats watching TV."

"You'll be protecting the family this time," Cord said. "That should make it interesting."

"Yeah, listen, since you're here, maybe you can help me with something. A friend of mine had some trouble with a couple of lowlifes the other day — one big, shaggy brown hair, the other one skinny with a long, hooked nose. One of them was named Virgil, not sure which one. I thought you might have crossed paths with them at one time or another."

Cord thought a moment. "Description

doesn't ring any bells offhand. Might come to me, though. If it does, I'll call you."

"Thanks."

Cord set his empty beer bottle down on the coffee table. "I gotta run. Nice meeting you, Samantha."

"You, too, Cord." She watched him walk out of the house, heading for the silver pickup parked out front, then turned to find Nick's blue eyes burning into her. Her breath caught and her mind went straight to sex.

"God, I want to take you to bed," he said.

Samantha's mouth went dry while the rest of her body turned hot and damp. "I want . . . want that, too, but . . . I just . . . I need a little more time, Nick, please." If she wasn't carrying his baby, she would already be back in his bed. But the child was more important. She had to make the right decision and to do that, she had to think clearly. Sleeping with Nick would only muddy the waters.

He nodded, released a slow breath. "So what did you find out about Alex Evans?"

Samantha reached out and took hold of his hand, ignored the little zing that raced up her arm. "Come on," she said, "I'll show you."

■ ■ ■ ■

Nick followed Samantha into the bedroom, careful to keep his eyes off the bed and his mind out of the gutter. Damn, he wanted her. Maybe it was just that she was a tempting little bit, and he hadn't gotten his fill of her in Las Vegas. Maybe it was just that she was there in his house and conveniently sleeping just down the hall.

Nick wished he could convince himself. Though he was drawn to her pretty, all-American-girl looks, long curly hair, and sexy curves, there was something about her that drew him more deeply. Her sweetness, maybe, her warm nature, or the way just being around her settled him somehow.

He didn't know what it was, but he had felt it from the start.

"I printed out as much as I could," she said as she sat down at his computer, returning his thoughts to Jimmy and the problem at hand. "First I pulled up Alex Evans's credentials from the office website." She typed in the info and he watched it pop up on the screen.

"At forty-four, he was the most junior partner in the firm," she said, "but he had a very impressive background. Born in Chicago in 1969, graduated University of Illinois in 1995, then got an accounting degree from the Keller Business School a year later. His first job was with Paxon, Reynolds Accounting in Chicago. In 2000, he moved to Fairbanks, worked for a firm up there. Moved to Anchorage in 2004 when he accepted the job with Jankowski, Sorenson."

Nick felt a frown forming between his eyes. "Wait a minute. Those dates don't jive with the info we have on Evanko. He couldn't have been in school. He didn't get out of jail till ninety-six."

She turned and flashed him a grin. "I know. What his online résumé doesn't say is that Alexi got his degrees through correspondence courses. It's public record. By the time he was released from prison, he had a bachelor's and an accounting degree."

"Jankowski, Sorenson had to know he was an ex-con."

"Maybe. But maybe he never mentioned that part of his past. He had to have a bachelor's degree to take the Alaska state CPA exam. That would have had to happen before he went to Fairbanks. Jankowski, Sorenson could have checked, found out he had what he needed to work for them. Maybe they just looked at his letter of recom-

137

mendation and the rest of his résumé, and there was nothing about the fact he had gotten his degrees long distance."

"Be interesting to see exactly how much the company knew about Evans before he went to work for them."

"Are you going to talk to them? If you do, that might be a problem for Jimmy."

Frustration rolled through him. "I know. We've got to move slowly. We can't afford to draw attention to what we're doing. I told Jimmy that. I told him he needed to do things as normally as possible."

"Was he okay?"

"Seemed to be. Jimmy trusts me. Now that I'm involved, I don't think he feels quite so alone." He drew her up out of the chair and into his arms, bent and began to kiss the side of her neck. She smelled like flowers and tasted like heaven. Heat rolled through him, settled low in his groin. He felt the tremor that ran through Samantha's petite frame and began to get hard.

Nick forced himself to let her go. "I need to get out of here for a while. The weather's going to turn bad. Let's go for a ride on the ATV."

Her light brown eyebrows went up. "ATV? Is that a motorcycle?"

Nick laughed. "Not exactly. It stands for

all terrain vehicle. It's got four wheels, not two."

"I've never ridden on anything like that, not even a motorcycle."

Nick grinned. "I have a hunch there're a lot of things you haven't done before. With any luck, I'll get a chance to teach you some of them."

Her cheeks colored prettily. Sometimes he thought she was even more naïve than he had first imagined. He didn't know why that pleased him, but it did.

"We won't go far, just around a little of the lake, maybe stop and have an early dinner in town before we come home."

"I got so involved I forgot to thaw the trout, so that's probably a good idea."

"Grab your jacket and meet me out back."

"Okay." Samantha headed one way and Nick headed the other.

Maybe a little fresh air would clear his head. It wouldn't be as good as sex, but for now it would have to do.

CHAPTER ELEVEN

Seated on the back of the four-wheeler, as Nick called it, Samantha tightened her arms around his waist and kept her cheek pressed against his wide back. Her thighs hugged his, while her crotch nestled against his tight behind.

Her heart was thundering. She was trying to ignore the faint throbbing between her legs from the vibration of the engine and the seam of her jeans rubbing her most sensitive spot. She forced herself to concentrate on the scenery. Off to the left, Fish Lake stretched for miles along the grassy path Nick raced along toward town.

They weren't going very fast, he said, only about twenty-five miles an hour, but it seemed as if they were flying. The engine noise roared through her head, making her ears ring. By the time Nick pulled up in front of The Sleepy Moose Pizza Parlor, her legs were so stiff from gripping him so hard, she could barely unwind herself from around his body.

Sensing her dilemma, he swung a long leg over the front of the machine, hopped down, and lifted her off.

"So what did you think?"

What did she think? Her mind had fogged out miles ago. "It's . . . umm . . . an interesting way to travel."

He grinned. "Good for hunting and fishing. I guess you'd rather ride in a car."

"Or walk. I walk everywhere in San Francisco. It's very good exercise."

He opened his mouth, looked like he was going to make a comment about a different, more enjoyable kind of exercise, but didn't. "So that's how you stay in shape?" he said instead.

Samantha nodded. "I also do yoga three or four days a week. It keeps me limber."

Those hot blue eyes went dark. "I remember," he said gruffly, and glanced away.

Samantha could feel her cheeks heating up. Forgodsake, she'd had sex with other men. Well, only one besides Justin, but still. There was just something about Nick Brodie that brought out the wicked part of her nature. A part she hadn't really known she had.

"Let's get some pizza," he said, reaching

out to take her hand. "The day's almost gone. Tomorrow, we'll start digging again." As he tugged her toward the door, he looked back at her over his shoulder. "By the way, I really appreciate your help on this thing with Jimmy."

"I'm glad there's something I can do."

He nodded, led her into the restaurant, which had the head of a huge moose hanging on the wall behind the bar. An odd assortment of baseball caps decorated its massive horns.

"Good Lord, I had no idea a moose was that big!"

Nick just smiled. "Alaska moose are the biggest in the world. Their antlers can be seven feet across." He grinned. "You don't want to run into one in the woods. They can be more dangerous than a grizzly."

Samantha felt a chill. "Are there . . . are there any around here?"

Nick shrugged his shoulders and a memory suddenly struck of him naked, of how wide those muscular shoulders actually were. A sweep of lust washed through her, along with a rush of embarrassment. Samantha glanced away.

"This is Alaska," Nick said. "Moose are pretty much everywhere."

Confirming her initial feeling that Alaska

was the last place on the globe she'd want to live.

Nick reached over and caught her hand. "Hey, you aren't in any danger. If for some reason you run across a moose, you just back slowly away and leave him alone. Like most animals, they won't bother you if you don't bother them."

Samantha looked up at the gigantic head on the wall. "I'll keep that in mind."

"So how about a beer?" Nick asked, helping her up into a high-backed bar stool at the long wooden bar.

"I . . . umm . . . think I'm more in the mood for a Coke."

He turned to the bartender, ordered an Arctic Devil for himself and a Coke for her. At least he hadn't asked her why she wasn't drinking. But then they hadn't drunk all that much when they were in Las Vegas either.

"Arctic Devil?" She cocked an eyebrow in his direction as the bartender, an older guy with long, silver hair tied back with a piece of leather, slid a bottle of beer across the bar.

Nick just laughed. "It's from an Anchorage brewery. Named after the wolverine. If you like malty beer, it's great."

She smiled. "Bud Light is about the limit

143

of my beer-drinking sophistication." The bartender set a Coke on the bar in front of her. Samantha picked up the frosty mug and took a sip.

Nick glanced toward the kitchen, inhaled the aroma of tomato sauce and garlic. "Man, that smells good. What kind of pizza do you like?"

Samantha took a look around the room, checking out the food. About half of the tables were filled, a mixture of kids and adults, some couples, mostly families. All wore jeans, most had on hiking boots. Their burgers and pizza looked good. "Whatever you want is fine."

Nick cast her a glance. "I don't suppose you like pepperoni?"

She grinned. "I love pepperoni. I pretend it's chicken so I don't have a guilty conscience."

Nick laughed. He ordered a supreme, all the veggies, double mozzarella, and pepperoni. He picked up his beer, she grabbed her Coke, and they walked over and sat down at one of the empty tables.

Nick took a swig of his beer. As he set it back down, his gaze wandered out the window and his expression subtly shifted, turned darker than it was before.

"You're thinking about Jimmy," she said.

144

"You're worried about how to approach the investigation."

He seemed surprised she could read his thoughts, but for whatever reason, she'd felt a connection to Nick Brodie from the start.

"You're right. I feel like my hands are tied. The police have the info I need, but I can't bring them into this — at least not yet."

"What about Cord? The two of you worked together. Can you trust him?"

"Cord's my best friend. I'd trust him with my life. In the past, I have. I just hate putting him in the middle of something when it has to stay unofficial."

She sipped her Coke, wished it were a glass of white wine. "Cord said you were a very good detective. You never told me why you left the force. Cord seemed to think you just wanted a long vacation."

Nick rubbed a hand over his jaw. This late in the day, it was dark with an afternoon beard. "I told you I was a Ranger. I was in Iraq and Afghanistan. I've seen a lot, done a lot of things, but I always felt I was doing something good, that I was helping protect our country. Can you understand that?"

"I suppose I can, yes." The hero gene, she thought. She'd been right to think Nick had it.

"Then I went into police work. I was dealing with a totally different element. People weren't fighting for a cause. They were just greedy, or perverted, or cruel. Some of them were flat-out sadistic."

"There are a lot of good people, too."

"I know that. But the job is to catch the bad guys. The last case I worked involved the disappearance of a young girl. She was only thirteen. Turned out she was the victim of a serial killer. He'd murdered two other girls in Seattle before he came to Alaska."

"Did you catch him?"

He nodded, tipped up the bottle and took a drink of beer. "We caught him — though I wound up in a beef with my superior over cutting legal corners. So what if I cut through a shitload of red tape? We caught him. Unfortunately, not before he'd killed that young girl. I decided it was time to get out. Find something that made me happy instead of giving me nightmares. I had enough money to take some time off so that's what I did."

"That's how you ended up in Vegas, right?"

He nodded. "My brother, Rafe, figured I needed a break so he bought me a plane ticket." Nick smiled. "I'm glad he did — since I met you."

Samantha thought of the hours she had

spent in bed with Nick and heat stirred low in her belly. "So . . . now that you've quit, what are you going to do?"

He sat back in his chair. "That's the bad news. I don't know. This thing with Jimmy, it's got my juices flowing. I feel like I'm doing something useful again."

"You've got time to figure it out. Meanwhile, you're helping Jimmy, and that's a very important job."

He nodded, looked up as a teenage girl with a long red braid walked out from behind the counter carrying their pizza. She set it down on the table along with a couple of paper plates.

"Enjoy," the girl said.

Each of them grabbed a slice and slid it onto a plate. Samantha picked up her slice and bit into it, but when she looked at Nick, he was staring out the window again.

She reached over and touched his arm. "You'll figure it out."

Nick looked back at her and grabbed a piece of pizza. "I have to," he said. "I'm all Jimmy's got."

And Samantha knew right then that Nick Brodie would be a very good father. She had to tell him about the baby — and soon.

The bite of pizza she had taken suddenly stuck in her throat.

■ ■ ■ ■

Nick didn't sleep worth a damn. Again. When he wasn't thinking of Jimmy and Mary and how to collect information without setting off alarms, he was thinking of Samantha, frustrated and aching to have her.

He woke up crabby and needing a caffeine fix, headed for the bathroom, came out a few minutes later, and pulled on his jeans, wandered shirtless and barefoot down the hall. He was halfway to the kitchen before he caught the aroma of fresh-brewed coffee. The sizzle of frying bacon made his mouth water as he walked into the kitchen.

Samantha turned and smiled at him. She was wearing the green canvas apron again over jeans and a soft pink cable knit sweater. It gave him a funny little kick to see her there, looking so much at home.

"I figured you'd be busy today," she said. "A good breakfast is the best way to get started."

"Oh, man. Bacon and eggs? Are you kidding me?"

"Actually, it's bacon, and a cheese and veggie soufflé. Kind of a compromise. I hope that's okay. Oh, and I made biscuits."

"Jesus." He walked over and hauled her into his arms, gave her a quick, hard kiss. "That sounds great. I thought you'd still be sleeping."

"I woke up early." She glanced away and he wondered if her night had been as restless as his. If she hadn't slept, it didn't show — the lady looked good enough to eat. Nick inwardly groaned at the image that brought to mind.

While Samantha finished cooking, he set the table, then went in, took a quick shower, and dressed. He was walking back down the hall, towel-drying his hair when he heard a knock at the door.

"I got it," he said, recognizing Cord's familiar three short raps. He opened the door and his friend walked into the living room. "Your timing, as usual, is perfect. Samantha's just putting breakfast on the table."

"We need to talk," Cord said. "I found those guys you were looking for."

Worry filtered through Nick at the dark look on his best friend's face. "We can talk while we eat."

"What about Samantha?"

"She knows what's going on."

"Well, you damn well better tell me."

Nick just nodded and Cord followed him

into the kitchen. "We've got company," he said.

Samantha glanced up and smiled. "Hi, Cord." She set a couple of steaming plates piled high with food down on the table. "Don't worry, I fixed plenty. Kind of a habit I learned from my mom." She went back to fill a plate for herself, then sat down at the table to join them.

"So what did you come up with?" Nick asked, digging into the soufflé, barely suppressing a groan of pleasure.

"Samantha, this is great," Cord said without answering. "So your mother taught you to cook?"

"She taught me the basics. Since then, it's become kind of a hobby."

Cord flicked a glance at Nick, winked at Samantha. "You want to get married?"

She flushed and Nick clenched his jaw. His friend was way too good-looking and a little too impressed with Samantha.

Cord grinned. "Just kidding, okay?" He took another hefty bite. "This really is great, though."

"Thank you," Samantha said.

Nick decided to let the conversation wait, keep things easy until they'd finished breakfast. He didn't want to spoil a meal this good by talking about murder.

He buttered a light, perfectly golden-brown biscuit and slathered on some honey. They talked about the weather and Samantha's first ride on an ATV, which she described as "harrowing" and made him grin.

When breakfast ended, they all got up and carried their plates to the sink. He considered leaving Samantha out of the conversation with Cord, but she seemed to have guessed his friend was there with information, and her look said that wasn't going to happen.

Besides, he needed her help on the Internet, never his long suit. The more she knew about the problem, the more help she could be.

"Coffee's ready," she said as a fresh pot finished brewing on the counter. She filled their cups and one for herself, and they all sat back down at the table.

"So what did you find out?" Nick asked again.

Cord's easy smile slid away. "I kept thinking about the skinny guy with the long, hooked nose. His description was niggling at the back of my mind. I dug through some old mug shots and spotted him. Name's Cyrus Crocker. Knew him from back when I was working burglary. That put me onto his accomplice, a big guy named Virgil Turnbull. They call him The Bull. He and Crocker pulled a couple of jobs together, minor theft, breaking and entering, got off with ninety-day sentences."

"Doesn't fit what they seem to be into now," Nick said.

"Which is?"

"Strong-arming a kid. Threatening to kill him and his aunt if he doesn't keep quiet."

"About what?"

"Murder."

Cord's dark gold eyebrows went up. "The kid saw it?"

"No, but he figured it out. He was asking questions, digging where he shouldn't have been. Turnbull and Crocker came after him, knocked him around and stuffed him in the trunk of their car, told him if he didn't keep his mouth shut, next time they'd kill him — and his aunt."

"You aren't talking about the kid up the street, the one who does odd jobs for you?"

"Yeah. Jimmy Evans. He's a good kid and he's in trouble."

"Sounds like it. So you think Crocker and his buddy, The Bull, killed someone and Jimmy figured it out?"

"No. If the vic was murdered — and it looks damned likely — it was done by a pro. Coroner ruled natural causes. Heart attack, but the guy was only forty-four years old."

"It happens."

"If it was a heart attack, why did Bull and Crocker threaten Jimmy?"

"Good question. Word is those two are out of the burglary business and on the payroll, working for Connie Varga. You recognize the name?"

"*Christ.* Connie Varga aka Constantine Bela Varga. Yeah, I know the name. Guy's into everything from drugs to prostitution."

"That's right. But the way I understand it, Connie's only a middleman. No one knows who the big boss is — or if there are more than one. Whoever it is, he's got plenty of juice. If he wanted to make someone dead, he could."

"So could Bela Varga."

"So who's the vic? Wait, a minute. It's gotta be Jimmy's dad. You mentioned he died before you left, and I saw the article in the newspaper."

"That's him."

Cord didn't look happy. "All right, let's hear it."

Nick sighed and started talking.

Samantha sat quietly as Nick told his friend about Jimmy Evans and his aunt, Mary. About Alexander Evans, alias Alexi Evanko.

153

He mentioned Evanko's criminal record and what little else they knew, reminded Cord of the danger Jimmy and Mary would be facing if the wrong people found out Nick was investigating Evanko's death.

"The thing is until we come up with something concrete, it's just a twelve-year-old kid stirring up trouble for one of the most prestigious firms in the city."

"From what I read," Cord said, "one that heavily supports the police department."

"Yeah."

"Add to that, you weren't exactly Mr. Popularity when you left — at least not with Captain Taggart. You cut corners on your investigation, didn't go through channels."

"I caught the fucker, didn't I? I only wish I'd done it sooner."

Samantha sucked in a breath. Nick rarely swore, which told her how hard the case had been on him.

Cord just nodded. "That's right, you did. And if you hadn't, he'd still be out there killing kids." He took a drink of his coffee. "Look, I'll do what I can without authorization, but there're limits to what I can get."

"I know."

Cord slugged down the last of his coffee and got up from the table. "I've got to be getting back. I'll keep you posted." He was

154

just about to leave when a fresh knock sounded at the door. Samantha spotted Mary standing on the porch.

"It's Jimmy's aunt," Nick said to Cord. "She doesn't know anything about this."

Nick walked over and opened the door, stepped back so Mary could come into the house. She was wearing a long, gray wool plaid skirt, boots, and a burgundy sweater, her glossy black hair swinging loose around her shoulders. She looked elegant and exotically beautiful. Samantha couldn't imagine why Nick wasn't attracted to her.

"Everything okay?" he asked, worry clear in his face.

Mary smiled. "Jimmy seems much better. I just came over to thank you for talking to him."

"No problem. We're friends."

"I'm Cord Reeves." Cord smiled and extended a hand. It didn't take a brain surgeon to see the gleam of attraction in Cord's hazel eyes. "I'm a friend of Nick's. We worked together in the Anchorage PD."

"You're a policeman?"

"Detective. I work the vice squad."

"I'm Mary George. I live up on the hill. It's nice to meet you."

"You, too, Mary."

If Cord had been about to leave, now he

seemed eager to stay. "We were just having a cup of coffee," he said. "Would you like to join us?"

Samantha bit back a smile. "I just made a fresh pot," she said.

Mary shook her head. "I really can't stay. I was just out for a walk. As I said, I wanted to drop by and thank you both. I really appreciate your helping Jimmy."

"I'll keep an eye on him," Nick promised.

Mary turned, smiled at Samantha. "You were great the other night. When Jimmy didn't come home, I was frantic. But you were there to talk to, keep me steady."

Samantha smiled. "We all need someone once in a while."

Mary nodded, turned and started for the door.

"It's beginning to rain," Cord said. "I was just leaving. Why don't I drive you home?"

Mary glanced out the window, saw the sky had opened up and a light rain was falling. "If you're sure you don't mind."

"It'd be my pleasure." Cord turned to Nick. "Keep in touch," he said, and then the two of them were walking outside, running through the rain, Cord helping Mary into his pickup.

Samantha looked at Nick. "I think he likes her."

Nick's smile looked relaxed for the first time that day. "That's good. Now I don't have to worry about how much he likes you."

Samantha laughed.

"Ready to go to work?" Nick asked, tipping his head toward the hall.

Samantha's chest squeezed. Work in this case meant finding a murderer. "Ready as I'll ever be," she said. And that was the truth.

CHAPTER TWELVE

Before heading back to the computer in his bedroom, Nick helped Samantha carry the empty coffee mugs into the kitchen.

"Is there any chance we could look at Alex Evans's home computer?" she asked as she loaded the cups into the dishwasher.

"That's a good idea," Nick said, wondering why he hadn't thought of it himself. But now that he had left the department, he was a little off his rhythm. He needed to get focused, get his instincts back on track. "Maybe we'll find something that can give us some insight about what the hell Evanko was into that got him killed."

"Of course if he had that kind of information, the killer would probably have erased it."

"Maybe. We aren't all computer geniuses, though, and since his death was ruled of natural causes, there was no real reason to worry about the cops digging around, looking for something that might lead to an arrest."

"So how do we get to it? We can't just ask Mary."

"No, we need to keep her out of this. We'll get Jimmy to help us. As soon as he gets home from school, I'll call him, see if he can get her to take him for pizza or something. That would give us enough time to get in and out of the house. He can leave the back door open."

"That sounds good. In the meantime, let's see what else we can find out."

They returned to the bedroom and Samantha sat down at his computer, started hitting keys.

"Alexi Evanko, born in Chicago to Ukrainian immigrant parents," she said. "No siblings. Convicted of armed robbery along with a man named Richard Spicer, sentenced to seven years in Statesville Prison. Got out in June of ninety-six."

They knew some of that, not all. "See what you can find on Spicer." He watched her typing, never missing a key stroke. He was more a hunt-and-peck kind of guy.

"Here's an old newspaper article. Looks like Spicer was given a lesser sentence for turning state's evidence against Evanko. Served two years and got out in 1990."

She typed and clicked, typed and clicked, pulled up another article and started reading, then sat back in the chair. "Wow."

He leaned closer. "What?" He tried not to notice how good she smelled, like flowers and the clean scent of soap.

"It says Richard Spicer was shot in an execution-style murder three months after he was released from prison. Happened in Chicago. No arrests made."

"See if they ever caught the guy."

She started searching, looking for follow-up articles. Found one dated a month later and started reading. " 'No leads in the cold-blooded murder of ex-convict Richard Spicer.' " She searched for newer information, shook her head. "I don't see anything. I don't think they ever arrested anyone."

"Could have been payback for ratting out Evanko. If it was, Evanko made friends on the inside, someone with enough clout to make it happen. We need to find out who his inmate pals were."

He picked up the phone and pressed Cord's number. Heard his voice on the second ring. "What's up?"

"I need the name of Evanko's cell mate at Statesville and anyone else he may have had connections to while he was there."

160

"I'm in the middle of something right now, but I'll head into the office a little later, see if I can find anything useful. Since it's supposed to be my day off, you owe me." Cord hung up the phone.

Nick turned to Samantha. "Cord's going to see what he can find out."

"Great. In the meantime, I can keep digging, but I really need to download some software. I brought my laptop, but I just use it for Facebook and e-mail, or putting marketing plans together. It doesn't have the kind of software we need."

"Go ahead. Get whatever you want."

"It won't be free."

"Just do it."

Samantha spent some time upgrading his system. His machine was almost new and it was a good one, but he mostly used it for e-mail, checking the weather, and writing reports.

Nick left her working and went outside to get some air. There was nothing he could do until Jimmy got home or Cord called with the information he needed.

Nothing he really wanted to do but take Samantha to bed.

Since that wasn't going to happen, he went out to the garage to work on his snowmobile. Tomorrow was the third of

October. It would be snowing soon.

He grabbed his toolbox and dragged the tarp off the snow machine. He hoped giving his Arctic Cat a tune-up would take his mind off sex, but he knew damned well it wouldn't.

"Guess what I found?" Samantha turned and smiled as Nick walked back into the bedroom. Her breathing slowed to a halt and she couldn't take her eyes off him. He'd looked good in Vegas. Amazing, in fact. But dressed in jeans and a blue flannel shirt that matched his eyes, a hint of afternoon beard along his jaw, he was the sexiest man she had ever seen.

He smiled. "Okay, I'll bite. You found the guy Evans had an argument with the day before he died."

"Go ahead, make fun of me. I didn't know he had a fight, but now that you've told me, I very well might have."

"You're kidding."

"I found a lawsuit filed against Alexander Evans a month before he died. The plaintiff was a man named Thomas Drummond. He and Alex were partners in a log home manufacturing business. He claims Alex used the real estate where the plant was sitting as collateral for a three-million-dollar loan, then diverted the money into personal bank accounts and unrelated companies. He was suing for malfeasance."

"Three million is a lot of money. If Evans stole it, that would definitely piss the guy off." He leaned down and kissed her. "Nice work."

Her face felt warm, along with other parts of her body. "Thanks."

"We need to check out Drummond, find out if he was pissed enough at Evans to kill the guy. Or more likely, pay someone to do it."

"You're thinking the man Cord mentioned, Constantine Bela Varga?"

"Not for the job itself, but somehow involved. We know Bull and Crocker are involved and Cord thinks they're tied to Varga."

"So we need to connect Varga to Thomas Drummond."

"Yeah. See if you can find a photo we can show Jimmy. He saw the guy who was arguing with his dad. That's what got him involved in this in the first place. We'll see if it was Drummond."

"All right."

"I'll go call Jimmy, figure a way for him to get us into the house."

Samantha went back to work as Nick

walked out of the bedroom. It didn't take long to assemble information on Thomas Drummond. He was the owner of Drummond Realty, a highly respected real estate company in Anchorage. He was married and had three kids, successful and very involved in the community, but she didn't get the impression he was wildly rich.

She printed the information and went in search of Nick, found him at the kitchen sink. As she walked toward him, the smile he flashed made her stomach float up beneath her ribs.

"While you were working earlier," he said, "I . . . ahh . . . took the trout out of the freezer. I mean, if you feel like cooking it. Or I can put it on the grill."

She smiled. "I'll cook. You've got cornmeal, right? For the hush puppies?"

He grinned. "Oh, yeah."

Samantha walked over and handed him the information she had printed off the computer, including a photo of the mayor of Anchorage standing next to Thomas Drummond.

Nick scanned the pages. "Looks like a law-abiding citizen, but you never know. I'll talk to Cord, see if he's heard anything that could connect Drummond to Varga. If the guy looks clean, maybe he'll talk to us, give

164

us the dirt on Evans."

"Won't that be dangerous?"

"If he isn't part of this, it shouldn't cause a problem."

"And if he is?"

He shrugged those broad shoulders. "We've got to do something. At the moment this is a fairly safe bet."

She nodded. "What did Jimmy say about getting us in to look at his dad's computer?"

Nick glanced down at his wristwatch. "It's all set. We need to leave in twenty minutes."

Nick walked up the hill to Jimmy's house, Samantha beside him. The rain had shifted to a light mist, making her fine brown curls even bouncier than they usually were. He wanted to grab a handful and haul her into his arms.

Instead, he caught her hand and kept walking, tugging her up the path to the top of the hill. The ground was muddy, narrow rivulets trailing down the hillside as they made their way up the gentle slope to the back of the house.

He glanced down at the new pair of hiking boots Samantha had purchased for the trip and proudly showed off to him. He wished she had also bought herself a thick pair of socks. He could tell by the way she winced with every other step that the boots were hurting her feet.

"I'll loan you some socks," he said. "The ones you're wearing are too thin for boots that heavy."

"Thanks. I guess I don't know much about hiking."

"It's all right. We aren't going far."

It was a little after seven. Jimmy had talked Mary into taking him out for pizza. Nick figured they'd be gone for at least an hour, plenty of time to get in and out of the house.

They reached the grassy backyard shaded by pines and made their way to the mudroom door. Nick turned the knob and pushed it open. Jimmy's golden retriever, Duke, rose from his dog bed next to the washing machine and trotted over to greet them, wagging his tail.

Nick ruffled his fur. "Some watchdog you are." If someone had broken into the house the day Alex Evans died, Duke wouldn't have paid the least attention, especially not on a Saturday afternoon when it had happened. Jimmy had been fishing with his friends. He'd been the one to find his father in the chair behind his desk.

"Jimmy said the study is on the main floor," Nick said, "just down the hall from the master bedroom." Over the years, he had been to the house a couple of times, but only in the living room. He led Samantha down the hall, found the study door closed. With a quick turn and push, he opened the door and they walked into an elegant, wood-paneled office. It was spotlessly clean, the plank floors polished to a glossy sheen, not a trace of dust on the furniture.

If Evans had been murdered, there wouldn't be much evidence left at the crime scene.

Nick took a long look around, noting the mahogany cabinets and the leather-bound volumes in the bookshelves. A mahogany file cabinet sat in one corner. Family pictures hung on the walls and sat in brass frames on the desk.

He glanced over at Samantha, who was carefully studying the array of photos. "These were all taken after he was married. Nothing from his life when he was young."

"I don't think he had much of a life back then." Nick picked up one of the photos on the desk. "This is Jimmy and his mother." He showed it to Samantha. "Her name was Cora. According to Jimmy, his mother was half Yupik. So is Mary."

"Is that an Indian tribe?"

"Eskimo. They live on the coast and up along the Yukon River. They have a tendency to give their kids old-fashioned names."

"Like Mary and Cora."

"That's right. And last names are sometimes also first names."

"Mary George."

"Exactly."

"So she's never been married?"

"Not that I know of." Nick reached down and turned on the computer beneath Alex's desk. Samantha sat down as the machine booted up. She started by looking at the icons, apparently trying to figure out what programs the machine was equipped with. She spotted one she seemed to like and clicked it up.

"Oh, my God!" A grin spread over her face. "You are so going to love this!"

"What is it?" He came up behind her, settled his hands on her shoulders, heard her soft intake of breath. At least he wasn't the only one feeling the attraction.

"Alex's home computer is hooked directly to the one in his office. All his files are here. What should we look for?"

"We need a list of his clients, people he did accounting work for."

"Thomas Drummond would probably be one of them."

"Maybe. Can we get into the client's tax records?"

"Sure can. Everything he was working on is in here."

While she searched, Nick went over and looked through the stuff in the file cabinet. He dug through fifty-plus manila folders, searched both drawers, but nothing caught his attention. Returning to the desk, he rummaged through the drawers, found nothing. The guy was a neatnik. Nothing out of place, the trash can empty. The only thing that caught his eye was an indentation on the message pad.

Grabbing a pencil, he used the age-old detective scribble technique, watched what looked like a name and number appear, tore off the page and stuck it in his jeans.

He looked at Samantha. "Having any luck?"

"I found a brand-new flash drive in the desk. I'm downloading all the information that might be useful."

"That's great. As my dad used to say, you're handy as a pocket on a shirt."

She stopped typing, smiled up at him. "I bet I would have liked him."

At her look of sincerity, he felt a pinch in his chest. "I bet you would have. I think he would have liked you, too."

"What about your brothers? Were they close to him?"

"My brothers and I worshipped our dad. He was a real mountain man. Taught us to love the outdoors as much as he did. Taught us the value of hard work and clean living."

She looked at him in an odd sort of way and for a moment, he thought she was going to say something. Instead, she shook her head and went back to hitting keys and clicking the mouse.

They continued carefully searching the office for the full thirty minutes he and Jimmy had agreed to, then Samantha pulled the flash drive out of the computer and handed it over. Nicked stuffed it into his pocket, along with the scribbled note.

"We need to go. Last thing we want is for Mary to get home early and find us snooping through her house."

She shut down the machine and waited for the screen to go dark. "I'm ready."

"How are your feet?"

She took a step and made a face. "I need those socks you promised."

"Soon as we get home." Though once she took off the boots, he'd rather she just keep going, peel off the rest of her clothes.

They made their way back through the house, making sure all the lights were off and everything was left the way they'd found it. Tail wagging, Duke walked them to the back door, then looked disappointed when they left the house without him.

"We need to see what we've got," Nick said as they started down the hill.

"Tell you what . . . you can look through the information while I cook that trout."

"And hush puppies, right?"

"Absolutely."

Nick grinned. "Can't beat that deal." He watched her hobbling along in the boots, couldn't stand it any longer, and scooped her up in his arms.

Samantha didn't resist. Just sighed and rested her head on his shoulder. Maybe he was winning her trust all over again.

Nick damned well hoped so.

CHAPTER THIRTEEN

By late morning of the following day, a freezing wind swept down off the mountain behind the house. Heavy pine boughs scratched against the windows and a fierce howling screeched through tiny cracks around the doors.

Samantha had been working on Nick's computer, going over the information she had downloaded onto the flash drive. But she didn't know much about accounting and neither did he. Nick had e-mailed the photo she had found of Thomas Drummond to Jimmy. The boy had texted back that Drummond wasn't the guy who'd been arguing with his dad.

So far, all Samantha had found that looked useful was Alex Evans's client list. Nick had gone over it and she had e-mailed the list to Cord, who was back at work in Anchorage. Without causing too much notice, he was trying to dig up information while still doing his job as a detective in the vice division.

Samantha looked up as Nick walked back into the bedroom, felt that funny little airless moment when seeing him made it hard to breathe.

"Recognize any of the names?" she asked, hoping she didn't sound breathless.

"A few. Some of them own businesses in Anchorage. Cord's doing his best to come up with something, but he's got his own work to do."

"I know. What about that name and number you copied off the message pad in Evans's office?"

"If it's a name, it looks like it starts with a D. Could be D R N I T N or D I N I T R I. I can't make it out. I dialed the number but it wouldn't go through. I couldn't read the last number so I was just guessing. I'll try again later."

"Let me see it." He handed her the paper. Samantha studied it, took a pen and wrote D M I T R I at the bottom. "*Dmitri.* It's a Russian first name. I knew a guy in college who spelled it that way."

Nick looked at the paper. "I think you're right. Not much of a lead but it's better than nothing."

"So did Cord find anything on Thomas

Drummond?"

"No connection to Bela Varga or his men."

"You mean Crocker and the man they call The Bull."

"That's right. As far as Cord could tell, the only connection Drummond had to any of this was the business partnership he and Alex Evans had formed — apparently one that ended in a lawsuit."

"So you think it's safe to talk to him?"

"There's always a risk when you're asking questions. But we need to move this investigation forward, and so far this looks like our best chance."

He smiled. "Besides, I'm going crazy stuck in this house. Drummond lives in an upper-middle-class neighborhood in Anchorage. I called his office and talked to him. I didn't say much, just that I was hoping he could give me some information on Evans. He's meeting me at his residence at two o'clock this afternoon."

"I want to go with you."

Nick shook his head. "I don't want you getting any more involved in this than you are already."

"You said it's safe. Take me with you." She smiled. "I'm going crazy stuck in this house."

He grinned as she tossed his own words

back at him. "All right. I didn't invite you up here to make you spend all day doing what you do in San Francisco. I think Cord would have turned up a connection if there was one. We'll go talk to Drummond. Maybe you'll catch something I miss."

She smiled, gave in to the urge, threw her arms around his neck and kissed him. "Thank you."

Nick didn't let her go, just looked down at her with those amazing blue eyes and the hint of a smile on his lips. "What if I expect some kind of payback?"

Samantha's wariness returned and her easy smile faded. She tried to ease away, but Nick gripped her shoulders.

"Jesus, I'm kidding, Samantha. I was thinking maybe you'd cook for me again. Dammit, don't you know by now, I would never ask you to do something you didn't want to do?"

She did know that. She wouldn't have come up here if she hadn't felt certain she could trust him, at least physically. "I'm sorry. I was being stupid."

"Who was this guy you were engaged to, anyway? He must have been a real assho— a real jerk."

"He cheated on me. From the very start, he wasn't the man I thought he was."

"Yeah, well, I'm different. What you see is what you get."

She was beginning to believe exactly that. "I'm glad to hear it. So far I like what I see very much."

Nick hauled her back into his arms and kissed her, soft and sweet. Just a brief touching of lips, but even that had her heart beating way too fast.

"I need to change," she said, reluctantly pulling away, forcing her mind to the problem at hand. "Drummond's a businessman. We need to look professional."

"Good thought."

Making her way back to the guest room, Samantha pulled on a pair of brown wool slacks, a turquoise cable knit sweater, and a pair of brown ankle boots. When she walked back into the living room, Nick was dressed in black slacks and a pale blue shirt that set off his eyes.

He looked like the guy she had met in Las Vegas, so handsome it made her knees feel shaky.

"You ready?" he asked.

She just nodded and let him lead her out to the garage where his Ford Explorer was parked. A few minutes later, they were driving the road around Fish Lake, the wind buffeting the SUV, dark clouds hanging over the mountains in the distance.

"Not exactly the perfect day for a drive," Nick said.

"At least we're out of the house for a while."

He looked at the cloudy skies overhead. "The weather's always unpredictable up here, worse as the year progresses."

"It must keep things . . . interesting." A nice way of putting it. Samantha thought the weather was interesting enough in San Francisco.

"We've got a stop to make after we see Drummond. I want to drop off a copy of the flash drive. I've got a friend who's an accountant. She'll know what to look for in those files."

"That's a good idea. I assume you feel you can trust her."

"I . . . ahh . . . know her pretty well."

Catching the subtle implication, Samantha's eyebrows went up. "You mean you know her *intimately.*"

Nick sighed. "It was a while ago. We're just friends now."

Samantha wondered if that was the way they would end up. *Just friends.* Unconsciously her hand came to rest on her stomach. Not just friends, but friends who shared a child.

If she ever worked up the courage to tell
him.

She leaned back against the seat. There
was time, she reminded herself. Meanwhile,
at least they were out of the house.

Thomas Drummond was exactly what Nick
expected. Six feet tall, medium build, silver-
tipped dark brown hair. He was late forties,
dressed in a dark suit, a yellow, button-
down-collared shirt, and a conservative
brown-and-yellow striped tie. Clearly he
had been at work and had taken a break to
meet them.

"You're Nick Brodie?" Drummond asked
as he answered their knock and opened the
front door.

"That's right. This is Samantha Hollis.
She's a friend. We'd like to talk to you about
Alex Evans."

"Come on in." He led them into a large,
well-decorated home in a nice residential
neighborhood on the outskirts of Anchorage. The house was gray, two stories with a
three-car garage. Nick figured it was in the
six to eight-hundred-thousand-dollar price
range.

"My wife is out shopping. The kids are in
school. I figured this would be the best place
for us to meet. Would you like something to

drink? Coffee or a soft drink, maybe?"

"We're fine."

"Why don't we sit down in the living room?" He led them into a step-down living area done in a gray-blue color, traditional furniture, a coffee table in front of the over-stuffed sofa. Nick and Samantha sat on the sofa, while Drummond sat in one of the wing-back chairs.

"Let me start by telling you the reason I agreed to see you," Drummond said.

"All right, why was that?"

"Because I knew who you were. I remember reading about you in the *Daily News*. You're the homicide detective who caught that serial killer."

Nick's stomach tightened. "That's right. But just to be clear, a few weeks after that arrest, I left the force. I'm involved privately in this investigation."

"And you're investigating Alex Evans? Why? The man is dead."

"I'm afraid I can't tell you that. What I can say is that I uncovered the lawsuit you filed against him alleging malfeasance. In it you claimed Evans stole funds that belonged to both of you."

"That's public record. It's also the truth."

"The two of you were partners," Samantha said, joining in the conversation. "You must have trusted him — at least in the beginning."

"Alex was my CPA. He knew my financial situation, knew I was looking for a good investment. He and his firm had a very good reputation in the community. When he came to me with the proposal to join him in the purchase of a log home manufacturing business, I agreed. We became partners. Alex managed the financial aspects of the company while I did the marketing. For a while we did very well."

"What happened?" Nick asked.

"The financial crash of 2008 hit us hard. People stopped buying homes. Log homes were no different. We hung on through the first few years, but little by little the business kept sliding downhill. Alex suggested we refinance the real estate and use the money to keep the business afloat until things turned around. Instead, he took the money from the loan and never paid any of the bills."

"You didn't realize what was going on?" Samantha asked.

"I didn't find out until the property went into foreclosure. I called my lawyer, but without forking up a lot more money, there wasn't much I could do."

"So you filed a lawsuit," Nick said.

"That's right. That's what my lawyer advised. But attorneys don't come cheap. I waited, tried to work things out with Alex, but it was no use. I filed the suit, but what good did it do? Alex is dead and his estate is in limbo. I doubt I'll ever see any of my money again."

Nick sat back in his chair, his mind going over the information. Until the theft of the money, Evans had maintained an excellent reputation. Something had to have changed.

"It sounds like Evans got himself into some kind of trouble," Nick said. "The only way he could bail himself out was to take the money from the loan."

"Do you have any idea what that trouble could have been?" Samantha asked.

Drummond's features tightened. "All I know is he wasn't the man I thought he was. I don't know what really happened. I doubt I ever will."

"Maybe I can find out," Nick said. "If I do, once this is over, I'll let you know."

Drummond seemed to relax. "That in itself would be a comfort. The man's actions destroyed my credit and took a huge bite out of my savings."

Nick rose from the sofa and Samantha stood up, too. Nick shook the Realtor's hand. "We appreciate your help, Mr. Drummond."

"It's just Tom, and I wish you luck in whatever it is you're doing." Drummond walked them to the door, paused as they stepped out onto the porch. "I have a twelve-year-old daughter," he said. "I rest easier knowing that scum you put in prison is off the street."

Nick just nodded. He did his best not to think about the case since it still gave him nightmares.

Guiding Samantha down the sidewalk, he helped her into the SUV. The wind was blowing up a gale, the clouds thicker than ever, but it hadn't started to rain.

As much as he'd enjoyed the drive, from the ominous look of the weather, he'd be damned glad to get back home.

Samantha studied Nick's profile as he drove back through Anchorage. His jaw was set, his eyes fixed on the road. The car shuddered against a heavy gust of wind and the sky opened up. Nick turned on the windshield wipers.

"You said you thought Alex got into some kind of trouble. That's why he stole Drummond's money."

"That's right. From the day he got out of

prison, the guy stayed out of trouble. Or at least stayed off the radar. He had a good reputation. A family. Something changed."

"What do you think it was?"

"Maybe he got involved with the wrong people."

"You mean Constantine Bela Varga?"

"Could be. Varga's goons came after Jimmy to keep him quiet about the murder. We have to assume Evans and Varga were somehow connected."

"Maybe you're . . . umm . . . lady friend will find something on the flash drive."

Nick sliced her a sideways glance. "She isn't my *lady friend*. Not anymore." Nick signaled, turned the vehicle off the main road into an area of apartment buildings.

He was there to drop off a copy of the flash drive to his *intimate* friend. Samantha hadn't thought much about other women when she had accepted Nick's invitation. Now she wondered just how many *intimate* friends he had.

It was before he met you, she reminded herself, but it bothered her just the same.

Nick pulled the big Ford up to the curb and turned off the engine. Grabbing his heavy wool jacket out of the backseat, he pulled it on, turned up the collar, and cracked open the door. "Stay here. I'll be right back."

He ran through the rain up under the covered porch, pounded on the door to apartment number four. When the door swung open, a tall, movie-star gorgeous blonde threw her arms around his neck. She had on a tight pair of jeans and a fitted sweater that showed off every curve. The running shoes on the end of her long legs said she was physically fit. Nick extricated himself from her hold around his neck, stepped inside and closed the door.

Samantha felt sick to her stomach. She thought of the baby. Maybe telling him wasn't such a good idea after all. Nick was a bachelor. A very popular bachelor from the greeting he'd just received.

Fortunately, only a few minutes had passed before the door opened again and Nick raced out into the rain, jerked open the car door, and slid back in behind the wheel.

He cast her a look. "I know what you're thinking but you're wrong. Her name is Lisa Graham. We dated a year or so ago. We aren't involved anymore. Like I said, we're just friends."

"Intimate friends," she reminded him darkly.

"Not since before I met you," Nick reminded her.

Samantha turned away. "It doesn't matter. I'm only here for two weeks."

Nick caught her chin and turned her to face him. "It does matter. I'm with you. For as long as this thing lasts. You're the woman I want. The only woman I want. Okay?"

She swallowed, felt near tears. *It's just hormones,* she told herself. She was pregnant, forgodsake. She looked at Nick and nodded. "Okay."

Nick leaned over and gently kissed her. "Let's go home," he said and started the engine.

They decided to eat before making the drive back home, though secretly Nick would rather have had more of Samantha's amazing cooking. They stopped at a little place in Wasilla called The Trout Club that served great burgers and fries. Nick placed their orders at the window, waited till the orders came up, then they sat at one of the Formica-topped tables to eat.

"So where are we in the investigation so far?" Samantha asked as she unwrapped her turkey burger and dug in. "Wow, this is really good."

Nick swallowed the bite he had taken. "We're further than we were two days ago.

We still need to find out who hired Evanko at Jankowski. And Cord should be calling with that cell mate info pretty soon."

"You think that could be important, but it might just be some guy who robbed a bank or something."

Nick grinned. "That's true. Now you see how boring detective work really is. We follow a lead till it hits a dead end, then look for something new, follow where that leads and hope we come up with something."

"I think it's interesting."

"I used to."

"Until it got too personal? That's what happened, isn't it? You started feeling what those parents were feeling when they lost their daughter."

Nick set the burger back down on his plate. "I guess that was part of it. Homicide's a bloody business. I just didn't want to do it anymore."

"I guess I can understand that. But when I think about what happened to my sister . . . I don't know. I wish there had been someone like you around to catch the man who killed her."

"You said they never found him."

"No. A few years later, there was a similar case where a girl was abducted and killed. The man was killed in a shoot-out. The police thought it might have been the same man but there was no way to know for sure."

"I'm really sorry," Nick said, knowing only too well how hard a tragedy like that could be on a family.

Samantha just nodded and they finished their meal in silence. The rain had slowed to a steady patter by the time Nick drove around the lake and pulled into his garage, then led Samantha into the house.

Along the way, he'd made a decision. He was going to lay off the seduction routine. It wasn't his style to press a woman the way he had been pushing Samantha. Of course, he couldn't remember wanting a woman the way he wanted her. Still, from now on, what happened between the two of them would be up to her.

In that vein, since they had already eaten, he suggested they watch an old movie on TV.

Samantha seemed relieved. "That's a great idea. Why don't I make us some popcorn? I saw some in your pantry."

He'd forgotten it was even there. "That'd be great — but it's got to have plenty of butter."

She grinned. "I swear — your cholesterol must be sky high."

"One sixty," he said, flashing her a grin.

Samantha rolled her eyes. "Life is never fair."

They made the popcorn together, then sat in front of his 42-inch flat-screen to eat it. They made out like teenagers for a while, and settled in to enjoy the movie. By the time *The Searchers*, an old John Wayne classic that made Samantha cry, was over, he was surprised to realize he had really been having fun.

They cleaned up the kitchen and went to bed.

Alone.

If it weren't for his worries about Jimmy and Mary, he would have fallen asleep feeling strangely content. Maybe he wouldn't even have had one of his ugly dreams.

CHAPTER FOURTEEN

The room was dark, just thin rays of moon-light slicing in between the curtains. The hour was late when Samantha awakened from the first deep sleep she'd had since she'd arrived. She didn't know what had roused her, but her heart was thundering, her senses on high alert. It took a moment to realize she was in the guest room at Nick's house.

As understanding settled in, she began to relax. That was when she heard the noise, the fierce, deep growl that sounded like an animal in pain. It was the sound that had awakened her, and it was coming from the room next to hers.

Grabbing her robe off the foot of the bed, she slipped out into the hall. The door to Nick's room was closed. She quietly turned the knob and looked inside. The curtains were open, the clouds had lifted, and a slash of moonlight lit the bedroom.

Samantha's eyes widened at the sight of Nick Brodie lying naked on the bed, the sheet thrown off and tangled around his long legs. His lean, powerful body glistened with sweat and his jaw was set in a hard, angry line. He made that same guttural sound low in his throat, like a tiger ready to attack its cornered prey.

He thrashed on the mattress, fighting some unseen foe, shoving the sheet farther down, and muttering something she couldn't understand. He was in the throes of a nightmare and wildly angry at someone.

"Nick . . . ?" She crept toward him. "Nick, wake up."

Reaching a hand out to touch him, she shrieked as he grabbed her, jerked her across his body, came up over her and pinned her to the mattress beneath him.

"Nick! Wake up!"

For several heartbeats, neither of them moved. His eyes were open, but he didn't seem to see her. Then he shook his head like a bear awaking from hibernation and looked down at her as if he couldn't believe his eyes.

"What the hell?"

"You . . . you were having a nightmare. It must have been . . . been a bad one."

He raked a hand through his wavy black

hair, looked down and seemed to notice for the first time that he had her pinned beneath him. Samantha's eyes widened as she realized he was beginning to get aroused.

"Nick . . . please . . ." She wasn't sure exactly what she was asking, wasn't sure she didn't want the situation to take its logical course.

"Christ." Lifting himself off her, he padded naked to the bathroom. She told herself to look away from all those gorgeous muscles and his heavy arousal, but her eyes refused to listen.

Nick closed the bathroom door and she heard water running in the sink. She climbed out of his bed and was tightening her robe around her when he walked back out of the bathroom, his black hair wet, a towel riding low on his hips.

"Are you okay?" she asked.

He sat down on the mattress, glanced at the red numbers on the digital clock beside the bed. It was three a.m. "Sorry I woke you."

"It's all right. What . . . what were you dreaming about?"

He sighed into the quiet. "Drummond mentioned the last perp I caught. I guess it brought the whole thing back. The young girl's body . . . what the crime scene looked like. It was one of the worst I've ever seen."

In the depths of his eyes, she could read what working that case had cost him. Knew from experience some of what he felt.

"It might not have happened if we hadn't had to follow the goddamn rules. So damned much red tape. If we could have cut through all the bullshit, we might have found the bastard before he killed her."

"Captain Taggart's rules?" she asked, remembering what Cord had said.

"The system's rules. Taggart's captain of the detective division. He's one of those guys who follows the rules to the letter. As far as I'm concerned, when someone's life is at stake, it's time to bend the rules."

She thought of her sister, wondered if Danielle might have been saved if she'd had a detective like Nick Brodie working the case.

She realized he was watching her, his gaze running over her body. She was standing in the moonlight and the robe she was wearing wasn't very substantial.

"You'd better go back to bed," he said gruffly, and she knew it wasn't a suggestion — it was a threat.

Her body started humming. Her mind filled with images of Nick lying naked on the bed, all sinewy muscle, flat, ridged stomach, wide shoulders banded with muscle, and narrow hips. Memories of a hard male member that told her how much he wanted her.

"Will you be able to sleep?" she asked, knowing sleep was no longer an option for her.

"No." Those laser blue eyes seemed to pin her where she stood. "What about you?"

There it was. The invitation she could no longer refuse. He could give both of them the sleep they so badly needed, give them the kind of pleasure she hadn't been able to forget.

She moved toward him, peeling the robe off as she approached the bed, letting it fall at her feet on the floor, leaving her in only her short pink nightie. "I think you have what I need to get back to sleep." Sliding her arms around his neck, she leaned down and kissed him.

With a heavy groan, Nick kissed her back. When he deepened the kiss, desire surged hot and wild through her veins. She remembered the coppery tang of him when he was aroused, the taste of virile male. His tongue slid into her mouth and she moaned, felt his big hands dragging her nightgown over her head and tossing it away, felt his palms sliding down to cup her breasts.

"I remember everything about you," he said against the side of her neck, "the feel of your skin, the softness of your lips, the exact shape and weight of your breasts. God, I want you."

She whimpered as his hands moved down her body, cupping her bottom as he kissed his way from her breasts to her belly. Kneeling in front of her, he kissed the inside of her thighs, parted her legs and used his mouth and hands with the skill she remembered. Her body quivered. She cried out as sensation dragged her under, plunged her into a world of dark pleasure.

She had almost reached her peak, her body tightening, craving release. She whimpered when Nick stopped.

"Easy, baby. Not yet. Soon, I promise. I want to be inside you when you come."

Her body flushed with heat. She remembered how good he was at this, the way he understood exactly how to heighten her pleasure. His towel fell away as he lifted her, settled her in the middle of the bed, then came down above her. Spreading her legs with his knee, he made a place for himself between her thighs.

It felt so natural to have him there, as if he was a part of her, as if he belonged there. His kisses were long and deep, and though she could feel the tension in every sinew of his powerful body, he held himself back, taking his time, making it good for both of them.

She was lost in sensation when he opened the drawer next to the bed, drew out a condom and sheathed himself, then continued his skillful assault. Nipping the side of her neck, he returned to her mouth, kissing her deeply, creating a delicious tension that rolled through her body as he slid himself deep inside. She thought of the tiny seed that grew in her womb, the faint speck of life their passion had created. Perhaps that was the reason it felt so right that he should be there, reclaiming the part of herself she had already lost to him.

She thought of the child, but when he started to move, all thought slid away and she was once more in that place of dark pleasure. Her body tightened with each of his powerful thrusts, spun farther and farther out of control. A sweet pressure quivered in her belly as he drove deeper, brought her closer and closer to the edge.

She cried his name at the stunning burst of pleasure that exploded through her body, bright as sunlight over the mountains. Samantha clung to his powerful shoulders, her nails digging in, thick waves of sweetness rising higher and higher, then cresting and slowly beginning to fade.

Nick didn't stop. Just drove into her until she reached a second searing climax. Another deep thrust and a low growl came from his throat. The sinews in his neck went rigid, his muscles vibrating with the force of his release.

For long seconds neither of them moved.

Then Nick lifted himself away, dealt with the condom, and lay down beside her, nestled her head in the crook of his arm.

Samantha thought of the baby and the tough decisions she would have to make. Lying sated in Nick Brodie's bed, she realized the enormity of what she'd just done. She didn't know she was crying until he leaned over and wiped a tear from her cheek.

"Samantha, honey, what is it? I didn't hurt you, did I?"

She shook her head. At the worry in his face, she thought of the child he had fathered. She had to tell him. Knew it was time.

"It isn't that. You were wonderful. But I. . . . I have to tell you something. I can't hold back any longer."

"What is it, honey?"

"I'm pregnant."

"What? You're —" He broke off, sat up in bed, and Samantha sat up, too, pulling the sheet along with her as she moved back against the headboard. Nick reached over and turned on the lamp on the bedside table. "What do you mean you're pregnant?"

"That's . . . that's why I came up here. I needed to see you, figure out what to do."

Nick started frowning. "Wait a minute. You aren't saying the baby is mine?"

Shock rolled through her. She could feel the blood draining out of her face. Swinging her legs to the side of the bed, she stood up, grabbed her robe off the floor and pulled it on.

"It doesn't matter. I felt obligated to tell you. Now I have. I'll be leaving in the morning." The moment she started walking, Nick was out of the bed and stalking her.

He caught her before she reached the door and whirled her around to face him. "I used protection. If you're pregnant, it can't be mine."

Her eyes welled. She'd known this might happen, known this could be his reaction. Somehow she had convinced herself Nick would be different.

"I said it doesn't matter. I don't expect anything from you. I just needed to tell you. Now I have." She jerked open the door;

Nick slammed it closed.

"You're pregnant. You've had the test and everything?"

"I went to a doctor. She confirmed the test. I don't know how it happened. It shouldn't have, okay? They were your condoms, not mine!"

His eyes drilled her for several heartbeats. Then the corner of his mouth edged up and his features softened. "The baby's mine. Of course it's mine. I could tell that first night, sex wasn't something you'd had a lot of experience with."

She worked to keep her eyes on his face. He was still naked, though he seemed to have forgotten. "Until that night, I hadn't been with anyone since I broke up with my fiancé more than a year earlier."

He nodded. "Your fiancé. The a-hole. I remember. Are you okay? Is the baby okay?"

She swallowed, felt like crying again. "Everything's fine. The truth is I didn't want to be pregnant any more than you want to be a father. As I said, I don't expect anything from you. I wasn't even sure I was going to tell you."

"Wait a minute." His features went dark again.

"I had to find out what kind of man you were. I had to think of the baby."

198

"That wasn't your decision."

"I think it was."

"Bullshit. You should have told me as soon as you found out."

"Well, I'm telling you now. And now that I have, I'm leaving. All I need is a ride back to the airport in the morning." She jerked open the door; Nick slammed it closed again.

"You aren't leaving. You came here to find out what kind of man I am. Well you're going to find out that I'm the kind of man who isn't going to ignore his responsibilities. We've got plenty to talk about, and you aren't leaving until we've got this figured out."

She was furious. And oddly relieved. Still, she wasn't about to be bullied. "Fine, we'll talk in the morning. In the meantime, I need to get some sleep."

She pulled open the door and walked into the hall; Nick followed her out. "You're having it, right? You aren't considering —"

"No, of course not."

His shoulders relaxed. "Okay, then. All right." He glanced down, seemed surprised he wasn't wearing clothes. "We'll talk tomorrow."

Samantha turned and started walking. Nick disappeared into his room, reappeared with the towel he'd been wearing once more in place. At the door to her bedroom, he caught up with her, turned her into his arms and very softly kissed her.

"Don't worry, okay? We'll figure it out."

Her eyes burned. A lump swelled in her throat. "Okay," she managed to say. Pulling open the door, she walked into her bedroom. Her heart squeezed. At least she had done what she had come here to do.

So why didn't it make her feel better?

CHAPTER FIFTEEN

Dressed in jeans and a sweatshirt, Nick stood on the deck in back of the house the following morning, his cell phone pressed against his ear. A heavy white cloud hung over the mountain behind the house and the air was icy cold. Nick barely noticed.

"Hey, Dylan, it's Nick," he said as his brother picked up the call.

"Hey, bro, good to hear from you." Just the sound of his brother's voice was a comfort. Dylan was a year older than Nick, while Rafe, at thirty-four, was the oldest.

"Listen, something's come up. I thought I'd give you a call. How's Lane?"

"She's great. She thinks we should all get together for Thanksgiving. We could all meet here. Plenty of room and the lodge is really looking good."

Dylan had met Lane Bishop during a remodel of the old fishing lodge he had bought on Eagle Bay in the Alaskan peninsula. Lane was a Beverly Hills designer, the woman he had hired to do the interior, the lady he had fallen head over heels in love with and planned to marry.

"So Lane's, you know, adjusting okay?" Alaska wasn't an easy place to live. It was something Dylan had worried about over the weeks he and Lane had been working together on the lodge.

"Lane loves it here," Dylan said. "She's really excited about spending her first winter on Eagle Bay."

Nick thought of Samantha, tried to imagine her smiling as she slogged through the snow, her small feet in a pair of heavy leather boots. He tried to imagine her out on the frozen lake, grinning as she shivered inside an ice-fishing hut. But none of the images would come.

"So what's up with you?" Dylan asked.

"Remember the woman I met when I was in Las Vegas?"

"Sure. Samantha. You talked about her quite a bit. Wasn't she coming up for a visit?"

"She's here now." He glanced around to make sure she was still in the house, hopefully still sleeping. "The thing is, Dylan, she's pregnant."

"What? What do you mean she's pregnant?"

"Just what I said. Samantha's pregnant. That's what she came up here to tell me."

"Wait a minute, she's not telling you it's *yours*? You were careful, right? You used protection?"

"I was careful. But condoms aren't a hundred percent guaranteed."

"She *is* telling you it's yours. Is it?"

"Yeah."

"Not the slightest doubt?"

He thought of Samantha's colorless face when he had denied the baby, those big brown eyes filling with horrified tears. "No."

"Do you love her?"

"Hell, I don't even know her."

"So what are you going to do?"

"I don't know." He raked his fingers through his hair. "For chrissake, I don't even have a job."

"No, but you've got plenty of money."

"This isn't about money."

"No, it isn't."

"On top of that, I'm in the middle of a murder investigation. The timing couldn't be worse."

"I thought you were retired."

So many people had tossed those words back in his face, Nick almost smiled. "Whatever I do, I'm not going to shirk my responsibilities. Samantha says she doesn't want anything from me and I believe her. She's a successful career woman. She wasn't even sure she was going to tell me."

Dylan hissed out a breath. "Not good."

"Fortunately, she came to her senses." After he'd won back a little of her trust and they had wound up back in bed. "The kid is mine. I want some say in how he's going to be raised."

"Could be a she."

"Either way."

"Listen, don't do anything rash. Just take it slow and easy. You'll know what to do when the time is right."

It was good advice. Dylan was always solid as a rock. He looked up to see Samantha through the kitchen window, dressed for the day and heading for the pot of coffee he had made.

"I've got to go. I'll keep you posted." Nick hung up the phone and walked back into the house.

Samantha filled a coffee mug. "Hi," she said, her expression as wary as his own.

"Hi." He couldn't think of a damned thing to say. But then he'd never been pregnant before. "You okay? No morning sickness, nothing like that?"

"I'm okay. Listen, Nick, do you think there's any chance we could . . . umm . . . just pretend last night didn't happen?"

His mouth edged up. "If you mean the sex, I'm not going to forget that anytime soon." His gaze ran over her petite figure and an image arose of her feminine curves and sweet cries as he moved inside her. His body tightened. Oddly, now that he knew she was carrying his child, he wanted her even more than he had before.

"I meant the other . . ." she said. "The pregnant part. Is there any chance we could just go on doing what we were doing — getting to know each other?"

It sounded good. Too good. Could a pregnant woman actually forget about being pregnant?

His brother's words ran in his head. *Just take it slow and easy. You'll know what to do when the time is right.*

"Maybe," he said noncommittally, watching Samantha's reaction.

"We need to help Jimmy and Mary. Once we figure out what's going on with them, we can figure out what to do about . . . you know."

He grinned. He couldn't help it. "Yeah, I know."

"So is it okay?"

"What about sex? Because I still want you and I think you want me. I don't know much about . . . you know . . . but I know you can have sex right up till just before the . . . you know . . . is born."

She laughed. It broke some of the tension in the room. "Could we just play it by ear?"

He walked over and took the coffee cup out of her hand, set it on the counter. Nick drew her into his arms and kissed her, softly at first, then deeper. Lust wrapped around him and squeezed like a fist.

Jesus, when it came to sex, the woman had his number. They were both breathing hard when he let her go. It took a moment for him to realize his phone was ringing.

He pulled it out of his pocket, saw it was Cord. "Hey, man, what's up?"

"Evanko's cell mate was a Russian named Orloff. But here's the interesting part. Orloff worked for a guy named Milushev. You know that name?"

"Are you kidding? Milushev's one of the most wanted men in the country."

"That's right. A couple of years ago, when the feds got too close, he pulled up stakes and went back to mother Russia. Speculation is he's running his businesses from there."

"Jesus. Milushev definitely had the juice

to put a hit on Evanko's partner-in-crime, Richard Spicer."

"You got that right."

"And Evanko would owe him — big-time."

"Could be."

Nick looked up as the sound of a siren in the distance caught his attention. It was a rare occurrence this far out in the country. Following the sound, Samantha hurried out of the kitchen, crossed the living room, opened the door and went out on the porch.

An instant later, she rushed back in. "Oh, my God, Nick! Mary and Jimmy's house is on fire!"

"Gotta go. I'll call you back."

Nick hung up the phone and ran out of the house, with Samantha right on his heels. The two of them raced up the hill toward the fire. This time of day, Jimmy would be at school. Nick prayed Mary wasn't home, either.

Or that if she was, she had gotten out okay.

Bright red-and-orange flames crawled out one of the windows at the side of the house and smoke formed a thick black plume, rising in a column that climbed above the roof.

As she drew closer, Samantha's heart, already pounding with fear, kicked up another notch. Jimmy would be at school, but Mary. . . . What if she was still inside the house?

The fire truck was parked in front, the firemen already at work, hoses extended, shooting a stream of water onto the orange flames licking out of the window. A billowing cloud of smoke rolled out with the flames. It only took a second to realize which room it was.

"Oh, my God, Nick, it's the study."

"Stay here. I need to find Mary."

"Oh, God."

Nick took off running, but Samantha was right behind him. Her hiking boots felt clumsy, but at least she was wearing the heavy socks she had taken from Nick's dresser drawer so her feet didn't hurt.

Nick paused to speak to one of the firemen, then disappeared through the front door, where only a thin wisp of smoke trailed out. Samantha stopped beside another fireman.

"Is . . . is everyone out of the house?"

"We didn't find anyone inside."

"What about the dog? A golden retriever? He might have been in the mudroom."

The fireman shook his head. Beneath the brim of his helmet, his face was black with soot. "We didn't see any sign of a dog. The fire started in the office. We've been able to contain it there."

"Thank God."

Several minutes passed as she waited anxiously for Nick to reappear. She felt a wave of relief when she spotted him walking toward her from around the side of the house, Duke trotting along at his side.

"I checked the garage. Mary's car is gone. Duke was in the side yard. He was scared but he's okay. Apparently, there's a doggie door coming out one of the downstairs rooms. He's fine."

"The fireman said the blaze started in the study. They've been able to contain it there." She exchanged a glance with Nick. Lisa Graham was working on the flash drive, but they hadn't heard from her yet. Samantha wondered what could have been in the office that was worth setting fire to the house to destroy.

She glanced back at the big log structure. There were firemen inside. The flames were dying but smoke still rolled out the window. "You don't think whoever did this might have done something to Mary?" She couldn't help thinking of Jimmy stuffed into the trunk of a car.

"I don't think she was here, but we need to find her. Pulling out his cell, he started going through his contact list. "I've got Jimmy's number. Maybe he knows where his aunt is."

Samantha stood nervously as Nick phoned the boy at school. He told Jimmy about the fire, told him that Duke was okay and that the fire department had the blaze under control. "Your aunt isn't here. Do you know where to find her?"

Samantha couldn't hear the reply, but Nick was nodding.

"Tell her everything is being handled, but she needs to come home." Nick hung up the phone. "Mary was at the school. Parent-teacher conference. Jimmy thinks she was heading straight back home. He's going to call her."

Samantha felt a surge of relief. "So they're both okay."

"Looks like."

Nick turned back toward the house. "I have a feeling whoever started the fire was watching the place, waiting for an opportunity to get inside without being noticed. They aren't worried about Jimmy causing any more trouble, but maybe they decided to play it safe, get rid of any evidence that might still be in the office."

"Thank God we got the flash drive."

His features hardened. "Yeah."

Samantha turned as a silver pickup roared to a stop behind the fire truck. Cord threw open the door, climbed out of the truck, and strode toward them.

"What's going on? Where's Mary?"

"She and Jimmy are both okay," Nick said. "Neither of them was home when the fire started. Mary's on her way here now."

The tension eased from Cord's face. "I heard what Samantha said when I was talking to you on the phone. I was working a case that took me out to Birchwood so I wasn't that far away." He glanced over at the smoke still creeping out the window, looked back at Nick. "This isn't a coincidence, is it?"

"Not likely."

"I think it's time the two of us had a serious conversation."

Nick just nodded and the two men walked away.

Nick didn't bother to ask why his friend had come. He'd noticed Cord's keen look of interest the morning he had met the exotically beautiful woman who lived up on the hill. It was a look Nick had only seen on his friend's face once before. Her name was Jillian. Cord had fallen like a brick for Jill. The bad news was, she couldn't handle marrying a cop and eventually the relationship came to an end. Cord had never completely gotten over her.

Now he wore that same expression when he looked at Mary George.

"We need to bring in the cops," Cord said as soon as the two of them were far enough away that they couldn't be heard. "Someone's going to get killed."

"We bring in the police, someone is definitely going to get killed."

Cord shook his head. "We've got Jimmy's story. The kid was abducted and threatened, right? Now we've got a suspicious fire in his house. We should take this to Taggart, get the department involved in the investigation. Or maybe call the State Troopers."

"What about Mary and Jimmy? You willing to risk their lives?"

"We could get them a protection detail."

"There's no way Taggart's spending tax payer dollars with no more to go on than a kid's wild story and a fire that could have been an accident. And what about Jankowski, Sorenson? Taggart's not stirring up trouble with big donors like that — not without proof. Hell, we don't even have a murder victim. All we have is a guy who died from natural causes."

"We could protect them ourselves."

"We could. But we can't be two places at once. We need to follow the leads we've got."

Cord blew out a frustrated breath.

"We need evidence," Nick continued. "Something that'll support our claim Alex Evans's death was more than a heart attack. We get it, we can get them to exhume the body, find out what really happened."

Cord looked back at the thin trickle of smoke still drifting out of the office. "What about the fire? It's going to come up arson, right?"

"Maybe. But this is a local fire department, all volunteer. Unless these guys find a reason to suspect arson, it won't come up." There was a small fire station in Fish Lake, but it was kept locked unless there was a fire. Considering the volunteers weren't on anyone's payroll, they did a helluva job.

"Where'd it start?" Cord asked.

"The study. The fire department was able to contain it to just that one room."

"Was that where Evans was killed?"

Nick nodded. "He was sitting at his desk, leaning back in his chair when Jimmy found him."

"That's what Mary told me."

Nick's eyebrows went up. "I thought you just gave her a ride up the hill."

Cord shrugged. "It was my day off. We

213

went into Fish Lake and had lunch. We ended up spending a couple of hours together at the house before I headed back to Anchorage and went to work." He pinned Nick with a glare. "To dig up information for you, if you recall."

Nick ignored the jibe. "You didn't tell her anything, did you?"

"Hell, I didn't *know* anything. I still don't."

Nick turned at the sound of a car coming up the road, saw Mary's white Subaru Outback pulling up in front of the house. "There she is now."

Cord turned and started walking. Mary got out of her car, paused to look at the firemen putting up hoses, doing general cleanup. Cord reached her, drew her into his arms. Mary didn't resist.

Looked like the attraction was mutual.

Cord finally let her go. Though Mary was maybe five eight, Cord was still about four inches taller. Nick couldn't hear what they were saying, but he figured his friend was telling her the fire was under control and had only affected one room in the house.

The two of them started walking toward where Nick stood next to Samantha. Mary jerked to a sudden stop. "Where's Duke?" She glanced wildly around, a look of panic on her face.

"Duke's okay," Samantha assured her. "Nick found him in the side yard. He was right here a minute ago."

Mary turned. "Duke! Here, boy! Duke!"

When the dog barked and came trotting up to her, the worry drained from her face. Mary rubbed the retriever's golden fur, seemed to relax even more when she saw he was okay. "Thank you for taking care of him."

"No problem," Nick said.

"Do they know what started it?"

Nick and Cord exchanged glances. "Not yet," Nick said.

Mary's gaze went to the house. "It's going to be a mess to clean up."

"I'll help you," Samantha offered. "With two of us working, it won't be so bad."

"We'll all pitch in," Cord said.

Mary looked at the cluster of people who were becoming her friends and tears welled in her eyes. "Thank you." She glanced up as one of the firemen walked toward her, his helmet covering most of a soot-blackened face.

"Are you the owner?"

"I'm Mary George. I live here with my nephew, Jimmy."

"The fire destroyed the office, Ms. George,

but aside from the mess, the rest of the house is okay. Looks like there was lots of office equipment in there, computers, printers, scanners, stuff like that. There were a lot of electrical cords plugged into a single power supply. That's probably what started the fire."

"The room wasn't being used. Jimmy's father recently passed away. Alex had a lot of computer equipment. I should have checked, paid more attention."

"It wasn't your fault," Cord said darkly.

"We'll have to turn in a report," the fireman said, "but unless something else comes up, we've got all we need."

Mary nodded. "I really appreciate what you did. Thank you."

"I wouldn't try to go back in for a while. Better to let things cool down."

"Why don't you come over to the house?" Nick asked Mary. "We'll get some lunch and you can wait for the school bus there."

"All right."

"We'll start working on the house this afternoon," Samantha said. She turned to Nick. "If it's all right with you, I'll make supper for everyone tonight. I saw some hamburger in the freezer. I can make us a batch of spaghetti."

Nick grinned. "That sounds great. But

that's ground caribou in the freezer, not regular hamburger."

"Caribou?" Samantha's eyebrows shot up. "You expect me to cook a reindeer?"

Nick and Cord each boomed out a laugh. "That's Alaskan hamburger, honey," Nick said. "It's some of the healthiest meat on the planet." He slid an arm around her waist. "Come on, let's go home."

Walking next to him, Cord led Mary down the hill, Duke trotting along beside them. Nick thought of the fire and what could have happened if whoever had set the blaze had done it while Mary and Jimmy were home.

His jaw hardened. At least for now, everyone was safe.

CHAPTER SIXTEEN

As soon as lunch was over, Nick led the small group up the hill to survey the damage to the house. Mary called Jimmy on his cell and told him the firemen had left. She said they would be working at the house, cleaning up the mess when he got home from school.

"Let's get these windows opened," Nick said, "air the place out and get rid of the smoke." Aside from that, the house looked livable. They fanned out, going into the rooms on both floors, then Samantha and Mary got out cleaning supplies and started mopping up what looked like an ocean of water.

The good news was the door to the study had been closed when the fire started and the firemen had done their best to keep the destruction contained to that room. The blaze had burned up the office furniture and equipment, cabinets, books, photos and whatever else had been in there, but the damage to the rest of the house was minimal.

As Nick worked next to Samantha, wiping soot off the walls in the hallway outside the study door and doing other miscellaneous cleanup, he heard the school bus coming up the hill.

"That's Jimmy," he said.

"He's going to be upset," Mary said worriedly. "He just lost his father. He doesn't need more problems."

Unfortunately, at the moment the kid had trouble in spades.

"Let's wait for him on the porch." Nick urged Mary toward the front door. The two of them walked outside and stood at the rail to wait. The bus pulled up and the doors slid open. As Jimmy descended the steps, Nick waved and the boy hurried toward the house.

"What happened?" he asked, panic in his face as he climbed the front porch stairs.

Mary managed to give him a smile. "It's okay, Jimmy, it was only one room. Everyone's okay. Duke's fine." The dog trotted up at the sound of his name, and Jimmy's hand unconsciously sank into the animal's golden coat.

"The water is the worst part," Nick said.

"We're all pitching in to clean up."

"We won't have to move out or anything," Mary finished.

Jimmy nodded, but those dark, worried eyes swung back to Nick in search of answers and stayed firmly fixed on his face.

Nick tipped his head toward the stairs. "Let's take a walk, okay?"

Jimmy set his backpack down on the porch. "Okay."

"We won't be long," Nick said to Mary, who seemed grateful for his help. She and Jimmy were coming to know each other on a deeper level, forming closer family bonds. But it was going to take some time.

Resting a hand on the boy's thick shoulder, Nick guided him down the front steps. They walked through the pines, Duke trotting along beside them as they continued along the trail leading to the edge of the lake. It was quiet there, the wind calm, the pine boughs barely shifting above their heads. The lake stretched out before them, deep blue and smooth as glass.

At the water's edge, Jimmy stopped and turned. Nick could read the questions in his face.

"Was it them? The men who put me in the trunk?"

There was no sense lying. The kid needed

to know the truth. "Probably not the same two, but someone who works with them, someone who knows about fires. The blaze only burned the office. Whoever set it made it look like an electrical fire. They weren't trying to burn down the house, Jimmy, just get rid of any evidence."

The kid stared up at him. "But you got it first, right? When you went into my dad's office the other night?"

"We got what we could. I'm not sure exactly what we found, but we're working on it."

Jimmy nodded. "That's good." He kicked a loose rock, watched it sail into the water. "Do you think they'll come back?"

"I don't know why they would. They got what they came for. The fire burned up everything in your father's study."

"Maybe we should . . . you know . . . tell the police."

"If that's what you want, maybe we should. Cord thinks it's a good idea."

"Cord's a cop, right? I thought you weren't going to tell anyone."

"Cord's a detective, but he's also my best friend and a man I completely trust."

Jimmy said nothing.

"Look, Cord's helping me work the case. We had to have someone who could get the information we need. Cord's come up with some promising leads."

"I guess it's okay, then."

"Cord won't do anything that would put you or your aunt in danger."

Jimmy looked up at him. "So what do you think we should do?"

"I think it would be safer to wait, see what we can find out."

"Do you think we're going to find the guy who murdered my dad?"

"I do. Eventually we'll have enough evidence to take to the police. We just aren't there yet."

Jimmy turned toward the lake. A fish jumped, flashing silver and sending concentric rings fanning out toward shore. When he turned back to Nick, his features were solemn. "I think you're right. I think it would be safer to wait. Those two guys . . . they said they'd kill us. They'll do it, Nick."

Nick gave the boy's shoulder a reassuring squeeze. "Okay, then. We'll wait a little longer, find something we can give the police. I worked homicide with those guys for years. They're good men. We give them enough, they'll run with it. They won't quit till they find the guy who killed your dad and arrest him."

Jimmy stared up at the big log house on

the hill. Just the peak of the roof could be seen through the pines. "I bet it's a mess in there."

"Could be worse. The office will need to be gutted and completely rebuilt, but the rest of the place is okay. We'll finish cleaning it up, then Samantha's cooking dinner for all of us. Spaghetti." Nick grinned. "Reindeer spaghetti. She wasn't thrilled about that."

Jimmy laughed, the happy sound a kid makes when he thinks something is extra funny. It made Nick's chest feel tight.

"Yupiks eat caribou all the time," Jimmy said as they started back up the hill, the dog at his heels. "Mary says I have an uncle who can teach me to hunt."

"That's a handy thing to know in this country."

"If I could shoot, I could protect Aunt Mary."

Nick's stomach tightened. "You won't need to do that. If it comes to it, I can shoot. I won't do it unless I have to. But if I pull the trigger, I don't miss."

Jimmy said nothing till they reached the bottom of the stairs leading up to the front door. He paused for several long moments.

"I'm glad you're my friend," he said.

Nick glanced away. "Me, too," he said

gruffly, and they started climbing the stairs.

Samantha showed Mary how to make reindeer spaghetti — which, to Samantha's relief, turned out to be surprisingly good. Afterward they all pitched in to clean up the dishes, then Mary pulled her aside.

"I want to thank you for your help today. The house was a real mess, and you hardly even know us."

"It wasn't that bad and with all of us working together, it was kind of fun. You'll need to get a cleaning company out here to suck the water out of the carpet."

"I've already called them. I still appreciate your help. I can think of a lot more fun things to do than scrub floors and wash walls. And you even fixed supper."

"I'm glad I could help."

"I know you've already done enough, but I was wondering . . . I need to buy new curtains for the downstairs bathroom and replace a few other things that didn't fair too well with all that water. Do you think you would consider coming to Wasilla to help me shop? I'm really bad at decorating. We wouldn't be long, just a couple of hours."

Samantha glanced over at Nick, who was talking to Cord but watching her from the corner of his eye. He'd been doing that all afternoon.

"I love to shop. It's one of my favorite pastimes. What time do you want to leave?"

"The cleaning service is coming first thing in the morning. They should be done by ten. Why don't I pick you up then?"

"Perfect."

They walked into Nick's living room to join the men.

"I think we'd better be getting home," Mary said to Jimmy.

Cord stood up from the sofa. "You've got school tomorrow, right?" he said to the boy.

"Yeah."

"Come on, then. I'll walk you two home."

Mary flashed Cord a look of gratitude. "Thank you."

As the three of them left the house to head up the hill, Samantha closed the door behind them. She turned to find Nick watching her, the way he had been all day.

"What is it? What's going on?"

He rubbed his jaw. "I was just wondering. . . . I know we aren't supposed to talk about, you know . . . you being pregnant, but are you sure pregnant women are supposed to work as hard as you did today? Aren't you worried you might do something to the baby?"

She laughed. "In the old days, women worked in the fields till the day they delivered, then went back to work the next day."

"Yeah, well, we don't live in the old days. We live in the twenty-first century." The worry in those amazing blue eyes made her heart squeeze.

"Concern noted," she said. "But I doubt I'll have to scrub any more floors during the rest of the time I'm up here, okay?"

"I guess."

Since there was nothing more to say, she changed the subject. "We didn't hear from your friend Lisa today." With Evans's study destroyed and any other evidence with it, they needed to know more than ever what was on that flash drive.

"She said it would take a day or two."

"Any idea what she might find?"

"I wish I did. We're stalled till we hear from her. Or I figure out that phone number, or Cord comes up with something from Evans's client list."

"Since there's nothing we can do for a while, I'm going shopping with Mary for a couple of hours tomorrow morning. We should be back by early afternoon. You don't mind, do you?"

She could tell he was mulling it over, looking for any possible danger, finding no reason to object. "I don't see why not. It'll give me a chance to work on that phone number."

"Okay then." She glanced at the clock. "It's getting late and we've had a rough day. I think it's time we went to bed."

The muscles across his shoulders went tense. She could clearly read his thoughts, knew he wanted her, but he didn't say a word.

Samantha walked over and took hold of his hand. "Are you coming?" she asked.

Nick's gaze turned dark and hungry. Samantha gave a startled gasp when he scooped her up in his arms and started striding down the hall toward his bedroom.

While Samantha was shopping with Mary, Nick went in to work at his computer. Since his eyes kept wandering toward the unmade bed and his mind kept flashing back to the hot night he'd shared with Samantha, he walked over and made the damned thing before he sat down at his desk.

Clicking up his e-mail, he scanned the list of messages, replied to one from Dylan, who wanted an update on Nick's "baby" situation. Nick told him they were taking his advice and moving slowly. The next message was the one from Cord he'd been hoping to find.

Checked the names on Evans's client list.
No warrants, nothing worse than speeding
tickets on any of them. There are a few
small business owners. No problems I
could find. The rest are companies run by
corporations. Maybe Lisa can get in deep
enough to find out if there's anything there.

Good idea, Nick thought, hoping he'd get
more from his ex-girlfriend than Cord had
given him.

He went back to Cord's message and hit
reply. Thanks for the legwork. Keep in touch.
N.

Pulling out his cell, he punched in Lisa's
number, waited impatiently for her to pick
up. He remembered he'd spent a good
many hours waiting for the lady when they
had been dating. It wasn't his favorite pas-
time.

The phone clicked as she picked up. "Hey,
Leese, it's Nick. Have you got anything yet?"

"Hi, lover. I think I have something."

"Don't make me guess."

"You sent me Evans's accounting records.
I gave each of his clients a cursory look,
then went back and examined the accounts
that were more complex. I narrowed it down

to two that might lead to something."

"Which ones?"

"Northland Corp owns Sleep E-Z, which owns a string of cheap motels in Fairbanks and others scattered around the state. Sea-West owns twenty Captain Henry's Fish and Chips. They're fast-food restaurants located in Fairbanks and Anchorage."

"So?"

"You ever heard of Captain Henry's?"

"I don't think so. I've never eaten at one."

"That's the thing. Both these corporations pay taxes on a helluva lot of money. With income like that, they ought to be practically a household name, but they aren't."

"Go on."

"And there are all these money transfers, stuff going from one bank to another, in and out of the country, then some of it coming back."

Nick started nodding, though Lisa couldn't see. "It's called layering. Moving the dollars around. Makes them almost impossible to follow. Looks like Evans was helping them launder money. Whoever he was working for doesn't mind paying the tax, they just don't want to get caught doing whatever it is they're doing."

"Could be they took in a boatload of dirty, came out with a big wad of clean."

229

"If that's the case, the question is, what are they doing to make all that change — beside selling deep-fried fish and renting cheap-ass rooms?"

"And who are the guys taking all that money home with them?"

"Good question."

"Sorry, I can't help you with that. I'm only an accountant."

"You did good. Thanks, Lisa. You're a gem."

"That wasn't what you said last year when you dumped me."

"I didn't dump you. I thought we parted friends."

"Friends with benefits. I guess that's all we ever were."

It was true. As beautiful as Lisa was, she just didn't do it for him, except in bed. He had no complaint there. "Whatever we are, I really appreciate your help."

"No problem." Her voice lightened. "Let me know if you need anything else — anything at all — if you know what I mean." Lisa hung up the phone.

As Nick set his cell down next to his computer, he couldn't help comparing Lisa to Samantha. Physically, they were completely different, Lisa tall, slender, and athletic, Samantha petite and curvy, softly feminine. Lisa was a party girl, Samantha more of a homebody. He couldn't figure what it was that drew him to her so strongly, made him want her the way he did.

And the longer she was there, the better he got to know her, the more he worried they were completely unsuited.

He was ex-military. Ex-cop. No matter what job he took, that would never change. Samantha was a city girl, sweet and naïve and completely unfit for a life in Alaska.

Hell, completely wrong for a hard man like him.

On the other hand, she was carrying his child. He had a duty to that child, a responsibility. He wasn't about to ignore it.

The arguments went round and round in his head until he got up from the chair and padded over to his dresser. He needed some exercise, needed to go out for a run, come back and push a few weights.

Changing out of his jeans into a light gray, hooded sweatshirt and sweatpants, he shoved his feet into a pair of running shoes and headed for the door. He always thought more clearly outside, and Samantha wouldn't be back for a while. Nick headed down the front steps and started jogging along the road.

CHAPTER SEVENTEEN

Walking next to the cart Mary was pushing down the aisle of the Wasilla Target store, Samantha watched the tall woman picking up items to replace the ones that had been destroyed by the fire and the water from the effort to stop it.

Mary picked up a new burgundy bathmat for her powder room. "I love this color. It doesn't match what's in there now, but I was thinking of making some changes anyway." She tossed a set of matching towels into the cart. "I'm beginning to think of the house as mine and Jimmy's, not Alex's. Might as well do it now."

"That shade is going to look great with the wallpaper. You should pick up a few accessories to go with it, maybe a soap dish and dispenser, something like that."

"Good idea."

As Mary set to work choosing items, Samantha couldn't help thinking of Nick's house and how much cozier it would look with just a few simple touches. Spotting a pair of powder-blue curtains that would work perfectly with the towels in his guest bath, she reached over and picked them up. Nick only had an old-fashioned roll-down vinyl shade there now. She wondered if he would be angry or pleased if she bought the curtains, decided to find out and tossed them into the cart.

"I need a new rug for the entry," Mary was saying. "There's soot and dirt all over the old one — plus it's waterlogged. But I don't think I'm going to find the right thing here."

"I don't think so either. You need something that'll fit the log house theme of your home. You'll probably need to go somewhere that specializes in that kind of thing."

"They're building a Cabela's not too far away, but it isn't open yet. They might have something like that."

"Maybe. You could probably shop for it online."

"Oh, that's a great idea!"

As they continued down the aisle, Samantha spotted some interesting brown-and-turquoise kitchen curtains done in an Indian design. They looked masculine yet warm, and Nick didn't have anything covering the windows over the kitchen sink.

She picked up a package, guessed the size and figured they would probably fit, tossed them into the cart, then found the rods she would need in order to hang them and those in the guest bath. She would give the curtains to Nick as a gift. That way he couldn't refuse them. If he hated them, she'd bring them back.

"You're buying curtains for Nick's house?"

"Yes, but I'm not sure he'll want me to put them up. You know how men are."

"Those look like a guy. I think they'd be great."

"I guess we'll see."

"Are you . . . are you thinking of moving in with him?"

Samantha laughed. "Are you kidding? I work in San Francisco. I'm only visiting. Nick and I are just friends." Even as she said the word, it sounded funny on her tongue. She wasn't sure exactly *what* they were, but with a baby coming, they were way more than friends.

Mary cocked a disbelieving eyebrow. "I've seen the way he looks at you. Like you're dessert and he wants to eat you up. And if you don't mind my saying so, that's the same way you look at him. Or am I just imagining things?"

Samantha sighed. "It's complicated. Nick and I. I guess you could say we're in lust. We met in Las Vegas. The attraction we felt when we were there brought me here, but it can't go any further."

"Because you work in San Francisco?"

"It's more than that. My life is there. My family lives nearby. Besides, it takes a special person to live in Alaska. Clearly, I'm not that person."

"I was kind of hoping you'd be staying. I'm new to the area and female friends are hard to find. It's really a shame you have to leave."

Samantha felt an unexpected pang. "Yes, I guess it is."

On the way to the register, they passed the baby department. For the first time, Samantha felt the urge to prowl through the racks loaded with tiny garments, miniature shoes, sweaters, and down-soft blankets. It took all her will not to pick something out.

Which was crazy, since she had no idea if the child would be a boy or a girl. So far she'd been lucky. No morning sickness at all, not even tenderness in her breasts. But she was still in the very early stages.

They continued toward the check-out, and Samantha turned her thoughts in a different direction. "So what about you and Cord?"

Faint color rose beneath the high bones in Mary's cheeks. "He's really been nice."

"I would have figured him for a real heartbreaker, but he doesn't seem that way with you."

"He doesn't?"

"No."

"I could say the same for your Nick."

He wasn't her Nick, but Samantha didn't point that out. "I think he has a lot of women chasing after him."

"Maybe. But so far none of them have caught him."

Samantha smiled. "Even if I caught him, I'd have to let him go."

Mary grinned. "Sort of a catch-and-release kind of guy."

Samantha laughed. "Exactly."

They reached the register and separated their purchases, paid for them and carried the bags out to the car. The clouds had rolled in and the temperature had dropped dramatically since they had gone into the store. Shivering as they crossed the parking lot, Samantha wished she'd done a little more research on the weather and brought a heavier jacket.

"It's freezing out here," she said as they

climbed into Mary's white Subaru.

"The weather is really crazy up here. You never know what's going to happen. The forecast says we might get snow sometime this week."

"You're kidding, right?"

Mary just laughed. "You get used to it."

But Samantha knew she never would make it in the wilds of Alaska. She ignored the hint of regret that tightened her chest.

As the car pulled out of the parking lot and headed back toward Fish Lake, she turned away from the beautiful mountain scenery outside the window and glanced over at Mary. She and Mary were bonding. Maybe now was a good time to have a conversation about Mary's brother-in-law, Alex Evans.

"So how's Jimmy doing?" she asked, easing into the subject.

"Okay, I guess. Lately, he seems worried. I wish I knew what was going on."

What was going on was that the boy had been abducted and threatened and his house had been set on fire by the men who had killed his dad. But Samantha couldn't say that.

"What was his father like?" she asked instead.

Mary kept her eyes straight ahead, but Samantha noticed her fingers tightening around the steering wheel. "Alex loved his son."

"I believe that. You can tell by how much Jimmy loved him that he must have been a very good father."

"Yes, he was."

"Alex was married to your sister. Was he a good husband, too?"

Mary kept her eyes on the road. "Alex was obsessed with Cora. She was beautiful. Not as tall as I am, but her figure was perfect and her face could have graced any fashion magazine."

Easy to believe, since Mary, with her long, jet-black hair, high cheekbones, and sculpted lips, was equally lovely.

"From the moment Alex saw Cora, he had to have her. He was devastated when she was killed."

"Sounds like quite a romance. He must have swept your sister off her feet."

"You could say that. Alex asked her to marry him and Cora agreed. She didn't have any other choice."

A frown formed between Samantha's brows. "Was she pregnant?"

Mary started shaking her head. "It doesn't matter why she married him, and I'd rather not talk about Alex or my sister. From here on out, Jimmy's welfare is what's important."

Guilt washed through her. She really liked Mary. "I'm sorry. I didn't mean to pry." Well, she did, but only to help Nick and Jimmy with their investigation.

"It's all right." Mary smiled weakly. "It was just girl talk."

"That's right." But Samantha's mind was leaping ahead, wondering what had forced Cora George to marry Alexander Evans. Every day, the mystery of his death seemed to get murkier instead of clearer.

Mary dropped Samantha off at the house, her arms full of the purchases she had made.

"We'll have to do this again before you leave," Mary said through the open car window, apparently forgiving her for prying into her life.

"I'd love that. Maybe you and Cord could come over one night for supper."

"Maybe," Mary said noncommittally.

Samantha waved as she hurried off, shivering all the way to the front door. It was unlocked, but when she went inside, Nick wasn't home.

Since his car was still in the garage, she didn't think he had gone very far. He liked to get out in the fresh air, so maybe he'd gone for a run. Wherever he had gone, it gave her the perfect opportunity to put up the curtains she had bought.

Samantha grinned. Finally warm again, she set to work.

Nick jogged up the walkway, slowed to climb the front steps, crossed the porch and opened the door. He hadn't meant to be gone quite so long, but the air was crisp and clean and the exercise had cleared his head.

He glanced up as he walked across the living room and stopped dead in his tracks. Through the doorway into the kitchen, he could see Samantha standing on a ladder at the sink. He watched her a moment, hardly able to believe his eyes.

What the hell? Those were curtains she was hanging!

Anger swept through him. They were supposed to be figuring things out. Working on the details, getting to know each other. Baby or not, no way was she moving in, taking over his house, his life. What the hell did she expect from him? Whatever it was, it wasn't going to happen.

He stormed toward her. "What the hell do you think you're doing?"

Samantha shrieked and the stepladder tipped sideways. Nick rushed forward and caught her as she tumbled toward the floor. Swinging her up, he set her firmly on her feet.

"You shouldn't be up on a ladder in your condition. You almost fell and hurt yourself. I asked you what you're doing."

Samantha set her hands on her hips. "Until you scared the holy bejesus out of me, I was hanging curtains."

"I see that."

"I found the stepladder on the back porch. Along with your toolbox. The hammer and screwdriver were in there. I didn't think you'd mind if I borrowed them."

He couldn't seem to get his mind to work, to understand why Samantha would be hanging curtains in his kitchen. "Why? We haven't even talked about the baby. I can't believe you're already moving in and changing things around."

Those big brown eyes went wide and hot color rushed into her cheeks. "It was supposed to be a gift! I have no intention of moving in with you — not now or anytime in the future. You didn't have any curtains in here. I saw these at Target and thought they looked like something you'd like. I figured if you didn't, we could take them back and you could pick out something else."

241

Turning, she marched past him out of the kitchen, off down the hall to the guest room. Nick winced at the sound of the door slamming behind her. He looked over at the window. The curtains were turquoise and a warm shade of brown. There was an Indian design and nothing feminine about them.

And the kitchen did look better, cozier, the way a home should be. He'd told himself he'd get around to adding a few decorative touches, but he really had no idea where to begin.

He looked back at the curtains that fit the kitchen and his taste perfectly, blew out a long, slow breath. He was an idiot.

Heading down the hall, he knocked on the bedroom door. "Samantha? Honey, can I come in?"

"Go away."

No way was that happening. He opened the door and walked into the room, saw her sitting on the edge of the bed, her face wet with tears.

"I'm sorry. I like the curtains. They're a great gift, nice and masculine, the perfect color, exactly what I would have chosen." If he ever picked out a pair of curtains, which he never would have.

"I wasn't thinking," she said tearfully. "I helped my brother decorate his apartment.

242

I thought it would be nice to help you, too."

"Please don't cry."

She glared up at him. "I'm pregnant. It's hormones. I hate crying. It's one of the reasons I didn't want to be pregnant in the first place."

His mouth edged up. He felt an unexpected surge of protectiveness that made him want to hold her. He could see by the look on her face that wouldn't be a good idea.

She wiped away the wetness on her cheeks. "I'll take them down."

"Leave them. I like them. I really do."

Her features softened. Damn, she was pretty. She had one of those faces that was so cute you didn't get it right away, but then you did. Soft pink mouth, big brown eyes. He loved the way those fine curls felt in his hands. Just looking at her made him start getting hard.

"You really like them?" she asked. "You aren't just saying that?"

"No. I mean, yeah, I really like them." And the funniest thought had struck him as he'd stood there staring at the curtains on his window. His house felt a little more like home.

He walked toward her, drew her up off the bed and into his arms. "I'm sorry, honey. Forgive me?"

She pushed him away, not quite ready to forgive him yet. "I don't want to move in with you, Nick. I didn't come here for that."

"I know." So why did the thought not sound nearly as terrifying as it had just minutes ago?

"I live in San Francisco," she reminded him in case he hadn't gotten the message. "That's where my home is."

He knew that. Hell, she hadn't even been sure she was going to tell him she was having his kid.

"I just . . . I guess I'm not used to having a woman around the house." He reached for her again and this time she didn't resist. He kissed the side of her neck and the stiffness went out of her body. He nibbled an earlobe, heard her quick intake of breath. "I must admit it has its pluses."

He could feel the warmth of her breasts, smell her floral perfume. A rush of desire slid through him, thickened, began to pound through his veins. He was hard for her, aching inside his sweatpants. He flicked a glance at the bed, only a few feet away.

"Did you . . . umm . . . find that phone number?" Samantha asked, drawing away from him.

Nick sighed, tried to think of something

besides being inside her. "Not yet. But I talked to Lisa. Looks like Evans may have been laundering money. According to the numbers in two of his accounts, Northland Corp and SeaWest, both may be running shady operations. Evans was up to his neck in whatever was going on, and the kind of money we're talking about is plenty of motive for murder."

"Did she find out who owns the corporations?"

"No. She says that's not her bailiwick."

A smile lit up those big brown eyes and the desire he'd curbed rushed back full force. Nick clenched his jaw.

"I could do it," Samantha said.

"You can find out who owns those companies?"

"Marketing was my specialty. We were planning to expand. You need to know who you're dealing with, the names of your competitors, people you might need to talk to. It's tricky, but I could do it."

Nick leaned down and kissed her. "Honey, you get me that info, you can put curtains all over the house."

Her chin inched up. "Fine, but you're buying the next ones."

Nick laughed.

While he went in to shower and change,

Samantha went to work on his computer.

She started by simply Googling the corporate names. Neither Northland nor SeaWest had a website. Next she started digging around on pay-to-subscribe websites that provided information on businesses and corporations, like www.LexisNexis.com. The sites provided the names of subsidiary companies under the parent corporation, the names of the executives who ran then, their addresses and even their phone numbers.

She paid the membership fee to use one of the sites and went to work. Both corporate names popped up as legally filed corporations. She had figured they would be. But as she maneuvered around the site, she realized that the information she was collecting was useless.

She couldn't find any information on John Thompson, the president of Northland, or Vince Murray, the vice president, or Richard Curts, the treasurer. Same with Robert Donahue, president of SeaWest.

She needed more information. Samantha paused, her fingers poised above the keyboard. Nick was a cop. Well, an ex-cop, but once a cop always a cop as far as she was concerned. If he knew she was hacking into corporate records, he probably wouldn't like it.

On the other hand, he had said himself there were times rules needed to be bent. Jimmy and Mary were two innocent people whose lives were in danger. Yesterday someone had set fire to their house. As far as Samantha was concerned, it was time to bend the rules.

Her fingers settled on the keyboard and Samantha went to work.

CHAPTER EIGHTEEN

Nick was on the landline phone, the call ringing through when he heard the knock at the door. For the last two hours, he'd been dialing different number combinations, trying to make a name/number connection from the message on the scratch pad at Alex Evans's office. He hoped the area code was 907, which covered all of Alaska. If not he was screwed. Unfortunately, so far he'd gotten zilch.

He ignored the knock when someone picked up the phone on the other end of his latest call. "Hello, is this Dmitri?"

"This is Dmitri," a heavily accented voice replied.

"Dmitri Johnson?" he asked, making up a name so the man would think it was just a wrong number.

"No." The phone went dead.

Nick shot up a fist. He had a number and a first name. The reverse directory could give him a last name and address. If the number was unlisted, he'd have Cord get the info.

They were back in business.

Heading out of the kitchen, he hurried toward the door. When he pulled it open, his brother Rafe stood on the porch.

"Are you going to leave me out here in the cold all day or can I come in?" At six-four, Rafe was the tallest, and also the oldest of the brothers. He had Nick's dark hair, though not quite as black, and his eyes were brown instead of blue.

Nick grinned. "It wasn't locked. Come on in."

Rafe stepped into his living room, and Nick closed the door behind him. "I was expecting a phone call," Nick said, "not a personal visit. Dylan's never been good at keeping his mouth shut so I figured I'd hear from you sooner or later."

"This is family business. He's worried about you." Rafe glanced around to be sure no one could hear him. "He's convinced some little hussy is trying to take advantage of you."

Nick laughed and shook his head. "Samantha's about the farthest thing from a hussy you'll ever meet. Come on, I'll introduce you."

Nick started down the hall, reached for the door to his room. Rafe came to an abrupt halt behind him. "She's in your bedroom? It's the middle of the day."

Nick grinned up at him. "Since when did you turn into a prude? You don't think it's okay to have sex in the middle of the day?"

"Why don't I just wait in the living room?"

Nick couldn't help laughing. "She's working on the computer, helping me dig up information. If you talked to Dylan, he probably told you I'm investigating a murder."

"Actually, he didn't mention it. He was concerned about your impending fatherhood. And frankly, so am I."

"Take it easy, okay?" Nick turned the knob and shoved open the door. Samantha sat in front of the computer, pounding away on the keyboard. "Can you take a break for a minute? I want you to meet my brother."

Samantha's gaze flew to the doorway. Shoving back the chair, she slowly came to her feet. Her gaze went to Rafe, caught the thundercloud of disapproval carved into his features, and her face went pale.

"You . . . you told him about the baby?"

"Not exactly. Dylan did."

She stiffened, drilled Nick with a glare. "You told your whole family? How could you? We haven't . . . haven't even really discussed it yet."

Nick looked at Rafe and wanted to punch him. He hadn't realized how badly this was going to go down.

Samantha started for the door, but Rafe stepped in front of her. "We need to talk about this."

Samantha's whole body went rigid. "I'm not talking to you about anything."

"Get out of her way, Rafe," Nick warned, trying to hang on to his temper. "Now." Rafe, being the oldest and no fool, stepped back to let her pass.

Nick waited until she'd made it as far as the hall, then went after her, caught up with her on the way to the guest room and turned her around.

"I needed someone to talk to, okay? I called Dylan. He's engaged to be married. I figured he and Lane would be planning to have kids someday. I thought he could help me figure things out."

"I haven't mentioned it to my family. I can't believe you called your brother. He probably thinks I'm trying to trap you into marrying me."

It was exactly what he thought. Nick hoped once Rafe got to know Samantha, he would realize that wasn't the case.

"You didn't tell your family," he said, "but you talked to someone, right? Your friend, Abby? Someone else you trusted? You probably needed advice as much as I did."

Some of the stiffness went out of her shoulders. "You're right. I did talk to someone. Abby is my best friend. She helped me get over the shock."

"Dylan and Rafe are *my* best friends."

She sniffed. "I suppose you told Cord, too."

"No. And I won't discuss it with anyone else until we decide how we're going to handle things. Okay?"

When she finally nodded, he slid an arm around her waist, turned her around and led her into the living room. Rafe was standing rigidly by the door.

"I'm sorry," Samantha said to him. "I'm just . . . I'm not handling this whole thing very well."

Rafe's dark gaze ran over her from head to foot, taking in her bouncy nutmeg curls, petite figure, and her pretty, all-American-girl face with its slightly freckled nose. There was no way he could think she was anything but what she seemed, sweet, maybe a little emotional in her current state, and sexy as hell.

"I'm the one who should apologize," Rafe

said. "I shouldn't have stuck my nose in. I'm not usually that way."

Except when it came to family, Rafe was pretty much a loner. But he had helped raise Nick and Dylan after their mother had died. He was protective of the people he cared about, and that hadn't changed.

Samantha smiled. It lit up her whole face. Rafe blinked at the change. "You were worried about Nick. I have a brother I worry about all the time. Can you stay for supper? I bought a chicken while I was shopping. I thought maybe chicken cacciatore with some parsley buttered potatoes. Or pasta if you'd rather. I could make enough for all of us."

Nick wasn't completely sure he liked the slow, answering smile that slid over his brother's too-handsome face. "I wish I could, but I've got to be getting back."

"You sure?" Nick said, only a little reluctantly. "Samantha's a really great cook."

Rafe looked past him to the window over the sink and something seemed to click. "She put up the new curtains?"

He felt the heat rising at the back of his neck. "They were a gift, okay? You don't like them, too bad."

Rafe grinned. "Oh, I like them. I like them a lot."

Nick couldn't figure out why his brother was grinning like a fool. The urge to punch him rose again.

"Before I head back, what's the story on this murder you're involved in?"

Happy for a neutral topic and one he needed to concentrate on, he invited Rafe to sit down in the living room. Nick spent the next half hour filling his brother in on Alexi Evanko and his son, Jimmy, and the case that had become so personal to him.

Samantha sat quietly while the brothers talked. She remembered Nick saying Rafe was the oldest, the brother who ran a charter fishing fleet in Valdez. It occurred to her that a man as protective of his family as Rafe was a man she could like very much.

"Right before you got here," Nick said to him as he finished summing up the case, "I got a new lead. Evans wrote a name and number on the scratch pad in his office. I finally got it unscrambled."

"You got it?" Samantha blurted out excitedly.

"Yeah."

"Were you able to get his last name and address?"

"Not yet. I'm hoping they'll show up in the reverse directory."

"Where's the number?" she asked. "I'll find it for you."

"It's on the kitchen counter."

She got up and started in that direction, stopped and turned back. "Oh, I found the name of the man who owns Northland Corporation and SeaWest."

Nick's head came up. "The same guy owns them both?"

"It looks that way. The information was buried pretty deep but I found it."

"What's his name?"

She pulled out the slip of paper she had stuck in the pocket of her jeans. "Luka Dragovich. Do you know the name?"

"It sounds familiar, but I can't quite place it. Cord might know."

"Aside from the chain of Captain Henry's, I also found a list of the motels he owns and where they're located. I printed it out for you."

"Great."

"Sounds like a lot of Russians are popping up in this case," Rafe said.

"Yeah. More every day. And the more there are, the worse this could get."

"You need to be careful."

"Always."

Rafe unwound his tall frame and stood up from the sofa. In a different, harder way, he was just as good-looking as his brother. He moved with the same air of confidence, exuded the same sense of power and control, and his broad-shouldered frame looked fit and trim. All in all, Rafe Brodie was a very impressive man.

"I've got to be getting back," he said. "It was nice meeting you, Samantha."

"You, too, Rafe."

He looked like he wanted to say something more, but didn't. "Take care, little brother."

"You do the same."

As Nick walked Rafe to the door, Samantha went into the kitchen and grabbed the paper with the phone number and the name *Dmitri* written on it. Once more seated at Nick's computer, she pulled a reverse directory up on the Internet.

The number came up as unlisted. Samantha wasn't surprised. If the man was a gangster, he would hardly have his number listed in the phone book.

Nick walked in as she got up from the machine. "Unlisted," she said.

"I figured. I'll call Cord. The police have access to unlisted numbers."

"Okay. While you do that, I think I'll do some yoga. I'm really feeling tied up, you know?"

His eyes darkened even as his mouth

256

faintly curved. "Tied up? I'd be happy to try that anytime you'd like."

She glanced at the bed, wondering if he was teasing or if he could be at least half serious. She caught the interest in those incredible blues eyes and desire trickled through her. What would it be like to be completely at the mercy of a virile male like Nick? What would he do to her? And God, how much would she like it?

After last night, one thing she knew for sure, pregnant women could still enjoy sex. She looked back at Nick, let her gaze run over his face, travel down that hard male body. She remembered the way it felt to have him on top of her, inside her. Her nipples peaked and Nick's blue eyes went hot.

"Either I'm reading your mind or you're reading mine," he said. Striding toward her, he hauled her into his arms and very thoroughly kissed her.

They might have made it to the bed if it hadn't been for the phone ringing in the kitchen. With the trouble swirling around them, there was no way Nick could ignore it.

"Jesus. I can't seem to catch a break," he grumbled. Kissing her one last time, he walked out of the bedroom.

Samantha sighed. Feeling even edgier than before, she headed for the guest room. Digging out a pair of snug black yoga pants and a tank top, she pulled them on and began doing her stretches.

She was an advanced student. Yoga was the way she kept her body flexible and toned. A few minutes into her routine, she began to relax. Samantha went into the lotus position, took several deep breaths, closed her eyes and let her worries slip away.

CHAPTER NINETEEN

The phone call was from Cord. "Just checking in," Cord said. "You come up with anything new?"

"Your timing's lousy, but I was going to call you. You in the office?"

"Sitting at my desk."

"That message I got from Evans's study, it's an unlisted number for a guy, first name Dmitri. The number is five, five, five, four, one, seven, four. I need his last name and address."

"Hang on."

Nick waited while Cord typed the info into his computer. A couple of minutes later, he came back on the line.

"Dmitri Fedorko. Number's in Fairbanks. Sonofabitch." Cord rattled off the street address and Nick wrote it down.

"Got it. I guess you know the name."

"Oh, yeah. Rumored to be connected to Connie Bela Varga."

"So our list of players is expanding. Now we've got Crocker, Turnbull, and Fedorko. Varga's in Anchorage, right?"

"Last I heard."

"Maybe Fedorko's the Fairbanks connection."

"Could be."

"Listen, it looks like Evanko was doing a little money laundering — or maybe not so little. Manipulating money for a couple of different companies that all track back to a guy named Luka Dragovich. You recognize the name?"

"Hell, yes. The feds have been trying to connect Dragovich with Milushev for years. He's a real badass. You're getting into some deep shit, my friend."

"Fedorko's in Fairbanks. That's where Evanko was working before he took the job in Anchorage."

"If he was working for Dragovich and some of that money he was massaging fell into his own pocket, that may have been what got him killed."

"Gotta be something like that. I figure he was walking the straight and narrow — at least where these guys were concerned — until things got tough in 2008. According to one of his business partners, he suffered some financial losses. Probably took money he figured to pay back, but somehow fucked up and got caught. Maybe he couldn't come up with enough to pay what he owed and they killed him."

"With these guys, he was a dead man the day he took the first dollar. Whatever he did or didn't do after wouldn't matter. You ready to take this to Taggart?"

He had to have his ducks in a row if he expected his ex-boss to get involved. "The only thing we really have is the flash drive. But even if we prove Evans was involved in money laundering, that doesn't prove he was murdered. And Jankowski, Sorenson could argue the information was taken illegally. We had permission to go into Evans's office, not permission to raid his companies' private accounting files."

"You're right. Taggart won't go for it. Maybe you could take it to Captain Caruthers."

"Caruthers runs Crime Suppression. Those guys go to PTA meetings and come up with community action policies. He's not going over Taggart's head on this and neither is anyone else. Not with what we have now. We need something else."

"Like what?"

"I don't know. I need to go to Fairbanks, see what I can turn up."

"If you can get in and out without making waves, it might not be a bad idea. You'd have to be careful. We still can't afford for anyone to know we're working on this."

He wondered when Cord had gone from helping him to working with him. Figured it had something to do with the lovely Mary George. Nick knew homicide, but Cord worked Vice, one of the best detectives in the division. Nick wouldn't be able to work this case without him.

"I'll send you everything I can find on Fedorko, Bela Varga, and Dragovich," Cord said.

"Sounds good. I'll keep you posted." Nick hung up the phone. Even as he walked out of the kitchen, his mind was working on the best way to approach the trip he needed to make. He'd call his friend, Derek Hunter, arrange a charter to fly him up, then rent a car once he got there. Derek was a bush pilot, like Nick's brother, Dylan. Derek, ex-military, was one of the best in the business. He was a good friend and a good man to know, since flying was the most common way to travel the long distances in Alaska.

Nick thought of Samantha and wished he could take her with him. It would give her a chance to see Alaska, the way he had promised. He didn't intend to get close enough to the bad guys to get him into trouble. Still . . .

The lady was pregnant. It was a stupid idea.

Figuring she was back at work on his computer, he headed down the hall. She wasn't at the desk, so he kept walking. The door to the guest room was open. Nick paused in the doorway, spotted her on the floor, and instantly went hard.

Jesus. The woman could do amazing things with that small, supple body. She went from holding a split position to placing her palms on the floor and lifting herself slowly, gracefully into the air. With her back to him, she didn't realize he was there, but she was concentrating so hard, he didn't think it would matter even if he spoke to her.

Next she lowered her feet to the floor, bent in half and caught hold of her ankles. Nick's groin tightened. The sight of that tight little ass in the air was more than he could stand. Striding forward he moved behind her, set his hands gently on her hips and let her feel him, hard as a stone.

She didn't flinch, just slowly straightened to an upright position in front of him, slid a hand behind his neck and bowed herself closer.

Jesus God. Nick pressed his mouth against the side of her neck and turned her around, softly kissed those full pink lips, then took the kiss to a deeper level. Samantha kissed him back with all the heat he had imagined when he'd been watching her.

The bed was just inches away. He eased her in that direction, imagined her bent over the way he'd found her, turned her to face the bed.

"Put your palms flat on the mattress," he said softly, firmly, giving her little choice.

She sucked in a breath, but did what he asked, knowing what he wanted. What he had to have after watching her.

"You have the most beautiful little ass," he said because it was his favorite part of her body. He smoothed a hand over her hips, slid the side of his hand between her legs, heard her soft moan.

Grabbing the waistband of her stretch pants, he peeled them down to her ankles, urged her to step out of them, then returned to his place behind her. Sliding his hands over her bare hips, he reached around and began to gently stroke her, found her amazingly wet and hot. Samantha arched her back like a needy little cat as he unzipped his fly and freed himself.

He didn't need a condom. She was already

pregnant and he was clean. His jaw flexed at the notion of being inside her unsheathed.

Nick hissed in a breath and an instant later, he was. "God, I love the way you feel."

She made a little whimpering sound as he gripped her hips and started to move. Slowly at first, letting her get used to having him inside her this way, then moving faster, deeper. He knew what they were doing was safe in her condition. Samantha wasn't the only one who knew how to Google. And he would never do anything to hurt her.

She arched her back to take more of him, let out a soft whimper as she started to come. Nick drove into her, faster, harder, deeper, until her passage tightened around him and she moaned as she reached her peak. Nick let himself go, his muscles tightening as he felt the first hot rush of pleasure. Samantha trembled as a second climax shook her, and his own release struck hard.

When the tremors fully subsided, he eased her up and turned her into his arms, very softly kissed her. He ran a finger along her cheek. "You make me crazy. You know that?"

She leaned into him, rested her head against his chest. "Sex was never really important to me. I never really enjoyed it until I met you." She looked up at him, straight into his eyes. "You set me free."

Nick cupped her face in his hands. "I won't do anything to hurt you or the baby. You know that, right?"

She nodded. "I know. Pretty much everything regular is okay."

He smiled back. "Yeah, I know."

She let out a long, contented sigh. "I'm kind of sweaty. I think I'll shower and dress."

He thought of her naked, warm water sluicing over her feminine curves. "How about I join you?"

Samantha grinned. "Okay. But it's way too cold to run out of hot water."

Nick grinned back. "Then I guess we'll have to hurry."

Samantha laughed and they headed for the shower.

The crackle of chicken browning in the skillet filled the kitchen, along with the smell of garlic and olive oil. Samantha stood at the kitchen counter next to Nick, chopping onion and bell pepper for the chicken cacciatore she had promised to make him earlier.

"Sounds like whatever is going on may have some connection to Fairbanks," she said as Nick grabbed a slice of pepper and popped it into his mouth.

"Yeah, that's the thing," he said around it. "I need to get up there. I talked to a friend of mine. Derek can fly me up tomorrow. I figured I'd rent a car once I got there. Since I need to do the stakeout at night, I'll have to drive back the next day."

Samantha turned toward him, holding the chopping knife like a weapon. "Wait a minute. You keep saying *I*. You aren't thinking of leaving me here?"

"You're pregnant, honey. I can't very well take you on a stakeout."

"That's what you're planning to do? Stakeout Dmitri Fedorko's house?"

"That's right. And spend some time checking out those motels Dragovich owns."

"You said you were staying overnight. You'll need to rent a room, right? Why can't I wait for you there? That way I could fly up with you, see what Alaska looks like. We could drive back together."

Nick shook his head. "It's a bad idea. These guys are criminals. Something might go wrong."

"If it did, I'd be safe in the motel room. I'm a big girl. Even if something happened, I could find my way home."

Nick's mouth edged up. "I can't afford to get too close, so nothing's going to happen. But it's still a bad idea."

"I want to go." If she went, on the drive back home, maybe the time would be right for them to talk. She was a little more ready for that to happen. "Say you'll take me with you."

Nick released a slow breath. "I'll admit I thought about it. You're only going to be here a couple of weeks and so far, I haven't been much of a host."

He'd been a fine host. She'd come to Alaska to get to know him, not run around out in the woods in the freezing cold. Not her idea of a good time.

But she didn't say that. "I want to go. I'll stay in the motel room. You do your stakeout and come back. The next day we'll drive back together."

He walked up behind her, slid his arms around her waist, leaned down and nuzzled the back of her neck. Yummy little chills raced up and down her spine.

"I shouldn't take you," he said, "but, dammit, I want you to go."

She turned and slid her arms around his neck, gave him a brilliant smile. "Then it's settled. What time do we leave in the morning?"

He returned her smile. "Derek's checking the weather. There's a storm coming in later in the week, but he thinks it's going to be decent flying weather tomorrow. We have to be at the airport at nine o'clock."

"How long does it take to get to Fairbanks?"

"It's right at three-hundred miles from Wasilla to Fairbanks, but only two hours by plane."

"Okay, I'll be ready." She eased out of his arms and returned to fixing supper, removing the golden brown chicken and setting it aside, adding the peppers, onions, mushrooms, and white wine to the pan.

"Man, that smells good," Nick said, inhaling the aroma as he walked over to the stove. "Looks like you made plenty, which is good since you're eating for two." His eyes traveled down her body, stopped at her waist. "Are you feeling okay? You haven't been sick or anything? I thought that's what happened when a woman got pregnant."

"I feel great. My mom never got sick either. She said she was meant to have kids. She said she was one of the lucky ones."

"When are you going to tell her?"

Samantha shrugged. She wasn't prepared to tell her family, not until she made a few more decisions. Maybe she wasn't as ready to talk about this as she'd thought.

"I'm not sure. I guess when I get back."

"I could . . . you know, come with you if

you want. When you tell them, I mean."

She just shook her head. "I'll be fine. Why don't you set the table or something?"

He smiled. He had the most beautiful smile. "Is that a polite way of getting rid of me?"

"I cook better when I'm on my own." That wasn't exactly true. She enjoyed having company while she cooked. She just didn't want to talk about her parents and the baby.

"Okay, I get the hint. I'll set the table then I've got an errand to run. I'll be back in time for supper."

"Perfect." But once he was gone from the kitchen, Samantha felt unexpectedly lonesome. Since when had she started getting used to having Nick Brodie around? How deep was she letting herself get involved with him?

Her chest tightened. She'd convinced herself this was just a trip to help her make some tough decisions. Now her emotions were coming into play. Maybe going to Fairbanks was a bad idea.

On the other hand, they still needed to talk.

Samantha shoved her worries aside and concentrated on finishing supper.

CHAPTER TWENTY

Derek kept his single-engine plane, a well-maintained Cessna 185, at a small private airstrip outside Wasilla. Nick arrived at exactly nine and spotted Derek making a physical inspection of the plane, getting it ready for takeoff.

Black canvas duffel in one hand, Nick grabbed Samantha's wheeled carry-on and they started across the tarmac. The red-and-white-striped Cessna seated four to six, depending on how it was configured. It could slow to fifty-five miles an hour for landing, which made it a great plane for getting in and out of the wilderness.

Nick dropped his duffel next to a wheel, reached out and shook his friend's hand. "Hey, Derek."

"Hey, Nick, good to see you."

"Derek, this is Samantha Hollis. She's visiting from San Francisco. She's coming with us."

"Welcome, Samantha." Derek grinned, flashing a mouthful of perfect teeth, giving her the once-over before reaching out to shake her hand. He was dark-haired and green-eyed, an incorrigible ladies' man. Nick had forgotten that.

She smiled. "It's nice to meet you, Derek."

"She's never been to Alaska," Nick said. "I figured she'd enjoy the scenery."

"It's a beautiful trip. And the sun's coming out between the clouds. Weather's changing tomorrow, but it should be okay today." He tipped his head toward the plane, his pride and joy. "Ever been up in one of these babies?"

She shook her head. "A small commuter is as close as I've come."

"Then you're in for a treat."

Derek loaded their bags and Nick helped Samantha climb aboard. "You want to ride in the copilot's chair?" Nick asked. "You could see out a lot better."

She quickly shook her head. "No, thanks, I'm fine back here." Settling herself in the seat, she snapped her belt in place as Nick climbed aboard. Instead of sitting in the copilot's chair as he usually did, he sat in the seat next to Samantha.

"You ready for this?"

She moistened her lips. "Sure."

He could tell she was nervous, but he figured she'd relax once they got into the air. He smiled. "You won't believe what you're going to see."

The smile she gave him looked a little wobbly. "I can't wait."

Nick frowned, beginning to regret his decision. She hadn't done this before and Samantha wasn't really the adventurous type.

"You don't have to worry," he said. "Derek's a really great pilot."

Another weak smile. "I'm sure we'll be fine."

A few minutes later, the final flight check had been made, Derek was flipping switches and the plane was beginning to taxi down the runway. Nick noticed Samantha gripping her seat, but she didn't say anything. By the time they got into the air, her face was pale.

"You okay?" he asked.

She nodded. "I'm okay. Taking off kind of scared me. Sorry, I'm new at this. I'll be fine as soon as I get used to it."

But half an hour later, as the plane dropped into a trough and climbed out again, she looked even paler than before. The plane vibrated, rocked, rolled, dipped, and swayed.

"Sorry, guys," Derek said. "It's rougher than I thought it would be. Nothing to worry about; just isn't as relaxing as I'd hoped."

Samantha closed her eyes.

"Are you getting sick?" Nick asked worriedly.

"A little, I guess."

Dammit, he knew he shouldn't have brought her. Samantha wasn't cut out for this kind of thing. Sitting on the floor doing yoga and . . . other things . . . was about as much excitement as she could handle.

"Keep your eyes open and fix your attention on the horizon. It'll help you keep your bearings."

She nodded, turned to stare out the window. Range after range of incredible mountain peaks spread out on either side of the plane, rising from deep green forests to barren granite slopes well above the tree line, then changing to sparkling white, year-round snow-covered peaks.

"That's Mount McKinley." Nick pointed toward the majestic white-topped mountain ringed with clouds rising into the sky on Samantha's side of the airplane. "It's twenty-thousand-feet high, the tallest point in North America."

Her attention sharpened. She smiled and

nodded. The plane had smoothed out a little and Samantha's nervousness seemed to ease. They were traveling mostly above Highway 3, the scenic route that stretched between Anchorage and Fairbanks. With mountain ranges in the distance along each side of the roadway, they could fly a little lower, avoid using oxygen.

He hadn't mentioned that possibility. Apparently Derek had taken pity on the first-time, bush-plane flyer and was taking the easier route.

Samantha turned toward him. "It's beautiful, Nick. I've seen pictures, but they can't begin to do it justice. I've never seen anything so spectacular."

Relief trickled through him. "So I guess you're feeling better."

"My stomach's settled down, but I'll be glad when we get there."

He might have smiled if the thought hadn't struck that he hoped his kid was a little more adventurous than Samantha.

His kid. The idea was just beginning to take root. He was going to be a father.

Whatever happened between him and Samantha, Nick was determined to be a good one.

The plane landed in Fairbanks — at last.

Once the wheels stopped rolling and the engine went still, Samantha finally relaxed. The men climbed out of the cabin and Derek went to work securing the plane while Nick reached up to help her out of the passenger compartment. Setting his hands at her waist, he swung her down to the tarmac as if she weighed less than nothing. Samantha had never been so grateful to have both feet planted firmly on the ground.

"So how did you like it?" Derek asked as he walked toward them.

How did she like it? She hoped he didn't notice the tremor that rippled through her. "It was . . . interesting. It really wasn't so bad once I got used to it."

Derek flashed a winning smile. "But you'd rather be on the ground, right?" With his dark hair and smiling eyes, he was extremely good-looking. She imagined women fell at his feet. As far as she was concerned, he didn't have anywhere near the sex appeal Nick had.

She flicked the pilot a sideways glance, saw Nick waiting to hear her reply, and told them the truth. "The mountains were amazing. One of the most spectacular sights I've ever seen and one I'll never forget. I'm really glad I got to see them. But you're right. I'm not much for flying."

Nick just smiled. "I've never been crazy about it, myself," he said. "Unlike my brother, I've always preferred jumping out of a plane to riding cooped up inside one."

He was talking about his days as a Ranger. The image of Nick stepping out into thin air made her stomach roll the way it had on the airplane.

"Unfortunately, flying's pretty much mandatory if you want to get around up here," he finished.

Nick was used to it, but Samantha never would be. Just one more obstacle between them.

From the plane, Nick led her over to the rental car agency to pick up the vehicle he had rented. The weather had shifted, a wall of clouds completely obscuring the sun. The already chilly temperature must have dropped twenty degrees.

Samantha shivered inside her jacket. In San Francisco, it was her warmest piece of clothing. Here it was like wearing a lightweight sweater.

Nick must have noticed. He dropped his canvas duffel on the asphalt and unzipped it. "I've got something for you." Pulling out a heavy dark green jacket with a fur-trimmed hood, he held it up for her inspection. "I got it yesterday while you were cooking supper. I think it's time you put it on."

The wind swept icily over her face, and she eyed the jacket with longing. "You didn't need to do that."

"Seriously? You're freezing. Put it on."

She didn't argue. She wasn't a fool. Sliding her arms into the sleeves, he settled it on her shoulders. It was plenty big, but it fit.

"I bought it loose enough to fit over a heavier sweater. You like it?"

She pulled up the hood, felt the tickle of the fur against her cheeks. For the first time all day, every part of her felt warm. Did she like it? She loved it.

"It's great." She snuggled deeper. "I'm kind of hard to fit. I can't believe you got the right size."

He grinned. "It's a kid's extra large. I figured it'd be just right." He zipped the jacket up for her, then grabbed his duffel and tipped his head toward the rows of cars in the rental car lot. "I've got one reserved."

Apparently he had a Wizard account. Samantha went inside with him while he picked up the keys, waited while he went to get the car. He drove up in a plain brown Chevy Malibu.

"Color won't stand out and it's got GPS,"

he said. "And front wheel drive — safer if the weather gets worse and the roads get bad."

She thought of the bumpy plane ride. *Oh, dear God.*

Nick tossed her wheeled bag in the trunk, zipped his duffel and tossed it in with hers, slammed the lid. Helping her into the passenger seat, he rounded the car and slid behind the wheel. She hadn't noticed the holstered pistol in his hand till he set it down on the console between them.

"You brought your gun?"

He picked up the weapon, slid it out of its holster, and showed it to her. "Glock 21 .45 caliber semi-auto. I got used to carrying this model when I was on the force."

"I thought you didn't expect any trouble."

"I don't, but it's always better to be prepared. These guys don't play games, Samantha."

"So it's loaded."

He grinned. "They aren't much good if they're empty."

She sat back in her seat as he shoved the gun back into its holster, set it on the center console, reached down and started the engine.

As he pulled out of the parking lot, Samantha sighed. "I feel so out of my depths up here. Alaska. Guns. Murder." She looked at him hard. "You."

Nick's gaze swung to hers. "I'm the same man you knew in Las Vegas."

"In some ways, yes. You're definitely the man who came to my rescue in the hall."

"I'm the man who took you to bed in Vegas. Same man here."

For the first time that day, her smile felt sincere. "Better. You're an even better lover than he was."

Nick laughed. "I think that's kind of a backward compliment."

She just smiled. Nick had been the perfect lover in Vegas. And he was a better-than-perfect lover here. She didn't say it because she figured he was confident enough in that area already.

"So where are we going?" she asked as the Chevy rolled along the road, her gaze going out the window to her surroundings. Unlike the mountainous terrain they'd been flying over, Fairbanks was relatively flat. The tallest buildings in the city were maybe ten or twelve stories, and they were few and far between. It seemed more an overgrown town than a city.

"That's the Chena River we just drove across. It wanders all over town. There's a place I like to stay right on the water.

Individual cabins, and you can park out front. I called ahead and made a reservation."

"That sounds good."

"We'll check in and then I'll drive by those motels on your list. There are only three in the area. The Snooze Inn. The Rest Haven. And The Waterfront. They're not in the best parts of town."

"Let's drive by now, check them out."

"No way. You brought your laptop, right? You can e-mail your family or something, keep yourself busy while I do some recon. That was the deal, remember?"

"Fine, but I'm hungry." She gave him a playful smile. "Maybe we could get some fish and chips. I hear Captain Henry's is really good."

Nick chuckled, seemed to be thinking it over. "I guess that couldn't hurt. Fish and chips it is."

Samantha leaned back in her seat. She might not be the adventurous type, but solving a mystery was something else entirely.

CHAPTER TWENTY-ONE

Nick stretched his long legs out in front of him as best he could in the cramped interior of the car. It was late and the wind was blowing. It had been full dark since seven thirty.

The fish joint he'd stopped at with Samantha had been nearly empty. The soggy fish and chips they'd ordered had really sucked. After they'd finished eating, he'd stopped at a FoodMart and picked up some snacks and drinks for Samantha to have with her while she was stuck in the cabin.

At least the motel was nice there among the trees, nothing fancy, but being by the river made it pleasant. As soon as he dropped her off, he went back to the fish joint, parked, and just sat watching for a while. The building was old and poorly maintained, the blue paint faded, grass growing up between the cracks in the parking lot.

Only a very few customers and nothing much else going on. After a couple of hours, he went to the second location. It was poorly situated on a dead-end street without much traffic. Nothing seemed to be going on there, either. One thing for sure, neither of them was overwhelmed with business.

The third Captain Henry's caught his attention. Same run-down building, same poor business locale off on a side street. But here there was plenty of activity, particularly at the drive-up window, money being handed over, bags of "food" going out.

By the look of the disreputable clientele, there wasn't anything to eat in those bags, but there was plenty in there to get high on.

Drug money in. Massage it through the international banking system. Clean money out.

Nick watched for nearly an hour. Business was definitely good. And highly illegal. But unless you were looking for it, the place seemed pretty much like any other fast-food joint.

From the fish place, he headed downtown. It was late afternoon when he drove by each of the three motels, checked out the neighborhoods, the streets around them, the layout of the buildings in case he needed to get away in a hurry. He didn't expect trouble, but he was always prepared.

Just before dark, he went back to check on Samantha, make sure she was okay. She was working on her laptop, doing marketing research for The Perfect Pup.

"I'm fine," she said with a smile. "Go find the bad guys."

He kissed her hard and left, tried not to dwell on how he would rather be spending the night in bed with her than sitting in the car somewhere, freezing his ass off in the cold.

As soon as it was dark, he headed for the address Cord had given him for Dmitri Fedorko. It was an expensive, custom-built home on an oversized lot in an exclusive area west of town.

The lot was fairly open. It would be hard to get close enough to the house to see what was going on without being spotted, but through the expensive, high-powered Leupold binoculars he'd bought himself for his thirty-second birthday in July, he could see a soccer ball lying in the front yard next to an overturned bike. According to the info Cord had sent, Fedorko had two teenage sons.

He also had a mistress he kept in an apartment in Fairbanks.

Married, forty-five-years old, the guy had

a rap sheet a mile long but he'd been clean for the past ten years. Or at least he hadn't been caught.

Nick watched till the lights all went out in the house. He never saw Fedorko, but Cord had e-mailed his photo. Dark hair, black eyes, rough skin, broad nose, and thick lips. He was ugly as mud. Nothing about him would attract the sexy, twenty-four-year-old blonde named Suzy Fox whose picture Cord had also sent.

Nothing except money.

Starting the engine, he eased away from the house and headed back toward town to check out the motels.

The first was a dive, The Snooze Inn. It was laid out in an L shape with parking spaces in front of the rooms. Curtains sagged at the windows and the once-brown doors had oxidized to beige.

It didn't take long to figure out what was going on. A car pulling up, a guy getting out and heading into one of the rooms, staying fifteen, twenty minutes, walking back out. Other cars, other guys, other rooms.

Prostitution was big business. Up here, nothing much happened in those rooms for less than three-hundred bucks, and a good working girl could churn through twenty guys a day.

Six grand. A helluva lot more if the lady was anything special.

He headed for the second motel. At The Waterfront, he spent an hour waiting for something to happen. Nothing did. It was after two when he left and headed for The Rest Haven.

The place was surprisingly neat and clean, a cut above the other two, recently painted, with shrubs planted in pots outside the doors. Same layout, but the glass in the windows was clean and the curtains weren't drooping.

Unlike the mostly empty rooms at The Waterfront, The Rest Haven was earning its keep. Better-dressed clientele, guys in jeans or slacks, and jackets from someplace other than the Salvation Army. The working girls here were undoubtedly a cut above, too, and each john was paying dearly for it.

Nick pushed the seat back and stretched his legs out in front of him, settled back to watch for a while, see if he could pick up something that might be useful. A couple of times, his eyes drifted shut and he damned near fell asleep. He wished he'd stopped for a cup of coffee.

He cracked a window so the cold would keep him awake and leaned back to watch. Maybe five more minutes had passed when one of the doors swung open and he caught a glimpse of the woman who worked inside. He trained his binoculars on the door, where she stood talking to the man who had gone in twenty minutes earlier.

Jesus. Not a woman. A girl. Couldn't be more than twelve or thirteen. Alaska Native, dark-skinned and pretty, though her features were gaunt and her expression strained. She was wearing nothing but a pair of white panties, a slender young girl, with little more than nubbins for breasts.

Nick felt sick to his stomach.

The man headed for his car and the girl shut the door. Nick watched the sleazy bastard slide behind the wheel of an expensive, newer model Cadillac coupe. Nick jotted down the license plate number.

There was real money in prostituting kids, sick as it was. No wonder the bucks were flowing into Dragovich's bank accounts.

Deciding it was time to leave before someone spotted him, Nick started the engine and headed back to the rented cabin. Back to Samantha. And the clean, unsullied world she represented.

It scared him to realize how eager he was to get there.

Samantha couldn't sleep. She had dozed off

and on, but she was worried about Nick. It was three thirty in the morning and he still wasn't back. What if something had happened?

Finally giving up, she slipped out of bed and pulled on her robe, padded over to the desk against the wall, where she had set up her laptop.

Ever since they'd arrived in Fairbanks, she'd been thinking about those motels. If something criminal was going on, the obvious thing would involve prostitution. She was sure that's what Nick was thinking and just didn't want her to know.

After he'd left, she'd started digging, reading every article she could find on the illegal trade, how extensive it was in Alaska and just about everywhere else. One particular article had caught her eye.

It was published in the online version of the *Alaska Daily News.* Sex Trade Moves From Street To Web.

The article explained that prostitutes or pimps put ads on sites like craigslist. Using the Erotic Services section, posting faceless women's photos, they offered to *stimulate mind and body,* with the disclaimer that *any money exchanged is for companionship only. Anything else that happens is a matter of choice between consenting adults.*

Samantha re-read the article now and bookmarked it to show Nick in the morning. She yawned. The king-size bed looked inviting. She only wished Nick was back to share it with her.

Turning off her laptop for the second time that night, she went to the bathroom, came out and headed for bed. The sound of a key in the lock sent a rush of relief running through her. She hurried over and pulled open the door, saw Nick standing on the other side and threw her arms around his neck.

"Thank God you're okay. I was really getting worried."

"I'm all right." He bent his head and kissed her cheek, unwound her arms from around his neck. She couldn't miss the worry on his face, or the feel of his pistol in the holster clipped to his belt.

"What happened?"

"I need to get back to Anchorage, but it's a long drive and I've got to get some sleep." He looked down and seemed to see her for the first time. "They're running drugs and women," he said darkly. "Only the women aren't women, they're underage girls."

Samantha's insides twisted. "Oh, my God." She tried not to think of her sister, that before Danielle had been murdered, she had been brutally raped. She rarely allowed herself to remember. "We have to stop them. We have to do something."

"That's why I need to get back. We'll sleep for a couple of hours, then get on the road."

She didn't tell him there was no way she could possibly sleep. Not when she knew what was going on in those motel rooms. "Why don't you sleep in the car? I'll drive for a few hours, then we can change places."

His shook his head. "It's not an easy drive and the weather's getting worse."

"I can handle it. It'll only be for a couple of hours; then you can take over."

"It's sleeting. I've got a hunch it's going to snow."

"I'll wake you if it starts snowing."

He hesitated, finally nodded. "All right. At least there won't be any traffic. Get dressed and pack your stuff. As soon as you're ready, I'll load the car."

She did so quickly, pulling on her jeans and a warm sweatshirt, tossing the robe and the rest of her clothes into the carry-on, putting her laptop in there with them. She could feel Nick's urgency. He needed to do something, take some kind of action. But he was bound by his promise to protect Jimmy and Mary.

He was a cop. He wanted to help those girls.

What he didn't know was that she felt exactly the same.

Five minutes later, they were packed and ready to leave. Nick grabbed his duffel and opened the door.

Out of nowhere, a barrage of gunshots rang out, hitting the door, sending wood-chips flying, tearing into the metal frame. Samantha screamed and Nick slammed the door.

"Get down!" His gun was already in his hand. He moved to the window, used the barrel to break the glass and cracked off two answering shots. "Get behind the bed and stay there no matter what happens."

More shots rang out, pounding into the walls of the cabin, knocking more glass out of the window.

"Call nine-one-one." He caught hold of the dresser and pushed it in front of the door. "And stay down until I come back for you."

"You can't leave! They'll shoot you!"

Nick's hard gaze fixed on her face. He looked like a man she had never seen before. "They'll shoot both of us if I don't get to them first." He headed for the window in the bathroom. Frantically, she dragged her phone out of her pocket and dialed 9-1-1, watching in terror as Nick slid the frosted window open, knocked the screen off, levered himself up, and slipped silently through the opening. Then he was gone.

Samantha pressed herself flat on the floor and started praying. When the operator didn't come on the line, she looked down at the phone and realized the battery was dead. Oh, dear God!

There was a phone on the nightstand on the other side of the bed. She was crawling across the mattress when shots rang out and more glass flew into the room. Fighting back a scream, she took cover on the floor on the other side of the bed and heard more gunfire, shots blasting from what sounded like different locations.

Just as she reached for the phone, a man started shoving at the door. She caught a glimpse of him as the dresser began to move, a huge man using his massive shoulder as a battering ram. He'd be inside any minute.

With a cry locked in her throat, Samantha dragged the desk chair over, grabbed the lamp off the table, and climbed up on top of the dresser. As the man stuck his head through the door, she swung the lamp, hitting his shiny bald pate dead-on. The pottery base shattered, shards went flying, and for an instant, he froze.

Then he shook his head like a big wet dog, and a violent curse erupted in a language she didn't understand, followed by, "You bitch!" Which she understood completely.

Fear shot through her. Jumping down, she threw all her weight against the dresser, trying to keep him out, but it was no use.

Samantha screamed as the door burst open, knocking her across the room. She saw the fury in those cold black eyes and the ruthless twist of his lips as he raised his pistol and aimed straight at her.

Two quick gunshots rang out. For an instant, the world seemed to stop. She was sure she must have been hit, but she felt no pain. Then the man's barrel chest blossomed red with blood and he fell forward, landing facedown on the carpet. Two perfect round holes bored into his back where the bullets had entered and passed right through. Blood formed a spreading pool beneath him.

Samantha fought a wave of dizziness and gripped the dresser to steady herself. Her heart was thundering, her chest clamped down so hard she couldn't force a breath of air into her lungs.

Then Nick was shoving through the door,

dragging her hard against him, holding her tight and driving away her fear. "Are you all right?"

She managed to nod.

"We need to go." He cast a quick glance down at the man on the floor, caught sight of the lamp she had cracked over his skull, looked up at her in amazement. "Jeez. Nice work."

Her chest was too tight to reply. Nick grabbed the black duffel and tossed it up on his shoulder. "Put your coat on, get your carry-on, and let's go."

"Is he . . . is he dead?"

His hard gaze fixed on the man on the floor. "He's dead, you aren't. Let's go."

"What about the police? I . . . I didn't have time to call them."

"Better that way." Gun in hand, he moved toward the door, stopped to check and see if it was clear outside, then started forward again. "Come on."

She zipped up her heavy parka with shaking hands, grabbed the handle of the carry-on and fell in behind him, moving on wobbly legs. She was glad for the jacket; it was freezing cold outside.

"Should I . . . should I drive?"

He looked at her as if she'd lost her mind and just shook his head. "Get in and buckle up." There wasn't a glimpse of the man she had been sleeping with, no teasing smiles or occasional grins. This was Nick Brodie, former Ranger, ex-cop, in full battle mode.

It took two tries to strap herself into the seat. Nick started the engine and jammed the car into reverse. They were just pulling out of the parking lot when headlights came on behind them.

"Fuck. Hold on." As his heavy leather boot slammed down on the accelerator, she jerked back against the seat. Shots rang out. Nick jerked his pistol, angled it out the window, and fired two shots back, then the car was fishtailing around the corner, accelerating wildly again.

Dear God, was this really happening?

She turned to look behind them, saw a black SUV closing the distance between the two vehicles. She shrieked as a shot crashed through the back window and glass flew everywhere.

"Keep your head down!"

She clamped a hand over her mouth to hold back a scream as the car slid around another corner and shot forward again. As they roared down the straightaway, Nick leaned out the window.

He fired off two shots, fired two more. "Hold onto the wheel!" Determined to help,

Samantha fought back her fear and grabbed the steering wheel. Gritting her teeth, she steeled herself, kept the car steady and centered in the middle of the lane as it roared down the highway. Nick kept his foot on the accelerator, leaned out, took careful aim, and pulled off two more rounds.

There was a loud pop. She glanced in the rearview mirror in time to see the front tire on the other car explode and the car start skidding, careening wildly from one side of the road to the other.

There was an embankment on the right. The SUV hit the embankment and shot into space, began to flip in midair, then came down hard on the roof and slid completely off into the mud at the side of the road.

The last thing she saw before they careened around a corner at what felt like a thousand miles an hour were the wheels of the SUV spinning uselessly, the headlights growing smaller and smaller as Nick drove farther and farther away.

CHAPTER TWENTY-TWO

Nick looked over at Samantha. Her face was pale and she was trembling. But there was a stubborn set to her features he had never seen before.

The heater was cranked full force but with the window broken, it was freezing inside the car. The road had iced up and there was nothing but darkness for miles. At least the tank was full.

"A man is dead," she finally said. "Don't we have to talk to the police?"

He tried to block the image of the big Russian pointing the barrel of his semi-auto at Samantha, an instant away from pulling the trigger. At the time, he'd just reacted, done what he was trained to. Now he looked at her and fear washed through him. What if he'd been an instant too late?

"I'll talk to them as soon as we get to Anchorage. I don't want to chance another run-in with those bastards."

"Who were they?"

"My guess? Part of the Russian mob."

"How did they know where to find us?"

He shook his head. "I don't know. I didn't spot a tail. Maybe they picked me up on a security camera somewhere and started watching my movements."

He glanced in her direction. She was trying to warm her hands by pressing them between her thighs but she was still shaking. He wanted to stop the car and make damn sure she was okay. He wanted to tell her how sorry he was for bringing this down on her, but stopping was out of the question. He couldn't take the risk.

He raked a hand through his wet black hair. The sleet was getting thicker, turning into snow. "Dammit, I knew better than to bring you along. It was a stupid, unforgivable thing to do. I'm really sorry, Samantha. Are you sure you're okay? What about the baby? You don't think anything could have happened?"

"I was scared, but I didn't do anything strenuous. I just climbed up on the dresser."

As worried as he was, he couldn't stop his lips from curving. "Yeah, just climbed up on the dresser and knocked some Russian gangster loop-legged. You were really great in there."

She didn't reply, which told him exactly how shook up she was. He felt a fresh pang of guilt. He still couldn't believe it. When the going got tough, Samantha had done what she had to, gone toe-to-toe with a three-hundred-pound Russian gorilla. She might be a white-knuckle flyer, but she had one helluva lot of guts when the chips were down.

He dug out his cell phone, saw there was service, tossed the phone to Samantha. "Find Cord's number in my contacts and get him on the line."

She worked his iPhone, listened till Cord picked up. "Sorry to bother you so late, but Nick needs to speak to you."

She handed him the phone. He had hands free in the Explorer, not here, but this was important.

"This better be good," Cord grumbled, his voice thick with sleep.

"Get Mary and Jimmy out of the house. Get them somewhere safe."

"I take it something went wrong," Cord said, instantly alert.

"Something went wrong. I'm not exactly sure what. One of their goons is dead, two more shot up pretty bad."

"How long have I got?" He could hear

Cord moving around, throwing stuff into a bag.

"Time to get out to the lake and pick them up, but I wouldn't wait. I'm not sure how long it'll take them to track me. I didn't leave much of a trail, but still . . ."

"Don't worry, I'm headed for my truck as we speak. You really think these guys will come after them?"

"I'm not sure. I got a hunch they think the kid knows more than he actually does."

"I'll take them up to my place. No one will find them there. Where are you?"

"On my way back."

"You need to talk to Taggart. You can't wait any longer."

"I know. I'm going there first."

"It's snowing here. There, too?"

"Yeah."

"Be careful."

He grunted. "Too late for that." Nick hung up the phone.

Samantha felt tired to the bone. The heater was on full blast but with the back window gone, it was still icy cold in the car.

"I'll stop as soon as it's safe," Nick said. "Unfortunately, there isn't much out here for the next hundred miles."

A shiver ran the length of her body.

"I wish there was something I could do to make this better," he said.

Her gaze swung to his. "You did something, Nick. You saved my life."

For an instant, his glance strayed from the road to her. "If I hadn't brought you in the first place —"

"I wanted to come. We have to stop these people. We can't quit until we do."

"As soon as we get home, I'm putting you on the first plane back to San Francisco."

Samantha shook her head. "I'm not going back. Not yet."

"What are you talking about? You almost got killed tonight."

"That wasn't your fault. I'm in this, same as you. I'm not leaving."

For the second time that night, he looked amazed. "I'm a professional. You work in a pet salon."

"I can do things on a computer you can't. I can help. Now we know what we're up against, I want to help those girls."

"Why?"

"Because my sister was one of them. She was twelve years old when she was taken. Before she was killed, she was brutally raped, just like the girls in those motel rooms. There was nothing I could do then to make up for what happened. Now there is."

"Samantha. . . ."

"I want this chance, Nick. I need to do this."

"What about the baby?"

Unconsciously her hand came to rest on her stomach. "From now on, I won't be doing anything dangerous. Just working on the computer, helping you figure things out."

Nick just kept driving. She could almost see his mind spinning, mulling things over, trying to make the right decision. She knew exactly how hard that could be.

The silence stretched between them for so long, her eyelids began to droop.

"You know, I'm kind of getting used to the idea of being a father," Nick said, jolting her out of her exhausted stupor.

The words were unexpected yet she had been thinking along those same lines, beginning to imagine herself with a child. "I'm starting to feel like he's real. Like he belongs to me."

"He?"

"I don't know why, but I think it's going to be a boy. It doesn't matter, though."

His mouth edged up in the faintest of smiles. "A girl who looks like you would be okay."

She shouldn't have felt so pleased but she did.

"The thing is, I can't imagine having a kid who doesn't have my last name," Nick said. "Boy or girl, it'll be a Brodie. I think we should get married."

Samantha's whole body went stiff. "What are you talking about? A man is dead. We're running from the Russian mob and you're proposing?"

"I wasn't actually proposing. It was just, you know, an idea."

"Well, it's a very bad idea. It's too soon to even be thinking about something like that."

She couldn't see his eyes in the darkness, but she could feel them zeroing in on her. "You really hate the idea that much?"

"I told you — it's too soon to talk about it." But the bitter truth was, no matter how much she cared for Nick, she wasn't cut out for a man like him. She would hate living in Alaska and he would hate living in San Francisco. It was a no-win situation either way. She ignored a little pang in her heart.

"I guess you're right," he finally said.

"Of course I'm right." But even as she said the words, she felt another pang. "It isn't time to make those kinds of decisions, and besides, right now we need to concentrate

303

on Mary and Jimmy and putting those terrible men behind bars."

His big hands tightened around the wheel. "True enough."

The car rolled along in silence. In the headlights, the road was white with a light coating of snow. Two parallel wheel tracks showed the way, cut through by the last car to travel the highway.

She flicked a glance at Nick, saw that he was watching her from the corner of his eye.

"You saw a man die tonight," he said. "That's not an easy thing to handle."

She hadn't really had time to process it yet, didn't really want to think about it. "As you said, he was going to kill me. Now he's dead. It was his decision."

"Yeah."

She could tell he was wondering if she really meant it. She tried to feel some sort of pity for the man who'd been shot, but none surfaced. There were bad people and good people in the world. One of the bad ones was dead.

She shivered, pulled the hood of her coat a little closer around her face, felt the warmth of the fur against her cheeks, and silently thanked Nick for his thoughtfulness. Leaning back in her seat, she tried to concentrate on something pleasant, a beach in Hawaii, shopping at Saks.

As cold as she was, she began to nod off. She must have fallen asleep because when the car began to slow and turn off the road, she jolted awake.

"Where are we?" she asked, stifling a yawn.

"Gas station. I need some coffee."

"Oh, God, you haven't slept all night. Let me drive for a while." But when she looked out the window, she saw nothing but a wall of white.

"I'm okay. Once I'm in the zone, I can stay awake for hours."

"Something you learned in the Rangers?"

"Yeah."

He pulled up to a gas pump and got out of the car. "Go inside and get warm. I'll be there in a minute."

She didn't hesitate, just unbuckled her seat belt and opened the car door. It was six a.m., but the sun wouldn't be up for a couple more hours. Nights were long this time of year in Alaska, and they would only get longer.

She headed for the door to the Bear Tooth Mercantile. The log building looked as if it had been there forever. The orange neon OPEN sign was lit, but they were the only customers. Samantha shoved through the door, ringing the bell.

"You look frozen, little lady." A burly, white-haired man with a long scraggly beard walked out from behind the counter. The place was rustic, with rows of canned goods and packaged bakery items, a small refrigerator section filled with cartons of eggs and milk.

"My name's Joe," he said, but it should have been Santa Claus. "Come over by the stove and sit down. I'll bring you a cup of coffee."

She felt a rush of gratitude. She must look even worse than she thought. "That sounds like heaven." She followed him over to an old-fashioned pot-bellied stove and sat down in one of the wooden captain's chairs clustered around it.

"Cream and sugar?" he asked as he poured from the pot on the counter.

She usually drank it black but she could use a sugar boost, and the cream might help soothe her nervous stomach. "That would be great."

The white-haired man returned, ambling over with a paper cup he pressed into her hand.

"Thank you." Samantha warmed her fingers around the cup, took a tentative sip and felt like moaning in pleasure.

The bell rang above the door as Nick walked into the station. His jaw was still hard, but she didn't miss the concern in his eyes as they swept over her.

He returned his attention to Joe. "I've got a problem. I'm hoping you can help."

"Sure, son, what is it?"

Nick explained about the rear window, saying a rock had flown up from the road and knocked it out. Then the two of them walked through a door at the back of the store and disappeared.

Samantha made a trip to the ladies' room, then returned and sat quietly in front of the fire, letting the warmth from the stove seep into her, finished the last of her coffee. She was half asleep when Nick returned and gently took the cup out of her hand.

He stared at her for several long moments. "There's something I really need to do." Reaching out, he drew her to her feet and into his arms, wrapped himself around her and just held on. "Are you sure you're okay?"

Samantha relaxed into his warmth and strength. For the first time that night, she felt safe. "Better now," she said.

He kissed the top of her head. "We gotta go. I'm sorry."

"I want to get back, too, and I'm okay.

Really." She flashed him a slightly too bright smile. "What do we do about the snow?"

"Snowplow just went through, and Joe helped me fix that rear window. At least you won't be cold."

Relief flooded through her. She turned to the white-haired man. "You're a saint, Joe. Don't let anyone convince you otherwise."

Joe just smiled. "Roads are still gonna be icy. Drive careful, now."

"Thanks," Nick said.

The interior of the car was finally warm, and as the drive stretched on she drifted off to sleep.

The next time Samantha woke up, the car was pulling up in front of the Anchorage Police Department.

CHAPTER TWENTY-THREE

The snow had stopped and the sun was out. The temperature had risen enough to thaw the ground, turning the sidewalks slick and the roadsides muddy. Nick settled a hand at Samantha's waist as he led her up the front steps, through the familiar doors of the Anchorage PD, a two-story building on Elmore Road.

"Hey, Nick!" one of the detectives called out as he headed down the hall. "Finally decided to get your ass back to work, eh?"

"Hey, Wally. Not exactly." He walked up to the front desk and spoke to the female officer behind the counter, tall, dark-haired, and fit, with biceps that could compete in an arm-wrestling contest. "Trish, I need to see Captain Taggart ASAP. Tell him it's important."

"Sure, Nick. I'll let him know." She glanced down at Samantha, but spoke to him. "And you're here with . . . ?"

"Samantha Hollis, my fiancée."

Samantha opened her mouth, but Nick shook his head, warning her now was not the time. He was only a little surprised she didn't argue. Trish went to work on the intercom, relaying the news to his former boss. When she turned back, faint color marked her cheeks.

"Captain Taggart says it's about time he heard from you, and you're to . . . umm . . . get your ass back there right now."

Fuck. Apparently he'd already heard from law enforcement in Fairbanks. "Thanks, Trish."

"I gather your boss isn't happy," Samantha said as he urged her forward.

"Taggart's always mad about something." They walked down the hall. Nick opened the door to the captain's office and led her inside. It was spotlessly clean, every piece of paper filed away, the books perfectly lined up in the bookcase. The walls were lined with gold-framed commendations, Taggart's BA from the University of Washington, his masters in Police Science from UAA, anything and everything that said how great he was.

The captain rose from behind his desk, six feet tall, sandy hair touched with gray, athletic build. He prided himself on eating

310

healthy and staying in shape. He was a complete dick and one of the main reasons Nick had quit the force.

"Nice of you to drop by," Taggart said sarcastically. "I guess you figured I might have a couple of questions for you — like why you drove all the way to Fairbanks to stick your nose into a federal undercover operation. Your John Wayne routine damn near blew two years of hard work. What the hell did you think you were doing?"

Nick clamped down on his temper. Taggart always treated people as if he was the smartest guy in the room, which he never was. Nick took a moment to assess the news he was now involved with the feds.

"I was looking into a murder, trying to get enough evidence to convince you to open an investigation. While I was at it, I managed to stumble onto a human trafficking operation. But I guess you know about that."

He felt Samantha stiffen beside him. Probably couldn't believe the police would know what was happening to those girls and not do anything to stop it.

"I don't know what you're talking about," Taggart said. "There's a federal task force investigating Dmitri Fedorko for drug smuggling. Showing up at those fast-food places the way you did put Fedorko's people on alert. You could have gotten a federal undercover officer killed."

"Drug-running isn't the half of it. It looks like Fedorko and Connie Bela Varga may be working for Luka Dragovich. They're prostituting underage girls. Kids twelve, thirteen years old. I have a feeling they're hauling them in off the streets and forcing them into the life."

"I think they may be using the Internet," Samantha said, "advertising on erotic services websites. I saw a couple of ads for girls in the Fairbanks area when I was working online."

"Who the hell is *she*?" Taggart asked.

"I'm Samantha Hollis."

"She's my fiancée." Nick set a hand at her waist, making it clear she was under his protection.

"That's right," Samantha agreed, surprising him yet again. "I work with computers. I've been helping Nick gather evidence."

"For the murder I mentioned," Nick said. "Guy named Alex Evans. Looks like he was cooking the books for Dragovich."

"Alex Evans? The CPA who was a partner at Jankowski, Sorenson?"

"That's right. There's a chance they're all involved."

Taggart straightened to his full height, which still left him two inches shorter than Nick, something he undoubtedly hated. "You're talking about a highly respected accounting firm in Anchorage. One that is extremely supportive of law enforcement. Whatever you think you're investigating is over. You understand?"

Nick forced his jaw to unlock. "What about the girls?"

"The feds will handle this however they see fit. You stay out of it."

"So that's it?" Samantha asked. "That's all you're going to do?"

"That's right. And that's all you're going to do." He drilled Nick with a glare. "You hear me, Brodie?"

"What about the dead guy in the motel room? And the two I shot full of holes? What do you plan to do about them?"

"There is no dead guy. According to the feds, Fedorko's men picked up the body. No reports of gunshot wounds from any of the hospitals. You got lucky this time, Brodie." He smirked. "Though I imagine you're going to get one helluva repair bill from that motel you shot to pieces."

Nick's jaw tightened.

Samantha squared her small shoulders. "It's your job to protect people. Those girls

313

are just kids. You have to help them!"

"Get her out of here," Taggart warned. "Before I put you both in jail."

Samantha started to say something more, but Nick wrapped an arm around her waist and started hauling her toward the door. "Time to go home, sweetheart."

She sputtered something he was glad he couldn't hear as he pulled her into the hall and firmly closed the door.

"I can't believe that man. He's a complete —"

"Yeah, I know." Nick grabbed her hand and started tugging her down the hall. He didn't stop until they were outside the building and headed back to the car.

"Well, that went well," Samantha said as he loaded her into the rented Chevy.

"I wish I was surprised."

She looked up at him with those big doe eyes. As tired as he was, he felt a little kick. "Now I know why you quit."

Nick smiled, leaned down and kissed her.

Once they were back on the road, he drove a couple of blocks, then pulled out his cell phone and hit Cord's number.

"We just left Taggart's office. Everything go as planned on your end?"

"I've got Mary and Jimmy with me at the cabin. Mary's not happy about it. I haven't told her much. Hell, I don't know much."

"You got room for two more?"

"You bet. I figured you'd be heading in this direction. I stocked up on supplies in Wasilla along the way. How'd it go with Taggart?"

Nick scrubbed a hand over his face. "Looks like I wound up in the middle of a federal undercover op. From what I could tell, the agent's cover didn't get blown, so we're okay there. But Taggart's got his balls in an uproar. We aren't going to get squat help from him."

"So the feds are going after Fedorko?"

"That's what Taggart says. Unfortunately, they're focused on his drug operation. He's also running underage girls and it looks like both Fedorko and Bela Varga may be working for Dragovich."

Cord whistled.

"I'll fill you in when I get there."

"Turn off your phone. You don't want them tracking you. I picked up some throwaways we can use from now on."

"I'm on it. See you soon." Nick hung up and tossed his phone to Samantha. "Turn it off and do the same with yours. We don't want them using GPS to track us."

Ignoring the sudden pallor of her face, Nick focused his attention on driving while

Samantha turned off the phones.

Dropping the cell phones into her purse, Samantha leaned back in her seat. It had quit snowing hours ago, sometime between their stop at the Bear Tooth Mercantile and the police department in Anchorage. It was late morning now, the sun out, lighting a ring of distant white-capped peaks.

Samantha had come to appreciate the spectacular scenery in Alaska. She hated the cold and the isolation, but she understood Nick's attraction to the rugged high-mountain landscape. This was a man's country. And Nick was all man.

"We're going to Cord's house, right?" she said as the car headed north, back the way they had come.

"He's got a place near Hatcher's Pass. It's a big house so there's plenty of room."

"I gather that's where he took Mary and Jimmy."

"Yeah."

"I think Cord is as overprotective as you are."

Nick smiled for the first time that day. "That's a good thing, right?"

Her lips twitched. "Sometimes."

Nick used his turn signal, pulled around a slower vehicle, then moved back into the right lane. The earlier snow was mostly melted, but there were still patches of white on the ground.

"Cord's place is way off the road," Nick said. "His parents built it, left it to him when they died. He mostly uses it on weekends. It's a safe place for us to hole up. I don't want to leave you alone, and I have work to do."

"Then we're still working the case."

He flicked her a sideways glance. "What, you thought I was just going to quit? Taggart's an idiot. All he cares about is the glory. I've got a friend named Charlie Ferrell. He's FBI. Charlie'll help us if he can."

"Do you think Cord has an Internet connection at the house?"

"He's on satellite. He may be out in the wilderness, but these days you're only as far away as your Internet connection."

That was good because she had work to do, too. She wanted to get back on the Net, see if she could find an ad on an erotic website that connected to any of the motels the Northland Corporation owned around the state.

"How long will we be staying? I've got my overnight bag but there isn't much in it. Sooner or later, I'm going to need some clothes."

"I'll get us both some, but I need to make

sure my house isn't being watched. First we need to get rid of the rental car."

They headed for the car agency in Wasilla where Nick had arranged to drop the Chevy. He went inside and took care of the paperwork, paid for the broken window and miscellaneous damages, which included no small number of bullet holes. She worried about the questions he might have to answer, but then he'd been a cop, so she figured he'd know what to say.

"Derek moved the Explorer so we could get home." Carrying his bag and towing hers, he led her across the parking lot.

"Derek seemed like a nice guy."

"He's a good friend. We've known each other since we were kids." He spotted his big black Explorer, loaded the bags into the back and helped her climb inside. Locating his keys under the driver's seat, he slid behind the wheel.

"Are you sure you don't want me to drive? You must be exhausted. You haven't slept in over thirty hours."

"I'll sleep when we get to Cord's." Firing up the powerful V-8 engine, he pulled out of the parking lot.

As the SUV rolled down the highway, a sign reading TRUNK ROAD appeared, and Nick turned north. A few miles down the road, he turned again, ending up on Fishhook-Willow Road. At a place called Turner's Corner, Nick pulled up next to one of the gas pumps.

"I want to top off the tank."

"Good idea. I need to make a pit stop anyway."

He rounded the car and opened the gas tank, caught her arm as she walked past him. "You're still okay, right? You aren't feeling sick or anything?"

"I feel fine. Tired, but fine. I'll be right back." She went in and used the bathroom, bought a cup of coffee for each of them and two packages of those little white powdered donuts she loved.

Nick stood waiting next to the passenger door of the SUV. She handed him the coffee and a package of donuts. "I figured you could use something to eat."

He helped her climb in, took a big gulp of the steaming hot liquid and made a sound of pleasure in his throat. "Cord stocked up on groceries before he headed up to the cabin, but this is great." He took another sip of coffee, leaned down and gave her a quick kiss. "Thanks." As tired as she was, heat spread low in her belly.

Nick took another drink of coffee, ripped open the cellophane package with his teeth and wolfed down two donuts before she had time to fasten her seat belt.

The other four were gone by the time he got back in the vehicle and started the engine.

"It's not far from here," he said, wiping his mouth with his hand. "Sit back and enjoy the ride."

Samantha leaned back against the seat and fixed her attention on the view outside the window. The road was narrow, more like a bumpy asphalt lane. It was lined with trees, but the branches were bare except for a dusting of snow. She could see mountains sloping upward in the distance. As Nick drove toward Cord's cabin, she rested her head against the back of the seat and let the magnificent vistas soothe her.

She was just beginning to relax when Nick slammed on the brakes, throwing her against the seat belt.

"Sorry," he said, and pointed ahead. "Moose. Up here they pretty much own the road."

As if the huge beast didn't have a care in the world, the animal sauntered from one side of the lane to the other and gradually disappeared into the snow-dusted foliage. He was incredible, with antlers that must have spanned nearly six feet. Alaska was freezing cold, harsh, and amazing. The kind of place a masculine man like Nick would love.

And more and more, she understood how awful it would be if he felt he had to leave.

The thought ruined the rest of the trip.

CHAPTER TWENTY-FOUR

Cord's house near Hatcher's Pass stood two stories high, nestled deep in the trees, and had a wooden deck both front and back. It was a brown, wood-frame residence, not particularly attractive, and in need of a coat of paint.

Cord's parents had lived there, but after they died, he only came up a few weekends a month. Since he didn't use it often, he hadn't done much in the way of decoration. Still, it was sturdy and the roof was sound, a perfect place to get away from work and the pressures of life in the city.

Mary and Cord came out on the front deck as Nick drove up. Jimmy, in a long-sleeve Aces' T-shirt, walked out behind them, Duke tagging along at his heels. Nick grabbed the bags out of the back and followed Samantha up on the porch.

"I'm glad you're finally here," Mary said as they all trooped back inside out of the cold. "I want to know what's going on. Cord just said we had to leave. He said we were in danger and asked me to trust him. He said once you got here, it would all be explained. You're here now, Nick, and I want to know what's going on."

"Why don't we sit down?" Cord gently suggested.

Mary grudgingly allowed him to lead her into the simply furnished living room with its beige-and-brown high-low carpet, brown plaid overstuffed sofa and chairs. A wood-burning stove sat in the corner. There was a half-bath off the kitchen and laundry. A stairway led up to four bedrooms and two baths, all modestly furnished. Nick had stayed there a couple of times when he and Cord had hiked up in the pass.

"I'll tell you everything I know," he said, "but first I need to talk to Jimmy."

"Jimmy?" Mary turned an incredulous look on her nephew. "Jimmy, are you involved in this?"

The kid cast a pleading look at Nick, silently begging for help.

"Come on. Let's you and me talk first. Then we'll explain to your aunt, okay?"

When Jimmy nodded, Nick rested a hand on the boy's beefy shoulder and led him into the kitchen away from the others. "I wanted to talk to you first because you aren't going to like hearing what I have to say. I wanted to give you a chance to deal with it before we talk to the others."

The kid's black eyebrows pulled into a worried frown. "What is it, Nick?"

"I know you loved your dad. I'm sure he was a very good father. But being a good dad doesn't necessarily mean he was perfect. Your father made mistakes. He went to jail for them when he was younger."

Jimmy's dark face blanched. "That's not true."

"I wish it weren't, Jim. His real name was Alexi Evanko. He was Ukrainian."

"My dad was a CPA," Jimmy said stubbornly. "He went to college in Illinois."

"He got his degrees while he was in prison. Your dad was involved with some pretty bad people, Jimmy. You met a couple of them when they threw you in that trunk."

The boy shook his head. "That isn't right. Dad caught those guys doing something illegal. That's the reason they killed him."

Nick hated to disillusion the kid but there was no way around it. "I'm not a hundred percent sure why they killed him, son, but right now, it looks like he was helping them launder money. That means taking it from illegal sources and making it look legal.

There's a chance he got into financial trouble and stole some of that money. That's the reason they killed him."

Jimmy's whole body vibrated with tension. He started shaking his head. "I don't believe you. You're wrong."

"When you started asking questions, they got worried. That's why they burned your dad's study. They were trying to destroy any evidence that might be inside. But we'd already found it the night before. That evidence proves Alex Evans was involved in criminal activities, Jim. Like I said, it doesn't mean he was a bad father. It doesn't mean he didn't love you. I believe he loved you very much."

"My dad wasn't like that," Jimmy argued. "Ask Aunt Mary. She'll tell you the truth." The boy pushed past him and raced out the back door.

Nick let him go. With a sigh, he walked back into the living room, found Mary, Cord, and Samantha standing just outside the kitchen door.

"You heard?"

Mary nodded.

"I figured she was going to hear it sooner or later," Cord explained.

"I wanted to give Jimmy a chance to deal with the truth about his dad. I knew he'd take it hard."

"Thank you," Mary said softly.

"He went off by himself, but he's a smart kid; he should be all right. I figure he needs a little time to work things out. And deep down, he may have had suspicions about his father all along."

"He never said anything to me," Mary said, "but it's possible."

"Let's go back and sit down," Cord said. "I'm sure Mary has questions. I've got more than a few myself."

While Cord refreshed the fire in the woodstove, Mary sat down in one of the overstuffed chairs, and Nick tugged Samantha down on the sofa beside him. For the next twenty minutes, he filled Mary and Cord in on the rest of what had happened in Fairbanks, his conversation with Taggart, and what they had discovered so far.

When he was finished, Mary's beautiful face looked taut. "I suppose you expect me to be shocked, but I'm not. I knew the kind of man Alex was. I knew he was involved in all sorts of illicit activities. I never said anything because of my sister and Jimmy. And on the surface at least, Alex seemed to have changed. I figured whatever he'd done in the past didn't matter as long as he treated his family with respect."

Samantha spoke softly. "Mary, you told me Cora married Alex because she had no choice. I asked you if she was pregnant, but you didn't answer. Why did she have to marry him?"

Mary flicked a pleading glance at Cord. "I'm sorry, but I've said all I'm going to. I made a promise to my sister and I won't break my word." Rising from the chair, she crossed the room and hurried up the stairs. The sound of a door closing ended the discussion.

"Let me talk to her," Cord said. "Maybe I can get her to open up." Rising from his chair, Cord followed her.

When Nick yawned, Samantha stood up from her place on the sofa, caught his hand and tugged him up beside her. "You need to get some sleep. Is there a bedroom you can use upstairs?"

He nodded. She was right. The lack of sleep was beginning to dull his senses and drag him down. It was important he stay alert.

"Come on." Grabbing the bags he had left beside the door, he headed for the stairs, stopped to wait for Samantha to catch up with him, then continued on up to the second floor.

One of the bedroom doors was closed. He

could hear muffled voices, knew Cord was in there with Mary. The bed in the room next door was rumpled and there were kids' clothes scattered around. He walked past the bedroom Cord used when he came to the house, into a room at the end of the hall next to one of the two upstairs bathrooms.

There were twin beds inside, a nightstand between them. He tossed both bags up on one of the mattresses. "This okay with you?"

"Yes, but" — Samantha glanced around the sparsely furnished bedroom — "we're both staying in here?"

"It's not a secret we've been sleeping together."

"But Jimmy —"

"The kid's no fool and space is limited."

Her cheeks colored faintly. "You're right, of course. This is fine."

Nick reached for her, drew her into his arms. "You can go back home anytime you want. You'd be a lot safer back in San Francisco."

Samantha shook her head. "I'm not going. Not yet. Not until we make sure those young girls are safe."

"Are you certain?"

"I'm positive."

He shouldn't let her stay. He blamed it on her stubbornness, not his selfish desire to have her with him.

Not the fact he wanted her and wasn't ready to let her go.

Sliding his hands into her soft brown curls, Nick tipped her head back, bent his head and very softly kissed her.

"I want you to stay. I know I should make you leave, but I don't want you to go."

She reached up and cupped his cheek, ran her hand over the bristles along his jaw. "I'm not going anywhere. Not yet."

Nick felt a wave of relief.

He ignored the little voice that told him he was being a fool and both of them might pay.

Cord walked up to the slender woman who stood rigidly staring out the window. Outside, heavy black clouds were once more rolling in, blocking the last of a weak fall sun.

"Looks like it's going to start snowing again," he said.

Mary turned toward him. With her elegant features, coffee-with-cream complexion, and almond eyes, she was one of the most beautiful women he had ever seen.

"I don't mind the snow," she said. "Most people do, but I don't. Maybe it's because of my heritage."

"You were raised in Mountain Village, right? You and your sister?" It was a Yupik town on the Yukon River.

"That's right."

He reached out and tucked a strand of glossy black hair behind her ear. "You can trust me, you know? We're only trying to help you."

"I know that."

"We're trying to keep you safe, Mary. If you know something about Evans that will help us end this thing, you need to tell us."

Silence fell. Mary shook her head. "I wish I could — truly I do. But I promised Cora." She looked into his face and her fathomless black eyes filled with tears. "I promised her, Cord. How can I break my word?"

He traced a finger gently over her cheek. "Do you really believe your sister would expect you to keep a vow you made all those years ago when it puts you and her son in danger?"

Mary closed her eyes and the wetness spilled onto her cheeks. Long seconds passed before she looked at him again. She let out a slow, resigned breath. "You're right. Cora would want me to keep Jimmy safe no matter what I had to do."

"Then tell me what happened to her."

When she finally nodded, he led her over

to the bed and they sat down on the edge of the mattress.

The words began to spill out, softly at first, then with growing strength. "I'm three years younger than Cora. Our mother took off when she was ten and I was seven. Our father raised us, but he was a drunk. When he drank, he got mean, and he always picked on Cora. I don't know why. Maybe because she had the courage to stand up to him."

She looked past him back toward the window. The clouds were thicker now, and turning a purplish gray, a signal that snow was on the way.

"Cora stayed at home until she turned fifteen," Mary continued. "Then one night after my father slapped her for cooking something he didn't like for supper, she ran away. She figured he wouldn't bother me, and she was right. He needed someone to take over the cooking and cleaning, and he learned from his mistake."

"She never came back?"

Mary shook her head. "She made it as far as Fairbanks before she ran out of money. She was digging food out of a garbage bin when two men grabbed her and forced her into the back of their car." Mary stared down at the hands she had fisted in her lap.

"I've never told anyone this, Cord. Not ever. Cora made me promise on our lives."

"You're breaking that promise to *save* lives, honey. Jimmy's and possibly your own."

She swallowed and nodded. Took a deep breath. "Cora was beautiful. Even ragged and dirty, there was no mistaking how special she was. The men took her to a motel and an older woman cleaned her up, fixed her hair, and put on makeup. Cora was a virgin. They decided to sell her at an auction to the highest bidder. But Alexander Evans saw her. She was incredibly beautiful and he was crazy to have her. He was sixteen years older but he was determined, and the men he worked for wanted to please him."

"Go on . . ." Alex gently prodded.

"Alex took her home with him. He forced her to have sex with him, then kept her in his apartment. Cora lived with him for nearly two years before she accidentally got pregnant."

"With Jimmy."

"That's right. She was sure he would throw her out, but instead of being angry, Alex was ecstatic. He asked her to marry him. Cora knew what would happen if she refused, so she said yes."

"I'm sorry, Mary. For what you and Cora both suffered."

She stared past him out the window at the purple sky beyond. "My sister agreed to marry him, but she had one condition. That Alex get me out of Mountain Village and pay for my education, which he did. He made sure I got through high school, then went on to community college. Alex was obsessed with Cora until the day she died. And he loved his son. Jimmy was the only good thing that bastard ever did."

Mary turned and took hold of his hands. "You can't tell Jimmy about this — promise me, Cord. You can't tell him what his father was really like."

Cord squeezed her hands. "He's going to find out some of it. There's no reason he needs to know it all."

A weary sigh whispered out. "Thank you." Her soft smile made his chest feel tight. "I thought I'd feel terrible if I told you, but all I feel is relief."

"Some secrets don't deserve to be kept — not when it protects a man like Evans. Evans got exactly what he deserved."

"You're a good man, Cord. I appreciate everything you've done for Jimmy and me."

She was smiling at him softly, but all he saw in her beautiful dark eyes was gratitude.

He'd told himself she just needed time to get to know him. Now he wasn't so sure.

"You appreciate what I've done," he said, repeating her words, "but you aren't interested in me as more than a friend."

Mary's beautiful face filled with regret. "I wish it could be more than that. And I appreciate your friendship more than you could ever know. But all those things that happened to Cora, the way my father treated us, the men I dated over the years . . . I'm just not ready, Cord. Maybe someday I will be, but not yet."

He just nodded. Almost from the start, he had known the way she felt. It didn't change the way he felt about her. It didn't mean he would let anything happen to her or to Jimmy.

For the second time in his life, he was deeply attracted to a woman who didn't return his feelings. Maybe he wasn't cut out for a serious relationship. He should have been more careful, shouldn't have let his emotions get involved.

It wouldn't happen again, Cord vowed. He was fine the way he was. Aside from sex, he didn't need a woman.

With any luck, he never would.

CHAPTER TWENTY-FIVE

Samantha was exhausted. They both needed to get some rest, especially Nick. Deciding to sleep in one of his clean white T-shirts while he stripped down to a pair of briefs, Samantha surveyed the narrow beds in the room.

"I hate twin beds," Nick grumbled, hauling her into his arms and kissing the side of her neck.

Warm shivers raced down her spine. It was crazy. Nick desperately needed sleep. They both did. How could she possibly be thinking of sex?

"I wonder how much trouble it would be to push the beds together?" she heard herself saying, and clamped her mouth shut in utter disbelief.

Nick grinned. In less than a minute, he had the beds rearranged and Samantha working to redo the covers. Nick pitched in to help, and as soon as they were finished, he flopped down on the now king-size bed and tugged her down on top of him.

"We probably should be sleeping," she said, kissing the corners of his mouth. She could feel his heavy erection pressing against her thigh, and a soft ache started in the place between her legs.

"Yeah," Nick said with a sleepy yawn. "Probably." Samantha pressed her mouth against his chest, trailed soft kisses over a flat copper nipple. She'd started working her way down his torso when she realized his hand had quit moving up and down her back.

Raising her head to look at him, she saw his eyes were closed, his features slack, his body relaxed in sleep.

A soft pang slipped through her as she watched him. Thirty-plus hours of fighting bad guys and driving through a blizzard was a very long time, even for a tough guy like Nick. She gently kissed his mouth one last time and nestled against him, her own eyelids drooping. She'd only had a few hours of sleep herself.

Giving in to the fatigue dragging her under, she draped her arm over his powerful chest, snuggled against him and closed her eyes.

She wasn't sure how long she slept. At

least three hours, she figured. She didn't know what had awakened her, but when her eyes cracked open, she was still spread over Nick's chest, her arms looped loosely around his neck. When something hard nudged her thigh, she realized he was as aroused as he had been when they had fallen asleep.

One of his big hands moved under her T-shirt, tracing the line of her spine, continuing down over her bottom. His warm touch made her skin feel hot and tight, made her nipples peak, and the ache return between her legs.

Two could play this game. Samantha took up where she'd left off before they'd fallen asleep, kissing the side of his neck, trailing tiny love bites over his amazing chest and shoulders. Moving lower.

Nick groaned.

When she shoved his briefs down, peeled them off, and started working over his powerful erection, he hissed in a breath. Moving restlessly beneath her, he let her have her fun for several long minutes. She loved the power she felt, the way his muscles tightened as the heat continued to build. But Nick was a man who liked to take control, and it wasn't long before she felt his hands around her waist.

"Okay, honey, you want to do the work. Here you go." Samantha gasped as he lifted her up to straddle his hips. She could feel his heavy erection, braced her palms on his chest while he guided himself inside. His jaw clenched as she sank down on his rigid length.

"Damn, you feel good," he growled at the feel of her wrapping around him. She adjusted herself to take him deeper, then slowly started to move.

It felt better than good. The fullness, the closeness, the two of them moving perfectly together. Sensation rushed through her, shivered across her skin. Until she'd met Nick, she had never known this kind of pleasure. Every little movement sent ripples of heat into her most sensitive places, then spread out over her skin. She started moving faster, taking him deeper, heard him hiss in a breath.

"Easy, baby, I can't take much more."

But Samantha didn't want to wait. She wanted all Nick could give her. While his hands cupped her breasts, she rode him, didn't stop moving until the first climax struck, a hot wave that pulsed through her body and speared out through her limbs. With a soft sob, she gave in to it, let the rush of pleasure burn through her.

She barely noticed when Nick rolled both of them over, came up above her, and took control. Driving hard, his heavy weight pinning her to the mattress, in seconds he had her moaning, clinging to his shoulders as he carried her to a second stunning climax then followed her to release.

For long seconds they floated down, both of them lost in this brief respite from their troubles. Then Nick lifted himself away, settled next to her on the mattress and drew her snuggly against his side.

"I'm glad you're staying," he said softly, before his eyes slid closed and he was once more sound asleep.

Samantha closed her eyes against a rush of emotion. Respect for the man he was, a man who had learned the skills to protect himself and others. Trust that he would keep her safe. Admiration for his sense of honor and justice.

For the first time she realized that the deep feelings she held for Nick added up to one simple thing. *Love.* She had fallen in love with Nick Brodie.

And dear God, leaving him was going to break her heart.

Two hours later, while Nick was still sleeping, Samantha quietly eased out of bed, grabbed her robe and headed down the hall to the bathroom. After a quick shower, she quietly returned to the room, got dressed, pulled her laptop out of the suitcase and made her way downstairs. Amazingly, she didn't wake up Nick.

Since her laptop was fully charged, she sat down on the sofa and set it up on the coffee table. Connecting to Cord's Wifi, she booted up and checked her e-mail, found a message from her mom and three from Abby.

How are you doing? her mother asked. Haven't heard from you in a while. Hope everything is okay. Her mother went on to tell her about the shopping trip she and her friend, Margaret, had recently made to Nordstrom's. The chatty note rattled on, mentioning all the little things her mom and dad had been doing around the house.

It all sounded so normal, Samantha had to fight back tears. Nothing for her had been normal since her trip to Las Vegas.

She made some inane reply, assured her mom she was perfectly fine, then went on to read and reply to Abby's worried e-mails.

Don't worry. All is well here, and Nick is great. He said he thought we should get married. He was just being gallant, but it was sweet. Alaska is definitely not for me.

340

And Nick is a man's man so he could never be happy in San Francisco. I wish it could be different, but some things are just not meant to be. Sam

P.S. . . . at least I know he'll be a good dad.

She made no mention of the mayhem and murder surrounding her. She wasn't ready to go home, and once Abby knew the truth, she would insist Samantha leave.

Clicking off her e-mail, she brought up Google. She wasn't quite sure how to begin her research on porn sites, but there was no time like the present to start.

"What are you working on?"

Samantha paused and looked up to see Mary standing beside the computer. As lovely as she was, Samantha had never felt insecure around Mary. She seemed to have a way of putting people at ease.

"I've got a couple of things I need to check out. Did Jimmy come back?"

Mary nodded. "While you were napping. He has school on Monday, so we have another day before he starts missing classes."

"Did he seem okay?"

"He asked me if I thought what Nick said

about his father was true. I told him it didn't matter what Alex had done. The important thing was to remember that his father and mother both loved him."

"And you love him, too," Samantha said gently.

Mary glanced away. "I've never told him. I'm afraid he'll think I'm trying to be a substitute for his parents. But I love him very much. I loved him the moment I saw him in my sister's arms."

A noise sounded behind them and they both turned to see Jimmy standing in the kitchen doorway.

"I love you, too, Aunt Mary."

Mary made a small sound in her throat, walked over and wrapped the boy in a hug. "We'll get through this, Jimmy. We've got each other. That's more than a lot of people have."

He nodded. A little embarrassed, he backed away and called for Duke, who scrambled to his side. Both of them headed upstairs.

Mary turned back to Samantha. "Why are you still here, Samantha? After all that's happened, you should go back to San Francisco. You'd be safe there. With people like these, anything could happen."

"Maybe I should leave, but I'm not going

to. It's a long story, Mary. And complicated."

"We're stuck here. Nick's still asleep and
Cord's outside cutting wood. I've got time
to listen."

"All right." They went into the kitchen,
where Mary poured each of them a cup of
coffee, then they carried their cups back
into the living room and sat down.

"I'm staying because of my sister," Samantha said. "She died when she was twelve
years old." Samantha went on to tell Mary
about Danielle and how she'd been abducted, raped, and murdered. How they
had never found the man who killed her.
"This is my chance to do something for girls
like Danielle and that's what I'm going to
do."

"You lost a sister and so did I. I guess we
have more in common than I thought."
Mary went on to tell Samantha about Cora,
the story she had told Cord earlier. She said
she felt free of the vow she had made, now
that Alex Evans was dead.

"You mustn't tell Jimmy," Mary cau-
tioned. "He may find out someday, but he
isn't ready to hear it now."

"I won't say anything to anyone. I imagine
Cord will tell Nick, though. It might be
important to their investigation."

"I trust Nick."

Samantha smiled. "I do, too."

"Are you in love with him?"

A hard knot settled in her chest. "I can't be. We're just too different to ever make it work."

"I think he cares for you very much."

"Nick's extremely protective. I think it's just part of his nature. I hope it doesn't go any deeper than that. Neither of us can afford to get more involved than we are already." Ignoring the tightness that settled in her chest, she took a sip of her coffee. "What about you and Cord?"

Mary sighed. "I guess it's kind of a similar situation. Cord's a wonderful guy, but I'm not ready for a relationship. Not with him or anyone else."

"Life can be hard sometimes."

"I learned that a long time ago." They talked a little longer, then Mary changed the subject, bringing an end to the intimate conversation. "Cord bought some pork chops on our way up here. They're in the fridge. Maybe you'd be willing to fry them for supper."

"I'd love to. As soon as I'm finished with my research, I'll look around, see what I can find to go with them."

"Great." Mary rose from her chair. "I'd

better let you get back to work."

Samantha nodded. "I'd like to finish before Nick wakes up." Since he probably wouldn't think digging into erotic websites was a very good idea.

Setting her coffee cup down on the table, Samantha rested her hands on the keyboard and started typing. She wanted to see if she could find any erotic websites that linked to the group of motels owned by the North-land Corporation.

She almost smiled. Good thing she was using her own computer to dig up information, not Cord's. It might not look good for a police detective to be snooping around on Internet porn sites.

Bringing up Google, she typed in *craigslist,* went to the personals, and clicked on Anchorage, Alaska. She read the warnings and agreed to the hold harmless clause. But something must have changed because she couldn't find an Erotic Services section. There were plenty of personals, people looking for every sort of relationship, and some had extremely graphic photos, but mostly it looked like a lot of sad, lonely people seeking companionship.

She tried another avenue, typed in Erotic Services Anchorage, and a list of sites popped up on the screen: *Socialsex.com,*

Localadultpages.com, a website called *Naughty Reviews.* She clicked on the last one and her eyes nearly popped out as photos of a dozen naked women filled the screen. Some of them were even streaming live video.

Good Lord, it was like a giant shopping mall for sex! No wonder the police had trouble controlling it.

Resigned to viewing a lot of pictures she didn't want to see and would have trouble getting out of her head, she read the date of the posting, found the current ones, and started clicking on each photo, bringing up the woman's personal webpage. At the bottom of the page was a Contact Info section, giving a street address, city, and phone number.

Opening a software program on her computer, one that held the list of motels Northland owned and their addresses, she cross-checked the addresses of the women on the page.

Nothing matched the first group. Nothing matched on the additional pages on the site. She worked her way through the women's photos on the other two main websites, found nothing there. She was beginning to get discouraged when she pulled up Naked Naughties.com. Slogging through the photos, she was just about to give up — then bingo!

Finally, there it was! A near-naked photo of a woman using the name Ruby: black hair, smooth brown skin, attractive, somewhere in her twenties. She was offering her services as a masseuse, and the contact address matched an address for the Sunset Motel, one of the properties on Northland's list.

Her pulse kicked up. She took another, longer look at the photo. The woman was wearing a lot of makeup, but her almond eyes said she was probably Asian or Alaska Native. A map in the corner of the website marked her location by a red star on the Glenn Highway east of Eureka.

She telescoped out till she could see the surrounding area. The motel was north of Anchorage and east of Wasilla, not all that far from where they were now.

Her pulse spiked even higher as she considered the possibilities.

Trying not to get too excited, she went back to the website, started searching for another woman selling her wares in the same motel. Nick had said there were five women at The Snooze Inn in Fairbanks.

Samantha found a second woman in the same motel, a blonde with her legs spread and nothing on but a strip of black satin covering her crotch. Lacey offered her services as a massage therapist.

Hearing footsteps, she looked up to see Nick coming down the stairs, freshly shaven, black hair still damp from the shower, gorgeous blue eyes locked on her face. His lips curved into a slow, sexy smile. The bottom dropped out of her stomach the way it had when Derek's plane lifted off the ground.

"Hi . . ." was all Nick said, yet both of them knew exactly what the other was thinking.

Embarrassed by her train of thought, even more embarrassed by the graphic photos on the page, she minimized the naked pictures before Nick could see.

"I found something," she said. "A couple of things, actually."

She hated to show him, but she really had no choice.

Taking a deep breath, she moved over on the sofa so he could sit down in front of the screen.

On the sofa next to Samantha, Nick forced his mind away from her soft kisses, her sweet little body, and the great sex they'd just had.

"So what did you find?" he asked.

"A link from an erotic website to a motel owned by Northland." She clicked up the photo. Even as a kid, he had never been into porn, and all he felt at seeing the erotic pictures was disgust.

"There's a map," Samantha said. "The Sunset Motel is on the Glenn Highway northeast of here near Eureka. I found another woman who placed an ad for her services at the same location. There may be more."

"Can you verify the date of the posting? I think they're moving the women from place to place, using different motels around the state. It keeps the police off track. No way to know where they might show up next."

"Both of the photos were posted today."

Cord walked in with an armload of wood, his forehead beaded with sweat though it was freezing cold outside. He dumped the logs next to the wood-burning stove and brushed himself off.

"We've got something," Nick said, moving over so Cord could see what Samantha had found. "She's linked a couple of women to one of the motels Northland owns. Technically, the motels belong to Dragovich, but we have to figure Fedorko and Varga are running the women."

Cord studied the photo. "That makes sense."

"If we could talk to one of those girls," Nick said, "get her to cooperate, we might be able to get the feds to pull their heads out of their asses and start working on trafficking charges against Fedorko and Bela Varga. That could ultimately give them Dragovich."

"We could talk to the women," Cord agreed, "but we'd need help to do it. Backup of some kind. I could arrest the girls for soliciting, but once I take them to the station, they'll probably clam up."

"We have to do something," Samantha said. "This could be the break we need."

"Taggart won't like it," Nick said. "He'll be worried about upsetting the feds and tarnishing his sterling reputation."

"If I arrest them, I take them in. I'm still a cop, Nick, even if you aren't. And the guy is still my boss."

Nick released a slow breath. "All right, but we need to give him something concrete. If we get lucky, maybe one of the women will be willing to roll on someone higher up in the food chain."

"It'd be a gamble," Cord said.

"A big one," Nick agreed. "She'd have to be more afraid of jail than she is the Russians, and that isn't likely."

Samantha spoke up. "One of the women might help you if she thought you'd be willing to help her in return. If she was forced into prostitution against her will, even if it was sometime back, she might want to get out, make a fresh start somewhere."

Cord started nodding. "If she agreed to testify, she could go into witness protection, start a new life somewhere else. If protection isn't necessary, the Sister Mary Home for Women could take her in, set her up with a job and a place to stay. They've helped me with that kind of thing before."

"That could work," Nick said. "Which means our next move is to book an appointment with the massage therapists working at the Sunset Motel." The odds for success weren't good, but they had to do something. They couldn't hide forever.

It could work, Nick thought again. It could also fail miserably and put all of them back in danger.

Which was the reason it was time for him to send Samantha home.

CHAPTER TWENTY-SIX

"We need to talk."

The sound of Nick's voice drew Samantha's attention. Standing at the cutting board slicing tomatoes for the salad she was making to go with the pork chops, she paused. "What is it?"

He plucked the knife out of her hand and set it down on the cutting board. "It's time you went home, honey. I know you don't want to go. I know you want to stay here and help, but this thing we're planning . . . it could wind up leading the Russians right back to our doorstep."

He reached toward her, rested his hand very gently on her stomach, the warmth seeping through her clothes.

"You're carrying our baby," he said softly. "That's more important than revenge for your sister or seeing justice done or anything else."

Her heart squeezed hard inside her. "I

don't want to go, Nick."

"I know you don't. I wish you could stay, but you can't. I called the airport. There's a flight out in the morning. I booked you a seat. By the time you're in the air, Cord and I'll have a plan in place. We'll go in and talk to those women, see if we can get one of them to cooperate."

"If I stay, maybe I can help you convince them."

"You've been a big help already. You've given us solid information, stuff we couldn't have come up with on our own. You deserve to be in on this, but you have to do what's best for the baby."

Her bottom lip trembled.

"I promise I'll keep you posted every step of the way."

She looked into his hard, handsome face, and emotion tightened her chest. How could she have ever thought she wouldn't love him? She stepped into his arms and they closed tightly around her. Nick buried his face in her hair.

"As soon as this is over, I'll fly down to San Francisco and we'll talk about the baby, okay?"

Her throat closed up. She nodded, unable to speak.

"I'd rather not go back to my house right

now. There may be someone watching. I can pack up your things and send them down later. Unless there's something there you really need."

"My essentials are all in my overnight bag. My laptop is here and I have stuff to wear once I get home. I'll be fine."

He bent his head and very softly kissed her. "This isn't over, Samantha. You're going to have my baby. I don't take that lightly."

"I know."

He traced a finger along her jaw. "I'll let you finish dinner. Everyone's looking forward to it."

She nodded and turned away, wiped a tear from her cheek she hoped he wouldn't see. Instead of leaving, Nick turned her back into his arms and kissed her long and deep.

"This isn't over," he repeated gruffly, and walked out of the kitchen.

But Samantha knew that the moment the plane left the ground, it would be over for her. She swallowed against the painful ache throbbing in her heart and finished making supper.

The ride to the airport the following morning was silent and uncomfortable. As he drove the narrow road back toward the main highway, Nick kept glancing at Samantha, expecting her to say something, hoping she would, but she just kept her eyes on the road.

She was bundled into the cute little fur-trimmed parka he had bought her. It shouldn't have made her look the least bit sexy but somehow it did.

He wished he could think of something clever to say, something that would break the tension. He didn't dare speak for fear he would ask her to stay.

No way was he doing that. Last night, he and Cord had spent the evening making plans. He'd wound up calling Derek Hunter for backup. A former Marine pilot, Derek knew how to handle himself. Nick didn't need him to actually go in, just stay on the perimeter and keep an eye out, signal at any sign of trouble.

Last night, the three of them had driven to the motel and done surveillance. Nick counted four women in rooms along the corridor. No guards. These women weren't kids, they were pros.

This morning, he and Cord each made an online appointment for an hour-long "massage session" tonight. The fee was three-hundred dollars apiece. Instead of selling sex, the women were going to be arrested.

Or they could cut a deal. Nick prayed one of them would agree.

He glanced over at Samantha, sitting rigidly in her seat. He wished he could tell what she was thinking. She was going home and they still hadn't talked about the baby or the future, or any other damn thing. He still wasn't sure he'd passed the fatherhood test.

Biting back a curse, he forced his mind back to the present and fixed his eyes on the road. They were leaving Palmer, a small farming community on the Glenn Highway, when Nick heard Samantha's sudden gasp of breath. He turned to see her clutching her abdomen, bent over in the seat.

"What is it? What's the matter?"

She started panting. "I don't know." Her features contorted as she gritted her teeth against a wave of pain.

"Dammit, what's wrong?"

"It's . . . it's the baby. I had a few twinges last night, but I didn't think — Oh, God, Nick."

"Jesus! Hang on." He floored it, felt the rush of speed, the wheels spinning on the pavement, and fought to bring himself under control. "Hang on, honey. The hospital's not that far away. We'll be there in just a few minutes."

"I'm . . . I'm bleeding, Nick. Oh, God, I don't know what to do."

He clenched his jaw, pressed the gas pedal down harder, but there was a thin, slick coating of snow on the road and he didn't dare go any faster. What had seemed nearby suddenly felt miles away. He was in four-wheel drive, but he could still slide out of control. He merged onto the Parks Highway and floored it again.

Hugging her arms around herself, Samantha made little whimpering sounds, each one a stab in his heart. If something happened to the baby, he would never forgive himself. He had known the risk, but he had selfishly allowed her to stay.

Mat-Su Regional Medical Center appeared up ahead, a sprawling pink stucco building complex against the backdrop of Lazy Mountain, the peak now covered with snow. Nick followed the signs pointing to emergency, roared into the parking lot, and slid to a stop in front of the emergency entrance. Shoving the car into Park, he threw open the door.

"Don't move! I'll be right back!"

As he raced toward the automatic glass doors, he slipped on a patch of ice and nearly went down, caught himself and kept running, raced inside the building.

"I need help! Someone get a stretcher!"

The place erupted in activity and yet there was a calm control that kept his heart from tearing its way out of his chest.

"We're on it!" one of the doctors said as they moved toward the entrance. "What's the situation?"

Nick swallowed. "She's bleeding," he said, barely able to choke out the words. "She's pregnant." Then he fell in behind the doctors and nurses rushing out of the hospital, stood in terror as one of the white-coated men unfastened Samantha's seat belt and helped her up on the stretcher.

"It's all right," the doctor said in a soothing voice to Samantha. "We're going to take good care of you. Just lie back and relax."

She was crying and the sound wrenched Nick's heart. He gripped her hand and hurried along beside her, feeling completely useless as he accompanied the gurney back inside the emergency room. One of the nurses shunted him out of the way and the gurney disappeared behind a curtain.

For moments that seemed like hours, he just stood there, his mind mostly blank, worry pressing like a boulder on his chest. Finally, a little blond nurse took pity on him and gently guided him over to a cluster of chairs where he could sit down.

"Your wife is going to be okay," she said. "We're going to take very good care of her."

He swallowed, managed to nod.

"We'll need you to fill out some paperwork. Can you do that for us?"

Another stiff nod.

"Do you have her insurance information?"

He tried to think, but his brain felt foggy. He'd been in combat situations and been steady as a rock. Here he was completely at a loss.

"It might be in her purse," the nurse gently prodded. "Maybe it's in your vehicle."

His brain started functioning again. "I'll get it. I'll be right back." Heading out to the Explorer, he got in and started the engine, moved the car into a parking space. Her purse was on the floor of the passenger seat. He retrieved the bag and strode back toward the entrance.

The curtain was still drawn when he walked into the emergency room. There were people moving around, patients, doctors, and nurses. He could smell alcohol and the too-familiar coppery odor of blood. Before his mind could travel where those bad memories led, the little blonde reappeared.

"This way," she said, guiding him through

a maze of hallways. The hospital was impressive, with lots of stone and a big rock fireplace in the lobby. She led him to a row of cubicles, urged him to sit down in a chair at the counter in one of them. A heavyset, gray-haired woman appeared on the opposite side.

"I'll need name, address, and insurance cards," the buxom woman said. Her name tag read Hilda and it fit.

Forcing himself to focus, he dug Samantha's insurance cards out of her wallet, along with her driver's license. He passed them over and started on the lengthy task of filling out the necessary forms.

It didn't seem right that the name he gave the woman was Samantha Hollis and not Samantha Brodie.

Samantha awakened slowly. Feeling groggy and out of sorts, she forced her eyelids to open. She must have fallen asleep. Now she was flat on her back in a hospital bed, a curtain drawn around her.

At least she was no longer hurting.

Then it all came flooding back. The sharp, biting pain, the fierce cramping, blood oozing between her legs. She remembered Nick's wild ride to the hospital, slamming to a halt in front of the emergency room,

Nick racing for help. Fear sliced through her and an ache started throbbing in her chest. *Not the baby. Don't let it be the baby.*

She glanced wildly around, saw Nick sitting in the chair next to the bed, elbows propped on his knees, his dark head hanging forward in his hands.

She managed to speak but her voice quivered. "Nick . . . ?"

The sound of his name brought his head up. She had never seen him look so shaken, his features pale, his expression nothing short of ravaged. He came up out of the chair and reached for her hand, just held onto it for several long moments.

"They gave you something to stop the pain," he finally said, his voice dull and edged with emotion. "How are you feeling?"

"The baby. Nick . . . what happened to the baby?"

He swallowed. "I'm so sorry, honey. You lost the baby."

Her throat closed up. She felt a fresh wave of pain, but the ache was in her heart. All the way to the hospital, she had prayed the baby would be all right, that whatever was happening would pass. But from the first knifing cramp, she had known her body was rejecting the child. Tears stung her eyes and she felt the wetness trickle onto her cheeks.

"It's all my fault," Nick said hoarsely, drawing her attention back to him. "If I had sent you home the way I should have, it wouldn't have happened." His beautiful blue eyes looked so bleak, her heart clenched again, this time for Nick.

Samantha shook her head. "That isn't true, Nick. What happened wasn't your fault. We didn't do anything that would cause me to have a miscarriage. Not at this early stage."

A noise in the room drew her attention. "Samantha's probably right." A slender woman in white stood in the doorway, short dark hair, half-glasses dangling from a chain around her neck, clipboard in hand. "I'm Dr. Wallace. What you said, Samantha, is correct. Miscarriages — especially in the earliest stages — are a very common occurrence. It happens in more than twenty-five percent of pregnancies during the first few weeks."

Nick said nothing. She could see he still blamed himself.

"Having sex," the doctor continued, apparently reading his thoughts, "exercising, a mild fall, taking simple medications don't cause it to happen. Most often it's chromosomal abnormalities in the fetus. I would guess that's the cause in this case."

Some of the color washed back into Nick's face. "Are you sure?"

"I've given you the facts. It's hard to know for certain, but as I said, it's very common this early on." She walked over to the bedside and smiled down at Samantha. "The good news is, we didn't find anything that would preclude your getting pregnant again. Nothing that would indicate anything but a normal birth the next time around."

Samantha's throat tightened. A little sound escaped and Nick squeezed her hand. She realized he hadn't let go. "That's . . . that's really good to know," she said.

"You're going to be fine, Samantha," the doctor continued. "It's normal for a woman to have trouble dealing with a miscarriage, but if you stay positive and look toward the future, you'll be fine."

Samantha closed her eyes and leaned back against the pillow.

"How long before she can go home?" Nick asked.

"There's no need for her to stay. But she'll need a few days' rest before she resumes her normal activities."

"She was supposed to fly back to San Francisco today."

The doctor shook her head. "No chance of that. I'd prefer she didn't fly for at least a week. As I said, a miscarriage can be traumatic. She needs time to get back on her feet."

Samantha returned her attention to Nick. "I guess you'll have to put up with me for a few more days."

Leaning over the bed, he pressed a gentle kiss on her forehead. "I never wanted you to leave. I just wanted you safe."

The doctor tapped her pen against the clipboard in her hands. "I'll have the release papers prepared. As soon as they're ready, you can take Samantha home."

"Thank you, Doctor," Samantha said.

"I'll take good care of her," Nick promised.

The doctor just smiled. "I can see that you will." Her shoes squeaked as she crossed to the door and pulled it open, disappeared out into the hall.

Fighting not to cry, Samantha looked at Nick. "I should be glad this happened. We . . . both should. We didn't plan on having a baby. Now we don't have to . . . worry about it." She glanced away, tears leaking from the corners of her eyes. She swallowed past the thick lump in her throat. "Funny thing is . . . after all the worry, I kind of started . . . you know . . . looking forward to being a mother."

Nick glanced away. "Yeah. Funny thing." He released a deep, slow breath. "I'll get you checked out, then come back for you." Turning away from her, he strode out into the hall.

A fresh lump rose in Samantha's throat as the door slowly closed behind him. She shouldn't be feeling this way. She should be relieved. No more worry about the future. No more thinking about her relationship with Nick.

Samantha turned her face into the pillow and started to weep.

Nick checked on the paperwork, found out it would be ready in twenty minutes. While he waited, he walked outside the building to get a breath of fresh air.

The minute he stepped out the door, he filled his lungs, took in what felt like the first full breath he had taken since he got to the hospital. The temperature was in the low forties, the sky a dull pewter gray. He was glad for the chill that helped clear his head.

Pulling his throwaway cell phone out of his pocket, he dialed Cord's number.

"A problem's come up," he said when his best friend answered. "We have to abort the mission."

"What are you talking about? Everything's set."

"I'm at the hospital. Samantha had a miscarriage. She can't go back to San Francisco for another week."

"She was pregnant?"

He sighed, rubbed a hand over his face. "Yeah. Happened in Vegas. It's a long story. I'm bringing her back to the cabin as soon as she's released. If that's okay."

"Of course, it's okay, for chrissake. All right if I tell Mary? Samantha may need a woman to talk to."

"Good idea. I'll see you soon."

Nick ended the call. For long moments he just stood there, unsure exactly what to do. Then he phoned Rafe. He wasn't sure why. Maybe he just needed to hear his big brother's voice.

"Brodie," Rafe answered, not recognizing the caller on the disposable phone.

"It's me. I'm on a throwaway. Some things have come up."

He could almost feel his brother's worry antenna going on alert. "What kind of things?" Rafe asked.

There's a dead guy in Fairbanks and we're about to take on the Russian mob. "Samantha lost the baby."

"Damn. That's too bad, Nick."

"I got off lucky, right? No child support. No worrying about how the kid's being raised. I caught a break, right?"

A long silence fell. "I get the sense that's not the way you feel."

Nick swallowed. He took a deep breath and slowly released it, watched it turn white in the cold Alaskan air. "I don't know how I feel. The truth is, I was kind of getting used to the idea of being a father."

"She can have other kids, right? She came out of it okay?"

"Samantha's all right. She's pretty upset, but she's okay. She can't go home for another week."

"Good. That'll give you some time to figure things out."

"What's there to figure? She's going home. I'm staying here. That's all there is to it."

"Is it? You know, little brother, nothing's black and white. There are lots of alternatives out there if you look for them."

"Yeah, I guess."

"Listen, I've got a boat pulling out. I've got to go. Call me if you need me — and don't do anything stupid." Rafe hung up the phone.

The ghost of a smile touched Nick's lips. Shoving the phone in his pocket, he walked back into the hospital to collect Samantha and take her home.

CHAPTER TWENTY-SEVEN

It was late afternoon, the sky still overcast and grim. A fire roared behind the glass window in the wood-burning stove in the corner, keeping the living room warm. Having been fussed over by everyone in the house, including Jimmy, Samantha rested comfortably beneath a pile of blankets on the sofa. Her lower back was aching and she felt strangely lethargic, but aside from that, she was okay.

At least physically. She and Mary had talked when she'd arrived. Samantha was surprised how good it felt to speak to a woman who understood a little of the loss she felt.

"I'd love to have a baby someday," Mary had said. "But I'm not ready yet. In time, I hope I will be."

"I wasn't ready, either," Samantha said. "But as the days went along, somehow that changed." She fought back a fresh round of tears, felt Mary's slim hand wrap around her fingers.

"You're healthy," Mary said. "That's the main thing. When you're ready, you'll try again. Maybe that'll be soon, or maybe sometime down the road. You'll know when the time is right."

Though Samantha was comforted by the notion, she couldn't imagine having a child with anyone but Nick. She felt a soft pang in her heart. Having a baby with Nick was never going to happen. She needed some time to accept that.

She heard him before she saw him, talking to Cord as they walked out of the kitchen, one dark-haired, one blond, both tall and incredibly handsome.

"Have you called Derek and told him we'll be postponing the operation for at least a week?" Nick asked his friend.

"No. I'm not convinced we should do that. We aren't sure how long those women will be working that motel, and finding them again won't be easy. On top of that, I have to be at work Monday morning. We need to do this tonight."

"I'm not doing anything till Samantha is safe back in San Francisco." Nick smiled as he walked toward her. "How are you feel-ing, honey?"

"At the moment, hearing what you just said, I feel pretty rotten. I can't believe you're thinking of canceling your plans."

"What? You just lost a baby, forgodsake."

"That has nothing to do with it. You have to do the mission tonight. Until you resolve this, Mary and Jimmy are still in danger. And after what happened in Fairbanks, so are you."

"Samantha . . ."

"You know I'm right. You have to do this, Nick. You don't have any choice."

A muscle tightened in his jaw. "Even if we talk to those women, we might not be able to convince one of them to cooperate."

"You certainly won't be able to if you don't try."

"She's right," Cord chimed in. "We need to end this, Nick."

He raked a hand through his wavy black hair. "I don't like it. What if something goes wrong?"

"Something can always go wrong," Cord said. "Doesn't change what we need to do."

He flicked a glance at Samantha, saw the resolve in her face, and blew out a frustrated breath. "All right, you win. We go in the way we planned. But we leave Derek here with Mary and Samantha. We should have done that in the first place."

"If we do, we won't have a lookout."

"Yes, you will," Jimmy said from the bottom of the stairs. "I can do it. I'm the one who got us into this mess in the first place."

"I don't know if that's a good idea," Cord said, shaking his head.

Nick looked over at the tall woman standing next to the boy. "Mary?"

"I have to do this, Aunt Mary," Jimmy pleaded. "We can't just keep hiding."

Mary's gaze went to her nephew, and Samantha could see the love she felt for him.

"Jimmy's right," Mary said. "You've risked your lives to help us. We have to help, too. And I believe Jimmy can handle whatever you need him to do."

The boy seemed to stand a little straighter.

"All right, then," Nick said. "It's settled. We go in tonight, do what we need to. And hope like hell it works."

Mary held onto Duke's collar, keeping the dog in the house as the men headed out. Nick met Derek walking up the path as he, Cord, and Jimmy crossed the front deck toward the stairs.

"Change of plans," Nick said. "You're staying with the women. We need to be sure they're safe. Jimmy's taking your place as lookout."

Derek's brilliant green gaze slid over the boy. "You sure about that?"

Jimmy straightened to his near six-foot height. "I can keep watch. Nick says all I have to do is call him on the cell if I see something and need to warn him."

"We need you here," Cord said to Derek. "Nick's right about that. These women are important to us. We need to be sure they're safe."

"All right." Derek pulled a big semi-auto, Beretta nine mil from the clip holster hooked to the back of his jeans. He held up the weapon and dropped the clip to check the load, then shoved it back in. "I've got more firepower in my Jeep if it looks like I need it. You don't have to worry, I'll take good care of them."

Nick trusted that he would. Derek Hunter was one of the most capable men he knew. "If something happens and you need to leave, we'll rendezvous at the Salmon Lodge. You know where it is, right?"

Derek nodded. "Little place off the road near Goose Bay."

"The owner's a friend," Nick said. "Noah Devlin. Ex-Delta, though he may not admit it. He'll help if you need him."

Derek slid his pistol back into the holster beneath his flannel shirt. "Have fun," was all he said.

Nick headed for the Explorer. Cord and Jimmy loaded up while he went around to the driver's side, climbed in and started the engine. It took a while to reach the Sunset Motel, but as planned, they arrived just after dark, on time for their "massage sessions."

"I'm parking right here," Nick said to Jimmy, turning the SUV around for a quick getaway and pulling out of sight beneath the low-hanging branches of a pine tree. "You've got the night vision goggles, right?"

The boy nodded.

Nick tossed him the car keys. "You told me once your dad was teaching you to drive. If things go south, get in the car and get out of here. You got it?"

Jimmy shook his head. "No way. I'm not leaving you behind."

Nick stepped in front of him, used the voice he'd used in the Rangers. "This isn't up for discussion, Jim. I'm giving you an order. Things go bad, you leave. Got it?"

"Yes, sir."

"Good. You know what to watch for, right? Anything out of the ordinary. Anyone who shows up and heads for the rooms on the east side of the motel we're going into. That happens, we need to know."

"Okay."

"You got my number programmed into your phone?"

"Yes, sir."

"Good. Stay low and out of sight." Feeling the familiar adrenaline rush he'd always loved, Nick found himself grinning. "Keep the faith," he said and started walking. Cord smiled and joined him on the path leading down the gentle slope to rooms fifteen and seventeen on the east side of the Sunset Motel.

Nick stood on the threshold of room seventeen. The building was a single story, clapboard structure in fair condition. It was relatively open, just a few leafless trees between the motel and where he had parked the Explorer. Easy in and out. At least, he hoped so.

Nick knocked on the door, and a few seconds later, it swung open. A pretty, darkhaired woman wearing too much makeup and almost no clothes smiled and stepped back to let him in.

"Well, hello, handsome." She looped her arms around his neck. "I'm Ruby. What can I do for you tonight?" She was wearing a black lace thong and black, thigh-high stockings. She had heavy breasts topped by big brown nipples.

"You do massages, right?"

"Oh, yeah, baby. When I finish giving a good . . . massage . . . you'll feel relaxed in every part of your body."

"How much?"

She frowned, let her gaze run over him. "You're not a cop, are you?" He was in exceptionally good physical condition. No earrings. No visible tattoos. He knew he had the look. He could recognize it in other men.

"Ex-Ranger. I'm just looking for some company."

"The price was on the web."

"Three-hundred, right?"

"That's the base rate. Depends on exactly what you want."

"How about four-hundred and you answer my questions."

Her head came up and wariness crept into her features. "About what?"

"How about we start with Connie Bela Varga?" The Anchorage connection to Fedorko.

The color bled out of her face. "I don't know anyone by that name."

"Sit down."

She took one look at the hard set of his jaw and didn't argue. "What do you want?"

"I want to make you an offer, Ruby. You

can take the offer or go to jail."

"You said you weren't a cop."

"The guy next door carries a badge. Here's the deal. You tell me everything you know about Bela Varga and we don't arrest you. You give us something really useful, the deal gets sweeter. You've got ten seconds to decide, starting now."

He shoved up the sleeve of his jacket to look at his heavy black wristwatch.

"You're barking up the wrong tree," Ruby said. "I don't work for Bela Varga. I don't know anything about him."

He let the jacket sleeve fall back into place, fixed a hard stare on the woman. "All right. If you don't work for Bela Varga, who do you work for?"

Long seconds passed.

"I can stay here all night. Or I can have my friend take you in. What's it gonna be?"

"Fine, I work for a guy named Virgil Turnbull."

"He's the guy they call The Bull. Turnbull works for Connie. Give me something I can use, and I promise I'll help you. I can see you get a clean start somewhere else, get a job in some other line of work."

Her plump red lips curved up. "This is what I do, cowboy. I'm good at it, and I make more in a night than a waitress does in two weeks. You haul me in, I'll be out in twenty-four hours. Oh, one more thing. If I were you, I'd stop asking questions before Varga finds out and you wind up dead. Now arrest me or get out."

"You know he's running underage girls? Twelve, thirteen years old? They're just kids."

A shudder rippled through her. "I heard about it," she said a little more softly. "I don't hold with that kind of thing. But I can't help you."

"You sure this is the way you want it?"

"I'm sorry."

He didn't say more. The woman had made her choice. He hoped to hell Cord had done better. He headed for the door, pulled it open, and walked outside. Time was of the essence. There was no way to know if Ruby would call Virgil The Bull or another of Varga's henchmen.

He strode down the corridor and knocked on the door to room fifteen. Cord pulled it open.

"No dice," Nick said.

Cord motioned him into the room. "This is Lacey." He tipped his head toward the near-naked, bleached blonde leaning back in a chair, a cigarette dangling from between her fingers. "She doesn't have anything to give us, but she has a friend who needs the kind of help we can offer."

Nick felt a stirring of hope. "That so?" He smiled in her direction. "Hello, Lacey."

Blond eyebrows beginning to show their dark roots arched up. "Well, aren't you two a pretty pair? You boys are so yummy, I'd do you both for free."

Nick ignored her practiced smile. "Give us your friend's name. We'll do what we can to help her."

Lacey sighed and some of her bravado faded. "She goes by the name Crystal but her real name is Carol Johnson. She's got a ten-year-old kid. Evie's a real pretty little girl. Carol's sure they're grooming her for the life. She's desperate to get Evie someplace safe before it's too late."

"We can help her," Cord said. "We can be the solution to her problem."

"She might cooperate; I can't say for sure. She knows what'll happen to her if she goes against Bela Varga."

"If she helps," Cord said, "we can protect her and her daughter."

Lacey took a drag on her cigarette, blew out a slow stream of smoke. "Like I said, she might help you. She'd do anything for that kid."

"Where do we find her?" Nick asked.

Lacey sat up a little straighter. "You don't. I find her for you. I relay your message and set up a meet — for a price."

"How much?" Nick asked.

"Five-thousand. Cash."

"Three," Nick said.

Frosted pink lips curved into a smile. "Crystal works in Anchorage. It'll take me a couple of days to arrange things without causing suspicion."

"What about the woman next door?" Nick asked. "She knows we came for information. She might have called someone already."

"Ruby won't call anyone. She's afraid of Virgil. He gets off hitting women. Doesn't need a reason, any excuse will do. She won't say a word, and besides, I'll talk to her. She and Crystal are friends."

"You've got till Wednesday," Cord said.

"I'm not sure I can make it happen that fast," Lacey countered, shaking her head. Long, blond hair swung forward, exposing roots the color of her eyebrows.

"All right," Nick said. "But if we don't hear from you before the end of the week, we'll figure you're giving us the runaround and you won't like the consequences."

Lacey ignored the remark. "How do I reach you?"

Nick reached into his pocket, pulled out a piece of paper with the number of the disposable phone written on it. "You can reach me there." He handed her the slip of paper. "Call when you've made the arrangements."

"How do I get paid?"

"I'll leave the money with Crystal. That work for you?"

"Sure — assuming she goes for the deal." Lacey got up from her chair, stubbed out her cigarette in the glass ashtray on the dresser. "Now you'd better get out of here, before my next customer arrives."

Nick didn't argue. He couldn't leave soon enough. Turning up the collar of his jacket against the wind as they walked back to the Explorer, he thought of Samantha, and the tightness in his chest began to ease.

He told himself it wasn't because Samantha would be waiting for him when he got home.

CHAPTER TWENTY-EIGHT

Samantha watched Nick pace the floor. It was late Wednesday morning and still no word from Lacey or Crystal. Nick had given her the details. If Carol Johnson, alias Crystal Summers, could come up with information against any of the men involved in trafficking underage girls, the police would be forced to investigate. The feds would step in and once they were involved, the facts would be out in the open. Mary and Jimmy would be safe.

Hopefully Nick, as well.

Across the room, he checked his watch, his mood darkening with every passing minute. Jimmy was upstairs playing a game on his iPad, itching to get back to school, clearly as bored as Nick. Mary was trying to read a book, though the tedium of waiting seemed to be wearing on her, too.

Samantha was sick to death of being an invalid. She was feeling perfectly normal again and coming to grips with what had occurred — the end of a pregnancy that was never meant to happen in the first place.

Losing the baby still tugged at her heart, but she was learning to live with it. Life went on. She was healthy, and she was the type of person who looked forward not back.

Her focus now was on the young girls who were being so viciously abused. Though she'd been too young to do anything about what had happened to her sister, she might be able to help the girls in those motel rooms, who were being forced to do things no child should ever have to endure.

Nick paced the length of the room one more time. "Why the hell doesn't she call?"

"You told me it would take her a while to set things up. It's too early to give up yet. Why don't you go for a walk or something? You've got your phone. The sun's just come out. You look like you could use some fresh air."

And she had learned that Nick was a man who craved the outdoors. It seemed to run deep in his bones. He'd been out for a while every day, running, walking, hiking one of the nearby trails.

He turned toward the window, saw rays of sunlight streaming down through a hole in the clouds. "Maybe you're right. I won't stay long, and I won't be far away if you need me." Grabbing his jacket, he shrugged it on, stepped out onto the porch and closed the door.

Samantha stared at the place he had been, trying not to see him in the eye of her mind, tall and rugged, so damned sexy. She would never find another man like Nick. But maybe that was best. She'd be better off with a guy who enjoyed putting on a suit and tie, taking her out to a fancy dinner. A man who would escort her to a play or a lecture at the university.

She was never supposed to fall in love with Nick. He was never meant to be more than a fling, a guilty weekend pleasure. But the sad truth was, the thought of leaving him made her heart squeeze so hard it hurt.

Taking a shuddering breath, she sat up on the sofa, determined to think of something besides her unwanted feelings for Nick. She hadn't looked at her e-mail in days. She hadn't communicated with her family or Abby and if she didn't do it soon, they would worry.

Maybe when she finished, she would do a little more snooping, see if any of the people they were investigating showed up on Facebook. Fedorko had a wife and a girlfriend. Women loved to post photos and gossip.

Samantha opened the laptop sitting on the coffee table in front of her, booted up the machine, and went to work.

The Anchorage police station bustled with activity, uniformed cops and plain clothes detectives moving up and down the halls. Cord was one of them, striding along the corridor, heading for his desk.

"I need a word with you, Detective Reeves." The police captain stepped in front of him, just outside the door to his office. "In here." Smoothing back his silver-touched sandy hair, Raymond Taggart waited for him to walk in, then closed the door, crossed to his desk and sat down. Cord took a seat in a chair in front of him.

Since returning to work on Monday, Cord had been staying in his apartment. It was a relief to be out of the cabin, away from Mary. Away from feelings for her he didn't want to have.

The worst of it was, she was right. He'd been attracted to Mary George's exotic beauty and sweet disposition, but he didn't really know her. He'd done the same thing with the gorgeous blonde he'd asked to marry him last year.

It was time he started looking deeper, seeing past just the beauty to something more important. If he did, maybe he'd have better luck with women.

Still he was worried about Mary and Jimmy. He'd hoped the meeting with Carol Johnson, alias Crystal, would be arranged by now. He'd hoped to have something on the Russians he could bring to the captain.

No word from Nick meant neither Crystal nor her friend, Lacey, had called.

The captain's voice jarred him back to the moment. "I want to know what's going on," Taggart said. "I'm sure you know, and I expect you to tell me."

Cord sat up a little straighter. "I'm afraid I'm not following, sir."

"I want to know what's going on with your good friend, Nick Brodie. Last week he was involved in a shoot-out in Fairbanks. On his way back, he stormed in here with a woman, ranting and raving, determined to insinuate himself in the middle of a federal investigation. Not a peep from him since. You're his best friend. I figure you know what he's up to and I want you to tell me what it is."

Sonofabitch. He hadn't figured to be asked point blank. He did his best to skirt the question. "As far as I know, he's backed off. At the moment, he isn't doing anything." No phone call made that statement true. Unfortunately.

"Where is he? I want to talk to him. I sent a car to his house to pick him up but he wasn't there."

Cord shrugged. "Nick's not a cop anymore. He could be anywhere."

"What about the woman? Samantha Hollis, Brodie's fiancée?"

"Sorry, he doesn't keep me posted on his love life."

"Brodie made insinuations against Alexander Evans. Evans's son, Jimmy, and the boy's aunt, Mary George, live next to him up at Fish Lake. They weren't home either. I want to know where they are."

"From what Nick says, Alex Evans may have been involved with Luka Dragovich. Nick says Mary and Jimmy's lives were threatened. If they've left, wherever they are, they're probably safer than they were before."

"What's your interest in this, Detective? You realize if you're involved in any way, you could be brought up on charges of interfering with a federal investigation?"

"Look, Captain, at the moment, I don't know where anyone is. And I prefer to keep it that way."

"Well, I want to know what Brodie's up to. I'm assigning you the task of bringing him in. Arrest him if that's what it takes. If you want to keep your job, you'll make that happen as soon as possible. You understand?"

"Yes, sir."

Taggart waved his hand toward the door. "You're dismissed."

Cord clenched his jaw to keep from saying something he'd regret. He knew where Nick was. Hell, he knew where they all were. He just hoped like hell Crystal or Carol or whatever she was calling herself would agree to the meeting. And that if she did, she had the kind of information that would keep them all out of jail.

Because at the moment, it was beginning to look like there was a very good chance they could wind up there.

Raymond Taggart rubbed the back of his neck, the skin still warm from the anger pumping through him. Who the hell did Brodie think he was? Heading out his office door, he walked down the hall into the detectives' squad room and spotted his quarry behind the computer at his desk, typing up a report.

"Detective Archer, I need to see you in my office."

Archer surged to his feet. "Yes, sir." In his early thirties with red hair just beginning to recede and pale blue eyes, the detective was smart and eager to move up through the ranks. Ken Archer knew what needed to be done in order to get ahead.

Raymond strode down the hall back into his office, Archer close on his heels.

"Close the door," Raymond said.

The detective closed the door and took a seat on the opposite side of the desk.

"You and Reeves are friends, isn't that right?"

"We're friendly, yeah. We've gone fishing a couple of times. Went hunting once."

"I seem to recall you and another detective talking about a cabin he owns up near Hatcher's Pass."

"He's got one up there somewhere. I've never been there."

"I want you to find out where it is. Ask around. Use county records. Whatever it takes. I want the location, and I want it today."

"No problem. It shouldn't be that tough to find. What's going on?"

"I'm not sure yet, but I intend to find out. Get me that information, Detective. I expect to see it on my desk this afternoon."

"Yes, sir, Captain."

Raymond watched the detective leave the office, certain he'd come up with the location. Unlike Reeves and Brodie, Archer knew which side to be on when things got tough.

Raymond's mouth thinned. He'd been called on the carpet by the feds for the debacle in Fairbanks. He wanted Brodie's head for stirring up trouble. He wanted to make sure the bastard didn't cause him any more.

Reeves wasn't the sort to get in your face the way Brodie was, but he could also be a pain in the ass. And they were always looking for ways to circumvent his authority. He wasn't having it this time.

He wasn't letting either of them get away with it.

His neck felt hot again. *Not this time, Brodie.*

There was simply too much at stake.

After a ride on Cord's ATV that took him up the hill but still kept the cabin in sight, Nick walked back into the mudroom. The succulent aroma of a ham-and-cheese casserole hit him so hard his mouth watered.

When his phone started to ring, he frantically dug it out of his pocket and held it against his ear. "Brodie."

"It's Lacey. Crystal's agreed to meet you. Be at the Eagle's Nest Bar tonight at eleven p.m. It's on Wayburn. You know where that is?"

"I'll find it."

"Bring the money." Lacey ended the call. It was four p.m. Thursday afternoon.

Nick stuck the phone back into the pocket of his jeans and looked up to see Samantha standing in the doorway, an apron around her waist, wooden spoon in her hand.

He frowned. "You're supposed to be resting."

"I'm tired of Campbell's soup and I'm tired of resting. Was that Crystal?"

"That was Lacey. The meeting with Crystal is set for eleven p.m. I need to find the Eagle's Nest Bar. Mind if I use your laptop?"

"It's on the coffee table. Can I go with you?"

"You know you can't."

She smiled and he felt that little kick. He was beginning to get used to it.

"Just testing," she said.

He smiled back, went in and Googled the address for the Eagle's Nest Bar. A map popped up. He recognized the area. Blue collar, not too rough. Good entry and exit. A good place to meet.

On Monday, he'd gone to his bank in Wasilla and pulled out five-thousand dollars. Three for Lacey. A couple of thousand in case something unexpected came up. He wasn't hurting for money, and if this worked, it would be worth it.

He phoned Cord as soon as he had the info he needed. "We're on," he said. "Eleven p.m. tonight. Eagle's Nest Bar." He gave Cord the address.

"I'll see you there." Cord hung up the phone. There was an unfamiliar tension in his friend's deep voice. Nick wondered what it was.

"What time is supper?" he asked Samantha, and found himself wandering in her direction.

"Since you need to leave, seven o'clock."

Knowing he shouldn't, wondering if she would pull away from him the way she had been lately, he moved behind her, wrapped his arms around her waist. When she leaned back against him, he lifted away her hair and nuzzled the nape of her neck.

"I've missed you," he said.

"I've missed you, too."

"I'm really sorry about the baby," he whispered against her ear.

"I know." She turned into his arms and looked up at him. "Someday, there'll be other children for both of us."

He frowned. "You're saying that as if we'll

be having kids with other people."

She drew back to look at him. "What did you think, Nick? You know as well as I do, we're too different to make it work. It was just a weekend in Vegas. Nothing more. Someday, we'll each meet someone who suits us better."

Nick let her go. His heart was beating painfully, his chest clamping down. He wasn't ready to talk about this, wasn't ready to let her go.

"I've got to call Derek," he said. "He's coming to stay with you and Mary while I'm in town for the meet. I'll get something to eat while I'm there."

"Nick, wait. That didn't come out the way I meant. Please don't go."

He just kept walking. Samantha was right. They were nothing alike. Sooner or later it would all go wrong. They didn't belong together.

So why did it feel like they did?

CHAPTER TWENTY-NINE

Cord's silver Chevy pickup was parked in the lot outside the Eagle's Nest Bar. He'd backed into one of the spaces in case he needed to leave in a hurry. Nick did the same with the Explorer.

The bar was nothing fancy, just a brick building with a neon beer sign in the window. Country music filtered through the walls. Nick stepped up on the porch and shoved through the door.

Cord intercepted him just on the other side. "I don't think she's here yet."

"Let's get a table. Somewhere in the back where we can talk." They moved in that direction, the sound of their heavy boots on the old wooden floor masked by a Willie Nelson song coming from the jukebox next to the bar. The place was about half full, mostly working men, half-a-dozen women. There were always more men than women in Alaska.

He checked out the patrons, a beer-drinking crowd. A dozen different varieties were on tap behind a long, rustic bar lined with stools.

Nick sat down across from Cord in the corner. A flame flickered in a red glass candleholder in the middle of the table. Through one of the windows, he could see a group of smokers puffing away around a fire pit out in back of the bar.

When a waitress arrived, he ordered a pitcher of Alaskan Amber and three glasses, just to fit in.

"You got it, honey." The buxom woman in a short black skirt and white blouse sashayed back toward the bar, then returned a few minutes later and set the pitcher and glasses down on the table.

Nick filled two glasses and handed one to Cord, who took a drink, wiped the foam off his mouth, and sat back in his chair to wait.

Nick was sipping slowly, trying to make it last, when the front door swung open. Orange light from the neon beer sign illuminated the figure of a petite, black-haired woman.

"That's gotta be her," Cord said as she made her way deeper into the bar.

Nick frowned. "She looks pretty young to have a ten-year-old kid."

"She's heading this way. I guess we're about to find out."

The young woman who walked up to them had long, glossy black hair, dark, almond eyes, and an amazingly pretty face. She was clearly Alaska Native, one who looked more like a college girl than a prostitute.

She stopped at the edge of the table. "You're Reeves and Brodie?"

"That's right." Ever the gentleman, Cord rose and pulled out a chair. "I'm Cord. This is Nick. Have a seat, Ms. Johnson."

She sat down wearily. "It's been years since anyone's called me that."

"We can change that," Nick said softly.

Her black eyes gleamed in the light of the candle. "I'm really hoping you can. I have a daughter ten years old. I want her safe."

"You understand what we need in order to make that happen?" Nick asked, filling a glass with beer and setting it down in front of her.

She reached for the glass. "You want Connie Bela Varga."

"That's right," Nick said. "Can you give him to us?"

Her hand trembled as she lifted the beer glass and brought it to her lips, took a drink and set it back down on the table. "I was twelve when one of Bela Varga's men dragged me out of my mother's car while she was in the market. I've never seen her since."

"Jesus," Cord said. "Where's your mother now?"

"I don't know. I got pregnant when I was fifteen. By then I was in the life. After my daughter was born, I had a little more freedom. I sent a note to the village I'd lived in, but I never heard back. Mom drank a lot. I don't know if she's even still alive."

"If you help us, we'll find out," Nick said.

"We'll help you make a new start," Cord added. "You can be Carol Johnson again."

"He'll kill me, you know. He'll kill Evie, too."

Nick's stomach knotted. "We won't let that happen," he promised. "We'll make sure you're protected until this is over. If you testify, you'll be placed in witness protection. It'll mean a fresh start for both of you. If that isn't necessary, we know people willing to help you and Evie start over."

She nodded, her features resigned. "I'd rather be dead than go on the way I have been, living in constant fear for my child. I don't want Evie to live the kind of life I have."

"Then tell us what we need to know," Nick said.

"I can do better than that." She opened her coat and pulled out a small leather-bound volume. "This belongs to Connie Bela Varga. He starts a new book every year." Her lips curved into a grim smile. "He's not exactly into the digital age."

"Where'd you get it?" Nick asked.

"I got it from Connie's house. I'm there at least a couple of nights a week. Doesn't matter that I think he's a pig. Connie takes what he wants and he wants me. And keeping him happy keeps my little girl safe."

"For as long as it lasts," Cord said.

"That's right. I'm no fool. I know it's only a matter of time until he replaces me. What's going to happen to my daughter when that happens?"

Nick looked down at the book she had placed on the table. "What's in it?"

"Dates, times, names, and places. This is a list of names — girls his men picked up last year and where they found them. Most of them are underage. They sold some of them. If the girl resisted, they got her hooked on drugs. Some of them died, but others are still alive, still being held against their will."

Nick picked up the book, his fingers curling around the edge, biting into the leather. "We'll find these girls. We'll see they're released, try to get them back to their families."

"Most don't have families. They're runaways, girls from foster homes or abusive parents. But a few of them are like me. They were taken. They want to go home."

She stood up from her chair. "I have to go. I don't want them to know I was here."

Nick handed her an envelope. "Lacey's money's in there, and a thousand for you. My number's inside." The number of the disposable. "If anything goes wrong or it looks like you or Evie might be in danger, I want you to call. We'll have a place for you to go. Somewhere safe."

She nodded, swallowed. "Thank you."

"We'll be in touch as soon as we can work things out," Cord promised.

"How do I reach you?" Nick asked.

"I'll reach you. I'll call you tomorrow night. Will that be enough time?"

"If it isn't," Nick said, "we'll talk about it then."

Carol nodded.

Nick watched her cross the room, her shoulders a little straighter. She flicked a last glance in their direction as she shoved through the door and disappeared out into the darkness.

Nick glanced down at the book he still held in his hand. "We need to see what we've got."

Cord nodded. "Let's get out of here."

"We should be okay at my place," Cord said as they walked out the door. "We can figure things out when we get there."

Nick nodded. "Sounds good."

Half an hour later, they were sitting in the living room of Cord's apartment, a newer, nicely furnished second-floor unit with a vaulted ceiling. Cord always did have good taste.

"This information is invaluable," Cord said, flipping through the pages of the book a second time, then handing it back to Nick. "We need to get it to Taggart. There's no way he can ignore this kind of evidence."

"Before we talk to anyone, we need to make a copy. There's a FedEx Kinko's on Northern. I'll stop on my way back to the cabin. But I'm not going to Taggart. I want to talk to Charlie Ferrell first."

"You don't trust Taggart?"

Nick ran a hand through his hair. "I don't know. Something doesn't feel right."

"Then maybe I should tell you Taggart ordered me to bring you in."

Nick's head came up. "You're supposed to arrest me?"

"If I have to. I'm supposed to get you to the station one way or another."

Nick rose from his chair, his adrenaline pumping, his muscles suddenly tense. He and Cord were friends, but Cord was also a cop. And he didn't take orders from his superior lightly.

"Then I guess we have a problem. I'm not going in with you and I'm not giving Taggart this information."

Cord slowly rose to his feet. "Take it easy, Nick. I told the captain I didn't know where you were. As far as I'm concerned, I still don't."

Nick slowly relaxed. He should have known he could trust his best friend. "This needs to happen fast. I'll call you as soon as I talk to Ferrell."

"What if Carol Johnson calls and needs help?" After meeting her, neither of them seemed able to think of her as Crystal.

For the first time that night, Nick grinned. "Then I guess your cabin will just get a little more crowded."

Cord smiled and shook his head. "Keep me posted."

"Will do." Grabbing his jacket off the back of the chair, Nick shrugged it on. Shoving the book into an inside pocket, he headed out the door.

Derek Hunter stood at the cabin window. At half past midnight, Nick had phoned. He was running a little late, but he was on his way back up the mountain.

Mary and Jimmy were in upstairs rooms asleep, the dog in with Jimmy. Samantha had finally gone up to bed, but he figured she wouldn't be sleeping. She'd be waiting for Nick. It didn't matter that according to both of them, she was heading back home the end of the week. Samantha was clearly in love with him.

He wasn't sure how Nick felt. Hard to tell with a guy like him. In lust for sure. Maybe something more. Samantha was a keeper. He wondered if Nick had figured that out.

He scanned the area outside the window, looking for headlights. It was after one thirty. Nick should be back any minute.

He caught a flash of light on the road, a vehicle winding its way up the hill. He relaxed a little, figuring it was Nick's Explorer. Then he spotted a second pair of headlights rolling along behind the first. A little ways closer to the cabin, both sets of lights went off.

Unease rolled through him. Reaching for

the lamp on the table, he switched off the light, then cracked the window and heard the hum of engines driving toward the house through the darkness.

Fuck. Moving quickly, he grabbed the AR-15 he'd left in the car last time and decided to bring it in with him tonight. Now he was glad he had. He slung the weapon over his shoulder, pulled his Beretta out of the holster at his waist, checked the load, and shoved it back in. He watched the cars moving closer, caught an occasional glimpse when the moon broke through the clouds.

A pair of SUVs. He wondered how many men were in each. Leaving the window, he hurried up the stairs, banged on Mary's bedroom door, threw it open.

"Get dressed. Get Jimmy and get ready to leave. Stay in the bedroom until I come for you."

He pounded on Samantha's door. When he opened it, she was sitting up in bed, a book in her lap, reading by the glow of a tiny book light.

Her eyes widened at the sight of the weapon slung across his chest. "What is it?"

"Get dressed. We may have to leave. Turn the light off and stay in here until I come get you."

The light went off and she went into action even before he closed the door.

By the time he got downstairs, the cars were almost at the top of the hill. He shoved the window open and used the barrel of the machine gun to knock out the screen. The vehicles rolled to a halt near the deck out in front, and the doors swung open. Six men unloaded, all of them armed.

"Send out the boy," one of them called when they spotted him in the window. "Do that and we'll leave."

"What do you want with him?"

"That's none of your business. Send him out or we come in and get him."

Derek's jaw hardened. "Some of you will die if you try. Maybe not all, but more than a few."

One of them tipped his head to the side and two of them broke away, keeping low and circling toward the back of the house. Behind him, he heard footfalls coming down the stairs, turned to see Jimmy carrying one of Cord's hunting rifles.

"Cover the back," Derek said, hating to get the kid involved, but not having any other choice. "Shoot them if you have to." He turned back to the men out front, knew they had heard the exchange. "I'm not the only one in here with a gun. You sure this is what you want to do?"

Four big semi-autos pointed in his direction. "Send him out or we come in."

Derek held the semi-automatic weapon steady. He had used one in Afghanistan. This one was legal, not fully automatic, but armed with a Slide Fire, allowing him to pull off seven-hundred-fifty rounds a minute if he had to. "First man who moves is going down."

One of them said something into a two-way radio, the sound crackling through the still night air. Derek heard gun shots, semi-automatic pistol fire slamming into the back of the cabin. Then rifle fire, two shots fairly close together. *Jimmy.* Return fire shattered a window, pounded into the wooden walls. Derek held his position and prayed the kid was okay.

"Let's go." The men in front split up and started forward.

Derek pulled the trigger, sending a spray of bullets into the ground at their feet and scattering them even more.

"Last chance!" He ducked as shots slammed into the window frame, popped up long enough to spot his targets and lay down a row of lead that stopped them cold. Two men went down screaming as bullets tore into their legs.

Two down, four to go.

More shots echoed from the back of the house. Didn't sound like Jimmy's rifle, and it was coming up the hill from below. He smiled grimly. Looked like Nick had joined the party. Derek hoped like hell the kid didn't shoot him.

Out front, the men must have realized things were going sideways. The last two men fired off a couple of rounds as they helped their injured buddies limp over to the car. One of them jumped behind the wheel and started the engine. Gravel sprayed as the tires spun and the car shot off down the road.

Another man rounded the corner of the house from the back, blood oozing from a wound in his shoulder. Running flat out, he reached the second SUV and climbed behind the wheel. The car shot backward, whirled around, and roared off, disappearing down the hill.

Derek pulled his AK back through the window, turned and ran to the rear of the house. Jimmy was still pointing the rifle out into the darkness.

"Nick's out there," Derek said calmly, not wanting to rattle the boy.

"I saw him," the kid said. "He shot one of them. I shot one, too, but I didn't kill him. He took off into the trees."

As they looked out the window of the mudroom, Derek spotted the guy heading down the hill, moving through a cluster of pines. He was dragging his leg, frantically waving his arms, trying to flag down the second vehicle. The car finally slid to a halt, the man jumped in, and the SUV roared off down the road.

Nick appeared on the porch, his pistol holstered, his hands in the air. "Don't shoot, kid. It's me."

Derek smiled with relief. He'd done his job. All of them were safe. And he didn't even have to kill anyone.

CHAPTER THIRTY

Nick took a step back as Jimmy jerked open the back door and raced out onto the porch. "Nick!" The boy engulfed him in a bear hug, acting once more like the twelve-year-old he was instead of the man he'd been forced to become.

"I almost shot you," Jimmy said.

Nick just smiled. He'd signaled as he'd come up the hill, used an owl call they both knew to make sure the kid realized it was him. "It's okay, you didn't. You helped save your aunt and Samantha. You did good, Jim."

As they walked back into the house, Mary rushed forward. "Oh, Jimmy." She pulled the boy into a hug. "I was so afraid you'd be hurt."

"I'm okay, Aunt Mary." He hugged her back, then turned away, a little embarrassed. "I recognized one of them, Nick. It was the man who came to my dad's study the day before he was killed. You think that's why they were after me? Because he thought I knew who he was?"

Nick nodded as another piece of the puzzle came together. "Yeah, I do. I think they were afraid you'd figure out who he was, connect him to your dad, and go to the cops. Getting the police involved is the last thing they want."

"What . . . what are we going to do?"

Nick turned at the sound of Samantha's voice, saw her standing in the kitchen doorway. She was dressed in jeans, sneakers, and a sweatshirt, ready to leave at Derek's command. Her face was pale but her chin was firm.

His expression changed from relieved to fierce. He'd never forget the murderous rage that burned through him as he'd heard the echo of gunfire and drove wildly toward the top of the hill. He would have killed every last one of them if they had hurt her.

He drew her carefully into his arms. "You scared the hell out of me. You know that?"

Samantha leaned into him. "I knew you'd come. I never doubted it."

He would have come. No one could have stopped him. He closed his eyes, grateful he had arrived in time, and that Derek had made sure they were safe until he had.

He looked over Samantha's head to his friend. "I owe you one, buddy. A big one. Thanks for keeping them safe."

Derek just grinned. "I needed the practice. I was getting a little rusty."

"Derek and Jimmy held them off," Samantha said, clearly proud of the boy. "If it hadn't been for them. . . ."

The thought of what could have happened made a hard knot ball in Nick's stomach. "They were great." He tipped her face up and softly kissed her. "You okay?"

She nodded. "How did they find us?"

His jaw hardened. "Good question." On Monday when he'd gone to his bank in Wasilla, instead of going by his house for clean clothes, he'd driven to Walmart and bought jeans and T-shirts for him and Samantha. And he'd made damned sure he wasn't tailed.

"Who knew about this place besides you and Cord?" Derek asked.

"I don't know. Cord said Captain Taggart was trying to track us down. I'm beginning to think I know why."

"You don't believe the police are involved with the Russians?" Samantha said.

Nick rubbed a hand over his jaw, felt the roughness of his late-night beard. "I don't know what to believe."

Samantha turned, took in the destruction in the cabin. "You don't think they'll come back?"

"They were pretty well shot up," Derek said, "but they might regroup, bring in more men and hit us again."

The fury he'd felt as he'd driven up the hill returned. "If they do, they won't find us. We're getting the hell out of here."

They loaded their bags into Derek's Jeep Cherokee and Nick's Explorer. Then everyone piled inside the vehicles, including the dog, and they headed for the Salmon Lodge.

Nick roused his friend, Noah Devlin, out of bed, all six-foot-five, two-hundred-thirty pounds of him. Noah had thick brown hair and striking blue eyes. If he hadn't been solid as a brick and former Delta, his dimpled cheeks might have gotten him called pretty. As it was, no man would dare.

Noah made coffee while Nick dumped wood on the embers in the hearth, and the fire blazed to life. Then they all sat in front of the flames to decide their next move.

Noah took a sip from his steaming mug. "What about the woman you met with in Anchorage? You figure those guys are onto her?"

Nick mulled that over. "If they followed

her to the bar, she's in trouble. She seemed pretty canny though and I didn't see any sign of anyone outside. But we need to move on this as fast as possible."

They were sitting in the owner's cabin, a spacious log house behind the front office. Alaska Native artwork hung on the walls and a big rock fireplace dominated the room. The fire had burned down a little, lighting the room with a soft orange glow.

Noah sipped his coffee. "Clearly, they're willing to go to any lengths to get hold of the boy. It's not my call to make, but I think you might be better off splitting up."

Nick had been thinking that same thing. "Maybe. Depends if we can find a safe place for Jimmy and Mary to hole up while we deal with the problem."

"I know a place Jimmy and I can go," Mary said, speaking up for the first time since they had arrived at the lodge. "We can go to Mountain Village, where I was raised." Her Yupik village up along the Yukon. "We have relatives there, people who will protect us."

"Are you sure they'll take you in?" Nick asked.

"Jimmy has an uncle who's been wanting to meet him for a very long time. And we're family. They'll protect us. They've never forgiven themselves for what happened to Cora. They'd give their lives for us if they had to."

"With any luck, we'll get these guys before it comes to that," Nick said.

"Uncle Audrac told Aunt Mary he'd teach me stuff," Jimmy said, sipping a mug of coffee laced heavily with cream and sugar. "Like how to track big game and be a really good hunter."

Reminded of their conversation down by the lake, Nick squeezed the boy's shoulder. "I remember. You'll have to miss a little school, but with the information we've got, this'll all soon be over, and you and Mary can come back home."

Jimmy just nodded, his features glum. This was hard on everyone. Sensing the boy's distress, Duke curled in a ball at his feet.

"I'll fly them up," Derek offered as he walked back from the kitchen into the living room. "I've been up to Mountain Village so I know the route."

"What about the weather?" Nick asked.

"I just called. Weather's supposed to break. We can leave at first light."

Mary spoke to Samantha, sitting next to Nick on Noah's comfortable brown plush sofa. "Are you feeling well enough to fly home?" she asked.

"I feel pretty much back to normal. I'm a little tired, but other than that, I feel fine."

"She isn't going back," Nick said firmly. "Samantha was with me when I talked to Taggart so he knows she's involved. We don't know who we can trust anymore. We don't know how far this reaches. I want her with me. I want her where I can keep her safe." He pinned her with a look. "You okay with that?"

"Before tonight, I would have argued I'd be safe in San Francisco. Now the only place I really feel safe is with you."

Nick cupped her face between his hands, leaned down and softly kissed her. "I won't let them hurt you."

She gave him a tremulous smile. "I know."

Noah rose from his chair. "You've got a big day tomorrow. Why don't you all get some sleep? This time of year, we've always got empty cabins. I'll get you some keys."

For what was left of the night, Jimmy, Mary, and Duke bunked in one of the larger cabins with Derek, while Nick and Samantha took the smaller cabin next door. They hadn't been followed to Goose Bay. He and Derek had made sure of that. He felt safe, at least for now.

As tired as he was, Nick's mind churned. How had they been found? Who was responsible? What would the Russians do next?

It was almost dawn when he finally fell into a restless slumber.

Samantha lay in bed next to Nick in one of the lodge's rustic cabins. It was just getting light outside, the sky turning from black to a dark shade of purple. Nick was finally asleep, a heavy troubled slumber that made her want to hold him, comfort him.

Even as she'd slept, she had sensed on some level that he was awake. Perhaps knowing he watched over her was the reason she had been able to sleep so soundly.

Now she wanted to do the same for him, to let him rest and regain his strength. He had pushed down the covers, leaving him naked to the waist. Watching the rise and fall of his hard-muscled chest, the tightening of the sinews across his abdomen, she felt desire flare for the first time since she had lost the baby.

Last night, as tired as they both were, she had felt an urge to join with him, simply to feel safe and protected, the way he always made her feel. But he didn't try to make love to her and in a way she was glad.

This morning was different. As she watched him, she felt a need that reached deep inside her. For a while that need had been buried beneath the loss she had felt, but she was young and strong. And whether she wanted to be or not, she was in love with Nick.

Her gaze wandered over his sleeping figure, his lips curved softly in slumber, thick black lashes forming crescents on his cheeks. Just looking at him made her heart ache. She had wanted Nick Brodie since she'd seen him in that Las Vegas hallway, tall and dark, with the most gorgeous blue eyes she had ever seen. She wanted him now.

Smiling at the thought, she dozed for a while, just to give him more time to sleep, awakened again and watched him a little longer. Knowing it was time to get up, she slid from under the blankets and headed for the bathroom to get ready for the day. Cranking up the heater, she spent a few minutes taking care of her needs and brushing her teeth while the room warmed up, then she turned on the shower and climbed beneath the fine hot spray.

The door to the bathroom opened and she heard Nick at the sink. She had just tipped her head back to rinse her hair when the plastic curtain slid open and Nick stepped into the shower. At the sight of his hard, naked body, her breath caught. He was just so completely beautiful.

She smiled up at him. "Good morning."

Nick leaned down and gave her a slow, very thorough, peppermint-flavored kiss. "I saw you watching me while we were in bed," he said, his eyes on her face.

"You . . . you did?" She felt warm all over, and it had nothing to do with the water.

"The way you were looking at me . . . it really turned me on."

She glanced down, saw he was aroused, and her breathing went shallow.

"I think you wanted me," he said softly. "Did you?"

Her heart was pounding. She'd wanted him then. She wanted him now. "Yes . . ."

Nick claimed her mouth in a ravaging kiss that grew deeper and hotter by the second. Bending his head beneath the warm spray, he suckled her breasts, first one and then the other, while his hands slid over her water-slick hips, slipped between her legs to stroke her. She was wet and ready, had been all morning as she had watched him.

"God, I want you," he said, and then he was lifting her up, wrapping her legs around his waist, sliding himself deep inside. He was big and hard and he filled her completely. With a whimper of longing, Samantha locked her arms around his neck and let him take her, let him drive deeper, harder, until her body began to tighten around him and she was reaching the crest, climbing the peak and tipping into glory.

"Nick . . ." she cried out the instant before she convulsed around him, the pleasure so deep and intense she felt as if she drowned in it.

Nick kissed her deeply and let himself go, his muscles tightening as his own release struck. At the last moment he withdrew, spilling his seed outside her body, ending any chance of another unplanned baby. Samantha felt a moment of loss that disappeared as she looked into those blue, blue eyes.

Resting her head against his shoulder, she clung to him as the seconds ticked past. Then the water began to grow cold and the moment was lost.

Nick kissed her one last time and turned off the shower. He stepped out first, grabbed a towel and wrapped it around his waist, grabbed one for her and gently enfolded her in the softness.

"I didn't hurt you or anything?"

She shook her head. "No." He'd been careful. He was always careful with her, always looking out for her. Knowing she would have to give him up made her feel like crying.

"We better get dressed," he said. "We've got a lot to do."

Samantha towel-dried her hair as best she could, leaving it to dry in curls that hung down her back, then followed Nick out of the bathroom. Grateful he had gone shopping for something clean to wear, she'd been only a little surprised the clothes actually fit.

"What are we going to do first?" she asked as she pulled on soft blue jeans and a long-sleeve pink T-shirt. She smiled at the words Girl Gone Wild stamped on the front, and figured it had come from the teen department.

"First I make sure Derek gets Mary and Jimmy off safely." Nick smiled darkly. "Then I call the FBI."

Nick followed Derek to the airport. It didn't take long to get the plane loaded and ready to leave.

Mary walked over and hugged him good-bye. "Thank you for everything you've done, Nick. I don't know what would have happened to us if you hadn't been there to help."

"Just stay safe until this is over."

She nodded, turned and headed for the plane.

Jimmy stuck his hands in his pocket and stared down at his heavy leather boots. "I'm really sorry, Nick. I never meant for any of this to happen."

Nick draped an arm around the boy's shoulder. "None of this is your fault, Jim. You ran across some bad people. Bad people do bad things. With any luck we'll find them and bring them to justice."

Jimmy looked into his face. "Thanks, Nick."

"Take care of your aunt."

The boy just nodded. Whistling for Duke, he and his golden retriever ran for the plane.

Nick waited till the Cessna began to taxi down the runway, then headed back to the Explorer. Samantha was with Noah. No one knew where they were, and she'd be safe with his friend. Still, he couldn't completely relax until he was back at the lodge.

CHAPTER THIRTY-ONE

The disposable rang as Nick opened the car door and slid in behind the wheel. As the Cessna lifted off the runway, he dug the phone out of his pocket. "Brodie."

"It's me." Cord's voice came over the phone line. "You were supposed to call. What's going on?"

Nick's fingers tightened on the phone. "Maybe that's something I should be asking you."

"What the hell are you talking about?"

"You might want to make a trip up to your cabin. It's a little more ventilated than it was yesterday afternoon."

Silence fell. "What happened?"

"The Russians showed up. Shot up the place pretty bad. Got pretty well shot up themselves. I keep asking myself how they knew where to find us."

"Is everyone okay? No one got hurt?"

"Thanks to Derek and Jimmy, they're fine.

So you didn't tell anyone where we were?"

Cord fell silent again. This time, Nick could almost feel the wheels spinning in his mind. "Taggart was looking for you. He knows we're friends. Maybe he found out about the cabin. It wasn't a secret. Maybe he told someone and the Russians got wind of it. Hell, I don't know. But I sure as hell didn't say anything. You've got two women and a kid up there. Do you really think I'd do something that could get them killed?"

Nick scrubbed a hand over his face, blew out a weary breath. "No." Cord was his closest friend. Nick trusted him with his life. "And it makes an odd kind of sense that Taggart's involved. He always likes to see himself as smarter than everyone else. He could be feeding the Russians information, helping them stay one step ahead of the feds. There's big money in drugs and women. The payoff would be huge for that kind of help."

"I'm not sure I buy it, but I guess it's possible. I presume you've got everyone somewhere safe — and for now I don't want to know where that is."

Nick felt the pull of a smile. "They're safe."

"What are you going to do?"

"My next call goes to Charlie Ferrell. I'm

hoping he can step in and take charge, make this whole thing come together. I'm not a cop anymore and I don't want to be. I just want this over and everyone safe."

"Sounds good. If I find out anything useful, I'll let you know. If there's anything you need, call me."

"You got it."

As promised, Nick's next call went to Special Agent Charlie Ferrell. In the eye of his mind, he could see Ferrell's big hulking frame in a wrinkled black suit with his phone pressed against his ear. Late forties with salt-and-pepper hair, he and Nick had first met during a kidnap-murder investigation a few years after Nick had become a homicide detective.

They had worked together again on what had turned out to be Nick's last case, the brutal murder of a thirteen-year-old-girl by a serial killer. Nick had gained a deep respect for Charlie, who had taken the girl's death almost as personally as Nick had. Ferrell was a man Nick totally trusted.

After a few quick pleasantries, he cut to the chase. "I've got something for you, Charlie. It's got to do with the Fedorko investigation and it's big."

"I thought you were retired."

"I'm not retired. I'm just looking for

something to do besides get shot at."

"If you're dicking around with the Russians, it doesn't much sound like you've found it. How big are you talking about?"

"What I've got will break your case wide open. I think you've already connected Fedorko to Bela Varga. You also know both of them work for Luka Dragovich. I've got enough to bring Bela Varga down. Good chance he'll roll on Fedorko. Get them both, you might even snare Dragovich."

Charlie fell silent. "Sonofabitch," he finally said.

"There's a catch."

"Always is."

"I've got the information you need but I want something in return."

He grunted. "So what have you got and what do you want for it?"

"I've got Varga's log book, showing dates, names, and places of some of the girls his men have abducted. Mostly Native girls, a lot of them are underage. He's running kids, Charlie. The guy is the scum of the earth."

"Worse, as far as I'm concerned."

"I've also got a flash drive that connects the dots between Dragovich and money laundering through international banking accounts. On top of all the other goodies, I've got a witness. One of Bela Varga's women. She was abducted when she was twelve years old."

"Holy shit."

"Exactly. Listen, Charlie. The girl has a ten-year-old daughter. She's terrified Bela Varga will force the kid into the life. She wants safety for herself and her little girl. She wants to start over. I told her we could make that happen. In the meantime, she and the kid need protection."

"That's it?"

"Just get the girl and her daughter somewhere safe until this is over. Once it is, you can put her in WITSEC or we can connect her with a group that'll help her start a new life somewhere else."

"When can you bring her in?"

"The sooner the better. The Russians are breathing down my neck. People are in danger. I need to make this end."

"Pick a time and place, and we'll be there."

Relief filtered through him. "Expect to hear from me by tomorrow."

"You got it."

Nick signed off and shoved the phone back into his pocket. The moment Carol called, he could put the plan in motion. He hoped to hell she called soon.

■ ■ ■ ■

Snug in the cozy cabin Noah had assigned them while she waited for Nick, Samantha sat in front of her laptop, set up on a knotty pine desk as yellow as the sun. The log cabin was rustic but charming, with a pine bed and dresser, and a wrought-iron lamp with a parchment shade.

Clicking up her e-mail, she began reading the replies she had received from the last batch of mail she'd sent. The first came from her mother.

Hi, honey. How are you? I've tried to call, but your phone keeps going to voice mail. Are you sure everything is okay?

Guilt slipped through her. She and her mother had always been close but the pregnancy had thrown her. She didn't want to talk about it over the Internet or on the phone. There were too many emotions involved, too much she needed to explain. She'd have to wait until they were face-to-face, which with any luck would be fairly soon.

Her heart squeezed. Going back to San Francisco would give her the chance to explain things to her family, but it would

426

also mean leaving Nick. It was going to be one of the hardest things she'd ever had to do.

Shoving the unwanted thought aside, she typed in her reply.

Everything okay here. Just extremely busy right now. Sorry, my phone isn't working right. I'm trying to get it fixed. I'd really like to come see you and Dad as soon as I can get time away from work. Till then, I'm missing you both. Love, Sam.

She punched the Send button and watched the message wing off into cyberspace.

Abby's e-mail was simple and straight to the point.

No more bullcrap, Sam. What's going on?

She smiled and started typing.

Hiding from the Russian mob. Been in two shoot-outs, one where a man was killed. Oh, by the way, I'm in love with Nick and leaving him is going to break my heart.

With a sigh, she went back and deleted the message. Typed in:

Staying in a quaint mountain cabin. Can't say I like Alaska, which is bun-freezing cold, gray, and snowy, but the scenery is fantastic and things are never dull. How are you and Mr. Tall-blond-and-handsome? He still in the running for stud of the year?

The reply came right back, which meant Abby was in front of her machine.

Mr. Tall-blond-and-handsome has a new name. Mr. Tall-blond-and-shitty. He is out of the running, for sure. Can't wait for you to meet Luke.
He's really great. Gotta go. Dogs calling.
Ab.

Typical Abby. She specialized in man-trouble and never seemed to tire of the game. Samantha wished she was close enough to get one of Abby's great, everything-is-going-to-be-okay hugs. But Abby wasn't there and the problems that she and Nick, Jimmy and Mary were facing weren't going to be solved with a simple hug.

She answered a few more messages, including one from her brother, Peter, telling her more about his current lady love. She warned him not to blow it and told him to have fun.

After she finished her mail, she did a few basic yoga routines, just to start getting her body back in shape, then went back to doing what she did best, digging around on the Internet.

Facebook and all the other social media held a treasure trove of information. If she looked long enough, dug deep enough, there was always something out there to find.

The tiny cabin at Salmon Lake Nick shared with Samantha was beginning to feel claustrophobic. Pacing back and forth, he waited impatiently for the call from Carol Johnson. It didn't come until after supper, a meal of roast moose, potatoes, and carrots. Since Samantha had been cooking, the food had been delicious and Noah had been impressed.

Now that supper was over, they were back in the cabin, Nick lying on the bed, trying not to think about seducing Samantha, at least not until after the call he was waiting for. Relief hit him when the phone started ringing. He dug the disposable out of his pocket and pressed it against his ear. "Brodie."

Across the room, Samantha glanced at him expectantly. She looked so pretty, he felt an ache in his chest. He forced himself to concentrate on the call.

"Nick, this is . . . Carol Johnson. Evie and I . . . we're ready whenever you are."

Finally. "How about tomorrow afternoon?"

"That would work. Connie's out of town, so he won't be expecting me to come over tomorrow night. You've got things set up?"

"I've arranged for you to be taken into FBI protective custody."

"All right. Where are we meeting them?"

"A café near the Eagle's Nest." He figured she'd be okay with the location since she had arranged the first meet. "That work for you?"

"Yes. Will you be picking us up? I don't trust anyone else."

"I'll be there. What's your address?"

Carol rattled off an address just a few blocks from the café, probably the reason she had picked the bar for their first meeting.

"I'll be there at one thirty," Nick said. "I'll be driving a black Ford Explorer."

"All right, we'll be ready."

"And Carol . . . ?"

"Yes?"

"Everything's going to be okay."

He heard the slight catch in her voice. "I'll see you tomorrow," Carol said softly, and the call ended.

Nick punched in the number for Charlie Ferrell. "We're on for tomorrow. Two o'clock." He'd given it a lot of thought. He preferred daylight so he could keep an eye on their surroundings.

"Where?"

"There's a little café on Wayburn. Marty's. It's a locals' joint."

"I know where it is."

"There's a parking lot on the right. Nice and open. There's usually people around so we shouldn't stand out, but not too many. We'll be able to tell if any uninvited guests show up."

"Sounds good. I assume you'll be bringing the book and the flash drive."

"I'll have them with me. Look for my black Explorer." Nick hung up the phone. Setting the disposable on the nightstand, he walked over to Samantha, who rose and went into his arms.

"Is everything ready?" she asked as he nuzzled the side of her neck.

"Should be."

She drew back to look at him, reached up and smoothed the frown lines from his forehead. "Then why are you still worried?"

His mouth edged up. She was beginning to know him too well. "Old habit, I guess.

I'll stop worrying once Carol and Evie are safely in FBI custody." He bent his head and very softly kissed her. "In the meantime, let's go to bed."

Samantha slipped her arms around his neck and kissed him, long, hot, and deep, making him instantly hard. "Good idea," she whispered, kissing him again.

Though making love to Samantha would help take his mind off Carol and her daughter, two o'clock tomorrow couldn't come soon enough for Nick.

CHAPTER THIRTY-TWO

The mid-October afternoon was dreary, a leaden sky hanging low on the horizon, an icy wind sweeping down off the snow-capped mountains in the distance. Near the outskirts of Anchorage, a sleeting rain began to fall and Nick turned on his windshield wipers.

He was anxious to pick up Carol Johnson and her daughter, hand them over to the feds for protection. Once word of the evidence against Bela Varga and Fedorko got out, there would be no need to worry about Jimmy's safety, no reason for the mob to go after him or Mary.

The nav system in the Explorer directed Nick to the address Carol had given him. He spotted a small figure at the window as he pulled up in front of her first-floor apartment, a four-unit stucco building with patches of snow on the lawn in front.

An instant later, the curtains fell closed,

the front door opened and Carol appeared, looking even smaller and more vulnerable than he remembered. With a quick survey of the area, Nick got out of the Explorer and headed up the sidewalk to her porch.

Carol motioned him inside the apartment, which was neat and clean, furnished simply with a tweed sofa and two matching chairs. Inexpensive framed posters of Alaska hung on the walls. A wheeled carry-on sat on the plain beige carpet next to a smaller wheeled bag with pink-and-purple hearts on the front.

"This is Evie," Carol said. "Evie, this is Mr. Brodie. He's here to help us."

"Hello," the girl said shyly. She was petite like her mother, with Carol's same shiny black hair and almond eyes, but her skin was lighter, her features more refined, evidence of a Caucasian father. Even as young as ten, it was clear the girl would turn into an exotically beautiful young woman. In a year or two, as her figure began to blossom, she'd be every pervert's sick fantasy.

Nick's jaw tightened. He forced himself to smile. "Hello, Evie. It's nice to meet you." He looked up at Carol. "We need to go."

Dressed in jeans and a dark blue cable knit sweater, Carol grabbed the handle of her carry-on while Evie took hold of the bag with the hearts on the front. "This is all we're taking."

Nick nodded his approval. He'd been worried they would try to take too much with them. He moved to the window, checked up and down the street but saw nothing that seemed to pose a threat. As he pulled open the door, his hand went to the Glock .45 in the holster on his hip, but aside from an occasional car rolling down the block, the street remained clear.

In minutes, the bags were loaded, Evie sat in the back with a seat belt fastened across her lap while Carol was belted into the passenger seat.

"We aren't going far," Nick said. "A place called Marty's Café."

"I've been there," Carol said. She managed to smile. "Evie loves their pancakes."

"I want to drive by first," he said, "make sure nothing looks hinky."

Carol's lips trembled, but she nodded. He could read her fear in the stiff way she sat, the way her gaze assessed the street outside the window. With the sleet continuing to fall, there weren't many people on the road. Few cars passed them as they rolled toward the restaurant.

The sign for Marty's Café appeared on a single-story building up ahead. Nick drove slowly past, spotting a few diners at tables on the other side of the gold lettering on the front window. He counted six cars in the parking lot, including an unmarked brown Dodge Charger. A plain dark blue Chevy Tahoe, another feebie favorite, sat at the curb across the street. Both were empty.

Two men stood at the edge of the lot, their collars turned up against the wind, hands shoved into their pockets. He recognized Charlie Ferrell as one of them. Two more agents were positioned partway down the block.

Nick breathed a sigh of relief. The feebies were there in force. Carol and Evie would be safe.

"Oh, my God, don't stop! I know one of those men!"

The terror in Carol's voice had him pressing on the gas, easing the car in between two others, turning when he reached the corner.

"Four of those men are agents, Carol. Did you see someone else?"

"The blond man. He was standing next to the big man at the edge of the parking lot. I saw him at Connie's. I saw them talking. I think he was someone on Connie's payroll. Oh, my God, Nick, I didn't know he was FBI."

"The big guy's Charlie Ferrell. He's a friend. Are you sure it was the man standing next to him? You need to be absolutely certain, Carol."

"I got a very good look at him that night. Blond hair, blue eyes, extremely well dressed and very good-looking. It was him. I'm absolutely sure."

Nick bit back the dirty word locked behind his teeth and kept on driving. He didn't stop till he reached the edge of the city, pulled over to the side of the road and phoned Ferrell.

"Where the hell are you, Brodie? We saw you drive by. We figured you were making a sweep, going around the block and coming back, but you never showed up. What the hell's going on?"

"Carol spotted a rat. I don't know his name but he was the blond guy standing next to you. She saw him with Connie Varga when she was staying at his house."

"Bullshit. That's Ford Sanders. I've known him for years."

"Snappy dresser, blond, blue-eyed and good-looking?"

"Shit."

"As I understand it, you've been one step behind Bela Varga and Fedorko for years. Maybe Sanders is the reason."

Charlie's voice came out hard. "If he is, you can bet I'll find out."

"I'm not bringing Carol in until I'm sure she'll be safe." Nick hung up the phone.

"Mom, what's happening?" Evie's frightened voice reached him from the backseat.

"It's okay, sweetie," Carol said, turning so she could talk to her daughter. "We just have to wait a little longer."

Nick wondered what explanation the woman had given the child about all of this. Whatever it was, Evie seemed to understand the two of them were heading for a new life somewhere else. When he glanced over at the woman in the seat beside him, she was silently crying.

"What are we going to do?" she asked.

Nick's jaw hardened. "For now, you and Evie are going to take a little vacation. There's a place I know you'll be safe."

A faint sob came from her throat.

"Charlie's a good man," Nick said. "He'll figure this out. We just have to wait until he does."

With that, Nick stepped on the gas, heading back to the Salmon Lodge. At least Noah would be happy. He was about to get more new business.

Samantha was getting bored. She had done

everything she could to come up with new information on Constantine Bela Varga or Dmitri Fedorko. Fedorko's wife, a woman named Helga, and his girlfriend, Heather Austin, had been her best hope. The only thing she'd come up with was their names.

Heather wasn't into social media as far as Samantha could tell, and Helga Fedorko only communicated with members of her immediate family. And all they talked about were their kids.

With a sigh, she turned off her laptop and rose from the desk. Outside the window, she could see Noah at work, his face gleaming with sweat as he swung a heavy wooden ax, splitting wood for the winter, tossing it into a stack off to one side. Some of the snow had melted, but the sky was iron gray, and there was still a layer of white on the ground.

She started to turn away, to pick up the mystery novel she had borrowed from Noah, anything to keep her mind off Nick and what was happening in Anchorage. The sharp echo of a gunshot had her whirling back to the window, gasping as the heavy ax slipped from Noah's big hand. She watched in horror as he crumpled slowly to the ground, a gusher of blood erupting from a wound on the side of his head.

Dear God, Noah! She started running, cried out as the door crashed open and two men burst into the cabin, both of them carrying big black, semi-automatic pistols. One was balding, short but wide, built like a tree stump, the other had brown hair and might have looked innocuous except for the blue ink tattoo of a spider's web on the side of his neck.

Fear shot through her. For an instant she stood frozen. Then she thought of the window in the bathroom, grabbed the lamp on the desk, picked it up and hurled it at the tattooed man's face, heard it crash on the floor as she flew past him across the room toward escape.

The short man rushed in front of her and slammed the door, blocking her way. Grabbing her wrist, he spun her around, shoved her arm up behind her back and pushed her into the middle of the room. Shaking all over, Samantha fought to control her terror, fought back the image of Noah lying on the ground, bleeding into the snow.

"Well . . . look what we have here." The tattooed man's voice held the trace of a Russian accent.

"Who are you?" She took a shaky breath, rubbing her wrist, determined to brazen it out. "What do you want?" What was hap-

440

pening to Noah? What would the men do to her?

The short man walked over to the laptop sitting open on the desk. "Looks like that new software the boss installed did the job," he said. No accent. Just a smug look on his puffy, dish-shaped face.

"What software?" she asked, but a sick feeling sank into the pit of her stomach.

The tattooed man stared down at her. "I believe it is called a Trojan horse. A smart girl like you must have heard of it. This one is new, a very sophisticated model, highly classified by the federal government. It goes on alert when someone trespasses in a place he should not be. It seeks out the intruder's server, then tracks backward until it finds the guilty party and uses GPS to relay his location."

Dear God forgive her, she had brought the men here with her digging. Her heart squeezed at the memory of Noah lying in the snow. She prayed she hadn't gotten him killed.

A dark smile played over the Russian's lips. "I believe it worked very well, would you not say, Ms. Hollis? It brought us straight to you."

Her head came up. "How do . . . how do you know my name?"

"It is quite amazing how easy it is to get information if one has enough money. You are Brodie's woman. Your man has caused us a great deal of trouble. But we are certain, once he knows you are with us, that trouble will end."

The room seemed to spin. Samantha fought for control. Nick would be back. She just needed to delay until he could get there. But what if she led him into terrible danger? What if they shot him the way they had Noah?

"Get her moving, Roman," the short man said. "We need to get out of here."

"Get your coat, my dear," the tattooed man, Roman, said. "We would not want you getting cold."

"What about Noah? At least let me bring him inside. He could freeze to death out there."

The short man barked a laugh. "It's a little late to worry about that." Grabbing her parka off the back of the chair, he tossed it in her direction. "Put it on, or we take you the way you are."

Fighting not to tremble, she stuck her arms into the sleeves of the hooded jacket and pulled it on. Roman jerked her in front of him and pushed her out the door. The broken lamp crunched beneath her feet.

Pretending to stumble, she reached down and picked up a jagged piece of glass, stuck it into her coat pocket.

There was nothing she could do as they dragged her toward the black sedan with its engine running in the parking lot.

A third man came down off the hill and ran toward the car, a rifle with a scope in his hand. As the short man shoved her into the backseat and slid in beside her, the third man popped the trunk, tossed the rifle inside, and slammed the lid.

He rounded the car to the driver's side while Roman got into the passenger seat. "Very nice shooting, Markov," Roman said to the driver. "Now let's go."

As the car drove away, a hard lump rose in Samantha's throat. She closed her eyes and started to pray, first for Noah, that by some miracle he would live. Then for herself. That God and Nick Brodie would find a way to save her.

CHAPTER THIRTY-THREE

The drive back to the Salmon Lodge finally came to an end. Nick pulled the SUV into the parking lot and turned off the engine. He and Carol got out, then Nick helped Evie out of the car.

Walking around to the back, he retrieved their two bags, and the book and flash drive he'd stowed in a small canvas satchel.

"We need to get you into one of the cabins." Leading them toward the registration office connected to Noah's log house, he walked up on the porch and pulled open the door. Not finding Noah inside, he left the luggage and led mother and child on into the living room. The fire had died and he didn't see anyone around.

"Noah!" he called out as he set the canvas bag on the dining table. "Noah, where are you?" When no answer came, unease filtered through him. He turned to Carol. "Stay here. I'll be right back." Pulling the Glock

444

from his holster, he headed through the house toward the cabins in the rear. Across the yard near the woodpile, Nick spotted Noah lying in the snow, the side of his head covered in blood.

Jesus, Noah! Adrenaline shot through him, slamming his pulse into high gear. Noah was down. Where was Samantha? Gripping the gun in both hands, he dropped behind the covered gas barbeque sitting on the back deck and scanned the area around the house.

Nothing. Keeping low, heart pounding like a hammer against his chest, he started for the steps, heard light feminine footsteps behind him, knew Carol had come to the back door.

"Oh, my God!" she cried, spotting Noah's bloody, unmoving body in the yard.

"Stay inside." Weapon in hand, Nick moved off the porch, heading for the little cabin where he had left Samantha. His stomach balled into a hard, tight knot at the thought of her bleeding or dead like Noah.

Nick pulled himself under control. It took sheer force of will to narrow his focus and go into the zone. Drawing on his years of training, he settled. Rock-solid calm now, he moved quietly toward the cabin next to the one he shared with Samantha, found nothing, checked the area around it, and moved back toward the little cabin.

As he neared the front door, he noticed it was open, standing slightly ajar. Dread curled in the pit of his stomach. Nick ignored it.

Flattening himself against the wall beside the door, he took a quick look through the window but saw nothing. Weapon at the ready, he turned, raised a booted foot, and kicked the door wide open.

A shattered lamp, glass shards scattered over the floor, the shade bent and lying next to the bed, but no sign of Samantha. He checked the bathroom, found nothing, took a deep steadying breath and fought to control a fresh round of fear. If they'd wanted Samantha dead, she would be.

She wasn't dead, she was alive and she needed him.

Nick steeled himself. He'd be no good to her if he didn't get himself under control. Forcing his mind back into the zone, he strode back to Noah, went down on one knee beside him. Carol Johnson knelt next to him, a kitchen towel in her hand, carefully wiping the blood from the side of his head.

"He's breathing," she said. "We need to get him inside, out of the cold."

Nick checked Noah's pulse, found it steady, took a look at the wound. "Gunshot. Probably a rifle. Doesn't look like the bullet pierced the skull." A theory confirmed by Noah's deep groan.

The big man stirred, tried to sit up. "Samantha . . ."

"Take it easy." Nick urged him to lie back down. "You've been shot. I think it's a graze, but we need to get you inside where it's warm."

"What about . . . Samantha?"

Nick's jaw hardened. He forced out the words. "They took her. Let's get you inside."

Together, Nick and Carol helped him get on his feet, up the back porch steps, and inside the house. They started for the bedroom, but Noah shook his head. "Living room. Warmer in there."

As they headed in that direction, Nick noticed the fire was blazing again and the heat had been turned up. "Good job," he said to Evie, who stood watching from a few feet away.

"We need to get him out of those wet clothes," Carol said. By now Noah was shaking so hard, his teeth were chattering. "Evie, honey, why don't you go get some blankets?"

The girl hurried out of the living room as

Carol started stripping off Noah's wet jacket and the flannel shirt beneath it. Evie returned a few minutes later with blankets she had taken off one of the beds, including a thick down comforter.

"He'll be warmer with nothing on," Carol said, eyeing the comforter.

She was right. Down worked best utilizing the body's own heat. With Carol's help, Nick got Noah out of his heavy work boots, jeans, and long underwear. They settled him on the sofa in his briefs and pulled the warm down comforter all the way up to his chin. The rest of the blankets were piled on top.

As Noah lay there with his eyes closed, Carol searched the medicine cabinet in the bathroom and came back with antibacterial ointment, gauze, and a wrap-around bandage. In minutes, she had the gash cleaned and dressed, and a bandage wrapped around his head. Noah hadn't moved.

Carol reached down and gently laid her palm on his forehead. "He's still ice cold." She pulled the comforter over his head so his breath would help warm him. "If you think it's necessary, I'll take off my clothes and get in there with him."

Noah's low rumble of mirth made both of them smile with relief. His head came out from beneath the comforter and dimples formed in his cheeks. Some of the color had washed back into his face. "As nice as that offer sounds, I don't think it'll be necessary."

"I guess you're feeling better," Nick said.

"I've got the mother of all headaches but I'm pretty sure I'll live. What about Samantha?"

The sound of her name pierced the barrier Nick had built around his emotions. He had to think clearly, had to stay focused if he was going to save her.

"Thanks to a rat named Ford Sanders, they know I've got the ledger and the flash drive. Until they get them, I don't think they'll hurt her."

But there was no way to be sure.

"Never saw it coming," Noah grumbled. "I must be out of practice."

"Sniper," Nick said. "If the guy had been a halfway decent shot, you'd be dead."

Noah grunted. Closed his eyes against the pain and let himself drift off.

Time seemed to crawl. While Noah dozed on the sofa, Nick paced back and forth in front of the fire, waiting for the call he was sure would come. He considered phoning Charlie Ferrell, but until he heard from the Russians, he didn't want to do anything that might get Samantha killed.

He was sure they would call, but it was nearly an hour before his disposable phone started to ring. Taking a slow, steadying breath, Nick pressed the phone against his ear. "Brodie."

"Nick . . . ?" The fear in Samantha's voice cut into his heart like a blade.

"I'm right here, baby."

"They . . . they shot Noah. Oh, God —"

Before she could finish the sentence, the phone was snatched out of her hand. A man's voice with a slight Russian accent came over the line. "As you just heard, we have something here that belongs to you."

Nick's fingers tightened around the phone. "You hurt her, you touch her, you're dead."

"Do not despair, my friend. Your lady is fine — at least for the moment. As I was saying before I was so rudely interrupted, we have something that belongs to you. And you also have something that belongs to me."

"I'm listening."

"Bring me the book and the disk. In exchange you will get your woman back. Oh, and of course you must bring the boy, Jimmy, and the woman, Crystal."

Nick's chest tightened. "Jimmy doesn't know anything. He saw one of your men at his house, that's all. He doesn't know the guy's name or anything else. Jimmy and his aunt are gone and they won't be back anytime soon."

Silence fell. "I thought that might be so. At times, my men can become overzealous. We'll leave the boy alone, but you must bring the woman." He chuckled, the grating sound running up Nick's spine. "The young girl, Evie, is worth a good deal of money to me, but as I sense there are limits to how far your conscience will allow you to go, you may keep the child. In all things, there are times concessions must be made."

Nick clamped down on the rage burning through him.

"Bring Crystal," the Russian said sharply. "The book and the disk, along with any copies you may have made. Take them to the Sunset Motel. I believe you know where it is."

Nick thought of the two women he and Cord had pressed for information. Lacey had tried to help Carol, but what about the woman who called herself Ruby? Had she betrayed Carol and Evie?

"I know where to find the motel," Nick said. "What time?"

"Nine o'clock tonight. And keep in mind that should you call in the authorities, a woman like your beautiful Samantha could be very useful to us. Perhaps she could take the place of my Crystal." His voice went hard. "Be there on time." The man hung up the phone. *My Crystal.* Had to be Constantine Bela Varga.

Nick turned to see Carol standing a few feet away, her face as pale as ash. Noah stood beside her, his massive chest bare, the blanket wrapped around his waist.

"She isn't going back to them," he said darkly, rightly guessing the Russian's intent.

Nick's features hardened. "Don't worry, we're going to give them something, but it isn't going to be Carol or anyone else." Pulling his Glock from its holster, he dropped the clip, checked the load, and shoved it back in. "It's five o'clock now. We've got four hours to come up with a plan."

Noah nodded grimly. "I need to put on some clothes."

"I'll help you." Carol draped one of Noah's powerful arms over her shoulder to steady him. Looking like the walking wounded, they headed off to his bedroom.

Nick thought of Samantha, the feelings for her that had grown deep and strong, how happy he was when he was with her. He closed his eyes, fighting to block any notion of what the Russians might be doing to her, and forced himself to concentrate on how he was going to get her back.

They needed help. There were people he trusted. It only took a moment to make his decision. His first call went to Cord Reeves.

Samantha huddled in the corner of the dingy motel room. Hands bound behind her, she shivered, though she was still wearing her hooded coat. Fear kept her adrenaline pumping. Fear for herself and for Nick. She knew he would come for her. Knew he would risk his life to save her. Standing up for others was a trait etched deep in the marrow of his bones.

Nick would come for her, but she didn't believe the Russians would let either of them live. The men had made no effort to hide their faces, though they knew Nick had been a police detective, not the kind of man who would look the other way once the exchange was made.

She glanced over at the other female occupant of the room, huddled next to her on the floor. The big Russian bruiser at the window had called her Lacey. From what Samantha could gather from snippets of conversation, a prostitute named Ruby had betrayed Lacey for trying to help Crystal and her daughter. Now Lacey was paying the price.

"Are you all right?" Samantha asked as a soft moan seeped from the blond woman's throat. The men had beaten her badly. Both her eyes were blue-black and puffed nearly closed, and her lips were cut and swollen. A trickle of blood oozed from her nose.

Lacey ducked her head and wiped the blood away with her shoulder. "They're going to kill us," she said, leaning her head back against the wall. "As soon as they get what they want, we're dead. Bull likes dishing out pain or he would have killed me already."

She recognized the name, Virgil Turnbull, one of the men who worked for Constantine Bela Varga. The Bull was out there now with the man called Roman, and the one named Markov, the man who'd shot Noah, ruthless men who would think nothing of killing them.

She tugged on the stiff rope binding her wrists and felt the bite of it cut into her skin. But while the guard had been staring out the window, she had twisted around enough to reach into her pocket and bring out the jagged piece of glass from the broken lamp in the cabin. Little by little, she was sawing through the rope, praying she would be able to get free before it was too late.

"Nick will come," she said to Lacey, ignoring the slick trickle of blood running through her fingers where she had accidentally cut herself. "You have to believe that."

"You're his woman. He'll come for you. I'm dispensable."

Samantha shook her head. "Nick isn't that way. He won't leave you behind."

Lacey snorted. "Have you looked around, Pollyanna? There are four of those big Russian goons out there, plus the one over by the window, and that short little fuck they call The Worm. And they've got enough guns to take on an army. Your man's as dead as we are."

Samantha's heart squeezed. She couldn't bear to think of Nick being wounded or killed. A memory arose of Noah Devlin on the ground, his lifeblood oozing into the snow. She said a prayer that he had somehow survived, took a deep breath and worked to summon her courage.

"I'm not giving up," she said, moving the glass shard back and forth. "You shouldn't either."

Lacey just scoffed. "You don't get it, do you? If these guys don't kill you, they'll use you. It won't be long before you'll wish you were dead."

If her hands had been free, Samantha would have covered her ears. She didn't want to hear Lacey's dire predictions. She had her whole life ahead of her. She didn't want to die. She had to stay positive, had to be ready to help when Nick came.

She tugged on the rope but it didn't budge. Samantha winced as the shard of glass sliced into her palm, but she kept on sawing at the rope.

CHAPTER THIRTY-FOUR

They sat in a group in front of the fire, Nick, Cord, Noah, and Derek. Weapons of every size and shape lay on the coffee table or the floor in front of them. Carol had put Evie in one of Noah's bedrooms, along with an iPad he had loaned her so the child could play games.

"So what have we got?" Nick asked, surveying the stockpile on the floor. Along with his Glock 21, he had a backup .38 Colt revolver and the KA-BAR knife he kept in the emergency gear box in the back of his SUV. If he'd had time to make the sixty-mile round trip to his house, he could have pulled a few more weapons out of the gun safe in his garage. But time was of the essence and the Russians were unpredictable. He didn't want to leave the others alone that long.

"I've got my Glock and my backup piece," Cord said. He used the same standard police issue as Nick, plus a .38 snub-nose. "I brought the thirty-ought-six and the Mossburg 12 gauge I keep up at the cabin."

Nick nodded. When he had phoned Cord, his friend had been at the cabin boarding up the broken windows from the recent firefight. Derek had been hammering nails beside him, saving Nick another phone call. Both men had immediately volunteered to help.

Derek reached down and picked up his Beretta nine mil, dropped the clip and checked the load. "I've got this little beauty and the H&K AR-15 I had with me up at the cabin."

"Nice," Noah said.

Nick's gaze swung in the big man's direction. "What about you?"

Noah lifted a pistol off the coffee table. "Nighthawk .45." He slid it into a holster and picked up another semi-auto. "H&K P30 nine mil." He holstered the weapon and set it on the table, reached down and hefted the automatic weapon on the floor at his feet. "AK-47 — little souvenir I picked up in Afghanistan."

Nick nodded. "Plus miscellaneous knives, a pair of tactical vests, and a couple of flash grenades. Not bad for spur of the moment."

"Since we've still got a little time," Noah

said. "Let's run through the plan once more." His head was still bandaged, but he seemed pretty much back to normal. This was good, because it was going to take all four of them to bring down the Russians and get Samantha out safely.

Nick looked at his watch. "Good idea." It was six thirty. Didn't get dark for another hour. They wanted to be there early enough to do recon and establish their locations, but not before it was dark enough that they wouldn't be seen.

They spread out the maps they had pieced together, one of them aerial views taken off Google Earth. The fact he and Cord had been to the motel helped them identify the best routes in and out, and where the Russians might have their men posted.

"We take three vehicles," Nick began. "Cord parks his pickup on this hill behind the building." He pointed to a spot on the map. "Noah parks his Durango on the lower road on the other side of the motel. I drive right up in front. When it's time to leave, if we can't get to one of the vehicles, we head for the others. If we have to leave one of them behind, that's better than not being able to get out. The keys will be on the floor under the driver's seat."

Cord pointed to a high point on a nearby

ridge. "I take my rifle and head up here, cover Nick from a distance."

Noah pointed out his position. "I locate to the north of the building, be ready to move to the east or west, depending on where the greatest threat appears."

"I hang back," Derek said. "Move in after Nick makes contact, cover him close up while he brings Samantha out."

"Once you have her," Noah said to Nick, "we all converge, cover both of you till you reach your vehicle or one of the others, then we get the hell out of Dodge."

"That's about it," Nick said. "We can only pray it goes down half as smooth as planned."

"Aren't you forgetting something?"

Nick looked up to see Carol standing at the foot of the stairs. "What would that be?" he asked as the men began smearing their cheeks with grease paint to camouflage their faces. All of them but him.

"Me," Carol said. "There's no way the exchange is going to happen if I don't go with you."

Nick started shaking his head. "No way. It's too dangerous."

"You want to know what danger is? Trying to live our lives with those bastards breathing down our necks. If this doesn't end now, tonight, Evie and I will never be safe."

"This is going to be hard enough without a woman along," Noah grumbled, staring at her, his forehead black with paint, black lines streaking down his cheeks.

"The odds of your getting close to them without me are slim and none, and all of you know it."

Since it was the truth, no one said a word.

"You men have risked your lives to help me and Evie," Carol went on. "This is something I have to do."

Derek looked over at Nick. "If we leave her in the car it might work. They'll see her and figure you're going to make the trade. You'll be able to use her as a bargaining chip."

"What about Evie?" Nick asked, pinning Carol where she stood. "What if something happens to you?"

"I talked to her. She's already in terrible danger. This is our chance to get out. We have to take it."

Nick glanced around at the men. Beneath the black stripes, their features were hard, but he could tell they were all in agreement. Not having Carol along was a problem they'd already discussed.

"All right, you go with us, but you stay in

461

the car. You don't get out under any circumstance. If I can't get back to you, one of the other men will. Can you do that?"

She nodded.

"One last thing." He looked at the others. "I called Charlie Ferrell."

Cord's eyebrows went up. "What the hell? Are you nuts?"

"I've worked with Ferrell. He's a straight shooter. He says they're playing Sanders, seeing where he'll lead them. But Sanders won't be told anything about tonight."

"I hope you know what you're doing," Cord said darkly.

"I know Ferrell." Nick's mouth edged up. "But just to be safe, I told him the meet was going down at ten."

Cord's face broke into a smile, and Noah boomed a laugh. The feds would undoubtedly show up early, so if the mission went off as planned, Ferrell and his agents would arrive just as Nick and the others were making their get-away with Carol and Samantha. They would be on their way back to the lodge, leaving the feebies to cover their withdrawal and pick up the pieces.

For the next few minutes, the men pulled on body armor, shoved guns into holsters and flash grenades into pockets. Nick glanced down at his watch. "You ready?" he asked Carol.

She grabbed her heavy jacket and pulled it on over the navy blue sweatshirt she was wearing with jeans and heavy boots. "I'm ready."

"Time to go. We need to do a little recon, then get into position."

Noah grabbed his AK-47. "Okay, boys," he said, shoving his big six-foot-five-inch frame up from the sofa, the black streaks on his face making him look like a monster from hell. "Let's roll."

Samantha shivered. The cuts on her hand still stung, but she hadn't bled much. By now it had dried into a dark brown stain. With luck, the men wouldn't notice. The glass shard had done its job. A final hard tug would break the rope around her wrists and she would be free. She'd be ready to move when the right moment came.

"What time is it?" Lacey asked from her place on the floor.

Samantha raised her head enough to see the red numbers on the digital clock on the nightstand. "Eight forty-five." She had heard the men talking, knew Nick would arrive at nine, bringing the ledger and the flash drive. She couldn't imagine him bringing Carol Johnson, handing her over to these cruel, vicious men.

"Almost nine," Lacey said.

The words had barely left the woman's mouth before the door swung open and two men walked in from outside, joining the ugly man at the window. She recognized the one with the spiderweb tattoo. *Roman.* The other man was equally tall, with a ruddy, pockmarked complexion. *Markov.* The man who'd shot Noah.

A shiver of fear ran through her. Whatever was going to happen was going to happen soon.

"Time to go, ladies," Roman said, hauling Lacey to her feet. "We will be leaving as soon as this is over."

Markov reached for her but Samantha shook him off and rose by herself. Lacey flashed Samantha a glance, her thoughts clear on her face. *This is it. They're gonna kill me and prostitute you.*

Samantha ignored her. Instead she went peacefully, letting Roman lead her out into the cold. The motel consisted of two rows of rooms, back-to-back, one row facing east, the other west. Lights lit the corridor beneath an overhanging porch that ran the length of both buildings.

The short man, The Worm, she thought with a dark tug of satisfaction, had been with Roman at the lodge. He stood just outside the door, next to a big man with thick shoulders, shaggy brown hair, and pig eyes. By the sound Lacey made when she saw him, Samantha knew he was The Bull.

She dragged her gaze away, fixed on one of the others. He was medium height and build, well-dressed in a long, gray overcoat, an expensive maroon cashmere scarf around his neck. He stood beneath the overhead light as if he had no reason to hide, as if there was no one in the world he was afraid of. Hard, gray eyes fixed on her face and a chill slid through her. The devil himself had eyes like those.

She knew without doubt the man was Constantine Bela Varga.

He ignored her as if she weren't there, turned and said something Samantha couldn't hear to one of his men. A fingernail moon cast dim gray light over the landscape. Enough to glimpse the Explorer parked on the street in front of the parking lot.

Her stomach cramped. Nick was there.

Her heart started pounding. She fought to keep from trembling. There was someone sitting in the passenger seat. Dear God, it had to be Carol. Seeing Lacey's battered face, Samantha could only imagine what the men would do to the woman who had betrayed her powerful lover, the devil who patiently waited to deal with her.

Samantha's gaze searched the darkness. Her heart squeezed as she spotted Nick, standing ten feet in front of the SUV, close enough to converse with the men, but not so close they could touch him.

He held a small canvas satchel in one hand, his other hand out of sight in the pocket of his coat. "The book and the disk are in the bag." He tossed it into the space between him and the other men. "The girl's handcuffed in the car. Let Samantha go and you can have her."

Samantha stared at him, unable to believe her ears. "Don't do it, Nick! They'll kill her!"

"Shut up or we'll kill you, too," The Bull warned. One of the men hurried over and picked up the bag, unzipped it and looked inside. "What about copies?" he asked.

"I didn't have time to make any," Nick said.

Samantha knew that wasn't true. Lisa Graham undoubtedly had a copy of the flash drive she had worked on, and Nick had said he'd copied the ledger. She shifted her thinking. Nick was planning something. She needed to stay alert, be ready to help him when the time came.

Roman shoved her forward. For a moment, she was afraid the rope would break too soon. "Here's your woman." Roman turned to the Russian with the pockmarked face. "Markov, go get the girl."

"Not until I have Samantha," Nick said. "Come to me, baby."

She started moving, her heart pounding so hard she could hear it in her ears. She took two steps before Roman fell in beside her, pressed his gun into her ribs. "Stop right here." He spoke to Markov over his shoulder. "Get Crystal out of the car."

Samantha looked at Nick. There was something in his eyes she had seen before. A darkness that seemed to well up inside him. He was in warrior mode. Nick was ready. Samantha prepared herself. Now was the time to move.

Nick recognized the determined glint in Samantha's eyes the instant before she jerked at the rope binding her wrists. The rope went flying, Samantha turned and shoved the big Russian as hard as she could and started running. Nick jerked his pistol out of his pocket, dove toward her, knocking them both to the ground, firing at the same instant. Two quick taps took the Russian down, the sharp reports followed by a barrage of gunfire from the men hidden around the motel backing him up.

His bullet hit the Russian square in the chest and he went down hard, his gun flying out of his hand, landing uselessly on the ground. Nick was back on his feet, firing off more rounds as he and Samantha raced for the cover of the SUV. Carol had ducked out of sight in the foot-well of the passenger seat to ride out the firestorm of lead filling the air around them.

The Explorer was only a few feet away. Nick grunted as a bullet slammed into his back, and he heard Samantha scream. Shots pinged off the SUV as they rounded the bumper and reached safety on the opposite side behind the front wheel.

"Nick!"

He could hear the fear in Samantha's voice. "I'm okay, baby, I'm wearing a vest." At her look of relief, he couldn't resist a quick hard kiss before he popped up and fired off a few more rounds.

A rifle shot from Cord's location took out one of the men. "That's Markov," Samantha said as the man rolled on the ground in pain, shouting obscenities in Russian.

Nick shoved her head back down. "Stay low and stay close," he commanded.

"The man in the gray coat is Bela Varga,"

she said, undeterred, as the Russian in the long, gray overcoat ducked out of sight in one of the motel rooms. Noah moved into position. The AK belched a stream of bullets, and the Russians scattered even more.

"What . . . what about Lacey?" Samantha asked. "We can't leave her here. They'll kill her."

Just then Derek moved, firing as he rounded the corner of the motel. Nick pounded the area with gunfire, laying down cover. Cord's rifle echoed from the hilltop. Noah fired a couple of bursts as Derek motioned to Lacey, who crouched in the corridor. He laid down cover fire as she ran toward him. Derek pulled her around the outside of the building to safety.

Gunshots erupted from every angle. Derek popped up, ripped off a stream of bullets from his AR-15. The Russians fired back, and a shot winged Derek, took him down to one knee. Clutching his shoulder, he ducked back out of sight behind the building.

Nick checked his watch. Nine thirty. Where the hell were the feds?

The fleeting thought occurred that maybe Cord was right, and Charlie was the turncoat. Then he heard the sound of a bullhorn, coming from the south end of the motel.

"This is the FBI! You're under arrest! Lay down your weapons!"

Their answer was a barrage of Russian gunfire. The perfect time, Nick figured, to make their escape. Ferrell knew they'd be bugging out. They just needed to get safely away.

Opening the rear door of the Explorer, he slid into the backseat, tugged Samantha in behind him, then climbed over into the driver's seat next to where Carol crouched in the foot-well and started the engine.

In minutes he was roaring down the hill, heading back toward the lodge. Two familiar sets of headlights fell in behind him. They were on their way home. The Russians would live or die, depending on the choices they made in the next few minutes. Samantha was safe. Carol and Lacey were safe. Derek needed medical attention, but they weren't far from the hospital.

Nick couldn't be sure it was over until he spoke to Charlie, but with luck, Bela Varga would soon be in FBI custody. The feds would have the evidence Nick had collected, and Carol would testify.

In the rearview mirror, Nick caught a glimpse of Samantha in the backseat, her face as pale as glass, her expression hard as steel. The lady was amazing. Nick wished he could hold her.

Instead, he drove up in front of the emergency room at Mat-Su Regional Medical Center, this time for a friend with a gunshot wound.

Thinking of the Russians who'd been shot full of holes, he figured the place would be doing a booming business tonight. At least the women were safe and Samantha was back with him where she belonged.

Nick almost smiled. He'd been in a shootout with half a dozen gangsters. Derek was wounded, Nick was sporting a bruise the size of Moscow, and he was back in front of the hospital emergency room.

Sometimes retirement could really be a bitch.

Chapter Thirty-Five

Derek's gunshot wound was a through and through. His shoulder had been patched up and he had been released. The doctors had kept Lacey overnight for observation. Nick hadn't realized how badly she'd been beaten until he'd seen her battered face in the lights of the emergency room.

He'd still been at the hospital when he'd gotten a call from Charlie Ferrell. According to Charlie, the Russians who came out of the shoot-out alive were all in custody. In a show of bravado, Connie Bela Varga had taken on the feds and gone down in a burst of gunfire. He'd landed flat on his back with a bullet in his chest and one in his leg, but the bastard was still breathing.

Tomorrow, Ferrell and a couple of FBI agents would arrive at the Salmon Lodge to bring Carol and Evie into protective custody.

Until then, Nick and the rest of the group

were all spending the night at the lodge.

It was two o'clock in the morning when they sat in Noah's living room, the guys still too jacked up to sleep. Carol was upstairs with Evie, but Samantha sat next to him on the sofa. Nick wasn't ready to let her get more than a few feet away.

A nice fire roared in the big stone fireplace. Maybe eventually, they'd all calm down enough to go to bed.

"Since I've been shot at twice today," Noah said, "I figure I deserve to know how all this came down."

Cord took a sip of his coffee. "I think you owe him that much," he said to Nick as Samantha brought out a fresh pot of coffee and refilled everyone's cups. He glanced back over at Noah. "Though I warn you, it's complicated."

Noah shrugged his massive shoulders. "Hell, it's only two a.m. The bars don't even close till five."

Nick smiled. "It all began with Jimmy. The kid who lives next door to me." He explained about the boy's belief that his father had been murdered, how the mob had figured he knew more about his dad's death than he actually did and come after him.

"They tried to scare him away. When that didn't work, they set his house on fire,

473

destroying any evidence at the crime scene."

"How did you get the flash drive?" Derek asked.

"Samantha got into the client accounts in Alex Evans's office. She downloaded the info. Being a friend and a CPA, Lisa Graham took a look, discovered Evans had been laundering money for Luka Dragovich. He's one of the top people in the Russian mob."

Noah whistled.

Nick explained about his trip to Fairbanks, accidentally getting the feds involved, and trying to convince Taggart to start an investigation into Evans's murder.

Nick told them about the connection between Bela Varga, Fedorko, and Dragovich, how the Russians were running drugs and trafficking underage girls.

"Of course, Taggart, wanting to big-deal it, blew me off," Nick said darkly.

"After that, things went rapidly downhill," Cord added.

"So how did they find out the kid was at your place?" Noah asked.

"Taggart wanted me to bring Nick in for questioning," Cord said. "Apparently he or someone in the department found out I had a cabin up near Hatcher's Pass. Since Nick and I are friends, whoever it was must have figured there was a good chance Nick had stashed the boy there."

"Which means either Taggart or someone in the department got that information to the Russians," Nick added. "Most likely through Ford Sanders, the dirty fed."

"So Ford also passed them the info about the disk," Noah said, "along with the ledger and the witness, Carol Johnson."

"Which led to one helluva firefight tonight," Derek finished, unconsciously rubbing the wound in his shoulder.

There was a lot more to it, of course, but Nick figured those were the basics, and it *was* two in the morning.

"Just one more question," Noah said. "How did they know you were here at Salmon Lake?"

"I don't know, unless . . ." Nick's head came up. "Jesus, every time I looked up, Samantha was digging around on her computer. Maybe they tracked her here."

"That's exactly what they did," Samantha admitted, regret stamped all over her pretty face. "They told me they used some new kind of Trojan horse. I'm really sorry, Noah."

"Not your fault, honey. None of this is anyone's fault but the bad guys'."

Nick reached over and caught her hand, brought it to his lips. Even at two in the morning, after brawling with the Russians, she looked good enough to eat. Nick didn't dare let his mind wander in that direction.

She smiled at Noah, and Nick read the relief in her face. And the exhaustion. Earlier he had cleaned up the mess in the cabin, hoping to ease some of Samantha's bad memories when he brought her back.

He stood up from the sofa, took her hand and pulled her up with him. "I think it's time we all went to bed. The feds will have a thousand questions tomorrow. In the meantime, we could all use a little sleep."

And he wanted nothing more than to climb in bed with Samantha, hold her close, feel the beat of her heart next to his and know she was safe.

He didn't need more than that. At least not tonight.

Monday finally arrived. Nick was back in his house and, damn, it felt good to be there. It was late afternoon. Special Agent Charlie Ferrell sat in the living room. He was a few inches shorter than Nick's six-foot-two, a big, bulky man, and solid beneath his slightly rumpled black suit.

"You were right," Charlie said from where he sat in a comfortable overstuffed chair. "Bela Varga rolled on Fedorko. Fedorko's singing some song-and-dance about false arrest, but there's a good chance he'll roll on Luka Dragovich to save his own ass. Varga and Fedorko are both facing felony charges of aggravated promotion of prostitution and sexual abuse of children, along with a laundry list of other charges a mile long."

"What about Ford Sanders?"

"So far he's lawyered up and keeping his mouth shut, but it's only a matter of time. Thanks to Carol Johnson, he's going down, one way or another." Charlie smiled. "She and Evie are doing great, by the way. We've placed them both in WITSEC. The marshals have taken them somewhere out of state; even I don't know where. They'll fly her back to testify if they need her, but by then she'll be established somewhere new. I think she's going to be okay."

"That's nice to hear," Samantha said from beside Nick on the sofa.

"What about the dirty cop in the Anchorage PD?" Nick asked. "He's gotta be the guy who tipped Sanders off to the location of Cord's cabin. Have they found the bastard yet?"

"Not yet, but Internal Affairs is leaning hard on anyone who knew anything about the case. Sooner or later, we'll find him."

"My money's on Taggart."

Charlie grinned. "Yeah, I remember how much you liked the captain when we were working that serial together."

"Guy's a real dick."

"Doesn't mean he's dirty. But if he is, he's finished."

Nick grunted. "Couldn't happen to a nicer guy."

Ferrell laughed and stood up from his chair. "I've got to go. Last night we made multiple raids on Dragovich's motels. We rounded up a batch of those young girls. With their help, we'll find the rest of them. We'll get the girls back home or somewhere safe."

"That's really good news," Samantha said, also rising.

"Thanks for everything, Charlie." Nick and Ferrell shook hands.

Samantha walked over, went up on her toes and kissed Charlie on the cheek. "Thank you."

"Just doing my job," Charlie said, his face a little red.

"Stay safe," said Nick.

Charlie smiled. "You, too."

Nick watched the man head out the door, turned and pulled Samantha into his arms. "It's over, honey. Now our lives can get back to normal."

Samantha looked up at him. "Haven't you figured it out yet, Nick? For you, that was normal."

He frowned. "What are you talking about? I'm not a cop anymore and I don't want to be."

"You're not a cop. Not in the literal sense. But what you did for Jimmy and Mary, for Carol and Evie — that's what you do. Investigating, protecting, solving crimes. It's in your blood and you're really good at it. That kind of work is what calls to you. You might think it isn't what you want, but I think it is. I think you loved every minute of what we were doing."

Nick reached out and caught her shoulders. "I didn't love putting you in danger. I didn't love seeing you with that big Russian's gun stuck in your ribs."

Samantha just shrugged. "There are hazards to any job." She smiled. "Besides, you saved me, didn't you?"

Thinking of those moments, he shifted against the ache in his back where that bullet had pounded into his tactical vest. "When I realized those thugs had taken you from the lodge . . . Jesus, Samantha, I never want to feel that way again."

She gazed up at him and something

shifted, darkened in her features. Her big brown eyes filled with tears. "You won't have to, Nick. You won't have to worry about me again. It's time for me to go home."

"No." He shook his head, feeling as if someone had just turned the room upside down. "We haven't talked. We need more time. We need to work things out."

She wiped at the tears that started rolling down her cheeks. "I have to go home. It's time, Nick. Past time if you want the truth. Talking isn't going to change anything. I have to leave. I need to be with my family, my friends. I've already arranged my flight. I leave at eleven forty-five in the morning."

Nick drew her closer, wrapped his arms around her. "I don't want you to go, baby. Not yet."

For an instant, she hung onto him and his world seemed to right itself. Then she pressed her hands against his chest and eased away.

"Try to understand, Nick. I have to do this. Don't make it harder than it is already." Reaching up, she touched his cheek, leaned up and kissed him, then turned and walked off down the hall.

Nick watched her small figure disappear into the guest room. Samantha was leaving.

Inside his chest, his heart felt like fifty pounds of lead. Finding enough air to breathe seemed an insurmountable task.

And yet he knew she was right. Samantha couldn't be happy in Alaska. And he sure as hell couldn't make it in San Francisco. Add to that, they were nothing at all alike.

Nick grabbed his jacket off the back of a chair and strode to the door. Maybe the cold would ease the ache in his chest. He hoped so. Nick walked out on the porch and stepped into the cleansing air of a chill Alaska day.

It was Tuesday. Today she was leaving. Samantha rolled her wheeled carry-on out into the living room. Last night's TV news had predicted a new storm coming in. She said a silent prayer that her plane would be in the air well before the weather changed for the worse.

She tried not to think of the turbulent flight back to San Francisco, and instead concentrated on how good it was going to feel to be back home. She hadn't seen her mother in weeks, hadn't talked to her parents in what seemed ages. She hadn't even told her best friend about her terrifying adventures in Alaska.

She hadn't mentioned that she had fallen

head over heels in love with Nick and that leaving him was tearing her in two.

There was so much she needed to say. So much heartbreak to get past. So much healing she needed to do.

As much as she had wanted to spend her last night in bed with Nick, she had stayed in the guest room, unable to fall asleep. Her heart was breaking. Every moment she spent with him only made her feel worse.

Since the moment she'd told Nick she was leaving, he had barely said three words. They had eaten in silence, then gone to bed early. Her flight was leaving at just before noon. After a stop in Portland, she'd be back in San Francisco by eight o'clock tonight. Back in her own home, back in her own bed, back in her own life.

Tears welled, burned behind her eyes. She was leaving so much behind. The baby she once hadn't wanted and then had come to love. The man she had fallen in love with and would miss for the rest of her life.

"Are you ready?" The sound of Nick's voice made her heart squeeze.

She pasted on a too bright smile. "I'm ready."

Nick grabbed her carry-on and tugged it out back to where his Explorer sat in front of the garage. Tossing the suitcase into the back, he opened the passenger door and helped her climb inside.

The ride to the airport was solemn. There was so much left to say and nothing important she would risk saying.

She struggled to find a neutral topic. "If I remember, you're supposed to have a big job coming up. Something Cord found for you before I arrived. Something to do with protecting a big, corporate executive?"

He nodded but didn't glance her way, just kept his beautiful blue eyes on the road. "That's right. Bill Foley's the CEO of Great Northern Petroleum. He's bringing his family up to look around. He's been spending so much time in Anchorage, he's thinking of buying a second home in the area."

"So you'll be guarding his family?"

He nodded. "His wife and two kids."

She thought of everything he'd done for Jimmy, the way he had risked himself to protect her. "They're lucky to have you," she said softly.

Nick turned the wheel and pulled the Explorer onto the shoulder of the road. He jammed the car into park, caught her shoulders and dragged her across the console into his lap, kissed her long and deep. Samantha felt a rush of heat and a constriction in her heart that made her ache all over.

"I don't want you to go," Nick said. "I want you to stay here with me."

She was trembling. She knew he could feel it, but she couldn't manage to stop. Dear God, she loved him so much. "Nick, please don't . . ."

A long sigh whispered out. Nick kissed her softly one last time and set her gently back down in the passenger seat. "I understand. I really do. I just . . . I wish things could be different."

Her throat ached. She wanted to tell him she loved him so badly, she had to press her lips together to hold back the words. If she told him, he'd push her even harder to stay.

But the straight truth was, if she stayed it would only make both of them unhappy. If not now, then six months from now, or a year. Sooner or later, the differences between them would ruin both their lives.

Nick settled back in the driver's seat and pulled the car out on the road. They didn't talk again until she was standing in the terminal, checked-in and ready to go through security, where Nick couldn't follow.

"I'll call you when you get home," he said.

She just nodded.

"E-mail me, okay? Let me know you're all right?"

Another brief nod. She couldn't take much more. She reached up and cupped his cheek, looked into his dear, handsome face, went up on her toes and pressed a last desperate kiss on his beautiful mouth.

"I'll never forget you, Nick Brodie." Fighting a fresh round of tears, she grabbed the handle of her carry-on and ran for the security gate. She was on her way home.

Samantha couldn't stop crying.

CHAPTER THIRTY-SIX

Nick had never been so eager to begin a new job. He was going stir-crazy sitting around the house. Being there without Samantha just felt wrong. Every time he looked at the curtains over his kitchen window, his chest squeezed so hard it hurt.

Sensing his dark mood, Cord had come over last night. They'd sat up drinking beer till midnight, then Cord had fallen asleep on the sofa.

Feeling groggy and out of sorts, Nick wandered into the kitchen the next morning and made a pot of coffee. As the aroma of the dark brew drifted into the living room, Cord roused himself. Nick heard the sound of bare feet padding toward the kitchen.

Cord yawned and raked a hand through his dark blond hair, making it stand on end. He was wearing his jeans, but his chest was still bare.

Nick didn't look any better in his brown terrycloth robe, a heavy beard along his jaw from two days without shaving. Worse yet, he'd had one of his bloody nightmares last night, something that had only happened once the entire time he'd been with Samantha.

"Do me a favor," Cord said with another yawn. "Shoot me and put me out of my misery."

Nick just grunted, poured a cup of coffee, and handed it to his friend.

"I look bad," Cord said, "but you look worse. I just have a hangover. You've got the dog-sick look of a man in love."

Nick's stomach churned. There was no use denying it. "You're right. I figured that out when I saw her standing next to that big goon with his gun pressed into her ribs." He took a long drink of his coffee.

"So why don't you do something about it?"

"Because it wouldn't work. Samantha hates it here and I sure as hell don't want to live in San Francisco. Aside from that, we're about as different as two people can get. Can you imagine Samantha on a fishing trip or flying into the wilderness to camp for the weekend?"

"No. I can't see that happening." Cord

scrubbed his head, then finger-combed his hair. "But somehow the two of you just seemed to fit."

They fit all right. In bed. Which was exactly what had gotten him into trouble in the first place. "Like I said, it wouldn't work. Now drop it, will you?"

"Take it easy, okay? I was just trying to help."

"You helped me get a job. I start in a couple of hours, by the way."

"You're right. Best way to forget a woman is to get your ass back to work."

"Exactly. Which reminds me, I need to get going."

Cord downed his coffee. "I've got to get on the road myself. You know, if you like the job, you might be able to hire on permanently, if that's what you want."

Was it? He didn't have a clue. "I'll think about it." But at the moment all he seemed able to think about was Samantha and how much he missed her.

Nick downed his coffee, waved good-bye to his friend, and headed for the shower. Maybe work would get his mind off the woman he couldn't have and help him start putting his life back together.

Nick wished he could make himself believe it.

■ ■ ■ ■

After a weekend trip to visit her parents in Sacramento, Samantha was back in her apartment. She had cleared the air and her conscience, told her family about Las Vegas and meeting Nick, summoned her courage and told them about the baby and how terrible she'd felt when she had lost it.

She'd told them about her grand Alaskan adventure, about being shot at, being abducted and held by the Russian mob. About how Nick Brodie had risked his life to save her.

"I don't know whether to shake the man's hand for saving your life," her father said darkly, "or shoot the sonofabitch for putting my little girl in that kind of danger."

Samantha laughed. It had happened so rarely since her return, the sound came out rusty. "Nick's a wonderful man, Daddy. I'll never meet anyone like him again."

She went on to tell them how protective he was, how smart and brave. How he'd sat by her side in the hospital, devastated because she had lost the baby. When she looked over at her mother, Isabel Hollis was frowning.

"Are you sure you're talking about a man

and not some super hero?"

Samantha smiled. "I didn't make him up. He's more than real, I assure you."

Her mom, a slightly taller, more buxom version of herself, with the same light brown hair, watched her closely. "Listening to you talk about him, it sounds very much like you're in love with him."

Samantha's heart squeezed. She fought the burn of tears. "It doesn't matter, Mom. We're just too different to ever make it work. We both agree about that."

Her mother reached over and caught her hand. "Oh, honey, I'm so sorry."

Samantha went into her mother's arms. She found herself crying and couldn't seem to stop. Her father, a mild-mannered man with a better-than-average understanding of women, quietly excused himself, leaving them alone.

"I love him," Samantha said. "I think I'll always love him." Her mother wiped away a tear of her own and held her daughter tighter.

She'd recover, Samantha knew. Broken hearts didn't kill you. You just wished you were dead.

On Saturday, she and her mom went shopping at the Arden Fair Mall, where they met her brother Peter for lunch at Seasons

52. Mostly Peter talked about his girlfriend, Heather, and the happier he seemed to be, the worse Samantha felt.

She left for home early Sunday morning. At least she had settled things with her mom and dad. And once she went back to work, she told herself, she could begin to get over Nick.

Nick stood next to a black Cadillac SUV with the words ANCHORAGE LIMOUSINE printed in gold on the side. The limo was there, along with him and another bodyguard, to haul Bill Foley's wife and kids around Anchorage.

Susan Foley was midthirties, dark-haired and attractive. Her daughter, Sarah, four years old, had dark brown hair like her mom, but it lay in rowdy curls all over her head. The little boy was three, chubby, and constantly grinning. They were great kids.

Nick felt a pang whenever he looked at them. By this time next year, he could have had a kid of his own. He could have been a father. For the first time in his life, he realized he wanted a family. A wife and kids like Bill Foley's. It wasn't going to happen anytime soon.

Nick moved away from the vehicle, his gaze searching the landscape, surveying the area around the house the Realtor was showing Bill's wife, a big, expensive log home on a small, private lake that came with the property.

His partner, Roy Wilson, was inside with the family. Nick took another lap around the house, checking the perimeter, but the area was secure.

The early winter storm that had dogged his days with Samantha had been replaced by a forty-five degree, brilliantly sunny day. Nick looked up at the clear blue sky and silently cursed his bad luck. The good weather didn't do him any good now that Samantha was gone.

The kids ran out of the house, followed by Susan, then Roy. Bill loved his family. Along with the billions he was worth came any number of threats to his wife and children. Bill was careful where they were concerned and Nick didn't blame him.

He opened the door of the SUV, and the kids climbed into the far backseat. Roy got in front with the driver, and Nick slid in after Susan.

"Beautiful house," he said, just to make conversation.

"Gorgeous." Susan looked at the log home through the windows as the limo drove away. "But we'd only be using it in the summer. It's just too hard living up here in the winter."

Thinking of Samantha, Nick settled back against the seat. "Yeah. Alaska definitely isn't for everyone."

"No, it really isn't. Bill loves it though. Me, I don't know. Summer would be okay, I guess."

"It's really pretty in summer," Nick said. But his mood had soured for the rest of the day.

A week later, the family left to return to their home in Seattle, and Nick was once more out of a job. Worse yet, now that he had spent time with the Foley kids, he felt Samantha's loss even more.

To make matters worse, every time he called, her cell phone went straight to voice mail. He left messages asking her to call him back, but so far, he'd had no word. No e-mail he'd sent had been answered. Nothing.

Clearly Samantha was avoiding him. She didn't want to see him, and knowing she was probably right to make a clean break didn't make him feel any better.

He was sitting on the sofa in his living room, brooding and feeling sorry for himself, when a familiar knock came at the door. Since it wasn't locked, his brother

Rafe walked into the living room.

"What's going on?" Rafe said.

"What do you mean?"

"Every time I call, you're too busy to talk. You've got one excuse after another. I figured the only way we were going to have a conversation was for me to drive up from Valdez."

Nick didn't bother to get up from the sofa. "Fine. You're here. Go ahead and talk."

Rafe grunted. "So I'm not imagining things. You're avoiding me, and I have a feeling it has something to do with Samantha Hollis. Right?"

"So what?" he growled. "She had to go home. We both knew she'd be leaving in a couple of weeks."

Rafe set his hands on his hips and glowered down at him. "I told you not to do anything stupid. Obviously you didn't listen."

Irritation trickled through him. He was the youngest Brodie, but he hadn't let either of his brothers talk to him that way in years. "What do you want?"

"I want to know why you let her go. Clearly you're in love with her. Did you bother to tell her that?"

Nick shot to his feet. "Dammit, Rafe, this isn't any of your business."

"Since you aren't denying it, I assume it's true. You're in love with Samantha Hollis. Crazy in love from the hangdog look on your face."

Nick glanced away. He loved her. He just couldn't have her.

His brother sat down in the chair and Nick sank back down on the sofa. "You can fix this, you know," Rafe said, the harshness gone out of his voice. "It isn't too late."

Nick sighed. Clearly the only way he was going to get his brother to leave him alone was to tell him the truth. "All right, fine, you want to talk? Here it is. I'm in love with Samantha. I'd marry her in a heartbeat if I thought there was a snowball's chance in hell she'd say yes. She won't. She hates it up here. She's a homemaker, not an adventurer. She doesn't like any of the things I like to do. Get it?"

Rafe seemed unconvinced. "That's it? The two of you are different?"

"That's plenty, don't you think?"

Rafe's deep voice softened even more. "Samantha is everything you've ever wanted in a woman, Nick. I can't believe you haven't figured that out."

"What are you talking about?"

"Ever since Mom died, you've wanted a home. A real home with a family of your own. It was one of the reasons you joined the Rangers. You wanted to belong. The Rangers were your family. Some of them still are."

"That's crazy. I had you and Dylan. I had a great dad."

"Four men living in a house together isn't the same and you know it. I knew Samantha was the woman for you when I walked in here and saw those curtains at your window. You loved them. I could see it in your face. You liked that she had done that, helped you make the place feel cozy. You liked that she cooked for you, that she made your house into a home. And you wanted that baby she was carrying. You can't deny it, Nick."

His chest tightened. Rafe had always been too damned perceptive. "You're right, I wanted it. It took me a while to get used to the idea, but yeah, I wanted the baby. I'd like to have a couple of kids someday."

"And a wife you love who loves you in return."

"Dammit, yes! I'd like to have a family. What's wrong with that?"

"Nothing's wrong with it. So why not now? Why not with Samantha?"

His chest was aching. He wished his brother would shut up and leave. "Because she won't live here, okay? And I can't make it in San Francisco. I could never be happy there."

"So find someplace else. A compromise. If she really loves you, she'll jump at the chance to make it work."

Nick said nothing.

"Come on, little brother. If this is what you want, go after it the way you have everything else you ever wanted."

Nick looked up at his oldest brother, one of the strongest, most solid men he had ever known. He thought of Samantha, his mind spinning, trying to figure out the logistics, see if there was any way he could make it work.

Rafe was still sitting there, waiting patiently for him to figure out he was right. As usual. Well, it wasn't the first time his brother had come up with a good idea, but it just might be the best one he'd ever had.

"Seattle might work," Nick said. "It's rainy there, but it rains in San Francisco, right?"

"That's right. There're some big, beautiful mountains around, and if you get a little ways out of the city, there're pine trees all over."

"I've been there. I liked it. And there's plenty of work."

Rafe started nodding, beginning to get

where he was going. "You're thinking of Ian. He's got the kind of job you were made for, and he'd be damned lucky to have you."

His cousin owned Brodie Operations, Security Services, Inc. "Boss, Inc." they called it, a company that specialized in private investigation, personal security, anything that required operatives with law enforcement backgrounds. The rich, dot-com folks were Ian's biggest clients. His cousin had always said there was a job waiting if Nick ever wanted it.

"Call him," Rafe gently prodded. "If she's the one, don't let her get away."

Nick started grinning. For the first time in weeks, a ray of light seeped through the gray, dismal landscape he'd been inhabiting. If Ian offered him a job, he'd take it. He'd fly to San Francisco and propose to Samantha the way he should have done before.

Over the next few hours, he convinced himself it would all work out, but after his brother had left and time slipped away, doubts began to creep in. Samantha had never said she loved him. Maybe she wasn't returning his calls because she was glad to be rid of him.

His chest went tight at the thought. One thing he knew for sure. If he went to San

Francisco, he wasn't leaving until he knew how she felt.

And if she loved him? Well, he damned well wasn't giving up until she said yes.

Chapter Thirty-Seven

Samantha stood up from where she sat in front of the computer in her office at The Perfect Pup. She'd finished her latest market survey and assembled the data she'd collected. They were expanding the chain, looking for new locations. She had plenty to do, but for now the day was over. It was time to go home.

She sighed as she packed up her desk and got ready to leave. Before she'd met Nick, she'd looked forward to returning to her cozy apartment, having a glass of wine and relaxing after work, or doing a little yoga, maybe pampering herself with a bubble bath or trying out some new recipe.

Since her return, she dreaded the hours in her lonely apartment.

"So you want to go for a drink with me and Luke?" Abby stood next to the desk in a pair of leggings, a short skirt, and boots that came to her knees. Samantha had been so lost in thought, she hadn't heard her friend approach.

"I like Luke," she said. "He's really great, but I'm just not in the mood." And when she was with the two of them, she missed Nick so much it was an actual physical pain.

"You sure? We'll probably get some sushi afterward."

Samantha grimaced. She might be a city girl, but she still hadn't developed a taste for raw fish. "Thanks, but no thanks." She rose from the desk. "You go ahead, I'll lock up." No use getting home any earlier than she had to.

Once the doors were locked and the lights turned off, it didn't take long to reach her apartment down the block. Samantha climbed the stairs and let herself in, went straight to the fridge and poured herself a glass of chardonnay.

"Hello, baby."

She jumped and nearly spilled her wine as she whirled toward the familiar male voice. "Nick!"

He rose from the chair like a shadow, stretching out his long legs, coming to his full, impressive height. He was wearing black slacks and a light blue shirt the color of his gorgeous eyes, reminding her of how handsome he had looked in Las Vegas.

Dear God, how could she have forgotten how beautiful he was?

"How did you get in?" she asked, knowing he'd charmed the manager or picked the lock. Nick was a man of many talents.

"I told the manager I wanted to surprise you. I guess she figured I was harmless."

She wanted to laugh. *Harmless* was the last thing Nick Brodie ever could be. She wanted to cry. Why had he come? Didn't he know how much it hurt just to look at him?

He reached down next to the chair he'd been sitting in, picked up a long gold box with a red satin ribbon tied around it, strode over and rested the box in her arms. A dozen long-stemmed red roses, their petals moist with dew, called to her through the clear, cellophane window.

"I tried to think of something more original," Nick said, "but the roses just seemed right."

Just as they had been before. "I love roses. They're . . . they're my favorite flower." She had to leave before she did something foolish like rush into his arms. "I'd better go put them in water." She hurried toward the kitchen, as if the distance between them would somehow protect her from the aching emotions roiling inside her.

She took the lid off the box with shaking

502

hands, reached under the sink and took out a cut crystal vase, set it on the counter. Nick walked up behind her, stood so close she could feel the heat of his tall, powerful body.

"I've missed you," he said softly.

Leaving the flowers in the sink, Samantha turned, tried to steel herself. "Why did you come, Nick?" Tears filled her eyes. "God, I wish you hadn't. I'm trying . . . trying to get over you."

He pulled her close, settled his mouth very softly over hers, stirring the heat and touching her heart.

"I don't want you to get over me," he said, wiping away a tear that tracked down her cheek. "I want you to marry me."

Samantha closed her eyes, unable to stop the flood of wetness. Nick's hand clasped hers as he towed her into the living room and settled her on the sofa.

"Just hear me out, okay?"

What else could she do? He was there and she loved him.

"I got a job in Seattle. My cousin, Ian, owns a security firm. They do personal protection, private investigation, stuff like that. Seattle's not that far from San Francisco. And it's not all that far from Alaska."

If she could have moved, she would have been in his arms. Her heart was twisting, squeezing, pumping hope through her veins. When she didn't answer, he started talking again.

"So . . . the weather's not that bad, and we could get a house big enough for your family to come and visit. You could maybe keep the job with your friend, Abby, work out of a home office."

Fresh tears welled. He would do that for her? Because the moment she had seen him standing in her living room, she had known she would do anything for him.

Even if it meant freezing her buns off in Alaska.

But she had to be sure that this would work for Nick, too. "Are you sure you could be happy there, Nick?" She wiped a tear from her cheek. "Seattle isn't your home."

"I've thought a lot about it. I'm not like Rafe and Dylan. Alaska is in their blood. When I was with the Rangers, I traveled all over the world, spent time in a dozen different places. Washington's got mountains and forests, and I'll be working at what I'm good at, just like you said."

She wanted this. Wanted to marry him so badly. "We . . . we have . . . nothing in common. I'm a homebody, you're a man's man, deep in your bones."

He bent down, pressed his mouth against

the side of her neck, made her yearn for him.

"We have a lot more in common than you think," he said. "We both like movies, right? And great food. And pizza, don't forget that. I can find men friends who like to fish, guys who like to ride snowmobiles and climb mountains. I don't need a woman to do that with me. I need a woman to come home to, one who'll give me children and make us a family."

Her throat closed up. Before she could speak, he pulled a blue velvet box out of his pocket, then went down on one knee in front of her. "I love you, Samantha Hollis. Will you marry me?"

She couldn't breathe. The ring was beautiful, a single glittering diamond, the setting perfect for her small hand. Leaning toward him, she wrapped her arms around his neck and just hung on. "I love you so much, Nick. I've been dead without you. I want to marry you more than anything in the world."

Nick slid the ring on her finger, stood up and pulled her into his arms. "We're going to make it work, baby."

"Yes." She smiled at him through her tears, started to grin. "Yes, yes, yes!"

Nick grinned back. "How about we do it

tomorrow?"

Samantha laughed and shook her head. "As much as I'd like that, you have to meet my parents and my brother. Some of my friends. Soon you'll be part of my family."

A slow smile spread over Nick's face. "I'd like that. I'd like that a lot." And then he kissed her, soft and deep.

Samantha kissed him back with all the love in her heart. For the first time in weeks, she truly felt home.

CHAPTER THIRTY-EIGHT

Nick had talked Samantha into coming back to Alaska with him to help him move. So far they hadn't gotten much packing done, since they'd been spending most of their time in bed.

He found himself smiling. He'd met Samantha's family before they left California, and aside from a lecture from her dad about keeping her safe and never putting her in danger again, he seemed to have passed the test. He was getting married, and it couldn't happen soon enough to suit him.

A few things had happened while he had been gone. Jimmy and Mary were back in their house, Jimmy in school again. But the two of them would be spending the summer in Mountain Village so Jimmy could get to know the Alaska Native side of his family. Being in the Yupik village had given him a sense of belonging Jimmy had never really had.

Three days ago, the court had ruled in favor of exhuming Alex Evans's body. Though it hadn't happened yet, Nick was certain this time the coroner would find evidence of murder. And Jankowski, Sorenson, Petrova, and Evans was under investigation for money laundering and other possible criminal activities.

He looked up from the box he was filling with some of his high school athletic trophies to see Samantha walking out of his bedroom, reminding him of what they'd been doing in there less than an hour ago. His body stirred and he bit back a grin. He couldn't believe he was getting hard all over again.

"I need some more boxes," Samantha said. "The packing tape's on the coffee table. Can you make a few up for me?"

"Sure. I'll have to get the rest of the cardboard out of the Explorer. I'll be right back." She returned to the bedroom, and he headed outside. Grabbing the flat, unmade boxes out of the back of the SUV, he started toward the house.

Hearing the sound of a man's voice talking to Samantha in the living room, he paused at the back door. The voice sounded vaguely familiar but he couldn't quite place it, and he didn't like the guy's tone.

"Where is he?" the man asked sharply.

"Who are you?" Samantha asked. "How did you get in here?"

Nick moved quietly, setting the boxes aside and opening the back door, easing through the mudroom into the kitchen. He didn't know what the hell was going on, but his instincts were screaming, and he wished he could get his hands on his Glock.

"Door was unlocked," the man said. "Thoughtful of Nick. But of course this is Alaska. No one pays much attention to locks up here."

Flattening himself against the wall next to the fridge, Nick caught a glimpse of a red-haired man standing just inside the front door, over six feet tall, with very pale blue eyes. *Kenny Archer.* One of the detectives he had worked with in the Anchorage PD. A bad feeling crept down Nick's spine.

Archer smiled, but there was a hard edge to it. "I asked you where he is." Samantha gasped as Archer pulled a pistol and aimed it at the center of her chest. "I'm not going to ask you again."

Nick's hand balled into a fist.

"He . . . he went to town for . . . for . . ."

"I'm right here, Archer." Nick stepped into the open, and the gun swept in his direction. Very slowly, Nick raised his hands.

"You got a beef with me, Kenny, leave the lady out of it."

"I don't give a fuck about her. You're the bastard who ruined my life."

The muscles in Nick's jaw went tense. "So I guess Ford Sanders decided to cut a deal."

"That's right. He set me up to take the fall, but you're the bastard who stirred up this mess. You just couldn't leave things alone."

"I gotta say, I never would have figured you for the dirty cop, Kenny. I would have bet my last dollar it was Taggart."

"Taggart's a fool. He's not smart enough to know what's good for him. He could have been living the high life. If he hadn't been such a candy-ass, we both could have come out of this thing rich."

"Sorry it didn't work out for you." Nick turned his attention to Samantha. "Honey, why don't you go on out front and let Officer Archer and me work this out?"

Her eyes cut from him to Kenny and back. She didn't want to leave him. Dammit, would she ever do what he told her? Her dad was going to kill him.

"Go now," Nick said in his Ranger voice, wanting her safe and hoping like hell she'd obey.

Samantha turned and started walking.

"Hold it right there," Archer said, halting her before she had taken two steps. "You aren't going anyplace. Not until this is over. Now get over here next to Brodie."

She moved slowly, her eyes on Nick's face. When she reached him, he eased her a little behind him.

"So what's your plan, Archer? You're wanted for a lot of things, but at this point, murder isn't one of them."

"Shut up."

"You need to think this over, Kenny. There's always a chance you can make a deal, get a shorter sentence. Hell, you might even get off with no time served."

"Bullshit, Brodie. Thanks to you, I've got nothing but jail time ahead of me. Killing you is the only thing that makes this all worthwhile." Archer raised the weapon and every muscle in Nick's body went tense. He had to make a move.

"Wait!" Samantha stepped out from behind him, making his jaw go tight, making him want to paddle her sweet little ass. "I've got a plane ticket to Seattle in my purse. You could move up the date, go in my place. You could get away, Kenny. You could leave Alaska and not have to go to jail."

It wouldn't work. You couldn't trade places with someone on an airline. Not since 9/11. Which Samantha surely knew.

"You think I'm stupid?" Kenny said with a sneer. "Maybe I should kill you, too."

The slight distraction was the opening Nick needed. He launched himself at Kenny, knocking him backward, both of them crashing to the floor. Archer's semi-auto went off with a roar that shook the house and muffled Samantha's scream.

Nick's shoulder took the brunt of the landing and began to throb as he wrestled with Archer for the weapon, clenching his jaw against the pain, and slamming the man's gun hand against the floor, once, twice, three times.

Archer hung on. "I'm going to kill you!" he shouted, fighting with all his strength.

"You aren't killing anyone, Archer." Both of them froze. Nick looked up to see a man standing in the kitchen doorway, a gleaming, freshly polished, semi-auto in his hand. Captain Raymond Taggart. "Drop your weapon or I'll shoot you right where you are."

Archer hesitated.

"Do it now!" Two uniformed police officers, guns drawn, backed up the captain.

For an instant, Archer's finger tightened around the trigger. If the pistol went off, aimed the way it was, the bullet might hit

Samantha. Then Kenny's muscles relaxed and Nick pulled the weapon from his hand, tossed it across the floor out of reach.

He came to his feet and hauled Archer up, dragged him over and slammed him against the wall, had him spread-eagled before Taggart had holstered his weapon.

For the first time, Nick noticed the flashing blue and red lights of the patrol cars parked around the outside of the house. The captain tossed him a pair of handcuffs and Nick locked them around Archer's wrists.

"Get that piece of dirt out of here," the captain said to his men, and the uniforms came forward to haul Kenny's sorry ass away.

Nick walked over to Samantha and pulled her into his arms. "You okay?"

She swallowed, nodded. "I think I'm getting used to this kind of stuff."

His mouth edged up. The lady was really something, and he was one lucky sonofabitch.

He turned to look at Raymond Taggart. "I thought it was you."

Taggart smiled coldly. "I never liked you, Brodie. You're too much of a wild card. But I won't have a dirty cop in my department. I'm grateful you exposed Officer Archer for the scumbag he is."

"How did you know he was here?"

"I put a bug on his car. I had a hunch it was him after what happened up at Reeves's cabin. I wanted to see where he'd lead us. This morning, Ford Sanders turned state's evidence. He'd been holding out, trying to cut the best deal, which apparently he finally did. I wanted to be there when we collared Archer."

"Glad you showed up when you did."

Taggart just nodded. "I'll want a statement from you and Ms. Hollis. I'll need you to come down to the station."

"Samantha's had enough excitement for one day. I'll bring her in tomorrow morning."

Taggart's jaw clenched. He took a deep breath and slowly released it. "All right, tomorrow then." He started walking, stopped and turned back. "I heard a rumor you were leaving, moving to Seattle."

"That's right."

Taggart's lips curled into a smile that really wasn't. "Couldn't happen to a nicer guy," he said, and walked out of the house.

Nick looked over at Samantha and both of them burst out laughing.

EPILOGUE

It was mid-January, the dead of winter, but in Seattle the sun had broken through the cloudy skies and the temperatures had risen into the fifties. In Anchorage this time of year, a good day would reach the mid-twenties.

Nick smiled. The home they had found south of Bellevue in the suburbs of Seattle had been vacant, making it easy for them to close escrow and move in. The four bedroom, three-bath house sat on an oversize lot with plenty of trees, in a forested area near the Cougar Mountain Wildlands between Bellevue and Issaquah.

Since Brodie Operations wasn't that far away, the commute wasn't bad. Nick would be working freelance for his cousin's company, which meant he could be his own boss, specialize in P.I. cases and also take personal security details.

He could work in the office or out of his house. Which Samantha would also be doing. Her friend, Abby, had convinced her to start searching for locations for two new Perfect Pup dog-grooming parlors. Samantha was looking forward to the challenge.

And of course, she had already badgered Nick into agreeing to let her help with his cases. Nick hadn't told her he actually liked the idea, though he was sure her father wouldn't. They'd agreed to a don't-ask, don't-tell policy where her dad was concerned.

And since they had left Anchorage, an interesting thing had happened. After a review of recent events, Raymond Taggart had gotten so much grief from his superiors, he had taken a job in Minnesota. He'd been replaced with a woman. Nick had worked with the lady, who was a great choice for the job.

Nick was looking forward to getting back to work himself, but he wasn't working today and neither was Samantha. Today was their wedding day.

Wearing a black tuxedo and crisp white pleated shirt, he stood next to Rafe and Dylan, along with Samantha's brother, Peter, all of them decked out like penguins and, in Nick's estimation, looking extremely fine.

In the end, he'd agreed with Samantha's mother that her daughter deserved a full-blown church wedding with all the trimmings. Besides, he wanted to see her walking toward him in one of those long white gowns.

Later, he wanted to be the man who stripped her out of it.

Rafe leaned over and whispered, "Get ready. Here she comes."

The tempo of the organ music changed and the guests in the lovely little white chapel came to their feet. The organ player began the bridal march, and Samantha appeared in the doorway on her father's arm.

She was all white lace, a tiny waist above a full, gathered skirt, her pretty face and long nutmeg curls hidden beneath a sheer white organdy veil.

Jesus, she looked so beautiful he couldn't breathe.

Walking next to her father, who looked equally debonair, she followed Abby, her maid of honor, and a friend from San Francisco, all dressed in pink. The women moved to one side and Samantha stopped directly in front of him. Nick struggled to remember what he was supposed to do.

The minister said something his brain was too foggy to catch.

Her dad answered, "Her mother and I."

Then Nick was taking her hand, both of them turning to face the minister, a tall, bone-thin man with a leonine mane of perfectly groomed silver hair.

Everyone sat down and the ceremony began. "Dearly beloved," the minister started, repeating the words of the traditional service that Samantha had wanted, and which felt just right to Nick.

As the ceremony progressed, he figured he made all the right responses since Rafe didn't jab him in the ribs and Dylan didn't snicker. All Nick could think of was Samantha and how lucky he was that she was about to become his wife.

The rest of the service passed in a blur. He put a ring on her finger, proving she was his, and that was all that mattered to him.

He failed to keep track of the rest of what went on until the minister said, "In the name of the Father, and the Son, and the Holy Spirit, I now pronounce you husband and wife. Nicholas, you may kiss your bride."

He swept her into his arms and did so with gusto, kissing her soundly, a deep, open-mouth kiss that lasted way longer than it should have. He heard Cord whistle, heard Derek's laughter, and Noah's booming *"Hooah!"*

Nick was grinning when he let her go, and Samantha was blushing.

"Hello, Wife," he said.

She smiled up at him, looking so sweet his chest squeezed. "Hello, Husband."

The minister spoke to the crowd. "It gives me great pleasure to introduce Mr. and Mrs. Nicholas Brodie."

Sitting next to Mary, Jimmy whooped. Some of the women were dabbing their eyes, and his friends were cheering. He caught a glimpse of his new boss, his blond, blue-eyed cousin Ian, next to his wife, Meri. Dylan's fiancée, Lane Bishop, sat next to Dylan's little girl, Emily. Winnie Henry, the woman who had helped raise all three Brodie boys, was wiping tears from her apple-round cheeks.

Even Nick's cousin, Ty, and his wife, Haley, had flown up from L.A. for the wedding.

To say nothing of Samantha's entire family, a lot of whom Nick wouldn't meet until the reception, which was being held in a room the family had decorated behind the church.

Nick looked out over the sea of friends

who had come to wish him well and couldn't remember ever smiling so broadly.

He was married. He had found his perfect match, a brand-new family, and the job he was meant for.

A man didn't get any luckier than that.

AUTHOR'S NOTE

I hope you enjoyed Nick and Samantha in
Against the Sky, book two of the Brodies of
Alaska trilogy. If you haven't read Dylan's
story, *Against the Wild,* I hope you will.

Up next is Rafe's tale, *Against the Tide,*
another high-action, romantic adventure.
The owner of a charter fishing boat fleet in
Valdez, Alaska, Rafe is drawn to Olivia
Chandler, the new owner of the Pelican
Café. Rafe is intrigued by the beautiful
woman whose past is shrouded in mystery,
and the more she avoids him, the more he's
determined to have her.

Olivia can't allow the attraction she feels
for Rafe to grow, not when her very life
depends on keeping her identity secret.

But murder and intrigue are in the wind,
and Olivia and Rafe are drawn deeper and
deeper into the mystery they must work
together to solve — before it's too late.

I hope you'll watch for *Against the Tide* and that you enjoy it. Till then, very best wishes and happy reading.

Kat

ABOUT THE AUTHOR

Currently living near Missoula, Montana, **Kat Martin** is the bestselling author of over fifty-five Historical and Contemporary Romance novels, currently an NYT bestselling author of the romantic suspense Against series. Before she started writing in 1985, Kat was a real estate broker. During that time, she met her husband, L. J. Martin, also an author with over 33 book length works. Kat is a graduate of the University of California at Santa Barbara, where she majored in Anthropology and also studied History. "I love anything old," Kat says. "I love to travel and especially like to visit the places where my books are set. My husband and I often stay in out-of-the-way inns and houses built in times past. It's fun and it gives a wonderful sense of a by-gone era."

To date, Kat has over fifteen million copies of her books in print. She is published in more than two dozen foreign countries, including Germany, Norway, Sweden, China, Korea, Bulgaria, Russia, England, South Africa, Italy, Spain, Argentina, Japan and Greece.

The employees of Thorndike Press hope you have enjoyed this Large Print book. All our Thorndike, Wheeler, and Kennebec Large Print titles are designed for easy reading, and all our books are made to last. Other Thorndike Press Large Print books are available at your library, through selected bookstores, or directly from us.

For information about titles, please call:
   (800) 223-1244

or visit our Web site at:
   http://gale.cengage.com/thorndike

To share your comments, please write:
   Publisher
   Thorndike Press
   10 Water St., Suite 310
   Waterville, ME 04901